Code Name:
Arc Angel

Code Name: Arc Angel

The Demise of the Devil

Bruce Jarvis

CODE NAME: ARC ANGEL
THE DEMISE OF THE DEVIL

iUniverse books may be ordered through booksellers or by contacting:

iUniverse
1663 Liberty Drive
Bloomington, IN 47403
www.iuniverse.com
1-800-Authors (1-800-288-4677)

ISBN: 978-1-5320-0003-4 (sc)
ISBN: 978-1-5320-0001-0 (hc)
ISBN: 978-1-5320-0002-7 (e)

Library of Congress Control Number: 2016911055

Print information available on the last page.

iUniverse rev. date: 07/11/2016

To my wife Joan who encouraged me to start, made recommendations, was my sounding board, and supported my effort to completion

To my children Michelle, John, and Anthony whose inquisitiveness as to status kept me going forward

To the "Greatest Generation" of men and women who won this war they never started or wanted

Contents

PROLOGUE

Germany's leader in September 1940 was Adolph Hitler. Europe was in crisis. After annexing Austria and the Sudetenland, Germany's armed forces had seized Czechoslovakia and then invaded and defeated Poland and Holland as well. Great Britain and France had declared war on Germany in support of Poland. However, Hitler's armies had not only invaded Belgium and France; they had all but defeated the French Army and the English expeditionary force. More than three hundred thousand men of that force, along with the French and Belgian Armies had been evacuated from the beaches of the French coast at Dunkirk. Amid a German attack on Norway, the Norwegian king and his government had left their country for London. Meanwhile, the Italians had declared war on Great Britain and France, and a new government, the Vichy, had been formed in France. It had negotiated an armistice with Hitler and Mussolini. The German Air Force, the Luftwaffe, was attacking Great Britain.

It was the second week of September 1940. Carlton Fuller had a full day of "honey do" to finish.

The telephone began to ring.

"Carlton, please answer the phone," called Maggie.

"Okay, I'll get it," Carlton shouted to his wife. "I'm on the porch painting the ceiling," he added loudly as he came down the ladder and headed to the front door. The phone was on the table in the hallway.

Carlton picked up the phone. "Hello."

"Hello," replied the person at the other end of the call. "My name is Bill Donovan; I would like to speak to Carlton Brausch." The caller emphasized the German name, *Brausch* with his slight German accent.

"My name is Carlton Fuller, not Brausch, as you said it."

"I apologize," the caller responded. "I would like to speak with you if possible."

"What's this all about?" Carlton continued. "Who are you?

"Who are you, a wise guy?" he repeated. And with that, he hung up the phone with a bang and stomped back to his work on the porch.

"Who was that?" called Maggie. "Why did you slam down the phone?" she asked quizzically.

"It was some goofball named William Donovan who wants to talk with me."

—〰—

So began one of the most intriguing, complex, and dangerous spy adventures of World War II. Carlton Fuller was recruited by the future director of the Office of Strategic Services (OSS), the forerunner of the CIA. The story is true, but some of the locations and some players' names are fictitious, as the CIA does not identify its operatives or where they've operated. The story was told to me by my father over a number of years, after he'd learned it from his friend Carlton Fuller, whose family is gone. The man was never publicly recognized, his story never told. We will never know the sacrifice he and his family made for the United States. He was one of the unsung heroes of the war.

We do, however, know the outcome of the story. The Arc Angel prevailed. The demise of the devil was achieved.

BOOK ONE

The Rise

ζɦe Beginning

$\mathcal{C}$ arlton was back on the ladder continuing his work painting the porch. The house he, Maggie, and the children lived in was over ten years old. He was thinking there were a few things, in addition to some painting, that the house needed. The linoleum in the kitchen and bathroom needed to be replaced. The carpet in the two bedrooms needed to be cleaned. The paint on the house was beginning to blister and peel. *Normal maintenance*, he thought. He had a busy day with the house. He wanted to get as much accomplished as he could before winter began. The telephone started ringing again. He was making good progress with the painting.

"Maggie, will you get the phone this time. I hate to climb down the ladder again. I have been up and down five times this morning."

"I can't. I'm up to my neck in washing and ironing. Please, Carlton, answer the telephone," called Maggie. "What are you waiting for? It has rung eight times already. Answer the damn telephone. Whoever is calling this time?"

"I'm afraid it might be that nut who called earlier," he said.

"I don't think so; it's been an hour since his call this morning. If it is, tell him you're not interested and hang up again," called Maggie.

"Okay, I'll get it," said Carlton. He came down from the ladder, walked into the hall, and reached for the receiver.

"Hello," Carlton answered.

"Hello, Mr. Fuller. This is William Donovan again. Please don't hang up on me again. Please, let me apologize for being so abrupt on my first call. I want to give you some explanation as to why I'm calling you."

"I'm sorry. I don't want any. Good-bye," Carlton replied.

As he was about to hang up the telephone, Carlton thought to himself, *The man said please twice. I'll hear what he has to say.* He put the receiver back to his ear.

"What?" Carlton questioned sarcastically. "Who are you? And what do you want? I'm very busy."

Giving Donovan a chance to talk was a fateful decision on his part.

"As I indicated earlier in my first call, my name is William Donovan. I was named by the president of the United States as coordinator of information in July of this year." Being a risk taker, Donovan took a shot, hoping that mentioning the president would get Fuller's attention. "I'm interested in talking with you because of your background, your heritage, and your family in Germany." Donovan continued, "I would like to meet with you."

"I have been estranged from my family in Germany for over twenty years. That is the reason I changed my name. They have no dealings with me." His interest was beginning to stir. "I don't understand. I have no dealings with them. I'm a lawyer, I have my own family, and I am a citizen of the United States. I don't even talk with the people in Germany. I have no idea as to what they are even doing there. Do you hear what I'm saying, Mr. Donovan? Why should I trust you? How do I know the president of the United States even knows who you are?" Carlton said sarcastically.

"I hear you, Mr. Fuller. I understand your concerns. I suggest you call your senator or representative's office and ask them who I am. Meet me at one of their offices if you like. What you just said is the reason I have a need to talk with you. Please, I only want to talk to you. It is important to me and to the country. Will you please talk with me ? I will send a car for you on Tuesday morning at nine a.m. If you won't come, I will continue to call you. I am very persistent."

"That is very presumptuous. Tuesday is not good; I will be in court Tuesday all day. I will meet with you, but I am very suspicious of everything you are talking about. The only time available this week is Saturday morning," Carlton explained. He was hoping that offering Saturday would get the guy to quit. It didn't. *Why did I agree to talk with him?* Carlton thought.

"Thank you, Mr. Fuller. I will have a car pick you up at your residence at seven a.m. Saturday morning. Your address is 3468 Randolph Avenue, Cleveland Heights, Ohio?" Donovan replied.

"Yes, that is correct," Carlton agreed. "Where will we be meeting at 7:00am?" he asked.

"We will meet at the Federal Bureau of Investigation Offices in downtown Cleveland," replied Donovan. "I appreciate your agreeing to meet with me. Thank you. Good-bye."

As Carlton was replacing the telephone on the hook, Maggie came into the hall and looked at Carlton. "I heard you agree to meet with the man. Why did you agree to talk with this guy?" she asked. "Who is he? What did he want? Where are you going Saturday morning at 7:00am? You don't get up until eight a.m. any day, let alone on a Saturday morning. Are you sure you made the right decision? The kids are meeting the Kramer kids at the park on Saturday. I was counting on you to take them and spend some time with them ... Now I will have to go with them and drive the car. You know how I hate to drive the car with the kids in the backseat."

"I'm sorry about Saturday morning, but it was the only day I had available this week except Sunday, and that's our day—you know, church and a great dinner together. It was his determination to talk to me. He was so insistent. Seems interesting to me. I guess it's the lawyer in me. Inquisitive about something I don't know anything about. Please support me on this one. I'll explain the whole meeting to you when I get home on Saturday. We will be meeting in the Federal Bureau of Investigation offices in downtown Cleveland. Now I have to finish painting the porch."

With a smile in her voice, Maggie kissed him on the cheek, looked him in the eye, and said, "Support you on this one. How many times over the years have I supported you on this one? Remember the cottage I supported you on at Lake Cable last summer? What a deal it was, a cabin located on the beach, summer breezes, warm water, sandy beach. Nothing but thunder and lightning, loss of power, and the coldest week of the year. Although you and the kids enjoyed macaroni and cheese almost every meal, I gained five pounds over that exciting vacation, and we couldn't go swimming because the water was too cold. Uh-huh. Why I still love you puzzles me, but I do and will forever." She walked out of the hall into the kitchen, chuckling.

As he climbed the ladder, Carlton smiled and remembered the beautiful blond he'd found at college. Maggie Bertrand. What a dish she was. She was as cute as a June bug with a turned-up nose and a wonderful smile and as pretty as a picture in *Collier's* magazine. He had been smitten instantly, but he hadn't even met her yet. He had talked about her with his buddies and asked them to help him figure out a way to meet her. Whatever it would be, it would be exciting.

Maggie and her friends had been at the college studying for finals near the end of their senior year. It had been a beautiful day during the spring of 1926. Carlton was twenty-six, and Maggie was twenty-two, and they were both in the prime of their lives. Carlton and his buddies had planned to splash the girls with buckets of water as they left the library that afternoon. After splashing the girls, they would retreat to the woods behind the library and hide, after which Carlton would emerge, pretending to suddenly see what had happened and come to the rescue. If the plan worked, Maggie would feel rescued and be impressed with Carlton. Carlton laughed to himself as he recalled the incident.

It all began innocently. The girls came out of the library. They came down the steps, and his buddies jumped out from the side of the steps and threw the water from buckets and soaked the girls. Their screams could be heard across campus. When Carlton heard the noise, he ran around the corner of the library, ran to Maggie's aid, and started to dry her off. The rest of the girls jumped on him and started hitting him as hard as they could, blaming him for throwing the water they'd been splashed with. He tried to explain, but they just beat him up. As it turned out, Maggie stayed behind and tried to comfort Carlton for the beating the girls had given him.

Maggie was drawn to Carlton immediately. He was about six feet tall, with blue eyes and the blondest hair she had ever seen on a man. He was outgoing in nature and loved the outdoors.

While they were dating, they rode bikes, went hiking, and enjoyed the theater and opera together. To Maggie, he was a perfect gentleman and paid complete attention to her when they were together. In the end, the means accomplished the end. It all worked out, and two years later, they were married. Carlton went on to complete law school and graduated two years following their wedding. Maggie and Carlton still laughed out loud when they recalled their "meeting," as they called it.

Carlton finally finished painting the porch. *What fond memories I have*, he thought as he cleaned his brushes and put his materials away.

He loved this woman very deeply and included her in all he did. They talked incessantly about the daily family activities and what was best for them and the children. She helped him with his career and stayed home to raise the children. Early on, it had been difficult, as they had gone through the Depression. He had been fortunate, as he was able to represent people who were unfortunate enough to go bankrupt. He'd ended up working for the city, representing it in collecting tax monies from industry. The job had paid the bills and put food on the table during the toughest times.

Carlton's practice had taken him many directions. He'd finally landed in an insurance office representing insurance companies in the claims process. Although he represented the companies, his philosophy was always to be fair, honest, and empathetic toward the client. He was successful.

Carlton's week was a very busy one. But, he could not stop thinking what Donovan might possibly want to talk to him about. His imagination was conjuring up all sorts of ideas, but they always led to dead ends. His life was very routine—work, go to court, do paperwork, go home, spend time with children, help wife, plan future, save money for children's college. It was, from his perspective, very boring and mundane.

It was Friday evening before his meeting with Donovan. "You're talking to yourself again," Maggie remarked as she waltzed into the living room to sit down to read the newspaper. "What's on your mind? You have been doing a lot of that this week."

"I was talking to myself, wondering out loud what this guy Donovan wants," Carlton replied.

"Donovan must be important if President Roosevelt has named him. Now I am also wondering what he wants to talk to you about. Sounds like something you should be proud of. Not everyone gets to talk to a presidential appointee," Maggie remarked.

"He is a mystery man right now. Please remind me to set the clock for five thirty a.m. I probably should take a bath and shave before I get picked up at seven. What's on the radio tonight?" Carlton mumbled.

"Well, if you give me the paper, I'll read the listings and tell you. Hopefully, not another presidential fireside chat. The president always scares me when he talks about the war in Europe. This guy Hitler the president keeps talking about makes me shake in my boots. He seems to be trying to conquer the world," Maggie replied.

"Thank the Lord that we are not in it. There are a bunch in Congress who want us to stay out of it. But we have to keep watch on what is going on. If for no other reason, we have to do it to protect ourselves. It doesn't seem that the war drums are beating yet. At least the newspaper isn't saying much about it. I wonder if we don't put to much faith in the *Cleveland Press*. It is Friday. Let's sit back and relax. It is time to enjoy our evening together. Have the kids gone to bed yet? It is awfully quiet in the house," Carlton remarked.

"You forgot they are sleeping over at your mother's house tonight. I'm sure she is spoiling them as usual," Maggie advised. "What should we do to enjoy ourselves? Should we go up early? What do you think, Carlton?"

"You're right. I probably should go to bed early. Seven a.m. comes early on a Saturday morning. I just don't know what this guy wants," Carlton responded sleepily.

The Meeting

A t 7:00 a.m., a knock on the door resonated throughout the Fuller house. Maggie looked through the window at the front doorway. "There's a soldier at the front door," she exclaimed.

"It must be the person Donovan sent to pick me up. He is right on time," said Carlton as he struggled out of the bedroom door, put on his shoes, and moved toward the front door.

Maggie opened the door. "Good morning, soldier. I bet your here to pick up my husband, Carlton."

"Yes, ma'am," the soldier replied. "Good morning, ma'am. I'm Major Best. Is Mr. Fuller ready? General Donovan is waiting. We don't want to be late getting to his office. General Donovan is very firm on being on time."

"He is, Major," replied Maggie. "Here he is now."

"Good morning. What's your name? I apologize. I missed it when you were addressing my wife. I'm still groggy; seven a.m. is early for me on Saturday mornings," said Carlton.

"Yes, sir. Major Best, sir," replied the soldier.

"It is a pleasure meeting you," Carlton said, shaking the major's hand. "Let's go, Major. We don't want to delay Donovan do we," he remarked sarcastically as he kissed Maggie good-bye.

The major opened the door for Carlton, who about fell into the car. And the major closed the door softly.

"Major, how long have you known Donovan? How much do you know about him? I need a little background about him before I meet him," Carlton said. "My name is Carlton Fuller. Sorry to be so flip; I'm hoping this meeting will not be a waste of time, both his and mine."

"I hope not either, Mr. Fuller. I met General Donovan and was assigned as his adjutant in early 1940 when President Roosevelt gave him a number of special assignments. I have been with him ever since. I can tell you one thing; he is held in the highest regard by President Roosevelt. Every time he is in Washington, DC, he has one or two meetings with the president. General Donovan is a hero also. He won the Medal of Honor for his action in World War I. In addition to that, he has many other medals for his service, both from the United States and many foreign countries. He has a nickname his classmates gave him in college. It is Wild Bill. I think it was for his actions on the football field. I would be afraid to ask him. I certainly don't call him that. He is married, has a family, and lives in a small town in Virginia—Berryville, I think. He has traveled extensively in Europe, meeting with many high-level politicians and keeping the President informed when he returned. I hope you have enough information, as we have just arrived at the office."

The building was a tall, featureless, granite public building.

"I will let you out. Just go in the doors straight ahead. Once inside, you will see the elevators. Tell the operator you are going to the fifth floor. Ask the operator where the Federal Bureau of Investigation offices are. He will tell you where the specific office is. When you get to the office, knock on the door, and General Donovan will open the door. Good day, Mr. Fuller. It has been my pleasure," the Major finished.

Major Best opened the door for Carlton, got back in the car, and drove away.

Here I am, downtown Cleveland by myself getting ready to meet with a war hero, presidential appointee, and world traveler, Carlton thought to himself. *I'm a little nervous; hell, I'm a lot nervous.* This would be like trying a case in front of the Supreme Court without being prepared. He entered the building and headed to the elevator operator.

Carlton approached the elevator operator. "Hello. My name is Carlton Fuller. I'm going to the fifth floor," Carlton said nervously.

"Howdy, Fuller. Strange name. Where are you going? Fifth floor. Get on. Let's go, or you will never get there," the operator said.

The ride was quick. When they arrived on the fifth floor, Carlton asked where the offices of the Federal Bureau of Investigation were.

The operator responded, "It is down the hall around the corner, fifth door on the right. Repeat after me."

Carlton repeated, "Down the hall around the corner, fifth door on the right."

"Perfect," said the elevator operator. He closed the door, and the elevator left.

Alone again, Carlton followed the directions. He found the door and took a deep breath and knocked.

He heard footsteps, and then the door opened. In front of him was a robust man, who introduced himself right away. "Hello, Mr. Fuller. I'm William J. Donovan. Please come in and sit down." His voice was vibrant and firm. Simultaneously, he reached out his hand and shook Carlton's with a strong grip. He offered Carlton a seat in a chair that sat in front of a desk.

Carlton noted the office was rather barren. It was furnished with a metal desk, some chairs, and an overhead light. A picture of President Roosevelt hung on the wall. Carlton thought the Federal Bureau of Investigations likely used the room as an interrogation office. Certainly, it was for temporary use by Donovan.

Thinking to himself, *This is a dynamic individual*, Carlton sat down in the offered chair. The chair was soft and comfortable.

Carlton responded, "Hello, Mr. Donovan. Happy to meet you. You sure are enthusiastic this early on a Saturday morning."

"It's my nature; I just made some coffee. Would you like a cup? Cream and sugar? Personally, I take mine black."

"I take mine black also. I never liked sweet coffee. I quit drinking milk products when I was young. Thank you for the coffee," Carlton answered. *A good start*, he thought.

"I'm sure you have been wondering why I wanted to talk with you. I apologize, but with the war going on in Europe, I didn't want to put what we are going to talk about in jeopardy. I want you to ask any questions you may have about anything we'll be talking about. It is important that you ask anything you feel necessary. Do you understand?" Donovan asked.

The meeting, apparently, is very serious and involves me, Carlton thought. What could it be? He drank his coffee and responded, "I think so."

Donovan began, "I have been working in secret with some of our European allies, trying to determine what types of people we will need should the United States enter this war."

Carlton's physically stiffened in the chair. *Enter the war?* he thought. *Congress is working to keep the United States out of the war. What is this guy talking about? What if I open my mouth about this conversation? What are the ramifications for my family or me? I don't think I want to go any further in this meeting.*

Donovan quickly responded, "I didn't know how you were going to react to that statement. I saw the look on your face and your physical appearance changed. Please let me continue before you walk out of the meeting. My European counterparts have been asking the president of the United States to enter the war since it started. The president has resisted, as he knows Congress would not entertain the idea of the United States entering this war. But the Europeans have been working hard to change his mind."

Carlton interrupted Donovan. "How do you know that I won't talk about this meeting to my congressman or my wife or anyone else?"

"I anticipated that question. Let me answer it this way. Following the meetings with your clients, you don't talk with your wife about them, do you? Remember client-lawyer privilege. I want to invoke that relationship now. You are an American, and you were raised by your mother. You are a successful lawyer. You have a wonderful family. You are living the American dream, like all of us Americans. I don't think you would want to lose all of these things your mother wanted for you or what you have achieved in your life, would you? It could happen, like it already has in Poland, Czechoslovakia, and Austria, and as it might in the future in France, England, Netherlands, Belgium, and the Nordic countries. The English have looked into your background and determined that you could be a future recruit. They have shared this information with me."

The bit about lawyer-client privilege surprised Carlton and set him back a bit. "Wait a minute," he exclaimed. "What's this about lawyer-client? This is not that kind of meeting."

"Oh, yes it is," replied Donovan. "I invited you to a meeting as a client, which I will swear to in court, and you agreed to the meeting as a lawyer, which I will also swear to."

This guy is slick as a whistle, Carlton thought to himself. *Be careful what you say.*

"What do you mean the English have looked into me as a possible recruit? Who are they to look at me? What right do they have looking at me?" Carlton said, getting perturbed. He was trying to keep cool, an important fact as he had learned many lessons in the courtroom.

"They certainly have no right to look into your background. But with them facing the Nazis, I'm sure we can't do anything about it. The English MI6 has talked with me about you as a recruit. They seem to feel you would be a good candidate," Donovan went on.

"It seems people have been making decisions about me without my knowing about it. They have been keeping the effort secret," Carlton noted. He was getting upset. He looked at his watch. Only twenty minutes had passed. It seemed like an hour. "May I have a glass of water, please?"

"Certainly. Major Best, please get Mr. Fuller a glass of water," directed Donovan.

Where did he come from? Carlton immediately thought. *These people are sneaky.*

"Yes, sir!" replied Major Best. He left the office to get the water.

While they waited for the major to return, Carlton continued, "What type of recruit?"

Donovan wasn't ready to answer that specific question yet. He didn't want to lie, so he dodged Carlton's question. "They were thinking about a foreign service job."

"If they asked me to take a job like that, would I be forced to take it?" Carlton asked.

"Absolutely not. They couldn't force you to do anything. It would be your choice of course," said Donovan.

"Thank you. I didn't think so," said Carlton.

The door opened, and the major came in with a pitcher of water and four glasses.

"Thank you, Major," said Carlton as he stood up and took a glass and watched the major fill it with water.

The major offered a glass to Donovan.

"No thanks, Major. I'll have another cup of coffee instead," Donovan said as he poured himself a cup of coffee.

"Let's continue, Mr. Fuller. I want to tell you what the British found out when they researched your background." Donovan then reached into a briefcase he had next to his chair and pulled out a sheaf of papers.

"You were born at three thirty a.m. at home, November 18, 1901," he continued. "Your mother, Mrs. Ellen Brausch was attended to by a midwife. Her name was Anna Smidt. You were one of two identical twins—two boys. Your mother had no problems with the delivery. Both boys were born perfect and very healthy. Your father, Fredrick Brausch, was in the living room getting drunk while you and your brother were being born. He was a colonel in the German Army. This was a high position in the German Army at that time. He participated in World War I as a colonel in the German Calvary. He retained his position in the peacetime army. He was given a position to manage the reduction of personnel and equipment following the signing of the Versailles Treaty. You were named Carlton after your great-grandfather on your mother's side. Your brother was named Horst after your great-grandfather on your father's side. Both of your great-grandfathers were deceased at the time you were born.

"When the midwife invited your father into the bedroom where you and your brother were born, he looked at the two of you and remarked, 'Oh my God, how will we be able to tell which one is which? They are identical twins. Ellen, how are you? Are you feeling okay? What do you think of our sons? How will we tell them apart?'

"Your mother and father started having marital problems when your father joined the Nazi Party in 1918. Your brother was very close with your father, and you were very close to your mother. You and your brother learned to speak the English language fluently, as well as your native tongue, German. This was at your mother's insistence. She wanted to prepare you both for international business careers. You were more of the intellectual type that your mother catered to and held close to. Horst was closer to your father because of his Nazi military life. Your mother did not like the Nazi Party and made sure your father knew it. They argued about it continuously," said Donovan. "She sent you to college in 1918. She told your father she did not want you to become a Nazi like he and your brother were."

He continued, "Your mother's hatred of the Nazi Party peaked when the Beer Hall Putsch failed in Munich in 1923. A number of party members were killed, and your father just missed getting shot and killed himself. When your mother found out the details, she threatened to leave your father and divorce him. He apparently had no problem with the threat, as they divorced in 1924. You and your mother left Germany.

The two of you immigrated to the United States, both sponsored by her sister Gerda, who lives in Akron."

"Wait a minute. Where did all this detail come from? I knew about my going to college but very little of the other information. My mother told me nothing about the rest," Carlton responded angrily.

"The British are very thorough. They have more detailed information about you. I am not at liberty to provide any more answers to your question at this time," Donovan replied. "Let me go on please," urged Donovan.

Carlton took another drink of water and sat back in his chair. He was asking himself where all this information had come from. Why had the British gathered it? He decided to listen and ask questions later.

Donovan continued, "Your father continued to grow with the Nazi Party. The party leaders apparently liked his military background and leadership skills. He was given a job within the party to work with the Brown Shirts—Hitler's security personnel. That is, they did the dirty work for Hitler, under the guise of security, and evolved into the SS during the party's rise in power as they took over control of Germany. Your father was one of their leaders. Your brother worked closely with him after he graduated from school. He became a Nazi early in his life. He, like you, was the ideal German. You both have blond hair, fair complexion, and blue eyes. He had the perfect name—Horst Brausch. He became involved with the German Youth Movement and helped develop the core ideals and method of operation.

"The difference is that your future was molded by your mother. She spoke to you at home in German and made sure you spoke English outside of home. This enabled you to finish your schooling, attend Ohio State University, meet your wife Margaret, and get your law degree. You now practice law here in Cleveland and have many German immigrant clients, because you speak the language as well as they do." With that, Donovan stopped the information flow.

Carlton was overwhelmed with the information the British had gathered about his family and him. His mind was twisting and turning. If they could gather this information, what else could they do? What do they want from me?

"Well, Mr. Donovan, you know a lot about me and my family. I know very little about you, what you represent, and why we are talking here in secret. You told me early on in this discussion that, if I had questions,

I could and should ask as many as I wanted to. Well I have many, but I haven't thought about them all yet. I wouldn't be a good lawyer if I didn't prepare my, case would I?" said Carlton.

Donovan shook his head in agreement and thought, This is a thinking man. *He seems to fit the mold. Let's give him a chance to ask his questions and continue to evaluate him.* "Go ahead, Mr. Fuller, ask your questions. I will do my best to accommodate you. It's your turn. I have been doing all the talking."

Carlton began, "Well I'm going to give you an opportunity to talk a little more. Have another cup of coffee or a glass of water because my first question is a multifaceted one: Who are you? What do you do? What are your credentials? Where is this meeting going? What do you want from me?"

Donovan sat back in his chair, crossed his legs, and began. "My name is William Donovan. I'm of Irish descent and was born in Buffalo, New York. My given middle name is Joseph. My nickname is "Wild Bill," which I obtained while playing football for Columbia University. I graduated college in 1905, went to law school there, and went on to become a lawyer practicing on Wall Street. During World War I, I was a major in the New York 'Fighting 69th.' By the end of the war, I had been promoted to colonel. Following the end of the war, I was a US attorney in Western New York. Following that job, I was appointed a deputy assistant attorney general in the Antitrust Division of the United ... during this time, I ran as a Republican for the lieutenant governor and governor of New York and failed.

"I have had the opportunity to travel extensively in Europe and meet with many high-level politicians. This travel gave me enough insight to predict an oncoming war in Europe. I wanted a place in any wartime structure should the United States enter the war ... A close friend of mine recommended me to Roosevelt. This led to a special emissary function to meet with British leaders to determine their ability to manage the war—hence, my meetings with their critical leaders.

"Following my meetings with the president reporting my findings, I was given the assignment of managing the intelligence gathering functions of the army, navy, Federal Bureau of Investigation, US Department of State, and other interests who ran their own intelligence operations and were reluctant to share any intelligence they had gathered. I was named coordinator of information by the president in July of this year. It will be a tough job to coordinate the diverse agencies' intelligence, to say the least.

"I believe that dissertation answered the first three questions," Donovan concluded.

"Yes it did; very impressive, to say the least. I'm sorry I put you on the spot. But with the information you provided me, I had to know who you are. Now, the fourth question—where is this meeting going?" asked Carlton. "We have been here now over two hours with no end in sight."

"I'm sorry we are taking so long, but we had a lot of ground to cover. Hopefully, we have a short time to go," Donovan replied. "I have a lot of work to do combining all the intelligence work into one organization. I think we talked about that already—a new name, a larger group of agencies. Our meeting will last as long as you want it to. Let me continue. The war in Europe is continuing to escalate. The British are pushing us to enter the war. Congress doesn't want a war. The president is carefully monitoring what is happening in Europe and other places in the world. It is almost inevitable that we, the United States, will get involved. People will join or be drafted in service. I myself am looking for volunteers. That is what this meeting is about and why I am talking to you. Based on our and the British findings about you—your character, your coolness under fire, and your ability to speak fluent German—I, we, believe you could be a major contributor to the war effort and help ensure the defeat of the Nazis. We would like you to volunteer for service to your country in a civilian capacity."

"Hold on there, Donovan!" Carlton said incredulously. "What are you saying? You want me to be a contributor to the war effort. Why should I be? The United States is not a participant in the war in Europe. What do you mean, we are going to get involved in the war? You said you talk to the president, but who are you to know all this information and solicit me to participate in something that isn't happening? Where do you get the authority to ask me to give up my life to a war that we are not involved in? I'm being redundant, which I never am. I am a little upset at all this right now. I want to leave and go home. I have to think about this." Carlton got up and headed to the door.

"Please, Carlton, Mr. Fuller, I didn't mean to upset you. I knew what I said would impact you. But I had to let you know what the meeting was about and see your reaction. Please sit down and stay a little longer and allow me to provide more information to clarify what

I said. Let me offer you more coffee, water, or something stronger," replied Donovan.

After hearing the conversation and watching Carlton Fuller get up to leave, Major Best thought, *Man, what a job the boss has with this one.*

Carlton stopped, turned around, and asked, "What do you have that is stronger?"

"I have bourbon, scotch, and whiskey. What's your pleasure?" retorted Donovan.

"Scotch with water and ice," answered Carlton.

With that, Carlton sat down again, and Major Best went into the next room and came back with the scotch for Carlton and one for Donovan.

"Just like your brother," said Donovan. "Prost."

"Prost," said Carlton, returning the toast. "What do you mean just like my brother?"

"I told you the British were thorough," noted Donovan with a wry smile.

"I want you to think about it," he continued. "You are right. The United States is not in the war yet. You can't make a decision without talking about it with your wife. You may want to talk about it with your mother. Your decision will be the most important one that you have ever made. I fully understand that. But, please do not talk about the United States joining the war or the draft or the fact that people will be joining the service. Those were statements I made to impress upon you the importance of your participation. They were just rhetorical statements. The newspapers are full of the information I passed on to you. People are speculating that we will enter the war soon. We have had a number of people volunteer already. Same civilian capacity as you would be. A crisis is coming." With that last statement, Donovan stopped.

"I will talk about it with my wife and mother. You are the coordinator of intelligence for the United States. I assume you want me to volunteer for intelligence work?" asked Carlton.

"Yes, that is a correct assumption," responded Donovan.

"What would I be doing?" asked Carlton.

"That is a reasonable question, but we haven't fully determined the assignment," he lied. "You will be working for me and my office in New York, specifically for David Bruce. You would be trained in New Jersey, Canada, and other locations as necessary. Following graduation of your training, your assignment will be given to you. I will start the process to get you a top-secret clearance. That will give you enough time to make a decision. Remember our earlier discussion; consider this conversation one protected by lawyer-client privilege. I expect that privilege to prevail," Donovan added. "One other thing you need to think about. People in your neighborhood will be talked to by the folks working on your clearance. I'm sure they will be asking questions. Tell them you have no idea what is going on. That is all I can say at this time. Thank you for your time today. Major Best will take you home and let you know how to contact me when you make your decision. This will be a difficult decision. Take your time in making it. Call me with either yes or no, please. Major, please take Mr. Fuller home and make sure he has a telephone number to contact us," Donovan directed. With that, he extended his hand to Carlton.

The two men shook hands.

"Yes, sir!" replied Major Best.

"Before I leave, don't start working on any clearance for me. I don't want anyone sniffing around my neighborhood asking questions about me. I haven't volunteered for anything. Don't push, Mr. Donovan. I have a lot to think about," Carlton remarked as he left the office with Major Best.

Good News/Bad News

The ride home was longer than the ride to the meeting place had been. At least Carlton felt that it was. He was tired and wrung out. This guy Donovan knew more about him than he did. *He knew when I was born. He knew that I had a twin brother. He knew that we were identical twins. He knew our mother and that we were healthy after birth*, he reviewed. It went on and on. Donovan had even known his brother drank scotch and water with ice. The general had known what his father and brother were doing for the Nazis. He hadn't been able to ask enough questions. Donovan had done his homework.

"How are you, Mr. Fuller?" asked Major Best. "You and Mr. Donovan had a long day," he continued. "I thought you put the general to work today. He looked tired after you and he had finished the day. Normally, he isn't tired after his meetings."

"I'm doing okay. I'm tired also. It was a long day. It was a very emotional day for me. Not much time to rest between questions and answers. Is it always this way after his meetings?" Carlton replied. "I'm glad he was tired; he worked me over."

"I can't say, Mr. Fuller. He has a lot of meetings that I'm not invited to. I was at this one only because we are out of town. We are leaving tonight," said the major.

Carlton Fuller was looking forward to getting home and seeing his wife. He hadn't had a day like this since the last murder case he was involved with as a defense attorney. He had begun to drift off to sleep when the car lurched to a screeching stop. The major let out a line of nasty cusswords at the offending driver, who'd failed to stop at a stop sign.

"I almost hit the bastard. He didn't stop. I'm sorry, Mr. Fuller. If I had not stopped as quickly as I did, I would have T-boned him. Are you okay?" Major Best asked.

"I'm fine. If I hadn't grabbed the seat in front of me, I would have been on the floor. I had drifted off to sleep. It was just a natural reaction. I don't get to sit in the backseat of an automobile very often," replied Carlton.

"Here we are, Mr. Fuller. It was my pleasure meeting you, sir. Have a good evening, sir," Major Best said.

"You too, Major. Thank you for the ride," said Fuller. With that, he opened the door, got out of the car, walked to the front door, and opened it.

"Hi! I'm home, honey," called Carlton.

"Carlton, where have you been? You have been gone most of the day. What happened? You always call me when you are going to be late," said Maggie as she ran up to him and kissed him on the cheek. She was full of questions.

Carlton thought, *What do I do now?* Donovan had invoked client-lawyer privilege. He couldn't tell her much. He knew she would press him for answers that he couldn't respond to. "Hold on, honey. Give me a chance to go to the bathroom, sit down, clear my head, and get a scotch and water. Then I'll try to answer all the questions you have," he said.

Carlton returned to the living room and sat down in his favorite chair. Maggie was sitting on the edge of the couch, anxiously awaiting him. She was ready for answers to her questions. They always discussed his cases when he came home from the office or the courtroom. She was always a good sounding board. He was very lucky to have a wife who was willing to help and get involved if necessary. How was he going to handle this situation? He had been asked to volunteer to work for the government in a civilian role, to help with the war effort that the United States was not involved with yet. The man, Donovan, worked for the president of the United States. The role he was being asked to play had not been defined for him, with the exception that it would involve Germany because he was fluent in German. He would be trained in New Jersey, Canada, and other locations as necessary. Trained in what? There were too many unknowns. What would he tell Maggie? This would be the toughest thing he'd had to do—to lie very carefully to Maggie. He thought to himself, *Well here we go.*

"It was a very grueling meeting. I met with two people. Actually, I met with one. The other person was the major. He sat outside the office and listened. He was the other person's aide. They were very interested in me. I, in turn, was very interested in them. They were from Washington, DC. We talked about the war in Europe and its impact on the United States. I was very surprised about what Germany had been doing over the past few years. Apparently, the Nazis have invaded a number of countries, and there may be others in their sights."

He went on. "Honey, we knew about some of this from the *Cleveland Press*."

Maggie interrupted. "Where was your meeting? What did they want of you? Why did they question you?"

She was very inquisitive, he thought. "The meeting was at the Federal Bureau of Investigation building on the fifth floor. They were interested in my background as a lawyer and my ability to speak the German language," Carlton told her.

"Your ability to speak the German language?" Maggie asked. "Why?"

"They explained that, with the Germans pushing the war in Europe, they were looking for German-speaking Americans," explained Carlton.

"How did they know that you spoke German?" asked Maggie.

"They told me they had researched backgrounds of a number of Americans who had immigrated to the United States from Germany and found my name," responded Carlton.

"That makes sense," Maggie replied. She seemed to quiet down with that answer. She relaxed a bit.

Carlton went on, "We talked about my family in Germany and when the last time I had visited them was. I told them I hadn't seen them or heard from them for a number of years. They indicated that the British were pushing the United States to get into the war. I told them we had read that in the *Press*." Carlton was feeling more relaxed. "What have you made for dinner, honey?" he asked. It was a question to divert Maggie from asking more detailed questions. It worked.

"Oh, I made beef stew. Did you have lunch?" she asked.

"No, but I bet that stew is good. You know I love your stew," Carlton responded.

"I'll go and set the table. You get ready for dinner," said Maggie.

"Thank you, honey," replied Carlton.

He started thinking about the meeting and what Donovan had said when he'd asked if he would be interested in joining him as a civilian volunteer. He would be working for some guy named David Bruce. He would be trained in New Jersey and Canada. Then what? he asked himself.

He had more questions. He needed to call the number they had given him. *I'm just a lawyer who speaks German.*

He was also hungry, and the stew smelled good.

Thank God Maggie hadn't asked any more questions tonight. Maybe she had something else on her mind.

It was September 1940, and his docket was full. The leaves had started to fall, and the house had to be readied for winter. He was going to be busy before the holidays, but he had to call Donovan with a decision of sorts.

Following dinner, Carlton picked up the *Cleveland Press* and started to read the evening paper. The more Carlton read about the war, the more he started to resent his ancestry. He thought to himself, *This has been going on since 1936.* There were thousands dead, countries were being taken over, and Jews were being persecuted. What was going on? Why was Germany doing this? Carlton was embroiled in his thinking about the war going on over in Europe. Since the meeting with Donovan, what he was reading in the evening paper had taken on a new significance.

"Honey," he called to Maggie, "have you been reading about what has been going on in the war in Europe?"

"Yes, I have," Maggie said. "I'm glad we're not sending people over there to fight. I'm glad we aren't involved."

"What are you doing?" asked Carlton.

"I'm listening to the radio. I'm involved in a mystery program that is very complicated. Some of these programs scare the bejeebers out of me," answered Maggie.

"Then why do you listen to them?" called Carlton.

"I get tired of reading the newspaper and listening to the news on the radio about what is going on in the world. Listening to the mystery stories gives me mental relief. They relieve the stress that I get thinking about war," said Maggie.

"I understand. Seems as if I just started to worry about the United States going to war. Sorry I bothered you. I'm going to get a nightcap. Would you like one?" asked Carlton.

CODE NAME: ARC ANGEL

"No, honey. I won't be able to sleep if I have one," Maggie replied.

As he was pouring his scotch, Carlton was thinking, *Sleep—I'm not sure I will be able to sleep tonight; too much on my mind.* He was thinking of Donovan. *Who is this mystery man? What does he want of me? What does he know that I don't?* His training as a lawyer was taking over his thinking process. He needed to do more investigating. *Where do I begin?*

Good question. The library was a good place to start. He decided to start with what Donovan said about himself.

The president had named him coordinator of information. The purpose of the office was to coordinate the gathering of intelligence by different government agencies. Was he looking for someone to help him gather or collect intelligence? Was he looking for people to volunteer to be spies or work with spies? *Why would I be working for David Bruce and not him? Who is David Bruce? Why now, as the United States was not at war? Why me?*

That last one was the question going round and round in his head. It was getting late. He told himself he should be getting on to bed. The decision could wait until morning. Carlton went to the bathroom, washed his face, put on the pajamas that Maggie had given him, and slipped into bed. He didn't want to wake up Maggie.

She stirred and said, "I'm awake. I have been waiting to tell you something. We are going to have a baby. Isn't that exciting?"

The ever-reserved Carlton jumped out of bed and shouted, "We are going to have a baby! *Exciting* isn't the word. There is no word except *happiness!* I'm going to be a father again. Number three. Oh my God."

With that he jumped back in bed. Then he put his arms around Maggie and kissed her full on the lips. He hugged her, and she hugged back and kissed him back. She was crying with joy. What more could they say that would express their happiness? They made love as they hadn't for some time.

The next day dawned bright and chilly. It was a perfect September, early fall day. Carlton stepped outside to check the weather, took a deep breath, and exclaimed to himself, *What a great day it is.* The fresh air made him feel full of himself.

The phone started to ring as he stepped back into the house. The phone's ring seemed louder than Carlton remembered.

"Carlton," called Maggie from the basement, "I can't answer the phone. I'm taking wet clothes out of the washing machine. Please answer the phone."

She was standing there in her robe looking as beautiful as possible. Oh how he loved this woman. She must have started washing clothes very early this morning.

"Okay," he responded. "I'll get it."

"Hello. This is the Fuller residence," Carlton answered.

"Hello, Carlton. This is your mother. I have bad news. Horst, your brother, just called me from Germany. He told me that your father had a stroke. He wants you to come to Germany as fast as you can get there to see your father before he dies. He indicated that he would arrange for your visit, given the situation in the world being what it is today. I told him you had no relationship with your father, but he insisted you come, as he said your father wanted to see you before he died."

"My God, Mother, the United States and Germany are at odds today. He wants me to come to Germany to talk to my father before he dies. I can't," Carlton said. "I would have to arrange to get a passport to travel to Germany. I don't know if the United States would let me travel to Germany, Mother."

"Horst said he would call you later this week with all the arrangements," said his mother. "I gave Horst your phone number," she continued. "He sounded so sad but so very German. I'm glad I had a chance to talk to him. It has been so long. I guess I'm getting old. I almost cried when he said, 'Hello, Mother. This is Horst.' He was speaking in German. Horst explained that your father was working at his office when he had the stroke. Horst said that the stroke left him paralyzed on his left side. He is very weak. Horst said he still could speak but very faintly. Your father wants to talk with you before he dies. Oh, Carlton, he is your father; please go before he dies."

He began to think; his mother had immigrated to the United States with him after she and his father had divorced. She had never remarried. Carlton suspected that his mother had never lost her love for his father. It was just the way she talked about him over the years that caused him to be suspicious. She was getting very emotional; she was crying now and becoming inconsolable.

"Mother, I will think about it. Please try not to be so emotional about this." He was trying to calm her down. "It will be a very difficult decision. The world situation will determine if I can make such a trip. The US government will make that decision for me. Do you want Maggie and me to come over and help you with dinner?" asked Carlton.

"Yes," his mother answered. "I'm very upset over this knowledge of your father being close to death. Would you and Maggie and the children come to have dinner with me?"

"We will be there at about five thirty," Carlton told his mother. "I'll see you then." He hung up the telephone.

He wanted to do what his mother wanted him to do. This was family business. How would he travel to Germany? What would the cost be? How could he and Maggie afford it? Would Maggie want to come with him? He would have to get a passport. His mind was going around in circles.

Carlton opened the door to the basement. Maggie was waiting for him at the foot of the steps.

"Maggie we need to talk. What are you doing?" asked Carlton.

"I am finishing washing the clothes. What's the matter? Who was that on the phone? Come downstairs. We can talk while the next load finishes," Maggie called up to him.

"What's on your mind?" she asked when Carlton had started down the steps.

"It was a call from my mother," Carlton started. "She was crying on the phone. She informed me that my brother, Horst, had called her. He told her that my father had a very serious stroke and wants to talk to me before he dies. She wants me to go and talk to him. She wants us to come to her house tonight for dinner to discuss this. I told her we would."

Maggie was shocked. "Your father had a stroke? He wants to talk with you before he dies? Where? When? Your mother wants you to go? What is going on? What did you say? You aren't going?"

Carlton grabbed Maggie by the shoulders and shook her slightly. "Hang on, Maggie. Please settle down. Let's talk about this. I just finished the call. Please settle down," Carlton said softly. "Please settle down, honey," he added calmly.

"Settle down? How did you think I would react?" Maggie asked angrily.

Now she was getting emotional, he thought.

"I'm sorry I reacted as I did. I was surprised and shocked all at once. Please tell me what is going on, so that I *can* calm down," Maggie exclaimed.

Carlton explained the conversation with his mother.

She thought that Horst had acted incredulously. "What? Is he nuts?" Maggie exclaimed.

"What a month, first finding out I'm pregnant, Donovan asking you to participate in a war that the United States is not involved with, and your brother asking you to go to Germany to talk with your father. What is going on?" Maggie asked. "I'm tired. I'm going upstairs to take a nap. We can talk about this tonight after the children go to bed. You go to dinner with your mother. I can't stand it when she cries. She will make me and the children start crying with her. Please, honey, try to understand." She shut off the washing the machine and turned toward the door to the upstairs.

"I'm trying very hard. I feel like you do. It has been a crazy month. I'm going to have a scotch. I'm going to relax for an hour. Then I will go to my mother's. I should be home later after we have dinner," he replied as he went up the basement stairs following Maggie. *What a day*, he thought to himself. There would be more tears this afternoon. And there would be more tears tonight when he told Maggie he was going to Germany to visit his father.

He would have to check for ticket prices and availability at the travel agency downtown. He would also have to visit the post office to apply for a passport. It was going to be a busy week.

Carlton finally arrived at his mother's house. He hadn't told Maggie of his decision. Her being pregnant would make it more difficult for her to understand. He would tell his mother while they were having dinner.

Carlton's dinner with his mother was a success. She had made Weiner schnitzel with purple cabbage and boiled potatoes. She baked bread and had gone to the German bakery and bought an apple crumb *kugan* for dessert. It was delicious. His mother was very happy that he had decided to visit his father. She offered to pay for the trip. He felt she wanted to make sure he would make the visit.

He explained to her that he had to visit the travel agency to find out the cost of tickets. He had to explain the passport process to her. He explained that, with the war situation in Europe, he did not know if the United States would let him travel to Germany.

Carlton realized that this visit had been easy, as he had already made the decision to visit his father. He thanked his mother for the wonderful dinner. He kissed her good-bye and left to go home. It was about 6:00 p.m.

The next discussion with Maggie was going to be a lot more emotional and teary. As he was driving home, he thought about how he was going to approach Maggie. He realized he couldn't concentrate; he didn't want to hurt her feelings. He had to find a way to let her down easy.

Carlton pulled into his driveway, still pondering the best way to tell Maggie. He almost hit the garage door. *Oh my God*, he thought. *What am I doing, you have to open the garage door before you pull the car into the garage.*

He stopped the car just in time, put on the emergency brake, got out of the car, and opened the garage door. *Finally*, he thought as he closed the door and walked to the house. He opened the side door and said, "Hi. I'm home." He was feeling a bit nervous, as he knew that Maggie would be upset.

"Hi, honey," called Maggie. "How did it go with Oma?"

"It went much better than I expected," he replied. "I need to discuss the situation with you.

"Where are the kids?" he asked.

"Upstairs listening to the Lone Ranger on the radio," she told him.

They sat down in the front room. Carlton began. "My mother gave me more details about what happened to my father. He had a very serious stroke. His entire left side is paralyzed. Horst told her that, although my father speaks very softly and slowly, he can be understood. He told Horst he wanted to talk with me prior to his dying. My mother wants me to go to Germany so badly that she would pay for the trip by selling her jewels. She begged me to go. I tried to tell her that I had to apply for a passport and also find out the cost of the trip. I indicated to her that I didn't think the United States would let me travel because of the war situation in Germany. I told her I didn't think I would be able to go because of all of the difficulties in trying to leave the United States to travel to Germany."

Maggie didn't react negatively this time. Apparently, the short nap had helped calm her down. Her comment shocked Carlton. "Honey, I understand. Check out the cost of tickets and apply for passports for both you and me. I want to meet the man who made you, and I want to be with you. You aren't going to make a trip to Germany without me. I'm sure that, between your mother and us, we can put together the money to get there and back. Your brother can put us up at his home."

Relieved, all Carlton could say was, "Okay."

They put the kids to bed and had a drink. Maggie, because she was

BRUCE JARVIS

pregnant, had warm milk. Carlton had a double scotch. He was still reeling from Maggie's reaction. Maggie was excited. She started talking about clothes for the trip and what they would be doing while they were traveling. She had never been out of the country. As a matter of fact, Carlton thought, neither had he. Her excitement was catching up with him. He couldn't wait to tell his mother. He would talk with her tomorrow. It was going to be a busy day. They headed upstairs to turn in.

Carlton couldn't get to sleep. He was thinking about the trip to Germany. Germany was at war with Europe and his father wanted to talk with him before he died. What would he do if he couldn't get a passport for him and Maggie? Poor Mother; what would she do if he couldn't make the trip? His mind was going in circles. It was going to be a long night if he couldn't go to sleep.

After coffee in the morning, Carlton asked Maggie where the telephone book was.

"It's in the cabinet that the phone is on in the hallway," she responded. "Why do you need the telephone book?"

"I need to find the addresses of the post office downtown and of a travel agency for our trip," he told her.

He found the telephone book and looked up the post office first. There it was. The address was 301 Prospect Avenue. Now, a travel agency. He found one called Cooks Tours, located at 173 Superior Avenue. *That's great,* he thought. Both were located downtown. *Two birds with one trip. Perfect.*

"Maggie I found the addresses. I'm going first to the bank to get some cash and then to the post office and travel agency. I should be home in three or four hours."

"Okay, honey. Be careful," she replied. "I'll get the kids off to school."

Carlton was driving home very disappointed. The person he'd spoken to at the post office had advised him that the United States was limiting the number of people traveling to Germany due to the war going on in Europe. "You must be approved by the State Department to travel anywhere in Europe," he'd been informed. "Your reason to travel must be a very serious issue." Carlton had tried to explain that his father was dying. That wasn't reason enough, he had been told. He'd left angry.

Next, the travel agent had explained that he first needed a passport.

Pan American Airlines flew to Marseille, France. The fare would be $673 round trip from Port Washington, New York. Train fare from Cleveland, Ohio, to New York, New York, would be $100 round trip for a coach car and $200 for a sleeping car. The travel agent didn't have the amount of the train fare from Marseille, France, to Berlin, Germany. She advised that the fares had changed since the Germans had taken over the trains in France.

No passport, no trip, he thought as he pulled into his driveway. It had been a disappointing day to say the least, he thought as he closed the garage door and walked to the house.

He walked into the house and called, "Hi. I'm home."

"Hi, honey," Maggie called. "What's wrong?"

"I need a drink. It was a very frustrating day. I wasn't successful at either the post office or the travel agency."

As Maggie went to the bar and fixed Carlton a scotch and water, Carlton told her the whole story.

She sat down. "You did have a frustrating day," she said. "Based on the costs you found out at the travel agency, we wouldn't be able to afford the trip anyway. The airplane trip sounded exciting, particularly since neither of us has ever flown. Spending the overnight portion of the trip in a sleeping car sounded romantic. I am looking forward to the trip more now than before after your explanation." Maggie tried to help Carlton get past his disappointment. She started contemplating ways they could solve the problem. "I've got it!" she exclaimed. "Call your friend Bill Donovan, the president's man. He wants you to do something for him. Why couldn't he do this for you?" she asked excitingly.

Carlton swallowed his drink. "You are right, Maggie. What a great idea. Maybe I can make a deal with him."

"Don't you dare volunteer for anything," Maggie replied. "Don't let Donovan talk you into anything. Based on what you told me about him, he is a slick-talking man."

"He has a mission to accomplish. I don't know what it is. But if the country goes to war, he has to fulfill it. That's what worries me about him," Carlton said. "I'll call him in the morning. Thanks, Maggie, for discussing this with me. Your idea to talk with Donovan is perfect. As a lawyer, I make deals all the time. Why can't I do this one for us?"

Privately, he was thinking, *I've never dealt with a man of this stature when I've made deals in the courtroom with other lawyers.*

He would plan a strategy and implement it!

Ḉꞣe Ḉall

Carlton reviewed in his mind how he was going to ask Donovan for his help in getting him to Germany. He placed the call to Donovan.

"Hello. Mr. Donovan's office. Miss Jordan speaking. How I may help you?"

"Hello, my name is Carlton Fuller. May I speak to Mr. Donovan."

"I'm sorry, Mr. Fuller. Mr. Donovan is out of the office at this time. May I take a message? I expect him back later this afternoon."

"Yes, please do. Ask him to please call me at home. He has my home telephone number."

"I will, Mr. Fuller. Thank you for calling."

What a polite person, Carlton thought. He wondered when Donovan would call.

It wasn't five minutes, and the telephone rang.

"Hello, this is the Fuller residence," said Carlton.

"Hello, Mr. Fuller. This is William Donovan. How are you? I have been waiting for your call. Have you made a decision regarding my request for your services?"

"I have Mr. Donovan. But before we get into that decision, I have another problem I have to make a decision on first," he replied.

"My brother, Horst, called my mother from Germany. He told her that my father had a very serious stroke. My father wants me to come to Germany as soon as possible and talk with him before he dies. Horst indicated that he would be able to make the arrangements with the German government to allow me and my wife to make the trip. He also said that my coming was very important to him and my father. Given the world issues today, I wouldn't have any idea first, how I would get there but second, could I even go? I know making the trip would require passport and transportations." Carlton went on to explain to Donovan the issues he had encountered and the frustrations he had gone through when he'd tried to make arrangements. The war complicated the entire issue.

"You are right calling me and explaining your reasons and frustrations, given the situation. It would be difficult to travel to Germany at this time, but I believe I can help. I do not know if your wife would be able to travel with you. The United States still has a diplomatic relationship with Germany. We have a chargé d'affaires in Germany named Leland B. Morris. Before we get to the details or finalize anything, I would like to meet with you. I'm available on Friday of this week. If you can make it, I will send Major Best to pick you up." Donovan added, "If I can make your trip happen, I will want you to help me out with a few things I need from Germany. Will you do that for me?"

Donovan was already thinking of the future. *This situation is perfect. I couldn't have set it up if I wanted to*, he thought to himself. *The Lord works in many ways.* "In addition, tell your brother when he calls that, if I can make the arrangements, you will be traveling on a US visa. He should coordinate your visit with our chargé d'affaires, Mr. Leland Morris, at our embassy. Please do not mention my name or my office to your brother."

Carlton was stunned at Donovan's positive response. "I'm sure I will be able to do the things you ask if the trip works out. I will clear my Friday calendar and plan to meet with you," he replied. "Thank you, Mr. Donovan. What time should I expect Major Best to be at my home to pick me up?"

"He will be there at nine a.m. I'm looking forward to our meeting." Donovan responded.

"Thank you, Mr. Donovan. Your answer to my questions and doubts are more than I expected. I hadn't planned to travel overseas ever. This trip will help my mother, as she will be comforted to know that I saw my father before he died. It will also satisfy my brother's concerns. Now all I have to do is help my wife through this decision.

"By the way, did I tell you my wife is pregnant with our third child? She advised me the evening following your and my first meeting. She is very concerned about your request. I have not made that decision yet. I hope you understand," Carlton said.

"Congratulations on the new child. It is always a joyous time for a family when a new child is expected. I will get started on your arrangements." Donovan stopped himself and thought... "If I can make this happen, you will travel as a diplomat working for the State Department and will be visiting the chargé d'affaires for me. This way, the trip itself will not cost you, with the exception of personal expenses. Tell your brother that the only way the US government will allow you to travel is on a diplomat's visa. This will also protect you from any harm by the German government. Thank you for calling. Good-bye."

As he hung up the phone, Carlton thought, *My God. What just happened.*

"Maggie where are you?" Carlton called. "We need to sit down and talk. I need your help to digest what just transpired on my phone call to Donovan."

"I'm in the kitchen starting dinner. The kids will be home from school shortly and will be looking for a snack. Can it wait until I deal with the kids?" she asked.

"It will have to. Please don't be too long," Carlton replied.

The family sat down and had dinner. The children were full of talk about school and their homework. Maggie made potato pancakes and served them with sugar and sour cream. They were delicious. It was getting later in the evening. Maggie took the children up to take a bath and get ready for bed. The hours since the phone call with Donovan had dragged, as Carlton wanted to talk with Maggie.

"Carlton," called Maggie. "Come up and read the kids a book and tuck them in for bed. They haven't had the opportunity to spend much time with you lately."

"Okay. I'm coming up," he replied.

"Hi, Daddy," the kids shouted in unison.

Carlton sat down and read the children two books and joked around with them. Carlton Jr. was six, and Charlotte was five. He was always amazed how they grew up a little more each day. "Good night, children," he said softly as he tucked them in with a hug and a kiss.

"Good night, Daddy," they each replied. "One more hug, Daddy," they shouted in unison.

Carlton complied.

Maggie was waiting for him as he came down the steps.

"Finally, honey, we get to talk. It has been a busy day for both you and me," he said.

"Kids first and then us," she said as she reached for Carlton and kissed him on the cheek. "What happened with your call from Donovan?" she asked.

Carlton explained the details to Maggie. Donovan had agreed that he would help Carlton get to Germany to see his father. Donovan had some things that Carlton would have to do for him while he was there. Carlton would be traveling as a diplomat. Donovan did not know whether or not Maggie would be able to make the trip. There were still some unanswered questions, but it was plain to Carlton he was going to be able to see his father.

Maggie's first comments were, "Aren't you afraid with all that is going on in Europe? How will you travel there? Where will you stay? Where will you meet Horst? I have a lot of questions and no answers. I'm starting to worry."

"So do I," Carlton replied. "I am worried too. I have a meeting scheduled with Donovan Friday morning. Major Best will be picking me up at nine in the morning. I'm sure many of the details will be worked out then. Hopefully, all the questions will be answered." They had been talking for more than three hours.

"How about a nightcap before we go to bed?" Carlton asked Maggie.

Maggie agreed "Sounds like we have an adventure ahead."

What a profound statement that would be.

Friday Morning

The doorbell rang. Carlton answered the door. It was Major Best. "Good morning, Mr. Fuller," said Major Best. "Are you ready to leave, sir?"

"Good morning, Major. Yes, I'm ready. Give me a minute to put on my hat and coat, and we'll be on our way," Carlton replied.

Maggie came over and kissed Carlton good-bye.

"Wish me luck, honey. See you later today," Carlton said as he closed the door and headed toward the major's car.

"How are you, major?" Carlton asked once inside.

"I am fine, sir. I have been very busy since you and General Donovan talked on the telephone this week. I have been working on a great deal of detailed information for your trip. The general is happy that you will have the opportunity to visit with your father before he passes. Be surprised, Mr. Fuller. I shouldn't have said anything regarding the trip."

"You said I will have the opportunity to visit my father! I'm going!" Carlton exclaimed. Oh, thank you, Major, for your help in making this trip happen. I am very excited that I will be able to make the trip. I am concerned about the travel and the situation in Europe. I am surprised that General Donovan was able to accomplish it."

"Sir, General Donovan can make anything happen. He is well respected and well connected. I have seen him accomplish what many cannot," replied the major.

"Have you ever been to Germany, Major?" asked Carlton.

"No, sir. Can't say that I have. I understand that it is a beautiful country," Best replied.

"Yes, from what I remember as a child, it is beautiful. The people are happy and strong. It is a country with much discipline," Carlton said.

"Here we are, sir. I'll be dropping you off. Do you remember how to find the general's office?" asked Major Best.

"Yes I do, Major. Thanks for the ride. I expect I will see you later."

"Yes, sir," said the Major as he opened the car door.

Carlton found his way to the general's office. He knocked on the door.

A young lady answered the door. "Hello. You must be Carlton Fuller. I'm Michelle Jordan. The general is waiting for you. Please come in. I'll take your hat and coat. May I get you something to drink?' she asked.

"No thank you," Carlton replied. *What an efficient young lady*, he thought.

"Hello, Mr. Fuller. Good to see you," General Donovan said. He extended his hand and shook Carlton's with firm pressure. "Please sit down; we have a busy day ahead."

"Thank you, General," replied Carlton. "I am looking forward to it with trepidation."

"I understand your concern. This is a large undertaking on your part. Let's begin. I have been successful in my endeavor to get you to Germany. In fact, more than just you will be traveling to Germany. Your wife will travel with you."

Carlton was speechless. He was so excited he couldn't speak.

"Let me continue. I have been in contact with the State Department to arrange for credentials for you and your wife to travel to and from Germany to visit your dying father. I have asked them to consider you a diplomat with a wife – who, rather than just attending his father, is there to review the situation in Germany for the State Department. I have explained my requirements to State and will be in touch with our chargé d'affaires, Leland Morris, in Germany to get his concurrence. I don't believe that will be a problem.

"Major Best and my secretary have been working on travel arrangements for you and your wife. Although traveling is very difficult to Europe, they have been successful in accomplishing the task at hand. In fact, I will be sending Major Best with you and your wife as an aide and protector. Hopefully, you will support his effort. He will be at your and your wife's service throughout this trip. Him being with you will enhance your status in the eyes of the Germans. I expect you will stay with your brother during your visit with your father. During the time you are with your brother, your wife will be spending time with Major Best touring the city and Germany as part of the diplomatic visit. Mr. Morris will make those arrangements. I have been doing all the talking. How about having a cup of coffee and time to ask some questions?" Donovan suggested.

"Whew, what a lot has happened since we talked. I am excited and overwhelmed. Yes, I will have a cup of coffee," Carlton replied. "Maggie will be beside herself. She won't believe she will be traveling with me. Major Best coming with us will be wonderful and make us feel a lot more comfortable in a difficult situation

"Thank you very much for you help, Mr. Donovan. I have a lot of questions: How will we get around while we are in Germany? What will the cost of the trip be? How do we reimburse you and the country for this opportunity? Who will take care of my children while Maggie and I are out of the country? I'm sure I will have many more questions before we begin our travel."

"Major, please bring in the coffee and a cup for yourself," Donovan requested.

"Yes, sir," said the major.

"Major, when we were talking in the car, you didn't mention that there was a chance for you to travel with us," noted Carlton.

"No, sir. I didn't. It was the general who had to say it. Not I." He winked.

"Shelly, please come in and explain the travel arrangements you have made and confirmed for the Fullers and Major Best," asked the general.

"Yes, sir," responded Shelly. "Mr. Fuller, you and Mrs. Fuller are leaving Cleveland for New York in three days. You will be leaving at six p.m. on the New York Central Train Lake Shore Limited from the Cleveland Terminal Tower terminal. You will have a sleeper car, Number 6. The train will arrive in New York City at ten a.m. Major Best will meet you at the station. You will travel to the Roosevelt Hotel in Manhattan to spend the remainder of the day and evening. The next morning, you will travel with Major Best to the Marine Air Terminal at LaGuardia International Airport in New York City. The three of you will catch a Pan American B-314 Clipper to fly to Marseilles, France, via Horta, Azores, and Lisbon, Portugal. The total flight time will be approximately twenty-seven hours. You will be provided with a private compartment on the aircraft. All meals and drinks are included. You will then travel to Berlin via train from Marseilles to Berlin. The Germans have assured us that your trip from Marseilles to Berlin will be safe. They will have an escort meet you in Marseilles. The escort will travel with you on the train. Once you arrive in Berlin, an embassy car will pick you up and take you to the embassy. Local arrangements for transportation while in Berlin will be made by the Germans. Local transportation for Mrs. Fuller will be managed by the embassy. Major Best will be with you throughout the travel. Your return will be handled by the embassy personnel at your convenience. All transportation is round trip."

"Wow, you have thought of everything. Thank you, Shelly, for your help," said Donovan.

"You are welcome, sir. That's what you pay me for," she said as she left the office.

"We have never traveled on a plane or train," Carlton replied. "What an adventure."

"Will you and Mrs. Fuller be able to make all the arrangements necessary in three days?" asked the general.

"If we want to make the trip, we will," said Carlton. "Now, sir, what do you want me to do for you?"

"I have a full schedule for you. Shelly will provide you with a detailed set of orders to review and memorize. Your first effort will be to understand both your father's and your brother's role within the Nazi regime. It is important that you learn and understand what they do and why. Meet their contacts. Try to understand their relationships. Meet their families. Try and establish a relationship with them. This information is important to the United States. I will meet with you and your wife following your visit to debrief both of you.

"Please make sure your wife understands her role. If she needs help with this role, I would be happy to discuss it with her. She will be traveling around Berlin and Germany with the major. Her local travel will be coordinated with the Germans by the embassy staff. The Germans will be showing her all of the positive things the Nazis are doing for the people and the country. Please make sure she looks beyond the obvious wherever she travels. Please make sure she meets Horst's family. Shelly will provide a package of information for both you and your wife to learn and understand during your trip over to Germany.

"During the trip, we will be monitoring your travels. You won't know this is happening. Should you have any difficulties during your travels, your point of contact is Mr. Leland Morris, the chargé d'affaires at our embassy. Major Best will do any damage control necessary, should that be required while you are in Germany. I don't expect that there will be any issues. But we want to be alert continuously while you are there. You are valuable assets to the United States. Have a good trip, and I will see you both when you return. Bon voyage!"

With that, Donovan shook Carlton's hand and left the room.

Shelly came into the room and said, "I will come out to your home in two days. I will have the detailed information package, all your tickets, your passports, and any other information necessary for your trip. Please have passport pictures taken of both you and your wife. I will attach them to the passport when I get to your home. If you have any questions regarding the trip, please contact me. Have a good trip. I'm sorry your father is sick. I will pray for him. I will see you in two days. Good-bye." Shelly left the room.

Major Best came into the room. "Well, Mr. Fuller, it seems we will be traveling companions," he said. "I'm looking forward to spending time with you and your wife. It will be an adventure for us all. I'm honored to be traveling with both of you."

"I'm very happy you will be with us during this trip to Germany. Please call me Carlton. Maggie and I are honored that Mr. Donovan decided to have you travel with us. Please take me home. This has been trying on my mind for a week. We have a lot to do in the next three days."

"Yes, sir," replied Major Best.

It was a quiet car during the ride home.

"Thanks, Major. We will see you next in New York at the train station. Have a good week," Carlton said as he closed the car door.

"Yes, sir. I will be at the station in New York picking you and Mrs. Fuller up. Have a good trip," the major replied.

Carlton opened the door and called to Maggie. "Hi. I'm home. I have a lot to talk about."

"I have been waiting for you nervously. Horst called while you were at your meeting. He wants to know what is happening. He contacted the US embassy and said they knew nothing. He said your father was holding his own but was getting weaker. He left a number to call him," Maggie told him.

They hugged.

"Sorry for taking so long," Carlton said, "but Donovan had a lot of information to discuss. Let's sit down and talk about the trip. The details are important, as Donovan has a lot for both of us to do."

Carlton spent the better part of an hour explaining to Maggie the details of the travel. He explained his role and Maggie's role. He explained that Donovan would be considering them assets of the US government while on the trip and that they would be monitored during the whole trip. He noted that Major Best would be traveling with them the entire time, except during the train trip to and from New York. He and Maggie would be considered a "diplomat and wife" while in Germany. The German government would be advised that they were to be treated accordingly. The purpose of the trip was for a diplomat to visit his dying father with his brother and family. It was also to review the status of the German state." He continued, "One last item. We must get passport pictures done quickly. Donovan's secretary will put them on the passports when she comes out here to our home in two days."

Initially all Maggie could say was, "Leave in three days?" and, "That Donovan wants his pound of flesh."

She was happy that Major Best would be traveling with them. She felt more secure with him around. She was looking forward to meeting Horst and his family. She wasn't looking forward to meeting Carlton's father under the circumstances but would do whatever was necessary to support Carlton. She had to think about her other role—visiting Berlin and seeing the state of Germany under Nazi control. Looking beyond the obvious was a mysterious request. She had to think about this.

Hopefully, Oma would take care of the children for the time they would be away.

What clothing to take? She would be a diplomat's wife. Wow! What did that mean? Maggie's mind was going a mile a minute. *One day at a time*, Maggie thought. We have a lot to do and very little time to do it in.

"Well, honey, we have a lot to look forward to and a lot to prepare for," she said. Would you contact your mother and ask her to stay here at the house with the children? I'll put together a grocery list. Then I'll go shopping and prepare our bedroom for Oma. The kids will be excited that we will be traveling to Europe. Having Oma taking care of them for a few days will be great fun for them. I will have to make sure that Oma knows how to operate our radio. That way, she can listen to all her shows.

I will talk with the children about our travel and Oma. They'll have to learn to listen to Oma's shows while we're away.

"You will have to change your schedule and contact all of your clients. Hopefully, you have nothing pressing. And we'll have to purchase some suitcases or trunks for this trip. I will start looking for a place to buy them. You'll have to go and get them. If I need clothes, I will go out and buy them. Will you need clothes? Whew, very exciting but very busy. I'll stop. I'm a little overwhelmed now."

"I know how you feel, Maggie. I feel the same way," said Carlton. "I need to get to the bank. Our initial expense will be high, and we will need cash to make the purchases. We will need traveling money for some meals, cabs, and other expenses. My clients will understand the visit to see my dying father. I will have to postpone a couple of trials. Hopefully, the judges will also understand. Since neither of us has ever taken a trip such as this, we will have either a great experience or a nasty one. Hopefully, the trip will be the former rather than the latter. We will be together, enjoying the ride with Major Best. It was my impression that Donovan was looking for a lot from us. When we return, he will debrief us personally. I think he stuck his reputation on the line for us, given the world situation today."

The next two days were full of shopping for clothes, suitcases, a camera, makeup, and groceries for Oma and the children, as well as getting their pictures taken.

Oma was excited that Carlton and Maggie would be traveling to Germany to visit his father. She hoped the visit would bring Carlton and his brother closer. She had completely forgotten about the war in Europe. She was also looking forward to spending the time with the children.

For their part, the children were excited that Oma was coming to stay with them.

By the time Monday morning came, it was time to finish up with the last-minute details and start reading the packages Shelly had brought over Sunday afternoon.

Maggie remarked after meeting the general's secretary, "Shelly must have worked overtime putting the packages together in such a short time. What a very nice woman. Donovan must be very happy having her as a secretary."

"Tell that to Donovan when we get back. I have a feeling she does a lot of overtime work for him. He is that type. Very demanding," Carlton replied.

Carlton was able to contact Horst. It was a good conversation. He asked Horst to speak English, and Horst complied without question. Horst was pleased that Carlton and his wife were coming to Germany. Carlton explained that the only way they could make the trip was with the help of the US government, as the United States was not issuing passports to travel to Europe because of the war going on. He explained that he and Maggie would be traveling as a diplomat and his wife visiting his dying father. Horst seemed concerned about their traveling on "official business" but replied that, since they were coming, he wasn't that concerned. That struck Carlton as interesting, but he let it go.

Horst indicated that he wanted Carlton and Maggie to stay with him while they were in Germany. Carlton let Horst know that, as long as they would be visiting their father, that would be okay. Carlton advised Horst that his point of contact was Mr. Leslie Morris the chargé d'affaires at the US embassy. Horst understood. He said he knew of Mr. Morris and would be in touch with him. He advised that the German government would do whatever it took to make the visit of Carlton and Maggie successful. The German government would fully cooperate with the US embassy requirements.

"Have a safe trip. I'm looking forward to seeing you both. My wife will be ecstatic. I know Father will be happy when I tell him you are coming. Although he is getting weaker, he has been waiting for you. I don't know how much longer he will last. Good-bye." Horst hung up the telephone.

Journey to Germany

he taxi stopped in front of the Terminal Tower on the public square side in downtown Cleveland. The area was bustling with people. It was drizzling outdoors. Carlton paid the taxi driver after he took the trunk and suitcases out of the back of the taxi. A redcap came out of the Terminal Tower building. He asked Carlton if he could take their trunk and suitcases to the train. Carlton agreed and said they were traveling on the New York Central Lake Shore Limited, Pullman sleeping car 6.

The redcap seemed very knowledgeable about the train. "Yes, sir" he said as he led the couple inside the building and down a slight ramp to the train station. The station was full of people hurrying to and from trains. Carlton hadn't realized how many people would be traveling.

Carlton and Maggie were transfixed at the station. It was so large, with shops and restaurants lining the sides of it. They had never been to the station or the Terminal Tower that housed it.

"This is absolutely beautiful, Carlton. I never knew this existed. We can see the Terminal Tower from our house. We have to bring the children and Oma down here to see all this. Maybe we can come down to lunch here after we get back. Do you think we could take a ride to the top of the tower?" she asked.

"I'm sure we can make a day of it. I agree with you; it is a beautiful station. Cleveland is proud of it. Where is the redcap with our trunk and suitcases?" asked Carlton. "I lost track of him."

"There he is, waiting I think for us. He is over at those stairways in the middle of the station," Maggie replied.

An announcement came from overhead speakers. "New York Central Train, Lake Shore Limited is now boarding on track 12. All aboard."

The redcap was waving at Carlton and Maggie to come over and go down to their train. They finally reached the redcap, and he led them down the stairs to the train and to their car. The porter was standing at the entrance to the Pullman sleeping car. Carlton thanked the redcap and gave him a dollar tip. The redcap thanked Carlton and left. The Pullman porter introduced himself as George and looked at their tickets. It was for duplex roomettes.

In the ticket package, Shelly had left Maggie a note. It said, "I know you are pregnant, so I requested duplex roomettes. That way, you will have the room to sleep comfortably. Have a good trip." It was signed "Shelly."

The porter took their trunk and suitcases, stored them, and led Carlton and Maggie to their roomettes.

Maggie remarked, "Shelly is wonderful to get us a roomette like this. They will be comfortable. Don't let me forget to thank her when we return."

"I won't forget. I'm looking forward to dinner," Carlton replied.

The porter let them know that dinner would be served at 7:00 p.m. He advised that he would set up the roomettes for sleeping at 9:00 p.m. He then left to attend to other passengers.

At 6:00 p.m. sharp, the conductor cried, "All aboard." And the train began to move. Their journey had begun.

At 6:30 p.m., the train was pulling into the Collinwood Yards to transfer engines for the trip to New York. An electric locomotive had pulled the train to the Collinwood Yards to transfer to a steam locomotive for the trip east. This was standard procedure at Cleveland.

"What was that loud noise?" Maggie said with a start.

"I think that was the new engine hooking up to the train," Carlton answered. He waved at the porter, who was in the aisle. The porter came over. Carlton asked him what the noise was, explaining that they were first-time travelers.

The porter explained the process and concurred with Carlton's explanation that what they had heard was the new engine hooking up.

"Thank you, George," said Carlton.

Maggie sighed with relief.

The Fullers enjoyed a filet dinner with all of the trimmings that evening. A businessman traveling to New York was their tablemate in the dining car. He asked Carlton what he and Mrs. Fuller were doing in New York.

Carlton responded by telling the man that he and his wife were celebrating their anniversary. Small talk continued for a while.

Maggie told Carlton she was getting tired. They left the dining car, headed for their roomettes, and retired for the evening. It had been a hectic three days.

At 7:30 a.m., there was a soft knock on the door of Carlton's roomette.

"Sir, it is seven thirty. We will be arriving in New York at ten a.m. Breakfast is at eight thirty." It was George, the porter.

Carlton knocked on Maggie's door.

She opened it and exclaimed, "What time is it?"

"Good morning, my dear. It's your wake-up call," replied Carlton. "It's seven thirty in the morning. Breakfast is at eight thirty, and we will arrive in the city at ten. How did you sleep?" he asked.

"I slept like a log. The train rocked me to sleep," she answered. "What's for breakfast?"

"I don't know, but let's get going and find out," Carlton answered.

Before they knew it, the porter was announcing that they would be arriving in New York City in fifteen minutes.

The porter had already moved their luggage from the train and placed it on the station platform. As he and Maggie left the train, Carlton tipped the porter two dollars and thanked him for his services. As they got off the train, there was Major Best, beaming.

"Good morning, Mr. and Mrs. Fuller. How was your trip?" He asked. "I have your luggage and a redcap. We are ready to go to the hotel."

"We are great, Major Best. It was a wonderful ride. The food was tasty, and we slept like babies. Let's hit the road," responded Carlton.

Maggie was beside herself. All this rush was exasperating.

Major Best was full of energy. "I was born and raised in Brooklyn. This is home for me. I thought I would give you two a guided tour of the city this afternoon if you re up to it," he exclaimed.

"What do you think, Maggie? Are you up to it?" asked Carlton. "We have never been here before."

"Let's get checked into the hotel. Give me a chance to freshen up a bit. I feel good after our train trip. I don't see why we can't let Major

Best be our tour guide this afternoon. I, like you, want to see the city," Maggie said.

Carlton and Maggie met the major in the lobby of the hotel. He hailed a cab, and off they went. It was one thirty, early in the afternoon, and the day was beautiful. The sun was shining, the sky was robin's egg blue, and the temperature was in the mid-seventies. What a day they had. It started with a trip on the Staten Island Ferry. When they returned, they caught another ferry out to the Statue of Liberty.

Maggie remarked, "Look how beautiful she is—how glorious she is. I feel overwhelmed." They went up to the crown and looked out toward the city.

Carlton was very emotional about the visit. He had tears in his eyes. "I remember when Mother and I passed the Statue of Liberty when we immigrated to the United States many years ago. What a beautiful sight she was as the ship passed by her," he said wiping his eyes.

When they returned to the ferry dock, they caught a cab to the Empire State Building. They went into the lobby to get tickets to travel to the top of the building. Maggie and Carlton were amazed at the speed with which the elevator reached the top of the building. When they opened the door to the observation floor, they both felt the height in the pit of their stomachs.

"Oh my heavens," said Maggie, "what a view! What is that across the river?" she asked.

"That is New Jersey," replied Major Best. "The river in front of us is the Hudson. If you look up the Hudson River to the right, you will see the George Washington Bridge. The smaller building there on the left is the Chrysler Building. And if we walk around the observation floor, you will see the East River and the Brooklyn Bridge. There is my hometown, Brooklyn," he continued. "If we continue all the way around, you can see Central Park, and beyond it is Harlem. Isn't New York a beautiful city?"

"It certainly is," replied Maggie. "You are certainly proud of your home town," she exclaimed.

"Yes, ma'am, I am," the major replied.

Following their visit to the Empire State Building, the major took the Fullers to Times Square. The lights were starting to be turned on, and the rush hour crowd was building. Carlton and Maggie were wide-eyed tourists. They couldn't believe the hubbub going on around them. Major

Best then took them to the theater district, where *Hold On to Your Hats* was playing at the Shubert theater, *The Dancing Years* was playing at the Adelphi, *Walk with Music* was playing at the Ethel Barrymore, and *Gondoliers* was ready to open at the 44th Street. Carlton and Maggie were fascinated with the lights and the shows playing. They both thought New York City was everything they had ever heard about it.

"Are you ready for dinner, folks?" asked the major.

"Yes, I am, Major. You have kept us busy and walked our legs off this afternoon. It is getting beyond our normal dinner hour. Where do we go from here?" asked Maggie.

"I have a special place I want to take you and Carlton for dinner. I am a personal friend of the owner. We are going to the Colony restaurant. It is a famous place here in the city, and you never know who you might see there. The food is terrific," replied Major Best.

They all hopped into a cab.

Major Best directed the cabbie. "The Colony please."

"Yes, sir. That's at Madison and 61st street," the cabbie responded.

"Yes, that is the location," said the major.

They arrived at the Colony. Major Best was excited as he led Carlton and Maggie under the restaurant awning. He met the doorman and asked him, "Is Mr. Cavallero in the restaurant this evening?"

"Yes, he is as always," the doorman replied.

"Thank you," said the major. He escorted Maggie and Carlton into the foyer of the building.

Maggie's first response was, "How elegant."

Standing at the reservations desk was Mr. Cavallero. He saw the major and shouted, "Billy, how are you? It has been sometime since I last saw you. What are you doing here?"

"Hello, Mr. Cavallero," the major replied. "I'm fine. How are you? I have brought my friends Mr. Fuller and his wife, Maggie, here for dinner. They are special people, and I wanted to take them to the best restaurant in the city."

The major and Mr. Cavallero hugged each other like father and son.

"It is so good to see you, Billy, and to meet your special friends. It is my pleasure, Mr. Fuller and Miss Maggie. You are being guided by a special boy, my Billy. Dinner is on me tonight. It is so good to see you, a major in the army. What a surprise. I will stop by your table in a while. Jacque, please take these folks to the special guest VIP table," he directed.

Carlton shook Mr. Caballero's hand, and Maggie smiled as they left and went to the table with Major Best.

"Your first name is Billy. We didn't know that," said Maggie. "Your relationship with Mr. Cavallero is special," she added.

"Yes it is, Mrs. Fuller. I grew up with his son. Mr. Cavallero is like a second father to me. I am very fortunate.

"My first name is William after my dad. Please call me Bill. Mr. Cavallero calls me Billy, like his son," replied the major. "Please look at the menu. The food is French."

Carlton and Maggie couldn't read the menu. It was all in French. Major Best translated for them and ordered their dinners. The dinner was very special and very good. Major Best ordered a French cabernet to complement the dinner, which began with a consommé, followed with a salad niçoise. The main course was rack of lamb with rosemary and thyme served with Barigoule vegetables. Dessert was gâteau m Kasson, a French flan. This was followed up with coffee and mints.

All Maggie could say was, "Ummmm!"

Carlton thanked the major profusely and tried not to belch. Maggie and Carlton were overwhelmed at the service and quality at the Colony. When Mr. Cavallero came to the table to talk with them and the major, they couldn't thank him enough. They had never been catered to like this before. They felt very special. They expressed their thanks to the major. He was embarrassed by all the attention and service they had received.

The major excused himself, as he wanted to spend a few minutes with Mr. Cavallero before they left.

When he returned, he said, "Mr. Cavallero expressed his thanks to you both for coming in tonight. He indicated that it was his pleasure to serve you both. I think we should be on our way, as we have a plane to catch at twelve fifteen tomorrow afternoon."

"I am getting tired," replied Maggie.

"Thank you, Major, for the wonderful day you provided for us. The tour was wonderful, and the restaurant outstanding. I too am tired. Let's get to the hotel," said Carlton. As they left the restaurant they asked the doorman to flag a cab for them.

When the cab arrived Major Best tipped the door man. As they got into the cab Major West replied, "I agree. We have a very long day ahead. We will be flying for twenty-three or twenty-four hours tomorrow,".

"Maggie and I have never flown before. Have you, Major Best?" asked Carlton.

"Yes I have. General Donovan and I flew to a meeting in Chicago last year. It certainly is a different way of travel. You get to your location very quickly. I know you will enjoy the trip. I understand the plane is very fancy inside."

Maggie put her head on Carlton's shoulder and fell asleep.

"We are looking forward to the flight. Maggie should be okay, as she is in the first trimester of her pregnancy. Do you think she will be all right?" asked Carlton.

"I'm sure she will. I will mention it to the pilot and his crew. I'm sure they will be careful during the trip," the Major answered.

"Here we are," said the major as he jumped out of the cab, paid the driver, and opened the door for Maggie and Carlton.

"Thank you, Major," replied Maggie sleepily. "See you in the morning. What time will you be coming by?"

"I'll meet you both in the lobby at ten hundred hours. We have about a forty-five-minute cab ride to the LaGuardia Marine Air Terminal. Get some breakfast before we leave," the major replied. "See you then. Good night."

"Good night," both Carlton and Maggie responded.

Maggie looked at Carlton and asked, "What time is ten hundred hours?"

"Honey, that's ten in the morning, army time. They tell time on a twenty-four-hour basis," replied Carlton knowingly.

Maggie was so tired all she could say was, "Hummmmm."

Che Flight to Marseilles

aggie and Carlton had breakfast in the hotel restaurant.
Right at 1000 hours, the major walked into the restaurant.
"Good morning, Mr. and Mrs. Fuller. You look rested and ready for our flight to Marseilles."

"I'm not sure," Maggie responded. "I'm a little nervous. I have never been on an airplane flight. I'm feeling a little apprehensive. Hopefully, my nervousness will go away."

"I'm sure it will, honey," Carlton said, trying to reassure his wife. "I'm nervous too. Remember, I have never been on an airplane either. We have each other and Major Best. We will be fine."

They caught a cab outside the hotel and were on their way to the LaGuardia Marine Air Terminal. Carlton and Maggie were all eyes as the cab drove through the city. They were in awe of the hustle and bustle of the place. *What a big city*, thought Carlton.

Maggie was thinking how busy the city was. It went on night and day. New York, New York!

Major Best was sitting in the front seat of the cab. He turned around and announced that they were arriving at the terminal. "We are arriving. Oh my God, look at the size of the seaplane sitting on the water next to the terminal. The terminal is a nice sized building, but the seaplane dwarfs it. Holy Moses!" he said as the cab stopped.

Carlton and Maggie looked through the cab's front window.

Carlton exclaimed, "I can't believe it; it is so big. Four engines! I'll bet the tail is forty feet high. The wings must be over one hundred feet long. How impressive. What kind of plane is it?" he asked.

"It is a Boeing 314," the cab driver responded. "It was built by the Boeing Corporation. The seaplane's wingspan is 153 feet. Its tail is only 28 feet tall. The seaplane is 106 feet long. The engines are a powerful sixteen hundred horsepower each."

"How do you know so much about the seaplane?" asked Maggie.

"When Pan American started flying from here, they opened the plane up for the public to see and tour. I learned all about the plane at that time. It is quite an aircraft. The plane is gorgeous inside. Boeing built the seaplane to compete with the ocean-going ships that carry passengers back and forth across the Atlantic Ocean," the cabbie explained. "It has all the bells and whistles. Have a good trip."

"We hope to. Thank you for the information about the seaplane. This is our first trip," Maggie said as she left the cab.

Carlton paid the cab fare and tipped the driver.

Major Best had a redcap taking their bags to the terminal for loading on the seaplane.

Maggie looped her arm under Carlton's as they headed to the terminal.

"What a beautiful building. Look at the frieze of flying fish on the side of the terminal," Carlton noted.

They had to check in at the ticket desk with their tickets and passports. There was a line of people who were on the same flight in front of them. Major Best was nowhere in sight.

"Oh Carlton!" said Maggie. "Look at the wonderful mural on the wall of the terminal. Its title is 'Flight.' The artist certainly captured its theme." She was getting excited now and couldn't wait to board the seaplane.

Major Best came out of door and was looking for Carlton and Maggie. "There you are. Have you checked in yet?" he asked. "I talked to the chief pilot and explained your situation, Maggie. He fully understands your needs. Should you have any issues during the flight, he indicated that his crew is fully capable of managing any situation that may happen. His stewards are both registered nurses. He will meet you both at the door as you board."

Carlton and Maggie completed the check-in procedure. It took a little longer than what they felt was normal. Maggie and Carlton told each other the process had been longer because they were traveling to Marseilles.

"Let's get to the gate. Pan American personnel are boarding passengers on the plane," urged Major Best.

Tickets and passports were checked again, and they all boarded the plane. The pilot was at the gate greeting all of the passengers as they boarded the plane.

"Good day, Mr. and Mrs. Fuller. My name is James. I will be your cabin steward. I will be at your service throughout the flight. Good morning. He gave the same greeting to Major Best. Mr. and Mrs. Fuller, you will be in the first compartment. Major Best, you will be in the second compartment. I will explain the facilities of the aircraft once you are seated and comfortable. Please enjoy the flight. If there is anything I may help you with, please do not hesitate to call on me." James led Maggie and Carlton to their compartment. He then led Major Best to his.

Maggie was impressed. James was very cordial and seemed very willing to help. "What a beautiful compartment we have," she said. "The colors are beautiful, and the carpet is so very thick. We have lounges to sit on. This is very luxurious. I can't wait for James to come back and take us through the airplane."

"I agree, Maggie. I wonder what the government paid for this trip?" replied Carlton.

"I'm sure Donovan will get this back in spades," noted Maggie.

The remainder of the passengers completed boarding. James came back to their compartment. "Hello again, Mr. and Mrs. Fuller," he said. "All the passengers have boarded and the door has been shut. We are getting ready to move out to the sound and get ready to take off. Is there something I may get for you before we start moving?"

"Yes as a matter of fact there is," Maggie replied. "I have to use the restroom. Where is it?"

"Oh, I will take you to the restroom. I apologize for not showing you the way earlier. I got caught up with the rest of the passengers," replied James, rather embarrassed.

When Maggie returned, the aircraft was already moving. Carlton was looking out the window watching all the boats on the water. "Honey, the bathroom is just beautiful," Maggie said, as if in awe. "It is very luxurious. And it's done in warm colors with gold fixtures."

"I just can't wait to see it," remarked Carlton rather sarcastically. "Come over to the window and look out with me. Look at the people in the boats looking at us. Hold on to me, as the seaplane is rocking a bit with the swells coming in from the bay."

An announcement came from the speaker in the corner of the compartment. "Good afternoon, ladies and gentleman. This is the pilot speaking. We have been cleared for takeoff. Please sit down in your compartments. We will be taking off in minutes. The loud noise you will be hearing will be the engines being revved up prior to takeoff. Once we begin our takeoff run, you might feel the aircraft rocking and bouncing before we get airborne. That is caused by the swell on the bay. It is nothing to worry about. We and the plane can handle that without a problem. I will let you know our flight plan once we get airborne and achieve our cruising altitude. The smoking lamp is out please. That means, in seaplane vernacular, put out all smoking devices. Once we reach cruising altitude, I will turn on the smoking lamp. Please sit back and relax. Here we go!"

Maggie and Carlton hugged each other, as the engine sound was roaring in their ears. They were white knucklers, as they had never flown before. The plane started moving faster and began bouncing and jouncing across the swells. All of a sudden, the movement stopped, and the seaplane was moving up into the air. Both Maggie and Carlton headed to the window. They were amazed as the plane rose from the earth toward the sky.

"Here we go," said Carlton as the aircraft gained altitude.

As the plane looped around gaining altitude, Maggie exclaimed, "Look at how beautiful New York looks from this high in the air. It looks like a small city. Oh, Carlton, how fortunate we are to be making this trip. What an experience we are having. We have to memorize the homework Donovan gave us while we are in the air," she added. "We have to be prepared for our mission when we get to France."

The pilot came back on the speaker again. "Ladies and gentleman, we will be flying north toward Newfoundland, and then turn we'll east toward the Azores. Our first stop will be at Horta, Azores. We will refuel at Horta and leave for our next stop, Lisbon, Portugal. We will top off our fuel tanks at Lisbon and then fly to Marseilles, France. Our total flying time to Marseilles should be approximately twenty-four hours. We will be cruising between eleven thousand and nineteen thousand feet. Our cruising speed should be approximately one hundred eighty-eight miles per hour. The level of flight will be determined by the smoothness of the air at the altitude we are flying. Our weather report tells us that our flight will be smooth most of the way. There is always a chance of some turbulence. I ask that, when you are in your compartment, you stay seated. Turbulence could cause you to fall or get bounced around your compartment should you be standing. We in the cockpit and all of our crew appreciate your flying with Pan American. We will make your trip as comfortable as we can. The smoking lamp is lit. Please relax and enjoy our service."

"Can you believe we're flying at between eleven thousand and nineteen thousand feet at 188 miles per hour," exclaimed Maggie. "I can't believe it. It doesn't feel any different than standing in our living room."

Carlton had to chuckle. She was right. *How amazing*, he thought to himself. "I think we need a drink to celebrate our first flight on a seaplane," said Carlton.

"I agree," said Maggie excitingly. "Where is James?" she stammered as the plane hit a small bump in the air.

James knocked as he entered their compartment. "May I get you folks anything to drink?" he asked.

"Yes, you can, James," Carlton answered. "May we have a bottle of champagne and three glasses, two for us and one for the major next door?"

"Yes, you may," replied James. "I have the finest French champagne available that Pan American could find. It is Moët and Chandon."

"Major," said Maggie as she knocked on the major's compartment. "Come join us for a glass of champagne. We are celebrating our first ride on a seaplane."

"I'm on my way," called the major.

James returned with the champagne and popped the cork. The wine spilled out the top of the bottle onto the compartment floor. James apologized for the spill but poured the wine quickly and handed the glasses to Carlton, Maggie, and the major. He then cleaned up the spilled wine.

"Prost!" saluted Carlton.

"Down the hatch," saluted the major.

Maggie didn't know what to say so she just drank her champagne down.

"Oh this is wonderful," said Maggie. "I never drank wine like this before. May I have a bit more," she asked James.

"Yes you may," James replied and poured another glass for Maggie.

"Maggie, be careful, please. Remember, you are pregnant," said Carlton.

"I will, Carlton. When I finish this glass, I'll sit down and relax. I don't think the wine will hurt the baby," she said.

"I think she will be fine," added the major as he finished his glass. "I'm happy we are here together on this adventure and mission. Can I join you both for dinner later this evening?" he asked.

"You may, Major. James, what time do you serve dinner?" Carlton asked the porter.

"About eighteen hundred hours New York time," said James. "I'll bring down a menu for you all later this afternoon. Is there anything else I can get for you?"

"There is that military time again. I can't figure it out. Now he has added New York time. I'm confused." Maggie responded quizzically.

The major chimed in. "It's very simple, Maggie. The military time clock starts at midnight and runs for twenty-four hours. Hence, zero zero zero one hours is one minute after midnight. Oh-one hundred hours is one in the morning. It goes on from there. So thirteen hundred hours is one in the afternoon and so on. Do you understand?"

"Yes, I think so. You explained it so simply and clearly. Let me see. Eighteen hundred hours is, ummmm, six in the evening. Now what is New York time? The porter said eighteen hundred hours New York time. I'm still confused. What time does the military use?" Maggie wondered out loud.

"The military uses Greenwich Mean Time as its basis for timekeeping. The reason it does so is the military operates around the world. Having a central point in the world where time officially starts every day makes a single time convenient around the world. Greenwich Mean Time is five hours ahead of Eastern Standard Time. The day always starts at zero zero zero one hours. Apparently, the flight crew on this seaplane also uses Greenwich Mean Time. If the time is eighteen hundred hours New York time, then it is twenty-three hundred hours Greenwich Mean Time. Are you still confused?" the major asked.

"No I'm not. Thank you for explaining the time differences for me. We will have to ask James when we see him at dinner what time the crew uses on our seaplane. Do you understand this time issue, Carlton?" Maggie asked.

"I thought I did until the major explained it," he replied. "Now I do. Let's get started reading Donovan's information. I have a feeling it will be complicated for both of us. See you for dinner, Major. Did the general give you a mission also?" asked Carlton.

"Yes, I have a package about two inches thick. We can compare notes after dinner. See you all for dinner," the major replied as he ducked out of the cabin.

The flight had been smooth as the seaplane traveled north along the East Coast of the United States. The weather was clear, and the sky was as blue as a robin's egg. After reading for a few hours, Maggie was looking out the window at the East Coast shoreline and thinking how beautiful it was from so high in the air. She thought about Donovan's assignment. It was simple: Absorb what the Nazis had done in the country. Try to look beyond what they are showing you. Understand how the people feel about the changes made. Talk with the people. Meet Horst's family and get to know his wife. *Very interesting*, she thought. *What is he looking for?*

"Ladies and gentleman," came the announcement through the speaker in the compartment, "This is your pilot. We will be turning east toward the Azores in a few minutes. We will be experiencing some weather on our flight to Horta. It shouldn't be too bad, but we may experience some light turbulence. You may want to take something if you think you may have an upset stomach. Ask your steward for some Dramamine to help you. Your steward will be bringing you menus for your dinner selections. Dinner will be served in the main lounge, which will be converted to a formal dining room. Following dinner, your steward will be asking you when you want your compartment made up for sleeping. Our estimated time of arrival at Horta is approximately oh-seven hours Greenwich Mean Time. Please enjoy your dinner and the remainder of your evening. If you have any question regarding the flight, please ask your steward. Thank you and good evening."

James knocked on the compartment wall. "May I come in?"

"Please come in, James," said Maggie

"I have your dinner menu for this evening. Our chef on this flight is Rafael Espinoza. He is Spanish. He trained in Barcelona at the Barcelo La Bobadilla Hotel located in Granada, Spain. Pan American hired chefs from five-star hotels around the world for their overseas flights. Pan American makes sure that our passengers on these flights have only the best of everything while flying with us. Dinner will be served at eighteen thirty hours New York time."

"James," said Maggie, "what time does the flight crew go on during this flight?"

"We go by Greenwich Mean Time, Mrs. Fuller. But I use New York time for our passengers, as most of them don't understand Greenwich Mean Time." James answered the question very diplomatically.

"Thank you, James. Please turn our beds down at twenty-one hundred hours New York time," said Maggie.

"I will, ma'am. Bon appétit," said James as he left the compartment.

Carlton had been involved with his mission information while Maggie and James were talking. Donovan's direction was very detailed. He wanted to know what Horst did for the Nazis. He wanted Carlton to get to know his daily routine—who he dealt with, who he knew, who he was friends with, who he confided in, how he dressed, what his rank was, and what his future in the Nazi Party and/or the army was. He was also to get to know his brother's wife—to understand what her role was and how she felt about the Nazis and Horst's role with the party. Carlton kept asking himself, *why does Donovan need this information?* Carlton was perplexed about it all. He wanted to know what Maggie and the major's missions were. After understanding their missions, maybe he would be able to make sense of this whole trip. The main reason for all this was for him to visit his father before he died. At least Carlton thought that was the purpose.

"Come on, Carlton. Let's go to dinner. We have to pick up the major on the way. You are really involved in your mission paperwork, aren't you?" Maggie asked as she reached out to Carlton for his hand.

"Yes, I am. Donovan has asked for a lot of information. Hopefully, I will be able gather as much as I can," he replied.

When they entered the lounge for dinner, Maggie remarked, "Oh, Carlton, look at the table they have set for us—china, silverware, candles, and more wine glasses than I have ever seen on a dinner table. Major Best, have you ever seen a table decorated like this one?"

"Can't say that I have, ma'am, except at the Colony," he replied.

The gourmet meal started with a soup and finished with a special dessert. There were four different wines, one for each course and after-dinner liquors with coffee. After each course was finished, the dishes and wine glasses were cleared, and the next set was provided. Carlton and Maggie had never eaten like this. The major explained that, while he'd worked at the Colony in New York, dinner was like this every night. All they could do was thank the waiters and James. Maggie wondered if every meal would be like this.

The conversation at the dinner table revolved around how different and delicious the food was. Maggie exclaimed again how fortunate they were. She couldn't wait until she could tell her family and friends about this treatment. At that point, the major advised her—to her disappointment—that Donovan had indicated that nothing of this trip was to be discussed with anyone except him.

When they went back to the compartment, Maggie was brooding and mumbling something about how she wouldn't have come if she'd known that before they left. Their beds were made when they returned from dinner. It was earlier than what Maggie had asked for, but both Carlton and Maggie were tired from all the excitement of the day.

The major studied his mission late until the night. And they all slept soundly until about 0100 hundred hours New York time, when the plane started bumping and jouncing back and forth. The aircraft had encountered some slight turbulence, which woke Carlton and Maggie up.

"What was that, Carlton?" Maggie asked sleepily.

"I don't know, but it was a little scary to me. I'll ring our steward. Hopefully, he will know what is going on," Carlton said as the plane bumped again and again.

A knock sounded on the wall. It was James. "You rang, sir?" he asked.

"Yes. What is all this bumping that is going on? It woke us up," explained Carlton.

"We have encountered a little turbulence. It is nothing to worry about, sir. We are flying through a slight storm. We should be past the storm in about ten minutes. The aircraft encounters turbulence from different things—mainly storms but, once in a while, different wind directions or wind shear we are unaware of. Is there anything I can do, sir?" asked James.

"Thank you, no, James," said Carlton. "Maggie, James said it's nothing we should worry about. It's just a slight storm. Try to go back to sleep," he said, trying to sound calm.

Maggie was already back to sleep. Carlton didn't go back to sleep until the plane stopped bouncing.

At 0400 hundred hours New York time, the pilot came on the speaker again. "Good morning, ladies and gentleman. I apologize for making this announcement early in your morning, but we will be landing at Horta, Azores, in approximately thirty minutes to refuel. I have been in communication with the tower at Horta. They indicated the sea is calm. We should have a smooth landing. Shortly, we will be reducing altitude and speed in preparation for landing. You will hear the flaps coming down. For those of you who are first-time flyers, I assure you the various noises you hear are normal. The smoking lamp is out. We will be in the water shortly. We will take off for Lisbon, Portugal, as soon as we refuel. Breakfast will be served after we reach our cruising altitude on the way to Lisbon. Thank you."

Maggie and Carlton were now wide awake, looking out the windows. It was daylight outdoors. The sun was shining, and the ocean was sparkling. It was a beautiful day in the Azores. The attitude of the seaplane changed as the nose pointed downward, and the sound of the engines changed. Maggie and Carlton were transfixed as the seaplane approached the water and touched down. It was a very smooth landing.

Following the landing, the aircraft moved through the water to the refueling docks at Horta.

They rang for James.

"You rang for me, Mr. Fuller," said James.

"Yes I did. What time is it here in Horta?" asked Carlton.

"It is oh-seven thirty hours Horta time. New York time is oh-four thirty hours," James answered.

"Will we be able to leave the plane while we are refueling?" asked Carlton.

"No, sir, I don't believe so. It will take about forty-five minutes to refuel. We are scheduled to leave quickly after the refueling is complete. You can deplane at Lisbon, as we are dropping off some passengers. Our schedule indicates the plane will be there for a longer period of time. The actual time will depend on the flying time to Lisbon," James responded.

"Thank you, James. The various times are confusing me. I will be happy when we reach our destination and only worry about the time zone we are in. Would you please bring us some coffee?" Carlton asked.

"I certainly will. The major also asked for some as I passed by his compartment," James replied.

The pilot came on the speaker "Good morning again. We will be finished refueling in about ten minutes. I will be starting the engines again shortly thereafter. Once we take off and reach cruising altitude, I will turn on the smoking lap, and you may light up if you wish. Breakfast will be served thereafter."

Maggie and Carlton settled back into their seats as the pilot started the engines. They sputtered for a minute but smoothed out quickly. The plane started moving from the dock out toward the harbor for takeoff. It wasn't bouncing or jouncing this time, as the water was smoother than it had been in New York. The engines roared and the plane moved quickly and rose smoothly into the air. They were on their way to Lisbon. After about twenty minutes, the pilot announced that they were at cruising altitude and that breakfast would be served in fifteen minutes. He added at the end of his announcement that the smoking lamp was lit.

James came in with the coffee that they had ordered earlier, before takeoff. "Sorry for the delay in bringing the coffee. I had to wait for takeoff before I could bring it to you," said James apologetically.

Following coffee Maggie, Carlton, and the major went to breakfast. The table wasn't as fancy as dinner, but the food was sumptuous again. Eggs, bacon, ham, and three different types of potatoes, along with melons and juices and coffee and tea were served.

Maggie commented, "If we continue to eat like this, I will be gaining more weight than the doctor would want me to. Isn't it wonderful?"

They all settled in for the five-hour flight to Lisbon. The sky was clear, and the flight was smooth. Maggie and Carlton fell asleep.

The major continued absorbing his mission ... He wondered about the war. What was happening in Europe? Hopefully he would be able to find an English-speaking newspaper while in Lisbon and get an update. If not, he would try to contact the American embassy and discuss the situation with the ambassador and his staff. He was concerned about what the Nazis were up to. Where and who were they attacking? What was America's status? It had been almost two days since he'd had any information. What was the status of the German bombing of England?

They had been in the air for about three hours, and the plane started to move a bit. Apparently they had run into a bit of turbulence. The engine sounds changed, and the major buzzed for James.

"Sir, you buzzed?" said James as he came into the major's compartment.

"Yes I did. I noticed that the sound of the engines changed, and we started moving again. What is happening?" the major asked.

"The pilot said there is a little weather below us, and he was increasing his altitude to settle down the aircraft. There is nothing to worry about, sir. This always happens between the Azores and Lisbon," James answered.

"Thanks, James. Sorry to bother you. Have you heard any war news?" Major Best asked.

"As a matter of fact, I did while we were at the Azores. I heard the Nazis were continuing to bomb Great Britain, and Vichy France was continuing to cooperate with the Nazis. The Free French in London continue radio broadcasting to France, encouraging the French people not to quit resisting the Nazis. I couldn't get a confirmation on that. I just overheard a conversation on the dock. Our people, that is our Pan American crew are concerned about the landing at Marseilles. I know that is especially concerning to you and the Fullers. I will try to get more information from the flight crew as we get on to France," James responded, giving the major more information than he'd expected.

"Please do, James. Thanks for the information," Major Best replied. He thought to himself, *I need to find out what is going on while we are in Lisbon.* He and the Fullers had a connection to make in Marseilles, and they had to get on to Berlin.

It wasn't another hour when the pilot came on the speaker again. "Good afternoon, ladies and gentleman. We will begin our approach to the Lisbon harbor for landing shortly. There is a little chop on the surface of the harbor. Due to the chop, our landing there might be a little bumpy. The aircraft will not have a problem handling the situation. I ask that you all prepare yourselves accordingly. The smoking lamp is out. Please put out all smoking materials. We will be spending approximately an hour to an hour and thirty minutes in Lisbon before we leave for Marseilles. If you wish to deplane, please advise your steward of your intensions. We will announce our departure time twenty minutes prior to departure. Thank you."

The pitch of the propellers changed, as did the attitude of the aircraft, as the pilot prepared for landing. Maggie and Carlton were again glued to the windows of their compartment. They were fascinated with the landings. The plane splashed down on the harbor water. Large waves splashed up the sides of the plane. As the plane slowed down, backwash from the hull rippled past the compartment windows.

Maggie exclaimed, "Oh my God. The water is going to wash over the entire airplane and sink us."

"No, I don't think so," said Carlton calmly. "The pilot said the harbor was choppy. I'm sure that is why the water splashed so high on the sides of the aircraft. See, as we are slowing down, the water isn't rising."

"It was a little harrowing to me," said Maggie.

About that time, Major Best stuck his head into their compartment and said. "Boy that was fun, wasn't it?"

With that comment, Maggie threw a pillow at the major. They all laughed.

The pilot came on the speaker again. "I apologize for the rough landing, ladies and gentleman, but the harbor had larger swells than we were told by the Portuguese air controllers. The plane is fine; it took the swells in stride. We will be moving toward the docks slowly. For those of you who are leaving us at this juncture, thank you for flying Pan American. Have a nice day. For those of you continuing on to Marseilles, we will be departing in approximately one hour and thirty minutes. The time will be sixteen hours Lisbon time or eleven hundred hours New York time. Please advise your steward if you will be deplaning. Thank you."

"Let's go out and get some fresh air, Maggie," said Carlton.

"Great idea, honey. I'm still a little shook up over our landing. My stomach is a little woozy. How are you feeling?" Maggie asked.

"I'm okay," he replied as he took her hand and led her to the exit door opening to the dock.

Major Best came by them on the dock. He advised them that he had to get to the American embassy. He would be back and would fill them in on what he was doing. Taxicabs were lined up on the dock waiting for passengers leaving the plane. "Enjoy the weather," he said as he climbed into a cab and left.

I wonder why Major Best had to go to the American embassy, thought Maggie. *Hopefully, the war isn't causing problems with our trip to Germany.* She continued thinking about what they were going to find in Berlin. She followed Carlton onto the dock. Pan American personnel were moving luggage and helping passengers leaving the plane. A number of military personnel were mulling around the dock. She thought of Major Best traveling in a strange city. What was going on? Her mind was visualizing various scenarios that only women could see.

"Carlton, what is going on here?" she asked.

Carlton was caught off guard by her question and responded

innocently, "Gosh, I don't know. Pan American is helping passengers who are leaving here in Lisbon get to their destinations and finding transportation for them. They are getting ready to top off the tanks of the seaplane to prepare it for our next leg of the trip to Marseilles. Why do you ask?"

"It seems strange to me—all of the military here, some with guns on their hips exposed for us to see. I'm very concerned," Maggie said.

"Enjoy the warm sun, honey. We haven't been outdoors for almost a day. It is certainly pleasant here in Lisbon. I'm sure that, with a war going on and so many strange people traveling here in Europe, the local military are very aware that anything that could happen at any given time," Carlton reassured her in a quiet voice, trying to calm down Maggie's concern about the hustle and bustle on the dock. He too was concerned about the open guns being carried by the local military.

They walked down the dock toward the city and noticed how beautiful Lisbon was from the dock. They stopped at a beverage stand, bought some tea to drink, and sat down on a bench they spotted on the dock. Maggie seemed to relax while they sat there. She enjoyed the views and soaked up the warm sun.

A taxicab came down the dock toward the plane and stopped where Maggie and Carlton were sitting. Major Best had returned.

"What time is it?" Major Best asked as he left the cab. "It seems I have been gone longer that I had envisioned," he said to the Fullers.

"You have been gone about an hour. We were getting ready to walk back to the plane. I'm sure they will be boarding us for our trip to Marseilles soon. How was your trip? What did you find out?" Carlton asked the major.

"Let's get to the plane. I'll fill you in on the latest news. A lot is happening in Europe. I also found out that the weather between here and southern France may be a little bumpy, as a low front is forming over Northern Africa," the major replied.

The Pan American staff had started reloading the passengers who were traveling to Marseilles. Maggie couldn't believe what some of the new passengers looked like. They looked shady, and some were dressed in military uniforms that were seedy, rather than sharp as Major Best dressed. These newcomers seemed very suspicious to her, and she snuggled up to Carlton. She tightened her grip on Carlton's arm as they approached the cabin door to enter.

"I'm starting to get afraid," she said as they settled into their compartment. "Hopefully, there won't be any problems on the plane while we are flying," she added.

"Don't worry, Maggie. We will be all right. I know the airline makes sure everyone flying will be okay. We have Major Best with us. I'm sure that he will help if necessary. Please calm down. You're getting me nervous. I'll ring for James and get us something to drink. A glass of wine should help. Let's find out what the major found on his trip to the embassy," Carlton said as he hugged Maggie to reassure her all was okay.

James came into the compartment, asking what was needed. He brought the wine into them as quickly as possible, noting that the wine was Portuguese.

The major came into their compartment and sat down. While they were drinking the wine, he explained why he'd needed to get to the embassy.

"I needed to find out the latest war news. I was concerned as to whether or not we would be able to continue our trip. Germany has almost complete control of France. A Vichy government has been installed to run France while the Germans occupy the country. The Free French under Charles de Gaulle are entrenched in London, England. They are radio broadcasting to France daily to encourage the French to continue to resist the Germans. There has been some bombing at Marseilles, but the port is still operating and the Marignane seaplane landing area is open and being run by the local port authority. We will be able to land safely. I understand that the Germans control the railroads in France. That is how we are traveling to Germany. It may be a harrowing trip, as the French Resistance is very active. We will get to Berlin safely. I have been assured of that. The American embassy in Germany is waiting for us to arrive. They have been reassured by the Nazi government that the trip will be safely made. I am sure the French underground have been advised that we are traveling to Germany on one of their trains. You two are special people."

The pilot was speaking again. "Ladies and gentleman, we will be starting the engines and moving out to the harbor to take off for Marseilles. The harbor is a bit choppy. Please settle down in your compartments as we take off. There is a little weather between here and our destination. I will keep you posted as we approach the weather. Flying time to Marseilles is approximately six hours. Your Pan American crew is preparing a wonderful dinner for you, which will be served at about eighteen hundred hours Lisbon time. Cocktails will be served prior to dinner. Please sit back, relax, and enjoy the remainder of your flight. The smoking lamp is out. I will turn it back on when we reach our cruising altitude. We will be taking off shortly. Thank you."

The engines started to roar, the plane started to move faster through the water, and the flight was airborne without incident once more.

"This pilot has done a wonderful job handling this large aircraft, hasn't he?" remarked Maggie. "I feel very comfortable flying now," she added sleepily.

Both Maggie and Carlton lay down to take a nap. They were worn out. It had been a short night yesterday. They fell asleep instantly.

"It is cocktail time, ladies and gentleman," came the now familiar voice of the pilot from the speaker. "Your stewards will be in your cabin to take your orders. We at Pan American want to show you our appreciation for flying rather than sailing to Marseilles. Although I can't spend time with all of you, we want to make dinner this evening a captain's dinner, just as if you were on a ship the evening before you reached port. Your chef and staff have gone all out this evening. Enjoy the celebration."

James came into their compartment, whistling the French national anthem, "La Marseillaise."

"I hope you don't mind," he said. "I want to show support for the Free French against those Nazis. The Nazis have taken France. I know they are killing French people. I love France and support the resistance. I hope you do not take offense with my being so patriotic and emotional. This war is taking a toll on me personally."

The Fullers were taken a little aback at James's brashness.

Major Best came in at the same moment and shouted, "Viva la France" with a French accent.

Maggie and Carlton burst out in laughter and joined the celebration that James had started. They all ordered wine and stuffed mushrooms. It was the beginning of a celebration. Following cocktails, Maggie, Carlton, and the major followed James into the lounge for dinner. They couldn't believe the table again. It was set as it had been the previous evening. Dinner began with fresh shrimp and ended with baked Alaska. The beef was chateaubriand done medium rare served with sumptuous fresh vegetables and a béarnaise sauce. The wine was a French cabernet.

"I have never eaten like this in my life," exclaimed Maggie.

Both Carlton and Major Best agreed. They finished dinner just as the plane began to bump.

James indicated that this must be the patch of weather the pilot had mentioned before they'd taken off. Hopefully, he said, the turbulence wouldn't be heavy.

For the next hour, the plane bumped and moved across the sky. Maggie started to feel a little woozy and prayed that she wouldn't get sick.

All of a sudden, the plane stopped bouncing, and the flight smoothed out. The pilot came back on the speaker again. "Ladies and gentleman, we have come through the bad weather and should have a smooth flight to Marseilles. Our estimated time of arrival is twenty-three hundred hours Marseilles time. The controllers at Marseilles advised us that the bay is quiet, the water is smooth, and we have been cleared to land. Based on our information from the Marseilles controllers, we should have a smooth landing. Please prepare yourselves for departure once we land. Please do not forget any personal items. We should be at the dock in forty minutes. The smoking lamp is out. Thank you again for flying Pan American."

Carlton was gazing out the window. "I see fires blazing down below. I wonder if that is Marseilles," he commented.

"Let me see," said Maggie as she crowded the window. "It looks like ships burning in the harbor. Will we be able to land? Will we be able to get to the dock? What is happening?" Her voice was tinged with alarm.

"Don't panic, Maggie; the pilot said we will have a smooth landing. I'm sure he wouldn't have said that if there were an issue," Carlton said with a bit of apprehension in his voice as he tried to calm her down.

The plane's engines pitch changed, and the its attitude turned to the down direction for their descent. They would be landing soon. Carlton and Maggie were holding onto each other tightly, as they had no idea what was happening outside in the harbor. The plane landed smoothly and moved through the water toward the dock. Major Best came into their compartment and assured them that they were safe.

"I was looking out the window of my compartment and saw the fire. It looked as if a couple of ships were on fire. There must have been an earlier disturbance before we arrived in the area. The fire did light up the bay, and I'm sure the pilot used the light for his landing. We will find out more when we deplane. Let's stay together and not separate. I understand we are being met by Germans and will be taken to the train right after we leave the aircraft," he said assuredly. The major was wearing his sidearm where it could be seen by all.

James came into their compartment to say good-bye and wished them a safe trip. The plane stopped at the dock. The docking area was lit up like a Christmas tree. Maggie and Carlton had gathered their things and headed for the cabin door to the dock. Major Best was right behind them.

They stepped out onto the dock and were almost blinded by the light. The Pan American folks directed them to the depot on the dock. They were told all departing passengers' luggage would be waiting for them after they'd cleared customs.

Maggie asked, "What is customs, Major Best? Why do we have to go through customs? It will delay us won't it?"

"Yes, Maggie, it probably will. But customs is an organization every country has. To make a long story short, every country has rules and regulations that travelers have to follow when they enter a country from another country. The customs personnel of each country will ask you some questions: Why are you traveling to their country? How long will you be in the country? Are you bringing any contraband into their country? They will want to see your passport. As long as you answer the questions honestly and have a clean passport, you will have no problems entering the country. Just get in line with the rest of the passengers, and all will be fine," Major Best explained to both Maggie and Carlton. He remembered that they had never done this before. He should have briefed them both earlier while they were on the plane. How stupid of him, he admonished himself.

"I'm sorry I didn't explain the process to you both before we landed. I forgot you are both rookies at this international travel," said Major Best, a little embarrassed at the whole situation.

"Thank you, Major," said Carlton. "Don't be embarrassed. We should have asked you first."

Ͼhe Ͼrain ͼo Berlin

fter they finished going through customs, the trio picked up their baggage and were met at the departure gate by a man in a German officer's uniform looking for the Fullers. Major Best interrupted the man and asked him who he was and why was he looking for the Fullers.

The man explained in perfect English that he was a German major who was responsible for escorting Mr. and Mrs. Fuller to the train for their trip to Berlin. He introduced himself to Major Best as Major Scheinhorst. He gave a one-handed salute and said, "Heil Hitler" to the major, after which he handed Best a letter. Major Best returned his salute with an American salute and introduced himself to the German major. They shook hands. Major Best explained to the German officer that he was there as personal assistant to the Fullers, making sure his role was very clear. He then read the letter.

"What does the letter say?" Carlton asked. "What is going on? Why a German officer?" He was getting concerned. And he didn't want Maggie to get upset.

Major Best explained the situation. Now that France was in the hands of the Germans, they had full control of everyone traveling through France and, in their case, traveling to Germany. The Germans understood that the Fullers were traveling to Carlton's dying father's bedside and were traveling on diplomatic visas. They wanted to make sure they reached their destination in Germany safely. Hence, they'd sent Major Scheinhorst and his group of men to be their escorts. "With the French Resistance active throughout France, the Germans want to make sure we are in their protective custody," the major concluded. "Our lives and theirs, the Germans', depend on our safe arrival in Berlin. A car is awaiting us outside the seaplane terminal with an escort to take us to the train station. From now on, we have to be careful of what we say, who we say it to, and how loudly we say it. Please understand, Carlton and Maggie, we are in a war zone. Until we reach the American embassy in Berlin, there will be many ears listening to what we say."

Both Maggie and Carlton nodded their heads. "We understand, Major," Carlton said. "Thank you for the explanation. Let's get going. It is late, and we're getting sleepy."

Major Best turned to the German major. "Let's get going, Major."

With that, the German clicked his heels, turned, and said to his men, "Achtung!"

They led the Fullers and Major Best to a Mercedes limousine that was waiting outside the terminal. There were four motorcycles in front of the limousine. They started up, and the motorcade left for the train station.

Maggie was beside herself. "Carlton we are in a motorcade with motorcycles escorting us. I can't believe it. Wait until I tell the children. How exciting. We didn't expect this."

"I know. I don't understand why either," Carlton replied. "Major Best, why is this happening?"

"I don't know either, Carlton. As I said, you folks are special people. I'm sure we will find out when we get to Berlin. We should be at the train station shortly. I'm hoping we can get some rest before we get to Berlin. This is all happening too quickly," Major Best answered.

When they arrived at the station, Major Scheinhorst advised them to follow him to the train. He would make sure they got to the correct train and sleeping car. If there was anything they needed, he personally was at their service. Carlton, Maggie, and Major Best thanked Major Scheinhorst for the escort. The German major explained to them that he and his men would be escorting them to their destination in Berlin. He and his men boarded the train first, followed by Maggie, Carlton, and the major, who were escorted to their sleeping quarters by the car attendants. Carlton and Maggie asked the car attendant for some tea, and Major Best asked for coffee. Following the beverage delivery, the train horn screeched as it left the station. Maggie and Carlton drank their teas, retired, and went to sleep quickly.

CODE NAME: ARC ANGEL

Major Best thought about the motorcade, the special handling by the Germans, and wondered what was up. Why are the Germans treating us like this? Who are the father and brother Carlton and Maggie are meeting? He dropped off to sleep with many questions running through his head and no answers.

The train sped through France, only slowing down to be rerouted because of damage caused by the Germans during the takeover of France in 1940. Because of the quickness of the Nazi takeover, the French railroad system was almost totally in tact. It was being used by the Nazis to carry their troops and supplies.

The train from Marseilles arrived in Paris at 4:30 a.m. French time. The sleeping car that Carlton, Maggie, and Major Best were on was transferred to a train traveling to Berlin from Paris as soon as it arrived in Paris. The Germans made sure their car moved quickly through the switchyard in Paris. Everyone was so tired they slept through the car transfer, not noticing the bumping and grinding of the car and the squealing of its wheels. At 0730 hours, the train slowed down significantly, as it was approaching the German border.

The car attendants knocked on the sleeping room doors and whispered softly in German, "Guten Morgen, guten Morgen. Es ist Zeit aufzustehen. Wir haben Kaffee und Fruehstueck fuer Sie. Sie sind gleich an der deutschen Grenze und muessen dort in einen anderen Zug umsteigen, der Sie mit nach Deutschland nimmt."

Maggie woke up. "Carlton, what are they saying?"

"They are telling us very quietly good morning, good morning. It is time to wake up. We have coffee and breakfast for you. We are arriving at the German border. You will have to leave this train and get on another one waiting for you in Germany," he replied.

Major Best had been awake for an hour before the train started slowing. He wanted to see what was going on outside the train. "Thank you, gentleman," he replied. "We appreciate your service. Let me wake up my friends. Maggie, Carlton, you need to wake up." He echoed the attendant's comments and asked them to hurry a bit.

"I'm coming," said Maggie. "Where is the restroom? Where can I wash my face? What's the hurry? I have to put on my makeup. I won't have anything to eat or drink until I finish my business this morning."

Major Best thought she sounded a little perturbed this morning.

The car attendant took Maggie's hand and helped her out of her room.

Even though they spoke different languages, they managed to communicate. He was able to explain where she had to go. She thanked him and hurried up the passageway to the restroom. Carlton stumbled out of their room and had the same issues Maggie had, except he wanted to shave before breakfast. The other car attendant led Carlton out the door and down the passageway in the opposite direction from the one Maggie had taken.

All Major Best could do was to thank the attendants. He gave each one of them an American dollar. They were beside themselves with the tip. They hugged the major.

At that time, Major Schienhorst came into the car and asked if anything was wrong.

"No, no, Major," explained Major Best. "It was just the hassle before breakfast. The attendants' service was wonderful. They were very helpful and patient with us all this morning. Mrs. Fuller wanted to look presentable before breakfast, which is her prerogative," he continued. "Mr. Fuller wanted to shave."

"I'm glad there was not a problem. Breakfast is ready for all of you in the next car back. Following breakfast, you all will have to leave this train and go through German customs. My men will carry your luggage to customs for inspection. Once customs have completed their checks, you will board a German train that will take you to Berlin. Please enjoy your meal. My men and I will be waiting for you on the next train. Good morning." Major Scheinhorst saluted Major Best, turned on his heel when Major Best returned his salute, and left.

When they returned, Major Best explained the situation to Carlton and Maggie.

At breakfast Maggie complained that they had to go through customs again. Why? What a hassle? Carlton tried to settle her down. He thought to himself, *Is it the baby? Is it the strangeness of how we are traveling?* She wasn't normally this unhappy.

Together, they left the train, walked into the German train station, and sat down on a comfortable bench. It hit them all at once. On the station entrance wall was a large German Nazi flag and, beneath it, a picture of Hitler. Two German soldiers in uniform, with rifles at their side, stood erect, apparently standing guard by the door. Maggie felt a shiver go up her spine.

After about ten minutes, the door opened, the soldiers snapped to attention, and a man in a black uniform came out the door.

"Hello," he said in perfect English. "My name is Lieutenant Weber. I am head of customs here. We have checked your personal goods. You are good to leave for Berlin. I apologize that we had to go through your luggage and personal things. We have to make sure no contraband passes the border from France to Germany. It is official business. I know you understand. Thank you for your patience. Good day." He saluted and said "Heil Hitler," turned on his heel, and left. The guards returned to a relaxed stance.

The train for Berlin was waiting for them.

"I'm sorry we had to go through your personal things. It is official business. What gives them the right to go through our personal things? Even you don't go through my personal things, Carlton. I'm so mad I could spit," said Maggie angrily and very sarcastically.

"They are the boss here, Maggie," Carlton explained in a strong voice. "They will do whatever they want to, whether or not we like it or not. These people are ruthless. We are diplomatic visitors here in Germany. We have to mind our manners. Remember our mission. It starts now. We have to watch what we say, who we say it to, and when we say it. We are being watched and listened to by all around us. Our friends are us. Even when we are in the US embassy, we have to be careful. I'm sorry, Maggie, but that is how it has to be. Don't you agree, Major?"

"You are right, Carlton. It is most important that we act our roles," Major Best replied.

"I understand completely, but his arrogance upset me. He looked at me with those blue eyes, and I felt undressed. The blaggard! They are evil," Maggie responded with venom in her voice.

The train had Nazi flags on each car and little red flags with swastikas on the engine. Soldiers with guns in their hands stood at the entrance to each car. As they boarded, Maggie was very uneasy. Carlton had a funny feeling in his stomach. Major Best was feeling very confident. It would be a very interesting ride to Berlin. The conductor called all aboard in French, the train's whistle screeched, and they were on their way to Berlin. They all looked out the windows of the train as it began to traverse Germany. They began to notice troops on the move and military equipment being moved on the roads heading east.

The train was packed with people. All were carrying bags, suitcases, and packages of food with them. The car in which Maggie, Carlton, and the major were sitting in smelled like a restaurant. German soldiers walked up and down the aisles of the train, making sure none of the passengers caused any trouble. Maggie suspected the soldiers were looking for someone. Periodically, they stopped and asked someone for papers.

After about an hour, Major Scheinhorst came through the train and asked if Maggie and Carlton needed anything. Major Best asked him if lunch was being served later that day and when they would arrive in Berlin.

Yes, lunch would be served for the diplomatic party in a private car ahead in about two hours, the German major explained. In the meantime, was there anything that anyone would like? The trip to Berlin should take about four hours or less. That would depend on how many freight trains would have priority to pass before the passenger train could continue. The war was causing the freight trains to carry many items required by the army. Hence, they were the priority. The time in Germany was 10:00 a.m.

"Carlton and Maggie would you like something to drink or eat before lunch?" asked Major Best.

"I'm fine. No thank you," said Maggie.

Carlton indicated that he would like coffee please. The major also told Scheinhorst that he would like coffee.

Major Scheinhorst replied, "I will get coffee. I will also advise you when lunch will be served." With that, he turned on his heel and left.

The conductor came down the aisle, muttering to himself about having to bring coffee to a group of Americans. Carlton and the major thanked the conductor for the coffee. They explained that Major Scheinhorst said he was going to bring the coffee.

"The swine," the conductor whispered under his breath. "Your welcome," he said and left for the next car.

"Oh, how beautiful the countryside is. Look at the farms," Maggie said. "They remind me of the farms in Ohio. How very impressive this looks. I'm still tired," she added. "I think I'll take a nap. How about you, Carlton?"

"I'm reading my orders from Donovan. I want to be ready to go when we get to Berlin. You go ahead and take a nap. It won't be too long before lunch," replied Carlton loudly to overcome the train's whistle, as it was passing a roadway.

"If I'm asleep, don't wake me for lunch," Maggie said. "I'm still full from breakfast."

The train made a few stops, letting off passengers and picking up new ones. A lot of German military men were traveling on the train. Some were going on leave, and others were returning to their units in the field. Everyone was speaking German, and the conversation was at a high pitch. That, along with the train noise, made it difficult to understand what someone was saying to you. Carlton couldn't believe Maggie was sleeping through this din.

An hour had gone by when Major Scheinhorst came down the aisle and told Major Best lunch was ready. He insisted that all three of their party come to lunch. Major Best shook Carlton's shoulder and asked him to wake Maggie and follow him and Major Scheinhorst to the next car for lunch. Maggie opened her eyes and looked a bit angry at Carlton for waking her up. Carlton shrugged his shoulders and kissed her on the cheek. She got up and followed him and Major Best down the aisle to the next car. When the car door opened, it was like night and day. The car was very quiet, and a table was set with china and linen. The lunch served was bratwurst, potatoes, and cabbage. It was served with a white German Riesling. Having a German husband, Maggie had made this combination many times. Major Scheinhorst checked with them to make sure they enjoyed lunch. He told them they could stay in this car until they arrived at Berlin.

Maggie thanked Major Scheinhorst for the wonderful hospitality. He bowed slightly to Maggie and left.

"The skunk," she said under her breath, as she had begun playing her role as a diplomat's wife.

As they drew closer to Berlin and deeper into Germany, they all noticed that there were more Nazi flags flying in the small towns they passed through. More war equipment was traveling on the country roads too. Not knowing what to expect, Maggie and Carlton were both getting a little nervous by the time the train slowed down as it approached the German capital.

The conductor came through the car and announced, "Wir werden in zehn Minuten am Berliner Hauptbahnhof ankommen, vergessen Sie bitte nicht Ihre persoenlichen Sachen im Abteil."

"Maggie," said Carlton, "the conductor said we will be arriving at the Berlin station in ten minutes; please make sure you leave nothing on the train."

Almost immediately, Major Scheinhorst came into the car. "I hope you had a satisfactory trip from Marseilles. I will be leaving you when you depart the train. Your luggage will be placed on the station platform for the Americans to pick it up. The American chargé d'affaires is meeting you on the platform. You will be going to the American embassy. Mr. Fuller, your brother will contact you there. He will advise you of your itinerary for the next days you will be visiting us here in Berlin. Please enjoy your stay here in Berlin and my country. Heil Hitler." He gave the German salute, clicked his heels, and left the car.

Major Best saluted and said, "Whew that is finally over. I can't wait to talk with some Americans."

"I agree," said Carlton. "He was very formal but concerned. I'm sure that he and his men were under a lot of pressure to get us here unharmed."

"I thought he was very nice. He was certainly very handsome in his uniform. His manners were impeccable. I thought he treated us very nicely," noted Maggie as she was getting ready to leave the train. "I'm being a diplomat's wife."

"Thank you, Maggie. Very handsome in his uniform—oh my heavens!" Carlton remarked with a laugh.

The train finally stopped. They left the car. As they reached the platform, an older gentleman and a young woman reached out to them and introduced themselves.

Amerizan Embassy

"Good afternoon. My name is Leland B. Morris. I'm the American chargé d'affaires here in Berlin, Germany. This is Miss Emily Sara Bayer. She is my aide. Welcome to Germany. It is our pleasure to serve you while you are here in Germany."

Leland Morris was a career diplomat. Recently, he had been appointed to his position. Maggie thought he looked very ambassador-like. He was tall and lean, had gray hair and wore wire rim glasses and a dark topcoat over a gray suit. *Very handsome-looking,* she thought. His aide was of medium height and had dark, curly hair. Maggie thought she was very pretty and dressed in the latest style. The Americans from the embassy were very well appointed. They certainly looked their roles. Maggie's initial impression was very positive.

"Good afternoon, sir. My name is Major William Best. I am traveling with these folks. May I introduce them—Carlton and Maggie Fuller."

Hands were shaken, and Miss Bayer hugged Maggie warmly. The party left the platform and headed into the station.

Mr. Morris informed them that the luggage was being taken care of by his staff and would be at the embassy when they arrived. The embassy car would be waiting for them outside the station. The Germans had sent a motorcycle escort for them. "The Germans are very concerned for your safety," he noted.

The Berlin train station was packed with people, soldiers, sailors, and officers of all German military services. Nazi flags of all sizes hung from the walls and kiosks. A large photograph of Hitler was mounted on one of the station walls.

Mr. Morris explained while they were on their way to the car that the decorations were very typical of many buildings here in Berlin. "The locals love their Führer," he said. The Nazis had many armed soldier stationed here in the station. They were unnerving for Carlton and Maggie. Mr. Morris explained that they must get used to the military in Germany, especially here in Berlin.

Once they reached the car, the driver held open the door for Maggie and Carlton. Major Best climbed in the front seat of the embassy limousine. After Maggie and Carlton were seated, Mr. Morris and Miss Bayer also entered the car and sat in the back with the Fullers. The driver gave the go-ahead to the motorcyclists to start the trip to the embassy. With red lights flashing, off they went.

"This is not normal for us here in Berlin," Mr. Morris explained. "We have been rather outcasts here since the United States recalled Ambassador Hugh R. Wilson in 1938 in protest of Kristallnacht. We try to maintain a reasonable relationship with Germany, but at times, it is difficult. Our president has stirred the pot a number of times. His relationship with the English leader Winston Churchill irritates Hitler to no end."

"What was Kristallnacht?" asked Maggie.

"This is not a very nice episode here in Germany," Mr. Morris began. "Kristallnacht means Night of Broken Glass. The Germans called it Reichkristallnacht. It was a series of attacks against Jews throughout Germany and Austria on November 9 and 10, 1938. The name came from the broken glass on the streets from destroyed Jewish stores, buildings, and synagogues. Authorities did nothing about it. Many Jews were beaten up, and many were killed during the attacks by paramilitary and non-Jewish citizens. It was a black day in German history."

"That is absolutely terrible, Mr. Morris," replied Maggie.

"I agree with you, Mrs. Fuller," said Mr. Morris. "Be careful while you are here what you say to whom. We don't know who is listening to us when we are out in public. There are many ears here in Germany willing to report you to the SS or the Gestapo."

"I'm sorry, but I don't know much about what is going on here in Germany. What is the SS or Gestapo?" asked Carlton.

"May I, Mr. Morris?" requested Miss Bayer.

"Yes, please do," replied Mr. Morris.

"There are three intelligence agencies here in Germany. They are the SS/SD, the Gestapo, and Abwher. The full title of the SS is Sicherheitsdienst des Reichsführer-SS or SD; it is the intelligence agency of the Nazi party in Nazi Germany. It was the first Intelligence agency established and is considered a sister to the Gestapo. The SD is an agency of the SS. In 1938, it was made the intelligence organization for the state and the party. The SD is headed up by Reinhard Heydrich, a former Navy officer appointed by Heinrich Himmler. The SS/SD is responsible for the detection and neutralization of enemies of the state.

"The Gestapo's official name is Geheime Staatspolizei, which means Secret State Police. The Gestapo, headed by Heinrich Müller, comprises the Secret Police of Nazi Germany and the occupied countries. They have the power to put people in prison without judicial proceeding. Their power is absolute. Both agencies are very dangerous and feared throughout Nazi Germany and the occupied countries. Both report to Heinrich Himmler. When and if you are around these folks, watch your back. Be careful what you are saying.

"The third organization is the Abwehr. It is headed by Admiral Canaris. Its official title is Amt Ausland/Abwehr im Oberkommando de Wehmacht. Their responsibility is to gather intelligence from humans, especially field agents and other sources. They report to the high command of the armed forces or OKW," Miss Bayer explained, adding, "I have been doing all the talking. Do you have any questions?"

Maggie spoke up. "You mentioned the OKW. Are they a spying organization like the SD or Gestapo? What is their function?"

"I apologize. I don't know much about the OKW. Their official title is Oberkommando der Wehrmacht. In English, it is Supreme Command of the Armed Forces. Its function is to coordinate operations among the three services—the army, the Luftwaffe, and the navy. The organization is under the command of General Wilhelm Keitel. His chief of staff is Alfred Jodl. Keitel reports directly to Hitler. That is all I know about them," Miss Bayer answered.

Major Best turned around and fully agreed with Miss Bayer. "The first two agencies she mentioned—the SS/SD and the Gestapo—are evil. I'm sure you both will be meeting some of these folks during your stay here. Please be very careful wherever you are. I will be a constant reminder for you both. Chances are you will know who the SS are, as most of them wear black uniforms with a silver SS either embroidered on or attached to their collars. They are very cocky and are feared by most. However, the Gestapo is made up of very sneaky people, who are dressed mostly in civilian clothes."

"Thank you, Miss Bayer, for the clarification. Organizations can be very complex," said Maggie. "Oh, I see an American flag flying in the breeze on a pole on the top of the embassy. How beautiful it looks. What a pleasure after seeing nothing but Nazi flags all morning. What a beautiful building you have, Mr. Morris. It is just gorgeous."

"Thank you, Mrs. Fuller. We fly the flag every day. It reminds us who we are and who we represent. The United States purchased an old castle two years ago to become our embassy. We needed a larger building to consolidate all our offices, which were spread out all over Berlin. The castle had to be completely renovated, as it had been completely burnt out inside. We spent an inordinate amount of money rehabilitating it. We are proud of our embassy now. The Germans would love to cover it with their flags."

"Miss Bayer, thank you for the detailed information regarding the Nazi intelligence and operations agencies. You certainly have a working knowledge of them and how they function." Carlton added, "Mr. Morris, I agree with Maggie's assessment of the embassy. It is just an outstanding building."

"You are welcome. I just scratched the surface for you," Miss Bayer said. "When I arrived at the embassy, my first assignment was to gather information about the agencies and provide a complete analysis of each agency. It was a difficult job, but I learned about a very sophisticated organization. I am at your service in the future should you have further questions."

"Thank you, Mr. Fuller," the ambassador added, clearly proud of the building. "We have had a bit of damage to the embassy caused by the British bombing of Berlin. We painted 'USA' in large, white letters on the roof in an effort to tell the British flyers this was our building, but to no avail. It was bombed anyway. We wanted you three to stay in the embassy while you are here in Berlin, but that won't happen. I have asked your brother, Mr. Fuller, if you can stay with him and his wife. He said, 'Yes of course.' He was very happy to blame the British for our bombing. Major Best, you will stay with me at my home. I expect that your brother will be here shortly, Mr. Fuller, to pick you and your wife up. Major Best, you will be able to use the limousine and our driver for your travels with Mrs. Fuller. If it isn't an issue, I will send Miss Bayer with you and Mrs.

Fuller. She is very familiar with the area. Just to let all of you know, Miss Bayer and I are aware of your missions here that were given to you by Mr. Donovan. We will coordinate your movement with the Germans. I apologize for the inconvenience." Mr. Morris added, "You will have to blame the Brits for the problem we face. I have been in touch with Mr. Donovan regarding the situation. He will talk to the Brits about their inaccurate bombing. He wishes you all good luck." Morris wore a broad smile on his face.

"Thank you, Mr. Morris, for your concern and cooperation," Carlton said expressing his appreciation to the chargé d'affaires. "I'm sure we will be all right staying with my brother. I had an opportunity to talk with him before we left for Germany. He expressed his wish that we stay with him the entire time we were here in Germany."

"I'm looking forward to having Miss Bayer with Major Best and me on my travels here in Berlin and the surrounding area," Maggie added warmly. "And I'm looking forward to meeting Carlton's family."

"I'm also satisfied with the arrangements you have come up with, sir," said Major Best. "I am not at all familiar with Berlin and the surrounding area. It will be a pleasure having Miss Bayer along with us on our travels. Thank you again for allowing the use of the embassy car and your driver.

"What is the latest status of the war, Mr. Morris?" he added.

"The Luftwaffe is still attacking Great Britain. Many civilians are being killed. The British are retaliating and bombing Germany. There is a lot of activity going on in the Mediterranean area. There has been agreement between the British and the Americans for America to supply fifty destroyers to the Royal Navy in exchange for bases in the Caribbean, Newfoundland, and Bermuda. That is the latest I have heard. I get bits and pieces of information in the diplomatic bag when it arrives. I will try to keep you up to date while you are here. We are arriving at the Embassy"

"Thank you, Mr. Morris for the update. It seems to be escalating," commented Major Best.

The group left the car and walked into the embassy. The lobby was done in dark woods. A picture of the president of the United States hung on one wall, and a US flag graced the other wall. A large skylight in the ceiling provided considerable natural light into the lobby. In the middle of the lobby was a large, circular table with a large bunch of very colorful flowers in a crystal vase, the facets of which reflected the light throughout the room.

Maggie had to comment how beautifully the lobby was appointed. At the end of the lobby was the receptionists' desk. Behind the desk, a door led to the inner workings of the embassy. At each side of the door, an armed Marine stood guard. Morris explained that it was necessary to have Marines at the embassy for security purposes. They walked past the Marines to Morris's office.

There, Morris served refreshments while they waited for Carlton's brother to pick them up. Maggie and Miss Bayer were talking about their families, and Carlton, Major Best, and Mr. Morris were discussing the latest politics when Mr. Morris's secretary knocked on the door. She announced that a high-ranking German officer named Brausch was here to pick up his brother and his wife.

"Please invite him to come into my office, Betsy," replied Mr. Morris.

In walked a German colonel. His uniform was impeccable, with an Iron Cross at his neck. His eyes were blue and his hair blond. He took off his hat and extended his hand to Mr. Morris and introduced himself, speaking in perfect English. "I am Colonel Horst Brausch. I am here to pick up my brother and his wife, Margaret."

Mr. Morris was taken aback when he saw the colonel. With the exception of the uniform, the man was a look-alike of Carlton Fuller—same height, blond hair, and blue eyes. *A spitting image of his brother*, Mr. Morris thought to himself. He extended his hand and introduced himself. "I'm Leland Morris, chargé d'affaires, United States; it is my pleasure to meet you, Colonel Brausch."

"The pleasure is mine, sir. That gentleman who looks like me over there must be my twin brother Carlton. Hello, Carlton. How many years has it been?" he asked.

Carlton and Maggie got up and walked over to Horst.

Carlton looked at his brother and said, "It must be at least twenty years, Horst. How are you? It is good to see you. Please speak English while we are here visiting you. My wife doesn't speak German. Let me introduce my wife, Maggie. Maggie, this is my twin brother Horst."

Maggie couldn't get over the likeness, the size, and the weight. They were very identical. With the exception of the clothes, one would not know the difference. She reached out her hand to shake Horst's. "I am very happy to meet you, Horst. Carlton has told me about you. I knew you were a twin brother. The likeness between the two of you is striking.

I am looking forward to meeting your wife and family. How is your father doing?" she asked.

"I'm overwhelmed, Carlton," replied Horst. "You have such a beautiful wife. You look so good. I didn't know what to expect. Our father is doing as well as can be expected, Maggie. Thank you for asking. I came here from the hospital. He is getting weaker but is happy both of you are here. I told him I was coming to get you both and bring you to his bedside. That brightened his spirits. I think we should get to the hospital as soon as we can. Don't you both agree?" he asked. "Mr. Morris, I'm sorry we have to leave so quickly, but our father is not doing very well. I want Carlton to spend as much time as possible visiting with him. Good to meet you, Mr. Morris." Horst shook Mr. Morris's hand, clicked his heels, turned, and left.

Carlton and Maggie thanked Mr. Morris and Miss Bayer, and Maggie told Miss Bayer she would see her soon. She took out a pad and pencil from her purse and took down the embassy telephone number. They shook Mr. Morris's and Miss Bayer's hands and then left the office and the embassy. Awaiting them was a black German Mercedes Limousine with a motorcycle escort. The embassy footman was helping the limo driver put Carlton and Maggie's luggage in the trunk of the limo. When they finished, they shook hands, and the driver got into the car.

Brausch Family

"**Z**um Charité Krankenhaus, bitte!" said Horst, directing the driver to take them to the Charité hospital.

The motorcycles started, and the limo followed.

As the limousine began to move, Horst addressed Maggie. "Maggie, when Carlton asked me to speak English because you don't speak or understand German, the first thing that popped into my head was my wife, Hildegard. I'm sure you and she will have an opportunity to spend some time together. I want to assure you. She speaks fluent English. Her father is an international businessman. He wanted her to speak English for that reason. I'm sure you and she will have no issues communicating with each other."

"Oh Horst, thank you for your consideration. I have been very concerned about the language situation since we started on this trip. You made me very happy saying that Hildegard speaks English. It will be wonderful not having either you or Carlton be an interpreter for me," replied Maggie.

"Horst, you introduced yourself as a colonel. What do you do in the Nazi organization to warrant the motorcycles and this beautiful automobile?" asked Carlton.

"Carlton, I don't warrant these items. They are for you and Maggie. You are special people. We want to make sure you are safe while you are traveling here in France and Germany. You are US diplomats. That is not the only reason. Our father was one of the original Nazi Party members and was one of the organizers of the Nazi Youth back in the twenties. He is very well respected and a personal friend of Hitler's. In fact, he started me in the movement. I just left the Hitler Youth organization and have been promoted to General Jodl's personal staff. Being that you are the son and brother to the Brausch family, you are very special people. General Jodl and his boss, General Keitel, made sure you both are safe. They made it clear to me that both of you are to be well taken care of. I hope you understand."

"Thank you, Horst. Congratulations on your promotion. I didn't realize what Father's background was in the development of the Nazi Party. Nor did I know of his relationship with Hitler. Maggie and I feel very safe here. We appreciate the concern you and the Nazi Party have for our safety. We also appreciate your letting us stay at your residence, in lieu of our staying in the American embassy due to the bombing damage. I have so many questions to ask. Hopefully, we will be able to talk in less formal circumstances. I hope you don't mind us speaking in English. Maggie doesn't speak or understand German," Carlton said, reiterating his concern over the language barrier.

"Thank you, Carlton, for congratulating me. I am a full colonel in the Wehrmacht. I still have to get my uniforms modified to reflect my rank. You and Maggie are the first people I have told. I have been too busy today even to tell Hildegard. I will try to answer all your questions if I can. We are approaching the hospital where Father is. The limo is slowing down. I hope the British won't be bombing tonight. Apparently, they are retaliating for Göring's Luftwaffe bombing England. Göring, that pompous ass, thinks he can beat the British by himself. He boasted the British would never bomb Berlin. Berlin is paying a small price for his idiocy. I apologize. I am only quoting my boss, General Jodl. Hitler spoke at a rally in Berlin. He promised the people that, if the British dropped bombs on Berlin, the Luftwaffe would drop many thousands of pounds more on their cities. Let's get into the hospital now that the limo has stopped." Horst continued his explanation as they entered the hospital. "The hospital has been missed by the bombs, thank God. Many wounded members of the military service are bedded here. This is one of the best hospitals in Germany. Apparently our antiaircraft fire has been so fierce that the British planes have to fly very high. That has definitely affected the accuracy of their bombing—hence, the damage their bombs did to the US embassy." He laughed heartily.

They walked for what seemed a mile through the hallways of the very large building. They entered an elevator, and Carlton's brother told the operator, "Dritte Etage, bitte," requesting the third floor.

"Shhh," whispered Horst as they approached room 399.

They all entered the room. A nurse was attending their father, who was under an oxygen tent. His breathing sounded labored.

The nurse spoke to him. "Herr Brausch, Sie haben Besuch. Es handelt sich um Ihren Sohn Horst und einem jungen Mann, der haargenau wie Ihr Sohn ausschaut, sowie eine junge Dame. Darf ich sie hereinlassen?" (Mr. Brausch, you have visitors. It is your son, Horst, a man who looks like him, and a woman. Would you like to see them?)

In a raspy voice, Herr Brausch replied, "Ja bitte." (Yes)

The nurse pulled open the oxygen tent, and Carlton and his father saw each other for the first time in some twenty years. They both started to cry, and then they reached for each other and hugged one another. Horst reached out and hugged them both. A German Army colonel, an American lawyer, and an old dying man, all of them crying, hugging over a hospital bed—it was a very emotional scene. Maggie, watching this scene develop, broke down herself, and the nurse had to leave the room.

Although she had seen this happen many times, this time the nurse broke down. She couldn't allow herself to be seen crying in public. *Discipline*, she told herself. Horst had told her the family story during one of his visits. She couldn't stop crying. She walked into a closet and closed the door so no one would see her crying. She was a nurse in the Nazi Army. How would her peers react?

After she calmed down she went back to room 399. All had calmed down except the father. He was still crying softly.

Carlton leaned over the bed speaking German, "Vater, hier ist meine Frau Margaret, ich nenne sie Maggie. Wir sind seit zehn Jahren verheiratet und haben zwei Kinder und sie ist mit unserem dritten Kind schwanger. Du wirst im Maerz nochmals Grossvater werden."

"Maggie, I said to my father, Father, this is my wife, Margaret. I call her Maggie for short. We have been married ten years and have two children. She is pregnant with our third child. You will be a grandfather again in March."

Mr. Brausch replied in a very weak voice, "Hallo, Margaret oder Maggie. Ich bin so froh, dass es Ihnen und Carlton moeglich war mich hier zu besuchen. Es tut mir Leid aber ich fuehle mich sehr schwach und kann nicht laut genug sprechen, damit mich jeder versteht. Doch es ist

15

fantastisch meine beiden Soehne wieder vereint zu sehen. Ich glaubte dieser Tag wuerde niemals kommen. Sie haben zwei Kinder und ein Drittes ist im Maerz unterwegs. Tolle Sache. Ich hoffe von Euch wieder zu hoeren, wenn es soweit ist. Ich bin wirklich sehr stolz."

"Hello," Carlton translated, "I am very happy to meet you Margaret, oh Maggie. I'm so happy you and Carlton were able to come and visit me. I'm sorry I am so weak. I can hardly speak loud enough for people to hear me. To see my boys together again makes me feel wonderful. I never thought that could happen again. You have two children and will have another in March. How grand that is. I look forward to hearing when that happens. I'm so proud."

Maggie could hardly hear him. She leaned over the bed to respond. "Mr. Brausch, I am so happy to meet you. I never thought I would have the opportunity to meet you in person. Our children's names are Carlton Jr. and Charlotte. I am carrying our third child, who will be born in March next year. We have been married ten years. Your son is a successful lawyer in Cleveland Ohio."

"Maggie, please don't be offended, honey. My father understands English but would rather speak and be spoken to in German," Carlton explained.

Mr. Brausch smiled as he responded to Maggie very weakly, "Danke, Maggie, ich weiss Du wirst Dich gut mit Horst's Frau verstehen. Ihr scheint Euch sehr aehnlich zu sein. Ich bin Ihnen sehr dankbar, dass Sie mich mit Carlton besucht haben. Als meine Jungs kleiner waren sahen sie sich aehnlich. Heute ist die Aehnlichkeit noch viel groesser. Richten Sie bitte meiner Frau aus, dass ich sie immer noch liebe. Ich bereue, dass ich ihr so viel Kummer bereitet habe. Nun fehlen mir die Kraefte weiterzusprechen, bitte haben Sie Verstaendnis."

Carlton translated again. "Thank you, Maggie, I know you will be happy to meet Horst's wife. You seem so much like her. I appreciate you coming with Carlton to visit me. When the boys were young, they looked alike. Now they even look more alike. Please tell my wife that I still love her. I am sorry I caused her so much pain. I can't talk much more now. Please understand."

Maggie saw a tear in his eye and responded, "I do, Mr. Brausch. I will tell Oma for you."

Maggie began to cry softly. Carlton, noticing Maggie's tears, hugged her and gave her his handkerchief. Carlton was a little surprised by his father's reaction to Maggie and by his repentance.

The nurse came over to Carlton and Horst. She asked them to leave, as their father had had too much excitement for one afternoon. She told them they could come back later that afternoon or evening. In agreement, the three visitors left the room, advising the nurse the two brothers would be back to visit in the evening. As they left, the nurse noted the striking likeness the two brothers had. *If they were wearing the same clothes,* she reflected, *you wouldn't be able to tell them apart.* She let it go and went on with her work. She had to dispense pills to Mr. Brausch and take his vital signs. She didn't want to wake him up. He was sleeping peacefully for the first time in weeks. She would take his vital signs and dispense the pills later.

The limousine left the hospital and turned left heading out a broad boulevard. Horst told them that he was taking them to his house to meet his wife and to give them a chance to freshen up before dinner. Maggie agreed that she certainly needed that opportunity, and Carlton concurred. The three made small talk as they traveled. Horst pointed out buildings they passed and explained that so many flags were flying because Hitler had just addressed a rally of Berliners, talking about the bombing of Berlin by the British. Horst talked excitedly about how Hitler had rallied the crowd with promises of the Luftwaffe's retaliation against the British.

The limousine turned down a street lined with beautiful houses with beautifully landscaped yards. Carlton asked Horst if he lived on this street. Horst said that he did, and just then, the limousine turned into a driveway leading to a Victorian mansion that was impeccably landscaped.

"How beautiful, Horst!" Maggie exclaimed. "The leaves are just beginning to change. It must be wonderful when the fall colors are in full bloom."

"Thank you, Maggie. Yes, it is beautiful in the fall. It is just as gorgeous in the spring when the trees are in full blossom. We are very fortunate to live here. The Jews were very reluctant to give it up," said Horst.

That comment hit Maggie like a flash of thunder. She grimaced and gripped Carlton's hand so hard he grunted. He looked at her and moved his head very slightly side to side, hoping Horst had not detected their reaction.

He hadn't. Horst was on his way out the door of the limousine.

Before they left the vehicle. Carlton whispered to Maggie, "Remember what we were told. There are ears everywhere. We must be careful what we say and to whom we say it—no matter how much we feel we are guests here. We can react to each other in private, but not openly in public. This is just the beginning."

She nodded her head in agreement.

Horst was waving to them and shouting for them to hurry up. He wanted them to meet his wife.

Carlton and Maggie walked up the stairs to the home's main entrance—two large, wooden doors with large, brass handles. Horst opened the doors to reveal a large foyer with tapestries hanging on the walls. The home was beautiful. From the foyer, they went into an entrance room with a stairway coming down to it. To the left was a drawing room, and to the right, Maggie saw what she thought looked like a library. Carlton couldn't believe his brother lived in a house like this one. He was impressed with the house but not with the fact that his brother lived in it. Who was the family who'd "given it up"?

Down the stairs came a beautiful woman with flowing red hair dressed in the latest fashion. "Hallo, Horst," she said. "Ich vermute, das sind Carlton und Margaret aus den Vereinigten Staten von Amerika" (This must be Carlton and Margaret from the United States.).

"Ja, dies ist mein Bruder Carlton und seine Frau Margaret" (Yes, this is my brother Carlton and his wife, Margaret), said Horst. And turning to the guests, he said, "Darf ich meine Frau Hildegard vorstellen und wuerdest" (Please meet my wife, Hildegard).

Then he smiled at his wife and added, "Du bitte in Englisch weitersprechen, da Margaret kein Deutsch versteht" (Please speak English, as Margaret doesn't speak German).

"I'm sorry for speaking German. From now, on I will speak English," responded Hildegard.

"It is a pleasure meeting you, Hildegard," replied Carlton. "I'm Carlton, and this is my wife Maggie, uh Margaret."

"Please call me Maggie. Margaret is so formal. I am very pleased to meet you, Hildegard. What a beautiful home you live in," said Maggie, trying to be as nonchalant as possible.

"Let's go into the library and have a glass of wine while the driver brings in your luggage," replied Hildegard. "I understand you both will be staying with us. That is wonderful. It will give us a chance to get better acquainted. Hopefully, the British won't be bombing again soon. Maggie, I had a telephone call from the American embassy saying they will be picking you up at nine in the morning for your tour of the city. I would sure like to go with you, if that is possible. I haven't been out of this house for a while. The social life is rather dull for us young folks here in the city. Isn't it, Horst? How has your trip been so far, Maggie? I have never traveled by plane. Was it exciting? I'm sorry. I have a lot of questions, don't I? I apologize for being so rude. Here comes the wine. Thank you, Ann."

"Please pour the wine. I hope you like white wine. We drink a lot of white wine here in Germany." Hildegard's tone of voice and mannerism made Maggie think of someone who was excited to have people to talk to.

They did a great deal of talking about the trip. Maggie explained the trip. She talked about the train, what sites they visited during their stay in New York City, the seaplane they flew in, and the train trip across France and Germany. Horst was interested in the seaplane.

Carlton was interested in how Horst and Hildegard had met and married. Hildegard was interested in everything American.

The afternoon was filled with continuous conversation. They all had a lot to catch up on.

After about an hour, Hildegard suggested that Maggie and Carlton refresh themselves and get ready for dinner. She took them to their bedroom and bathroom. From what Maggie saw, the entire house was done in antiques and impressionist paintings.

"How lovely and expensive," was her comment to Carlton.

He agreed. It was a wealthy Jewish family that had lost this house.

Carlton took Maggie into a closet in their bedroom. "Don't forget our mission," he said. "Remember what is being said. Remember what you see and where you have been. I just wanted to remind you, honey."

"I know, Carlton. My mission has been foremost in my mind ever since we got on the train," Maggie assured him. "I know that our friend Donovan will be very interested."

"Let's go to dinner. I'm famished," said Carlton as they left the closet.

"Me too," said Maggie.

And together, they headed down the steps to dinner.

The dinner was wonderful. Carlton and Maggie were full when they left the table.

Maggie asked Hildegard to explain the dinner to her—she wanted to take notes, which would enable her to cook it at home.

Hildegard was thrilled to oblige. "We started with Ochsenschwanzsuppe—in English, oxtail soup. From there, we had Wienerschnitzel, which is a veal cutlet that has been beaten and breaded with flour, bread crumbs, and egg. Then they are fried in hot oil until golden brown. They were served with Spaetzle or German dumplings, along with Rotkohl—red cabbage. For dessert, we had Apfelstrudel, or apple strudel. We drank French red wines that were very soft and smooth."

"Please give me the recipes, Hildegard," said Maggie.

"I will," Hildegard assured her.

Hildegard and Maggie were getting along very well. Carlton didn't know if it was the wine or just that Hildegard needed the companionship of another woman.

"Thank you for such a wonderful dinner, you two," said Carlton.

"It was such a traditional German dinner. We appreciate your hospitality. Horst, shouldn't we be getting back to the hospital?" asked Carlton.

"Yes we should," answered Horst, "Let me get the driver to pull up the limousine, and we will get started."

As Carlton and Horst were leaving the room, the ladies were heading for the drawing room with another bottle of wine and their glasses. Maggie was full. She had to be careful not to drink too much, as the doctor had warned her being pregnant was not the time to drink a great deal of wine. Plus, she continually thought about her mission. She also knew she was being picked up in the morning to go on her first tour. She didn't know whether or not she should invite Hildegard to join her.

Hildegard was feeling no pain. She poured another glass of wine for herself and Maggie.

"Maggie you mentioned your children at dinner. How many do you have?"

"I have two, and I am three months pregnant," Maggie told her.

From that point on, the conversation went on about family and living in the United States. Maggie didn't want to get into politics. She asked Hildegard about her house. Hildegard frowned and looked down at the floor.

"Did I ask the wrong question?" Maggie asked.

"No, no," responded Hildegard. "It's not really ours. It was given to us by the Nazis because of Horst's position in the party. I love the house and all the things in it. I love the servants waiting on me. The chef is wonderful. They are Jews who have no future here in Germany. We hope we can keep them with us. I am uncomfortable here. I cannot talk to Horst about how I feel. I tried, and he yells and shouts at me about the Nazi Party and their doctrine. He talks continuously about Hitler, the Führer. He has been promoted to a new position, and we will have to socialize with Jodl and his fat wife. He wants to spend more time socially with Himmler and his family. He wants me to become friends with these people. These people are evil. I hate them. I hate the Nazis. I hate Hitler for what he has done to Germany. I am a German, but I don't like Germany now."

With that, Hildegard poured herself another glass of wine. She was certainly flying high, thought Maggie. She tried to change the subject but to no avail.

Hildegard continued ranting on. "My husband grovels at the feet of these so-called leaders of the Nazis and of the country. His father is one of the originators of the party. I understand why our mother-in-law left him. I know why she took Carlton and went to the United States. Horst was his father's favorite. That is why Horst is what he is today. He is Nazi through and through. He has followed in his father's footsteps since he was a boy. He has secrets that he will not tell me or anyone. I have tried to be a wife and supportive, but I cannot do it. These people are killing Germans every day. They are killing people all over Europe. They are castigating the Jews, the Gypsies, the physically challenged, the mentally challenged, and the politically burdened. I will survive, but it will be very difficult.

"I'm sorry Maggie for going on like this, but I am not a Nazi. Today, when you arrived, I felt that I could talk with you about how I feel. Please don't let on to Horst or his father about this. Keep my feelings to yourself. I had to talk with someone about how I feel. There isn't anyone in this country I can talk to. The Gestapo is everywhere. People here in Germany would report you or me in an instant. They would pick us up, and that would be the end. Please be careful who you talk to," she cautioned. "I am at a point where I hate Horst for what he believes in and how he acts. He hasn't been physical with me, although he has threatened. I have to be very careful. We haven't made love for almost a year. I do not expect we will again. He probably will rape me one night when he is drunk."

Maggie was getting tired. She felt very badly for Hildegard, and she couldn't believe what she heard. Thank God the servants were gone. She and Hildegard were the only ones in the house. Life must be very lonely for her sister-in-law. *Hopefully, I can provide some womanly companionship for her over the next few days*, Maggie told herself.

"Hildegard, let's go to bed," she said gently. "I'm very tired. Who knows when Horst and Carlton will be home? Yes, you can go with me tomorrow morning. They will be picking us up early. Are you okay?"

"I think I'm very drunk. Would you help me up the stairs? Thank you for agreeing to take me with you tomorrow. If Horst asks me why I am going, I will tell him I am going to spy on you. He will like that. He will question me tomorrow night after we return," Hildegard replied.

"Of course I'll help," Maggie responded.

She put her arm around Hildegard's back and helped her up the long staircase to her bedroom. "Do you need help putting on your bedclothes?" she asked.

"No," Hildegard replied. "What time do we need to be ready in the morning?"

"About nine a.m., I think," Maggie said as she closed the bedroom door. "Good night."

"Good night," Hildegard said softly.

ℑ ᴀᴛ𝔥ᴇʀ

The motorcade was waiting for Carlton and Horst. It consisted of two motorcycles and a large, black Mercedes limousine. Horst directed the driver to take them to the Charité hospital.

"Horst please tell me about the hospital that Father is in. I am concerned about the treatment he is receiving," said Carlton.

"Charité is one of the largest hospitals in Germany. It is a teaching hospital and has had a number of Nobel Prize winners in residence. The nurses are all German Army, and there is a great deal of pride and discipline in the building. The care Father has been receiving has been greater than one could expect during a war," Horst assured Carlton. "Many wounded German servicemen are being treated at the hospital. Our Führer has demanded the best hospital service for our servicemen. They come before anyone else being admitted. I think you can feel comfortable in knowing that this is an exemplary service hospital."

"You certainly know better than me, Horst. What is the Hitler Youth you and father were involved in?" asked Carlton.

"It is an organization for the youth of Germany. It is made up of three groups—boys ages fourteen to eighteen, boys ages ten to fourteen, and girls from ten to eighteen. Obviously, it started small in 1922. The organization struggled early on. German politicians banned it, and it went underground. As Hitler rose in German politics, so did the German Youth. It became the official Nazi Party's youth group in 1926. The group was used to spy on church youth organizations' Bible studies and on various other church studies and just to cause political violence. The youth are the future pure Germans, and they will be future Third Reich soldiers. They were indoctrinated in racism as part of their training. They wear uniforms that look like those of the SD, only with one silver S on their collars. This aligns them with the SS. They are organized like an Army would be. They are trained to be future officers, technicians and labor leaders. They have their own monthly magazine called *Will and Power.* In 1934 a law was passed to outlaw all youth organizations except the Hitler youth group. The law further provided conscription of all German youth. By 1938 the group had over seven million members. They are a very active group in helping Nazism function," answered Horst.

"I'm dumbfounded, Horst. You have seven million members. Hitler has to be very proud of you and father," replied Carlton.

"Father and I are proud of what we have helped build. We have started building the future of Germany with pure Germans. We have a program that mates our older youth boys and girls to create purebred Aryan children, who will be indoctrinated into the Hitler Youth as they grow older. We are planning ahead to meet our Führer's goal of a thousand-year Reich populated with pure Aryans," Horst proudly proclaimed.

"I'm sure you are," Carlton said, shuddering to himself. *I will have a lot of information for Donovan to digest,* he thought. "It looks as if we are approaching the hospital," he added.

As they pulled up to the entrance to the hospital, the air raid sirens went off. A soldier came running out of the hospital and motioned for Carlton and Horst to come with him. "Quickly, quickly," he said.

The brothers followed the soldier into the hospital and down three sets of stairs to a basement bunker of sorts, which rapidly started to fill up with hospital personnel.

Carlton was thinking as he overheard conversations among doctors and nurses complaining about the British bombing Berlin. "Where is Göring's Luftwaffe? Aren't they supposed to protect us?" a nurse complained.

Carlton laughed to himself quietly as he thought about the people of this country. They are just like any country in a situation like this. They were complaining about the government.

Down the stairs came the soldier again. He announced the siren was a false alarm. A German plane was flying overhead. Someone had panicked and pulled the alarm switch.

Carlton and Horst headed to the elevator. They wanted to get up to their father's room. The door to the room was closed. When Horst knocked, a nurse opened the door and invited them in.

"Your father is sleeping rather soundly for a change," she told them in a whisper. "His breathing is not as labored as it was before. Please be quiet until I wake him to take his blood pressure and his vitals. If you would like some coffee, I will get it for you.

"I thought the air raid siren was going to awake him," she added. "Thank heavens it didn't. We have been having more false alarms lately. I guess the wardens are getting a little touchy."

"I have to check in with the night guard and let him know where I am in case Jodl needs me," Horst said as he left the room.

"Nurse, I'll have a cup of coffee," replied Carlton. "A little cream please would be nice if possible."

"Thank you, Mr. Fuller. I'll get it. Please don't say anything to the colonel, I am always a little nervous when the colonel is here," she added confidentially as she left the room. "He scares me and my colleagues. I should be used to him, but he gives me the heebie-jeebies."

"I understand. I won't." replied Carlton.

Mr. Brausch stirred as the nurse shut the door.

"Father, are you okay?" Carlton said. "Can I get you anything?"

In a raspy voice, his father responded, "I'm okay. Carlton, is that you?"

"It's me, Father. Horst and I came back to spend more time with you this evening. I would like to speak English, if that is okay with you. It's easier for me, as my German is a little rusty. Would you speak English?" Carlton asked his father.

"I understand. I will try to speak English," his father agreed. "My English, like your German, is a little rusty.

"Horst may not be back tonight," he added. "His new boss, Jodl, is working with his staff on a new plan for the services for next year. It is a very large undertaking. But it's something the Führer wants, and I'm sure it is top secret. Horst is very much involved in the planning process. I'm very proud of him. He has become an active cog in the planning wheel. He deals at the highest levels in the services. He talks with the Führer during the process. He keeps Jodl apprised of the Führer's desires. I hope you have an opportunity to meet Jodl and his staff before you have to leave."

Carlton noticed that his father's voice was starting to weaken.

The nurse came back with the coffee. "I see you are up, Mr. Brausch," she said. "I have to give you pills and take your vitals."

Carlton noted to himself how efficient this nurse was. It didn't take her three minutes to take his blood pressure and vitals. He was thankful his father had agreed to speak in English. Although he could speak German, English was a considerably easier language to communicate in. German was a very formal language. And he felt that, with Horst gone, now was the time to talk with his father.

"Nurse, could you leave us alone for a while. I haven't had an opportunity to talk with my father in private for over twenty years. I will call you quickly if I need help," Carlton said.

The nurse had to think for a minute but then concluded that leaving them alone presented no problem. "I will be just down the hall in the waiting room," she replied and left the room.

Carlton took his father's hand in his. "I don't know where to start, Father," he said. "I have many questions to ask you. What happened to you and Mother? Why did you let her go? How did Horst become a Nazi? What caused you to get involved with Hitler and the Nazi Party? What became of all Mother's personal belongings? Where do you live? Please do the best you can, Father, answering these questions. I know you are very weak. I'm hoping for the best."

"My son," his father started, "I will try very hard to answer all of your questions. I was almost killed in the Beer Hall Putsch during the fall of 1923. This was a time of chaos in Germany. We were living in Munich at the time. I was still in an army that had been very deflated in size. Inflation was very high. And jobs were difficult to find. Germany was still suffering from the Treaty of Versailles. Hitler joined the German Workers Party after the war ended. He had risen to the highest post in the party by 1923 and had a group of rowdy ex-army followers at that time. A high-level Bavarian politician was giving a speech at the Bürgerbräukeller beer hall. Hitler took the situation in hand and marched on the beer hall with his men. I marched with him.

"Push came to shove during the night. The result was the killing of nineteen Nazis and four police. I happened to be in the middle of the melee. I was bloodied. Your mother was at home taking care of you and Horst. When she heard about the Putsch and my participation, she hit the ceiling. From the beginning, she hated the Nazi Party. I joined it, as I felt that Germany was suffering. It is my opinion that Hitler had the answers for Germany then, as he does now. Your mother never understood that. Her hatred and my opinion obviously led to the demise of our marriage.

"Horst was always interested in the army, and I helped him nurture that interest. He has grown up believing what I believe. Your mother wanted you to have a university education and directed you in that direction. She took you and emigrated to the United States. I am so sorry that we couldn't bring you both up together.

"I live in Berlin. Your mother's personal things are still at my home. Her silver, china, formal gowns, typewriter, books, and so on remain there. I couldn't throw them away.

"My voice is going away," he said, winding down. "I am getting very tired. I hope this helps you understand."

"Thank you, Father. It does," Carlton replied. "But I will never understand Hitler and the Nazi Party. I know Germany was in chaos, but why didn't cooler heads prevail? Why all of the killing? Why taking over countries? Why the ideas about a superior race? Why the anti-Semitism? I'm happy I have had an opportunity to visit with you. I'm sorry you are so ill. I will pray for your soul, Father."

His father had dropped off to sleep again. Carlton didn't know if his father had heard him or not.

Just then, Horst and the nurse returned to the room. Horst was beaming. He turned excitedly to Carlton. "I talked to Jodl. He wants to meet you tomorrow. He said he would try to have Hitler visit his headquarters to meet you. He said Göring was in France with the Luftwaffe. He didn't know where Himmler and Goebbels were. He wanted them to meet you also. We have a big day tomorrow. How is Father doing?" he asked.

"We had a nice talk," Carlton replied, adding. "Father spoke in English. I was very surprised he was willing to do it. I know he would rather speak and hear German. I was grateful he agreed. It is so much easier for me. He is getting weaker. He went right to sleep when he finished talking."

"I'm getting tired. I need to sleep, Horst."

Carlton said good night to the nurse and left the room. Horst asked the nurse to call him should something happen to his father, wished her good night, and followed Carlton out the door.

The limousine was waiting with the motorcycles. They climbed in and headed toward the house Horst lived in. It was a wet evening. The rain had started while they were visiting their father.

"Thank God it's raining," Horst said. "The British won't be able to bomb tonight. What good luck we are having.

"Father spoke in English? That is strange. Normally he only speaks German. He must be very happy to see you."

There wasn't much conversation on the way to Horst's house. Carlton started dropping off as soon as the limousine started moving. With the rain coming down harder and harder, Berlin was quiet that evening. The driver had to slow down to avoid puddles.

Horst turned on his reading light. He was going through papers he brought with him from the office. "What?" Horst commented out loud.

"Are you okay, Horst?" asked Carlton, who'd been startled awake. "What's going on?"

"I'm fine," remarked Horst. "It was just something I read that shocked me. I can't believe it will happen. I'm sorry. I can't talk about it, but I couldn't help myself."

It was very dark when they arrived at Horst's house. No lights were on in the house. The women had apparently turned off of all the lights, expecting an air raid.

"Hildegard is finally learning. It has been difficult for her here in Berlin, especially since the Brits started bombing. We haven't had the chance to go out and enjoy ourselves. My job with the Hitler Youth has kept me very busy. Since the war started, we have been busy training the youth to shoot rifles, to fight fires, to be air wardens, to identify aircraft, and to shoot antiaircraft guns—all of this just in case they are needed to help out." Horst opened the front door. "This new job I have will be even busier. We are in the process of planning the next five years of activity for the services. The Führer is directly involved in all the details. It is a little bit unnerving having him with us every day and into the night. People get very nervous when he is around."

"Good night, Horst. I'm going to bed," said Carlton. "Don't stay up too late as we have a big day tomorrow," he added as he headed up the steps.

"Good night," Horst replied and echoed Carlton. "We have a big day tomorrow."

Maggie's Next Day

The alarm rang at 7:00 a.m. in Maggie and Carlton's room. She rolled over, picked up a robe, and stretched. *Oh its early,* she thought. *We are going on tour today. I told Hildegard she could come with us. I hope Major Best and Miss Bayer the lady from the Embassy won't mind.* She slipped on her robe, left her room, and knocked on Hildegard's door. She heard movement in the room, and then the door opened.

"Oh, good morning," said Hildegard, "I have a terrible headache. Must be from the wine we drank last night. I am so looking forward to our tour today. I have some special places I want you and your people to see. Let's get moving, get showers, get dressed, and have breakfast. I want to be on time. I think you said nine a.m. was pickup time. I advised the servants to have breakfast for us in about forty minutes."

"You are really excited to be going. And you have a headache. You are a better woman than I am," replied Maggie, "I'll be down for breakfast in about forty minutes."

Carlton had woken up when Maggie's alarm clock went off, but he hadn't even had a chance to say good morning to her, as she was off and running.

He was looking forward to spending the day with Horst. They were going to his brother's new office. Horst wanted to introduce him to the people he would be working with. He'd seemed especially interested in Carlton meeting Jodl.

Carlton caught Maggie as she was coming out of the shower. She was all wet as he hugged her and kissed her good morning. She looked wonderful. Her belly was just starting to protrude with her baby bump.

"You look so good this morning, Maggie," he said. "I could just keep kissing you. I'm going to Horst's office to meet his staff and Jodl. This should be a very interesting day. I can't imagine the Germans having me in their office where they are planning the war. But Horst insists that Jodl has invited me. What's your day going to be like?"

Maggie kissed Carlton warmly. "That's all you get, a wet kiss. We are going touring today. I asked Hildegard to join me."

A knock sounded on the door. Maggie went to dress, while Carlton opened the door a crack to see who'd knocked.

"Good morning." It was Horst. "Let's get going," he said. "We can get breakfast on the way to the office. Coffee is hot in the kitchen. We can get a cup on the way to the car. See you in twenty minutes."

Both finally dressed, Carlton and Maggie headed down the stairs to start the busy day. Each was having the same thought: *Remember your mission.* They were each acutely aware that they would have to report to Donovan when they returned.

Horst and Carlton were out the door quickly. Maggie and Hildegard had more time, and they were enjoying breakfast in the kitchen. The young kitchen servant brought coffee. Hildegard introduced Maggie to her. "Sara, this is Maggie Fuller. She is my sister- in-law from the United Sates. She and her husband are visiting my father-in-law, who is in the hospital."

"It is very nice to meet you, Mrs. Fuller," Sara replied.

"Very nice to meet you too, Sara," said Maggie, noticing the dark eyes and sad beauty of this young lady. The girl was dressed in a plain, light blue smock but had a yellow cross on her sleeve. *I wonder what that is,* she thought. *I'll ask Hildegard later.*

A car horn sounded outside the house. Maggie went to the front door saw the embassy car waiting. It was Major Best, accompanied by Miss Bayer.

Maggie waved as she and Hildegard left the house. "Hello, Major Best. I invited my sister-in-law to join us. I hope you don't mind. She has been ensconced in this house for a while and needed to get out. Major Best, this is Hildegard Brausch."

"Good morning, ma'am. It's a pleasure meeting you," said Major Best and, turning to his companion, added, "This is Miss Mayer from the US embassy staff."

Miss Mayer extended her hand to Hildegard. "It is my pleasure, ma'am. Please call me Emily. 'Miss Mayer' is so formal. We will be together all day today; no reason to be so formal."

"Thank you for being so gracious to me. It is a pleasure meeting you both. It will be nice not spending the day with Nazis looking over my shoulder," Hildegard commented sarcastically. "I have some very interesting places I would like for you folks to visit on your tour of Berlin—of course, after we visit those locations you have on your itinerary today."

"Where are we going to start?" Maggie asked Major Best.

"I thought a good place would be the Reichstag. It has an interesting history, particularly its recent history. What would you say, Mrs. Brausch?" asked the major.

"I agree wholeheartedly. It's a great place to begin our day. Please call me Hildegard; I agree with Emily, we don't need to be formal."

Carlton's Next Day

The Mercedes, along with its cavalcade of motorcycles was waiting for the brothers as they left the house.

"Must we have motorcycles?" Carlton asked. "They make me nervous."

"It gives us a high priority on the road. We have to travel about thirty miles to OKW headquarters, which is located in Zossan. With the roads full of military and civilians, the flashing red lights and sirens move the traffic out of the way. We will stop on the way to get some strudel and sausage for breakfast," replied Horst.

Horst continued. "Let me explain the organization for you. The OKW is the Supreme Command of the German Armed Forces. It has little oversight over the army, the navy, and the Luftwaffe. It is responsible for coordinating operations between the branches and subordinate only to Hitler himself. The OKW issues Hitler's orders to the services as directed by him. Hitler established the OKW in 1938, which led to the dismissal of the Reich War Minister and Commander of the Wehrmacht. This allowed Hitler to consolidate power and authority in his position as Führer.

"Currently, the OKW is led by General William Keitel, with Jodl as chief of the operations staff. We are composed of four departments. Wehrmachtfuhrungsstab, in charge of the operational orders, is headed by Colonel General Alfred Jodl. Next is Amt Ausland/Abwehr, charged with foreign intelligence and headed by Admiral Wilhelm Canaris. Wirtchafts und Rustungsamt deals with supply matters. And finally, Amtsgruppe Alllgemeine Wehrmachtsangelegenheiten handles miscellaneous business. I don't yet know who the leaders of the last two groups are. I'm sure I'll meet them soon enough."

"It seems to me that Hitler is a master at playing politics—using power and intimidation to achieve his end," Carlton commented after hearing Horst's description of the OKW.

"You are right, Carlton! He is a brilliant man. Have you read *Mein Kampf*? It explains his philosophy about the history of Germany and talks about how Germany and its people were treated after World War I. It discusses the purification of the German people and goes into depth on the Jewish issue and the influence of the Jews on Germany. Read it if you haven't. You are of German birth; it may change your mind about the Nazis." Horst was getting excited as he spoke about Hitler.

"I haven't read his book. It sounds as if the Nazi Party is treating it like a bible for the Germans to believe in. As of yet, I haven't given that any thought," replied Carlton somewhat sardonically.

Horst frowned at Carlton's reply.

They stopped at a small village bakery for breakfast. The food had been baked just that morning. The strudel was warm. The coffee was hot and fresh. The sausage was savory with just the right spices. *What wonderful food the local people cook and eat here in Germany*, Carlton thought.

The limousine and motorcycles drew a crowd in the village. The people seemed to be in awe of Horst as he got out of the limo, standing straight in his uniform with the iron cross at his neck. There was a lot of mumbling going on in the village. It seemed as if the local population did not see military brass of Horst's level very often.

Horst thanked the store owner and waved good-bye. He enjoyed the admiration the village seemed to give him. "We are almost to Zossan," he said. "The headquarters are underground. I am looking forward to you meeting the staff."

The limousine pulled up to a gate guarded by two soldiers. A major approached the limousine and immediately asked for identification. Once Horst was identified, the major snapped to attention and apologized to Horst for not knowing who he was. *Apparently, the major never received the message that Horst was the new staffer on board*, Carlton thought to himself. Not knowing who Horst was could have been a big mistake for the major.

Horst gave the major a sly smile and introduced Carlton, and they both went into the complex. As he led Carlton into the complex, Horst explained that they had to go underground. Soldiers with rifles or machine guns stood at every juncture of the hallway that led downstairs to the offices. It made Carlton a bit nervous.

It was the beginning of a long day for Carton and Horst. Carlton had never been to a location like this. There must have been hundreds of army and navy personnel on this planning staff. Carlton was introduced to all of the senior staff who Horst would be interfacing with.

When they finally met with Alfred Jodl, Carlton had met so many people he was getting tired. The general was very understanding and invited both Horst and Carlton into his large office to join him for lunch. Carlton was very impressed with Jodl. His uniform was perfect. Everything about him was perfect. His office was large. There was a picture of the Führer on the wall and a Nazi flag in one corner of the room. Jodl sat behind a large, wooden desk, and two plush, burgundy-colored chairs faced the desk. The large, oriental carpet covered about three-fourths of the floor. The general was very much aware of the reason for Carlton and his wife's visit to Germany. He wanted to make sure they were having a good visit with Carlton's father. He inquired as to his father's health.

Here is one of the Nazi's top generals and the leader of Hitler's planning staff. And he is interested in me and my father, thought Carlton. *Very impressive.*

Jodl went on to tell Carlton about his father's rise in the party and his accomplishments. He continued with Horst and his rise and success in the party, emphasizing Horst's work to build the future of the German Aryan race. He told Carlton to be proud of what his family had accomplished and elaborated on what else the family, now under Horst's guidance, would achieve. While Jodl was praising his family, Carlton noticed Horst beaming.

The meeting and lunch lasted two hours. The food was perfect and the beer outstanding.

Following lunch, Jodl excused himself and left for a meeting with the Führer.

As they walked out of the office, Horst remarked, "What a wonderful visit, don't you think, Carlton? What a man, what a leader, what a boss. I am going to be happy here. It will be long hours, but I will be in on the cutting edge of all of the war planning."

"Yes you will, Horst. I felt very gratified that Jodl praised both you and Father for your efforts. But it doesn't mean I agree with what is going on here in Europe. It is not my place to be agreeable one way or another. You and the German people are being gracious hosts to Maggie and me. I can't thank you enough for your help in allowing me to talk with Father. I want to thank you personally for your effort," Carlton said, hugging his brother as they left the hallway going up to the entrance.

Horst was taken aback by the emotion Carlton had displayed. "Why thank you, Carlton," was all he could say at the moment.

Meeting all these Nazis had made for a very interesting day for Carlton. He hadn't understood how committed they were to their missions. He was beginning to realize that the Nazi situation was deadly serious. He was beginning to believe that a world war had begun. What he didn't understand was when or why the United States would enter the war.

Horst was ready to head home. "What did you think of our day, Carlton?" he asked as they entered the hallway to leave the OKW headquarters.

"I am not a soldier or a service person," Carlton replied. "I find it unbelievable that so much of Germany's resources are moving forward in their effort to conquer Europe. The dedication of this OKW staff is amazing. It is a beehive of effort from the top of the organization to the bottom. It is so disciplined. And there is an attitude of success. I am concerned that the politicians of the world don't understand the motivation to succeed. But right now I am more worried about our father, Horst. Let's get back to the hospital, please."

"Good idea," said Horst and instructed the driver to take them to the hospital as they climbed into the limousine. "We will see Father and then get home to the ladies for dinner," he said to Carlton's.

The motorcade left quickly for Berlin.

It was quiet in the car as they sped on. Carlton was thinking of the day. His thoughts were of the United States and where it would be going in this conflict. Congress was against getting involved, Roosevelt was trying to help England, and the people had no idea what was really going on here in Europe. The entire situation was beginning to be quite disconcerting to Carlton. He could feel it beginning to cause stomach discomfort for him.

Carlton and Horst finally arrived at the hospital. They knocked softly at their father's door.

The nurse opened it. "Good evening, gentlemen," she said softly. "Your father has been restless all day. He's been sleeping, but he has been tossing and turning continuously. I had the doctor come in to check on him. The doctor said he was doing as well as could be expected. He felt there was nothing he could do at this time and advised me to keep him as comfortable as possible."

Horst left the room with the excuse that he had to check in. Carlton sat down next to the bed and took his father's hand. He said Our Father and Hail Mary prayers for his father, asked God to forgive his sins, and prayed that he would be comfortable.

"His hand is clammy," he noted to the nurse. "When was the last time you took his vitals?"

"About thirty minutes ago," she replied. "They were stable."

"Thank you for taking care of him, nurse," Carlton said. "I know he would be very satisfied with your service."

Horst came rushing back into the room. He seemed anxious about something. "I have to go back to the office quickly. Something big is going down. Jodl wants me there for the announcement. I told the limousine driver to take you back to my home when you are finished visiting. I have a car coming for me. Please apologize to the ladies. I don't know when I will be getting back. Have a good evening." His tone was excited, and he turned on his heel and left quickly.

What could it be? Carlton wondered He had seen a lot of action at the headquarters building while they had been there earlier.

He said good night to the nurse, adding, "Please let me know if my father takes a turn for the worse. I can be reached at Colonel Brausch's residence."

Once inside the limousine, he asked the driver to take him back to the colonel's home. The motorcade left quickly. It had stopped raining. The sky was clear, but the city was darkened, so as to not give the Brits any clear targets, should they decide to bomb Berlin tonight.

On the way to the house, Carlton wondered how the day had gone for the girls. He felt sure Maggie would have a lot to talk about tonight. Hopefully, she hadn't forgotten the mission. He certainly hadn't forgotten his. He had a lot to report to Donovan after today's visit. The limo finally pulled up to the house, and Carlton thanked the driver and the motorcycle drivers for their effort and went into the house. Maggie and Hildegard were waiting for him. Much to his surprise, Major Best and Miss Bayer were there also.

"Carlton, Hildegard invited Major Best and Emily to have dinner with us tonight. It has been a long and trying day. We learned a lot and saw many disconcerting things. We have a lot to discuss. But first, let's all have some wine and food. What do you think?" asked Maggie.

"I am all for that. Hi, honey. Hello, Major, Miss Bayer, Hildegard. My day was the same as yours—trying. A glass of wine and relaxation before dinner would be wonderful," he replied.

Carlton apologized for Horst not being there. He explained the situation. Hildegard stuck out her tongue and remarked with hatred in her eyes, "Those damn Nazis."

The cook served them a wonderful meal—pork roast and all the trimmings—among a friendly environment. Hildegard was smiling and pouring the wine. It was a wonderful atmosphere after a very serious and shocking day. They all seemed to need to let go and relax. The discussion of the day would come tomorrow. They needed to rest this night.

Major Best and Emily left after dinner to go back to the embassy. Maggie told Carlton that the two of them had drawn close over the last two days.

All Carlton could respond was, "Ummm!" He was tired and wanted to go to sleep. The day had been an eye-opener.

Loss and Closure

Carlton was awoken by the sound of someone rumbling around in the house. He got out of bed, put on his robe, and opened the door to the hallway. As he walked out of the bedroom, down the hall came Horst.

"I'm sorry I'm so late coming home," Horst said in a whisper. "Things are moving too quickly. It is three a.m. Is everyone okay?"

"Yes, we are okay," Carlton answered. "We missed you for dinner."

"I'm going to bed," Horst replied. "I have another early day today. I won't be able to spend time with you; I have to be back at Zossan early. We are beginning to implement a major effort within the week. Good night, Carlton. I'm glad we had a good day together yesterday."

As Horst disappeared into his room, Carlton couldn't help but think, *A good day together? I'm not sure of that.*

The telephone began to ring somewhere downstairs; Carlton didn't know where it was. He'd started toward the steps when Hildegard came out of her room. "That's the telephone," she remarked. "Who could be calling at this time of the morning? Damn Nazis!"

They ran down the steps to answer the phone. Hildegard reached for the phone. "Hello! Who is this at three in the morning?" she barked loudly in German.

After listening for only a moment, she gasped. "Oh! Oh! My God!" Then she handed the phone to Carlton. "It's your father," she said. "Here. Take the phone. They want to talk to Horst."

"Hello. This is Carlton Fuller," Carlton said. "I'm Colonel Brausch's brother. What has happened to my father?" Carlton paused, waiting for a response to his question.

"He has what? He has died? No, that can't be true we were with him yesterday evening. He had a stroke during the night and expired before the doctor could reach him. Yes, I know you did everything you could for him. I will advise Colonel Brausch. He will know what to do and who to call. Thank you again."

Carlton sighed as he put down the telephone and sat down. "He's dead, Hildegard," he said quietly. "He died following another stroke."

"I'm so sorry, Carlton," said Hildegard as she reached out to hug Carlton. He responded to her hug and hugged her back.

"Let me awaken Horst. He will make all the plans. I'm sure the military will have a large military funeral for your father. It will be taken completely out of our hands," she said and headed up the stairs.

Carlton started after Hildegard. He had to tell Maggie. *At least I had a chance to visit and speak with him,* he thought as he made his way up the stairs. *It gave him a chance to clear the air before he passed. He seemed satisfied to talk about his life. He made his apologies very humbly and seemed gracious and remorseful. Oma will understand and be forgiving.*

Maggie came down the steps. "Carlton what happened?" she asked. "I heard all the noise."

"Father died, Maggie. He had another stroke during the night. They couldn't do anything for him. The night nurse said they tried. But nothing could be done."

She hugged Carlton and tried to console him.

"I'm fine, Maggie," he told her. "I'm glad I had a chance to talk with him in private. He was very gracious and remorseful. He asked me to apologize to my mother for ruining our lives. I'm okay, honey. Please don't cry."

Horst came rushing down the steps and hugged Carlton. "We lost our father. All we have is each other," he said quietly. "I'm sure they did everything they could at the hospital. He was very weak. Did you have time to talk with him? Were you and he able to settle your differences? He and I had many talks throughout the years. He wanted to make sure he could tell you why he did what he did. He wanted to make sure you understood and would take his explanation back to Mother. I will take care of all the details. The military and the leaders of the Nazi Party will all be involved. It will be a large funeral because of his stature in the party. I will keep you and Maggie posted as to what your roles will be. Father was a hero in the party."

It was the first emotion Carlton had seen in Horst since he'd arrived here. "We talked, Horst," he told his brother. "I know how he felt. He tried to explain to me why he joined the Nazi Party. As a father, I'm not sure I fully could comprehend his motives. I will tell Mother when we get back that he still loved her. I will explain his apology to her. What will happen now?" he asked.

"I will call the military protocol office first thing this morning. They will prepare the funeral. It will be large and complex. They will want to ensure he has all the military rights he deserves. I'd expect many of the Nazi hierarchy will participate, as well as members of all of the military services. Hitler may even attend. Father was a personal friend of his. I'm sure there will be a cortege with horses, drums, and marchers. It will be a celebration of his life," Horst explained, adding, "I'm getting very tired. I'm going back to bed. Good night. It will be a long day tomorrow."

Carlton and Maggie went back to the bedroom. "Honey, are you okay? How are you doing?" asked Maggie again.

"I am fine. I have no tears. He was my father, yes, but he really wasn't, as I left him while I was a child. He was a memory who was very involved with affairs in his country. That was his legacy. He really did not have time for me or Oma. I'm afraid the Nazis will make a spectacle out of his funeral. They will give the population a hero to celebrate and mourn," replied Carlton.

Carlton and Maggie tried to retire, but sleep did not come easy for either of them. There was too much going on. They were both still reeling from their travels the previous day. The death of Carlton's father just added to their untenable situation. *I have to contact the embassy in the morning*, Carlton thought. *I have to inform Mr. Morris that my father has died. Maggie and I haven't had an opportunity to discuss her trip with Hildegard, Major Best, and Miss Bayer. My head is spinning.* He leaned down and kissed Maggie softly. She had finally fallen asleep. *What have I gotten her into?*

When Carlton woke up, Maggie had already left the room. He stretched and walked around the room, looking for some clean clothes. He looked out the window and noticed that it was raining again. *How apropos*, he thought. He had to contact Mr. Morris this morning.

When he went down for breakfast he found Hildegard discussing clothing for the funeral with Maggie. Horst had already left to see to the funeral arrangements.

"Good morning, ladies. Sorry I'm late for breakfast. What is the chance for a cup of coffee?" he asked.

Sara came into the room and poured him a cup. "I am very sorry for your loss, Mr. Fuller," she said, looking sad. "I understand how you feel when you lose a parent. I lost both of mine early this year during the Nazi attack on Poland."

"Sara, please do not engage in conversation with our guests," Hildegard scolded. "We have had this conversation before."

"Yes, ma'am," Sara replied sadly.

"Thank you, Sara. I am, in turn, very sorry for your loss," Carlton said. He wondered how her parents might have died. But he didn't make any further comments. He was aware the Germans had attacked Poland. How had Sara gotten here? Maybe Hildegard would tell him later.

"Hildegard, may I use the phone to contact the American embassy?" asked Carlton.

"Yes, you may," she replied. "Do you have the number?"

"I do. They gave it to me when I first visited there."

Carlton went to the phone and dialed the embassy number. Through the ring tone, Carlton heard some noise on the line. Just as the phone was answered, he heard the noise again.

"Good morning. This is the embassy of the United States. Miss Bayer speaking. How may I help you?"

"Hello, Emily. This is Carlton Fuller. May I speak to Mr. Morris?"

"Hi, Carlton," she said. "How are you? I'll get him for you."

"I'm fine. Thank you," he responded. He heard a pause on the line as she went to get the chargé d'affaires.

A moment later, the line clicked back on. "Hello, Carlton. This is Leland Morris. How are you today?"

"I'm fine, sir, but I have bad news. My father died during the night. He had another stroke. By the time the doctor arrived, he had already passed."

"I'm sorry to hear that," Morris replied with sadness in his voice. "You and your family have my condolences."

"Thank you, Mr. Morris. I appreciate that. I believe it will be a military funeral. My brother, Horst, is taking all the steps necessary for that to happen. I have the feeling the Germans will have a large funeral with a parade that will include marching groups from the military, a band, horses drawing a bier, and of course dignitaries marching behind the bier. I expect many of the Nazi hierarchy will be marching. My father was a Nazi Party hero. They will have crowds lining the street to mourn and celebrate him. Maggie and I, along with Horst and Hildegard, will be walking behind the bier. I would be honored if you, Emily, and Major Best would accompany us during the march and any ceremonies, sir," Carlton said.

"Major Best, Emily, and I would be honored to accompany you during the event."

"Thank you, Mr. Morris. I haven't heard from Horst yet as to when everything will take place. As soon as I find out the details, I will be in touch with the embassy to let you know. Following the funeral, Maggie and I would like to leave for home as quickly as possible. This visit has been very trying for us. We have seen and heard things that are incomprehensible. If you would take care of things for us, we would appreciate it very much."

"Please let me know as soon as you know the details. I have heard some rumors that Pan American is getting concerned about Germany bombing England. They are concerned that the Germans may mistake their aircraft for the enemy. I haven't heard anything from our government yet regarding that issue. I can understand Pan American's position. I await your call. My prayers are with you during this difficult time."

"Thank you, Mr. Morris. I will be in touch," said Carlton as he hung up the phone.

He walked back to the dining room.

"Hildegard, I was wondering about Sara. Where did you find her? What is the yellow mark she wears on her clothes? Where does she live? And how about the other servants?" Carlton asked. "I hope you don't mind my asking."

"No, I don't mind your asking," replied Hildegard. "You know how I feel about Nazis. Thank you for not asking while Horst was here. He would get upset if I talked about Sara in front of anyone. To make a long story short, Sara is a Polish Jew. She and her family lived in Krakow, Poland. Krakow was one of the initial cities bombed during the invasion of Poland. Sara was visiting an aunt and uncle outside of the city. When the bombs began to fall, she ran back toward the city to find her family.

She was knocked to the ground by the impact of a bomb. It knocked her out. She was found in a catatonic state by an Army infantry colonel friend of Horst's. He left her with the German medical group traveling with his division.

The medics revived her and brought her back to a somewhat normal state. Horst's friend contacted us, told us about Sara, and asked if we could use a servant. We had just moved into the house and needed help. He put her in a medical van with a German nurse, who brought her to us. This was all done undercover and unknown to anyone else.

"The yellow marking is a requirement; all Jews must wear it. It is a mark of disdain and humiliation. I hate that she has to wear it. But Horst demands it. I have taken in Sara as my daughter. She lives here in the house servant quarters. How I treat Sara is for me to know and not anyone else. Horst treats her with disdain. He treats her as if she is a nonperson. I hate him for it. It's a miracle I have her with me. The other servants are Jews from the Berlin area. They live in the Jewish ghetto here in Berlin. We are very fortunate to have them. With what has happened to many Jews here in Berlin, they are very lucky to be here with us. It's Horst's standing in the party that provides the privilege."

"It must be difficult for both of you. She seems to be a very sweet girl," interrupted Maggie.

"She is. She mourns for her parents and her country. We have had a number of discussions regarding that tragedy. I'm sure it will be very difficult for her to get passed it. It is difficult for me, as Horst would send her to the gas chamber if he had his way," added Hildegard. This further confirms Horst being a Nazi thought Carlton. He saw the look of distain in Maggie's eyes when she heard Hildegard's comment.

"Hello," Horst shouted as he came into the house. "It's still raining outdoors. I hope it stops before tomorrow. Tomorrow is the funeral. It will be an event. We will meet at the Prussian Victory Column at nine a.m. Goebbels is ordering a lot of publicity. He wants a crowd lining the streets. The cortege will begin at the Prussian Victory Column and will then move to the Brandenburg Gate, traveling the Charlottenburger Chausee. This avenue is very apropos for a Nazi hero, as it is lined with Nazi flags. It was used by Hitler after he returned from his Paris inspection earlier this year. It was picked by Goebbels himself to honor our father. He will ensure that the avenue will be lined with Germans saluting our father."

"I knew the funeral would be a spectacle," Carlton noted with disdain.

"We Nazis like spectacles—especially those that are held for our heroes," replied Horst proudly. "We will be marching behind the bier with all the dignitaries. Hopefully, Maggie will be all right walking that distance."

"I will be all right walking. Being pregnant, my doctor said I should walk every day. It is good for my diaphragm. Hopefully, the rain will stop," Maggie replied.

"I hope so. If it continues to rain, I'm sure every one of the dignitaries and mourners will ride in automobiles. The poor army, navy, and Luftwaffe personnel will march along with the band no matter if it is raining or not," said Horst. "The cortege, with the exception of the military marchers, will then be transported to the cemetery where the German hero Horst Wessel is buried. Our father, following a ceremony, will be interred there. We will receive friends and dignitaries here at my residence afterward."

"I invited the US chargé d'affaires, his aide, and Major James Best of the US Army to march with us. I hope that doesn't upset the Nazi plans for the funeral. The chargé d'affaires will be representing the United States at our father's funeral. I hope this will not be an issue," said Carlton rather bluntly.

"No, brother, I don't think so. Our relations with your country are strained but not cut off. If there are any issues with your invitees, I will talk with Jodl. I'm sure he will be able to resolve them. Hopefully, our military won't react to the US Army major attending," replied Horst somewhat sarcastically.

"I hope not, Horst. If they do, I will cause a scene your Führer won't want to be involved with," said Carlton loudly. He wanted to make sure Horst understood him clearly.

"Gentleman, please, you are acting like children," Hildegard cut in. "Tomorrow will be a glad and sad day. The Germans will celebrate a hero, and you both will mourn your father. All you have is each other. Let's quit bickering and prepare for tomorrow. Maggie and I have picked out our clothes. Horst, get a caterer to start preparing for tomorrow. You told everyone we will be receiving them here after the funeral. Get moving and prepare for that. I'm sure that will take you the rest of the day. I will talk to the servants and get them ready. They will be very busy. Carlton, I'm sure you can keep yourself busy with your embassy and travel plans.

Maggie told me you will be leaving soon after the funeral. Sara, please get some coffee and strudel for us. We have a busy day ahead."

Carlton contacted the embassy and advised Emily of the funeral plans. He told her of their desire to leave for home the day after tomorrow. He asked about the flight home. Emily had been in touch with the Germans regarding the train to Marseilles, which ran daily from Berlin via Paris. Emily was aware of the Fullers and Major Best requiring a reservation. The Germans were very cooperative and were waiting for a call from the American embassy to reserve seats on the train. Pan American had a flight landing at Marseilles tomorrow. They would hold the plane at Marseilles for the trio. It would be the last plane, as Pan American had been asked by the US government to cancel all commercial flights to Portugal and France. The plane would leave as soon as they arrived at Marseilles.

Carlton felt relieved. "Emily, please advise Major Best and Mr. Morris of the plans for the funeral, as well as our plans to leave. Thank you for all your help. Maggie and I are looking forward to seeing you, along with Mr. Morris and the major tomorrow for the funeral. We appreciate the three of you marching with us," replied Carlton.

"It is our pleasure, Carlton. I will finalize the travel arrangements for the three of you. I'll arrange for the embassy limousine to pick you up at the Brausch house and take you to the Berlin train station and fill you in on the details tomorrow morning. See you tomorrow. Good-bye," Emily said as she hung up the phone.

Ͳϩϵ Ϝυηϵʀλͷ

Ͳhe day dawned cool and breezy. The previous day's rain had stopped. It was a gray day, with the clouds scudding across the sky from north to south. It was a day of sadness for the Brausch family. It was a day of mourning for the Nazis. The military had gone all out for one of the original Nazi Party members. At the beginning of the cortege, a company of SS in their black, sparkling uniforms marched in a slow rhythm to the muffled beat of a drum corps. Black cloths covered the drums, enhancing the sound of the beat. The drum corps followed the SS. Behind the drum corps were three rows of soldiers, each carrying a red Nazi flag with a swastika flying in the cool wind. Following the flags came a Luftwaffe band, which would play at the cemetery. Behind the band came three companies of the military, one each from the Army, the Navy, and the Luftwaffe. Behind the military companies was the horse-drawn bier. The funeral bier that carried the coffin of their father was pulled behind a team of four black horses. A Nazi flag was mounted atop of the coffin. Following the bier was the procession of mourners—Carlton covered in a black topcoat; Horst in his army black uniform; and Maggie and Hildegard, also dressed in black. Walking with them were Mr. Morris, Emily, and Major Best. Behind them came the Nazi dignitaries, high-ranking military and political personnel.

Hitler designated the day as a day of mourning for the German people. Goebbels announced in the newspapers that the population of Berlin should line the streets to honor this Nazi Party founder. All of the party leaders were walking—Hitler, Göring, Jodl, Goebbels, Canaris, Axmann, Heydrich, Frick, and Himmler all turned out. Carlton was amazed at the turnout for his father. Hitler and the other leaders all took the time to introduce themselves to Carlton and Maggie. They all expressed words of condolence and sadness over the loss of this great man, as well as appreciation that the couple was here for Carlton's father. Each also noted how proud Carlton and Maggie must be of this man.

Carlton shook his head at the insincerity he felt when shaking the hands of the Nazis. He felt the day was an exhibition of an act of contrition for the people. They were all celebrating a life of an ordinary man who participated in the beginning of the Nazi Party. It gave the ordinary man in Germany an opportunity to mourn for his country's loss. The local population lined the flag-lined street. It was, as Carlton thought, a spectacle.

Once the cortege reached the Brandenburg Gate, it was transported to the Nicolai-Friedhof cemetery for the interment. This cemetery was picked by Goebbels.

Once everyone was settled, Goebbels gave the eulogy. Horst made sure Carlton knew that Goebbels had also given the eulogy for Horst Wessel here. "We should be honored," Horst bragged to Carlton.

Following the eulogy, a color guard of seven members of each service completed a twenty-one-gun salute. The band then struck up the German military lament "Ich hatt einen Kameraden" (I had a Comrade).

It was at this point in the service that Horst and Hildegard started crying. Carlton thought to himself, *How sad a song of remembrance.* Major Best came to attention and saluted. The Nazis stood at attention and gave the Heil Hitler salute. All of the military personnel at the gravesite sang with the band. Their doing so was a sign of respect for Carlton and Horst's father.

As the crowd sang, Carlton interpreted the words for Maggie:

Ich hatt' einen Kameraden (I once had a comrade)
Einen bessern findst du nit (You will find no better).
Die Trommel schlug zum Streite (The drum called to battle),
Er ging an meiner Seite (He walked at my side)
In gleichem Schritt und Tritt (In the same pace and step).

Eine Kugel kam geflogen (A bullet came flying):
Gilt's mir oder gilt es dir (Is it my turn or yours)?
Ihn hat es weggerissen (He was swept away),
Er liegt zu meinen Füßen (He lies at my feet)
Als war's ein Struck von mir (As if it was a part of me).

Will mir die Hand noch reichen (He still reaches out his
hand to me),
Derweil ich eben lad (While I am about to reload).
Kann dir die Hand nicht geben (I cannot hold onto your
hand).
Bleib dui m ew'gen Leben (Rest you in eternal life)
Mein guter Kamerad (My good comrade)!

Following the song's completion, the band and military marched off. The dignitaries left quickly thereafter. Horst explained that a major effort was taking place, and the leaders of Germany and the military were very much involved. He did not anticipate a large participation at the reception. The limousine and motorcycles were waiting to take them back to Horst's residence.

Mr. Morris, Emily, and Major Best would not be able to get to the reception. Mr. Morris advised Carlton and Maggie that he and Major Best would be picking them up early in the morning—at 6:00 a.m.—to get them to the station on time to catch the train to Paris. Although the Germans had said they'd hold the train in the morning, he didn't trust them. Carlton and Maggie hugged Emily. They thanked her for the time she'd spent with them and her effort in making all the travel arrangements for them.

It had been quite a morning. They were ready to get back to Horst's, get through the reception, finish packing, and get to sleep as early as possible. They had a long ride to get home.

The reception had gone well. Just as Horst had predicted, only a few personal friends from the military had shown up. Maggie and Carlton were happy about that, as they had met so many military personnel and their wives; they were tired of hearing military stories about Carlton's father. Horst reveled in the adoration of his father. The caterer set a wonderful table, and the wine flowed freely. The final visitors left the house early in the evening. Maggie had left the reception early. She'd told Hildegard she would be upstairs packing.

There was a knock on the door. It was Hildegard.

"Oh Maggie, I'm sorry to interrupt your packing," she said. "But, I wanted to talk to you privately. I have enjoyed your company these past few days. I will miss you terribly. You have given me hope and comfort. Please tell Oma I love her and will try to communicate with her in the future. Have a big, healthy baby. I wish you good luck and a safe trip home," Hildegard said as she hugged Maggie.

Maggie returned Hildegard's hug. "Hildegard, it has been a wonderful visit for Carlton and me. There are so many words I have to say but not enough time to say them. I wish you a long life. Stay safe. Take care of Sara. I know that, given the situation you are faced with, that will be difficult. I know you care deeply about her. May the day come when we will meet again." Maggie knew that might never happen.

By the time she was done, they were both crying. The hug they shared was long and warm.

"I will say good-bye in the morning. What time will you be picked up?" Hildegard said as she left the room.

"Six a.m.," replied Maggie.

"Thanks. I will have coffee ready," said Hildegard as she closed the door.

A few minutes later, Carlton came into the bedroom. "Honey, am I happy that the reception and the day are over. Are you as tired of the propaganda and the Nazis as I am? Horst cornered me when the last person left. He had to tell me how proud he was of Father. He was proud that all of the Nazi leadership had attended the funeral. He told me that never happens for anyone. His buttons were popping. He gave me a glass of wine and then toasted Father and the Nazis. I almost spilled my wine on him. Then he said something that turned my stomach. He said that, if the United States enters the war against us, we will be enemies. 'Then we will have to kill all of you.' I returned his words to him. I said, 'That works two ways, brother.' At that point I left him. Maybe he was drunk. He drank a lot of wine. I just don't know."

"Yes I'm tired," Maggie replied. "Hildegard came up to say she enjoyed our visit. I'm worried about her. She will have a difficult time coping with Horst and the hated Nazis. I'm sure Horst must have been drunk. Forget about it. I'm proud of you for replying to him as you did. We are packed, except for personal things. We can finish in the morning. Let's get to sleep. We have a long trip ahead of us. I love you, Carlton. What time should I set the clock for?" Maggie said as she put on her nightclothes.

"Thank you, Maggie. I love you to. Set it for five a.m. Let's get to sleep."

ϾꞪꝰ Ͼꝛⲓⲣ Ɦꝋⲙꝰ

He Embassy limousine was on time. Dawn was just beginning to brighten. The driver came out of the car to help with the baggage. Major Best stepped out to say good-bye to Hildegard. The family came out of the house, and Major Best Saluted Horst, who returned his salute with a Heil Hitler version. Horst and Carlton shook hands. Carlton asked him to ship Oma's personal goods to her, explaining that their father had them at his house. Horst agreed that he would try to do so.

Maggie couldn't bring herself to hug Horst. She shook his hand and thanked him for his hospitality.

Hildegard said good-bye and hugged Major Best. She then hugged and said her good-byes to Carlton and Maggie. She and Maggie were crying. Horst was frowning at all the emotion being shown by his wife. As the car pulled away, Horst reluctantly and Hildegard enthusiastically were waving good-bye. In the upstairs window, Sara was doing the same. Maggie noticed her immediately.

"Oh, Carlton," said Maggie. "Look who is waving good-bye to us. It is Sara. I feel so sad for her. Hildegard will have a difficult time with Horst about her staying in the house with them. He will be questioning their relationship. Maggie wants to adopt her as a daughter. I can't believe what Hildegard said Horst would do to this girl" Maggie waved back at Sara.

"The bastard. He is a Nazi through and through, isn't he? Did you see him strutting around during the reception talking with his military friends? He has been strutting like a peacock since we arrived here. I can't believe he is my brother," Carlton said derisively.

"Good morning, Mr. Morris, Major Best," said Carlton. "Emily, good morning to you. I didn't see you sitting in the backseat with the major. I was caught up in all the emotion of saying good-byes this morning."

"On the other hand," Maggie spoke up, "good morning. I see you all. And it is good to be with friends. What is this I see—Major Best and Emily holding hands in the backseat! What is going on? Mr. Morris, do you know why that is happening? I'm just kidding you both. It does look cozy back there."

"Let's change the subject," said Emily, blushing. "I have your travel plans. Let me go over them with you." She cleared her throat. "You will be leaving Berlin at seven thirty a.m. from the Anhalter Bahnhof train station to travel to Paris. You will not have to go through customs at the German-French border. The train will stop there but will pass through to Paris. Your train car will be switched and will travel directly to Marseilles. Once in Marseilles, you will go through French customs. Apparently, the Germans changed the routing of their trains. In Marseilles, when you leave the train, you will catch a taxi that will take you to the Pan American seaplane terminal, where your plane will be waiting. Once you arrive at the seaplane terminal in New York, you will be picked up by a government car and taken to the train station to catch a train to Cleveland. Here, Maggie, are all of your tickets and itinerary information. The Germans were very cooperative. So were the Vichy French. You two had someone looking out for you."

"I can't imagine who that may have been. Thank you Emily, for all of your work in putting these travel plans together for us," Carlton replied. "I noticed the hand-holding too. We will talk with the major about it on the way home."

"Carlton, the train station we are leaving from was one of the places Hildegard took us to on our tour of Berlin. She told us that the Nazis shipped hundreds of Berlin Jews to concentration camps from this and two other train stations in Berlin. The Nazis put the Jews on regular passenger cars under the guise of a trip to move them out of Berlin. The train then left for an undisclosed location, where the cars were transferred to another train that took them to various death camps. I shudder when I think of it. How cruel and evil. It makes me nauseous." said Maggie.

"You don't have to worry about that, Maggie," Mr. Morris assured her. "I have made arrangements with the German underground to place their people on this train with you. They will make sure you arrive in Paris on time. If something suspicious happens, they will identify themselves to you and take whatever steps necessary to get the three of you to Paris. The French underground will be with you on the train to Marseilles. They will be sure you arrive safely there to catch the plane. The three of you are very important passengers to the United States.

"We are arriving at the station," he pointed out. "Thank you very much for visiting us. I know you fulfilled your missions. The general will be happy to know you are on your way home. Have a safe trip and Godspeed."

"Thank you, Mr. Morris, for assuring us that our concerns are being taken care of. We appreciate your being with us during the funeral. Good-bye!" said Carlton. "Emily, thank you for everything you have done for us. Both Maggie and I appreciate your service and your friendship."

They all got out of the limousine. Carlton shook Mr. Morris's hand and hugged Emily.

Emily hugged Maggie. "Bon voyage," she said.

When it came to Major Best, he saluted Mr. Morris. He hugged Emily and gave her a long, passionate kiss. She was crying as they parted.

A German soldier picked up their luggage and put it on the train. The major gave him an American dollar as a tip. As the soldier left them, he said in a low voice to Carlton, "You all safe," and was gone.

The station was very busy. A lot of military personnel were traveling to Paris or beyond. All seats were full. Apparently, there had been a lull in the fighting, as many of the military were on leave. There was a buzz in the air about something. Carlton tried to strike up a conversation with some of the travelers but had no luck. All they wanted to talk about was going home, seeing girlfriends, seeing families, or just getting drunk, as they would soon be returning to their units and shipping out. They had no idea where they would be going or when. It would be a boring trip to Marseilles.

Carlton, Maggie, and Major Best had not had time to discuss the daytrip the latter two had taken with Hildegard and Emily. Carlton was anxious to find out where they'd gone and what they'd seen. Other than the train station visit Maggie had told him about, he knew nothing. However, they couldn't talk about it with all of the ears open in the train. That discussion would have to wait until they were on the airplane or when they were back in the United States. *In fact*, he concluded, *I'm sure it can wait until we brief Donovan.* Given the story about the train station, he felt certain Maggie would only want to talk about what they'd seen one time.

The train horn screeched, and they started moving. Thank God they were heading home. Carlton would talk to Maggie about her experiences when they got home.

Who should be walking down the aisle to meet them but Major Scheinhorst.

Carlton couldn't resist baiting him. "Major Scheinhorst, a sight for sore eyes. I thought we left you when we arrived in Berlin."

"No. You haven't lost me yet," the major replied. "I have the honor of escorting you and your party to Marseilles. I heard about your father. He was a hero. My condolences to you and your family.

"You will stay with this train car all the way to your destination this time," he added. "There will be a little delay in Paris, as the car must run through the Paris train station. The engineer has been instructed to make time. We don't want you to miss your plane. It is my responsibility to get you to Marseilles safely."

"Thank you, Major. Knowing you and your men are with us makes us feel very safe. We had a very interesting stay in Berlin. There is something big about to happen. What might it be?" said Carlton, hoping the German major might reveal something to him.

"Sorry, Mr. Fuller," replied the major. "I don't know what you are talking about. If I find out anything, you will be the first to know. Have a good ride. Food will be served in the next car. I'll see you all when you get off of the train."

"I appreciate that," said Carlton.

"I don't like that man," said Maggie. "He seems very cold and calculating."

"I agree with you," commented Major Best. "Just like all German officers."

The train made good time traveling through Germany. The roads going West were packed with military men and equipment. The food was average this trip. They ate the same fare the civilians were eating.

Carlton and Maggie asked Major Best many questions regarding his relationship with Miss Bayer. He blushed. He told them the relationship had blossomed quickly. He and Emily had had the opportunity to spend a lot of time together. He said it was love at first sight. He also indicated that Emily had provided him with a great deal of information on the Germans. She'd helped him with his mission from Donovan.

The train slowed down as it approached Paris. Maggie was very excited that she was able to see the Eiffel Tower. When they'd passed through Paris on the trip to Berlin, it had been nighttime, and they'd all been sleeping. Many of the military personnel left the train when it stopped at the Paris station. They didn't stop long. The horn screeched, and their car was switched through the Paris yard and picked up by the train going to Marseilles. They all had a chance to take a nap between Paris and Marseilles.

When they arrived in Marseilles, Major Scheinhorst came by to say good-bye. "It was my pleasure to escort you to your destination. I have new orders and will be heading West for a new adventure. Your limousine is waiting for you in front of the station. The driver has been instructed to take you to the Pan American seaplane terminal," he said as one of his military aides gathered their luggage. "Please understand," he added, "the driver doesn't speak English. He knows where to take you all. Bon voyage." With that, he clicked his heals, saluted the Heil Hitler salute, turned on his heal, and left the three of them.

"Good riddance," said Maggie. "It is time to fly."

They all agreed.

As they boarded the plane, a familiar face appeared. "Hello, Mr. and Mrs. Fuller. Hello, Major Best. How was your trip? We will be leaving soon, now that you all have arrived. We will be flying directly to Horta, Lages, to refuel and then home to the States. I'll bet you can't wait."

They all replied in unison, "Hello, James."

"What a nice surprise!" Maggie added. "And you're right. We can't wait to get home, James. It is so nice to see you.

"What's for dinner?" she asked.

"Pan American roast beef and all the trimmings," James said proudly. "Let's get boarded. The captain wants to leave as soon as you all are settled in."

The engines stared with a cloud of blue smoke. They sounded rough at first but smoothed out after a few seconds.

"What a great sound," the major remarked as the plane began to move.

"Ladies and gentleman, this is the pilot speaking," came the announcement over the speaker. "Welcome aboard our B314 seaplane.

We will be flying directly to Horta, Lages today. This will be the last civilian flight Pan American will fly from Marseilles to the United States. The crew will try to make the flight a special one. I know we will be flying for about twenty-five hours, so please make yourselves comfortable, as we are ready to leave. We have been cleared for takeoff. The smoking lamp is out."

The sound of the engines became louder, and the plane began to move through the water quickly. The bay must have been smooth, as the plane moved without a bounce on the trip down the bay.

Maggie shouted, "We are off," as the plane left the water and turned to the Northwest.

Once they reached cruising altitude, the pilot came back on the speaker. "We will be leveling off at seventeen thousand feet for our flight to Horta. The smoking light is lit. Please enjoy your dinner this evening."

After they took off from Horta, the plane encountered turbulence over the North Atlantic. It didn't bother Carlton, Maggie, or Major Best, as all three were sound asleep. The trip had taken its toll on all of them, and they were anticipating getting home.

It was early morning, about 6:00 a.m. Eastern Standard Time, when they were awakened by the pilot.

"Good morning. This is the pilot again. Sorry to wake you up so early, but we will be flying past the Statue of Liberty before we land. I wanted you all to take the time to view her from the air. She is a beautiful lady. I will reduce our altitude so that you all have a great view of her in all her glory. You will be able to see her from the port side of the plane. Following our pass by the statue, we will be turning around Manhattan Island to land on the bay by LaGuardia Field. The view should be spectacular. We will be landing in about one hour. Please prepare your personal items for landing and deplaning."

Maggie, Carlton, and Major Best moved to the left side of the aircraft.

They heard a knock on their doors. It was James with coffee and rolls. "Breakfast!" he shouted. "We are almost home."

It didn't feel like long before the pilot came back on the speaker. "It's the pilot again. We will be landing in five minutes. Please prepare to land. The smoking lamp is out. The bay is a little choppy this morning. I expect the plane to bounce a bit as we contact the water. It should not be an issue. The plane will rock a bit as we taxi to the seaplane terminal. Thank you for flying Pan American."

Major Best was the first one off of the plane. He made sure the Pan American luggage personnel brought the Fullers' luggage to a specific spot inside the terminal. By the time Carlton and Maggie met him, he had a redcap ready to take their luggage to customs. He told the redcap to wait for them to clear customs and then take their baggage to a taxi waiting at the stand outside the terminal. First, they had to clear customs. This was where he and the Fullers would be parting.

The major shook Carlton's hand and hugged Maggie. "I enjoyed traveling with you both," he said. "I believe we had a profitable trip. And we had a great time together. You are both some of the most wonderful people I have ever met. I will be seeing you again in Cleveland when we brief the general. Have a safe trip. By the way, your train leaves New York in three hours. Just tell the cab driver you want to go to Grand Central Station. I have taken care of the redcap. So long. See you in Cleveland. I'm going home for a few days. I have to put together my report and write to Emily." The major waved and went back into the terminal to get his luggage.

Maggie and Carlton said their good-byes to the major and followed the redcap to customs. Maggie was unhappy that they had to go through customs again.

Once they cleared customs, they followed the redcap to a cab waiting at the cab stand. The redcap put the luggage in to the cab, opened the door to the cab, let Maggie in first, and closed the door after Carlton was seated.

"Grand Central Station, please," said Carlton.

"Yes, sir," the driver replied.

The trip to Cleveland seemed to be longer than it had originally taken to get to New York. The dinner on the train was tasty. The wine was a New York Catawba, medium dry and very fruity. They both thought it was outstanding. They certainly weren't wine experts, but the wine tasted wonderful with dinner.

"Carlton, we had an adventure, didn't we?" said Maggie. "Our sister-in-law is quite a woman, isn't she? I'm sorry, but I don't like your brother. He is arrogant. I don't like the Nazis. They are trying to conquer the world. They are cruel, and they are murderers. I am glad you had a chance to visit with your father before he died, and I'm happy that Mr. Donovan gave us the chance to make this trip. I've been thinking about what he wants from you. Maybe I don't want to know. I haven't forgotten my mission. I have a lot of information for Mr. Donovan. I don't want to discuss it until we see him. I hope you don't mind."

"Honey, I agree. We did have an adventure," acknowledged Carlton. "And Hildegard is a special lady. You and she really hit it off. I don't like Nazis either. After spending time with my brother, I'm not sure I like him either. He strutted around like he owned the world. I appreciated what he did for my father, but the funeral was a spectacle that I resented. I agree with Major Best; the Nazis are evil. They have murdered thousands of innocent people with their false accusations and lies about why they are conquering Europe. A good example is Poland. Hitler's reason was that the poles were discriminating against the Germans who lived there. Our mission has been with me for the whole trip. We will brief Donovan after we get home. Are you as tired as I am? Let's get back to our sleeper and rest. We will be arriving in Cleveland at seven a.m. I'm looking forward to seeing the children. How about you?"

"I am too," Maggie replied. "I can't wait to hug them and tell them about our trip."

Carlton and Maggie were both up early. They were having breakfast when the train stopped at the Collinwood Yards to switch engines from a steam locomotive to an electric locomotive. Upon completion of the switch, the train continued to the Cleveland Terminal Tower station.

When they departed the train, Carlton tipped the porter who took their luggage off the train and gave it to a waiting redcap on the station platform. Carlton asked him to take their luggage upstairs and wait for them to direct him to their transportation. When they reached the top of the stairs that led into the station, they saw the children and Oma waiting for them. The children ran to them. What hugs they received. Maggie had tears in her eyes as she hugged both of their children. Carlton almost strained his back picking up both children to hug them both at the same time. Last but not least, up walked Oma. She too had tears in her eyes as she hugged Maggie first and finally her son, Carlton.

They were home.

BOOK TWO

The Demise

₩ɥɛ Dɛ𝔦Brıɛ𝔍

I t had been a busy time since Carlton and Maggie had come home from the trip. Carlton had to rebuild his schedule with his clients and reschedule his court dates. Maggie had to get to the doctor for her four-month visit. They both had to catch up with their children's lives and to tell them about their trip and its excitement. The children were fascinated with the train and plane portions of the adventure. Finally, they sat down with Oma and brought her up to date on the trip, her husband, and the funeral. That was the difficult part. It was very emotional for all of them. She was looking forward to receiving her personal goods from Horst. Carlton had to caution her not to get her hopes up too high, given the war going on in Europe. The trip had caused some chaos in their lives. It would take some time to get back to normal.

Shelly, Donovan's secretary, called Carlton a week after they came home and asked to set up a meeting to debrief him on their visit to Germany. "Good morning, Mr. Fuller. How are you today?" She sounded cheery. "Mr. Donovan would like to meet with you and Mrs. Fuller to debrief you on your trip. Would Wednesday next week be convenient?" she asked.

"Good morning, Shelly. We have been waiting for the call. Thank you for giving us this time to prepare for the meeting. Wednesday would be fine with us. Thank you for all of the effort you put forth to make the trip convenient and comfortable for us. Where will the meeting take place? And what time will it be?" replied Carlton.

"The meeting will be at the FBI building in downtown Cleveland at nine a.m. Major Best will pick you up at eight fifteen if that is convenient," she replied.

"That's fine with us. Shelly, thank you. Bye," said Carlton as he hung up the phone.

"Maggie, Shelly from Donovan's office called. Our meeting with him is next Wednesday at nine a.m. Major Best will be picking us up at eight. Have you completed your write-up?" he asked. "I just finished mine."

"Yes I have," she replied, "I wanted to make sure I covered the places Hildegard took us to that day. I'm looking forward to meeting Donovan."

"For the first time, I am too," said Carlton, "We have a lot of information to pass on to him. I'm sure he is going to ask me if I am ready to volunteer. Based on what we saw and heard in Germany, I am considering doing it. I hate what the Nazis are doing to the world and its peoples. The killing, the prejudices, and the excesses they have introduced. Innocent people are paying the price for a megalomaniac devil. How many more will die before it is all over?"

"Carlton, you're going to do what?" questioned Maggie. "Do not volunteer until we talk about it in detail. My God, here I am four months pregnant, and you're going to leave me alone and volunteer to fight someone else's war. I don't like the Nazis either. In fact, I hate what they are doing to the Jews and other helpless people. But I don't want to lose you to this war the United States is not even involved in. Please don't do this to me, honey," she said, crying loudly and collapsing in the chair.

Carlton rushed to hug and console her. "Maggie, I was just talking out loud. I have been thinking about the whole situation since we began this journey. I'm not doing anything yet. You and I have to discuss the issue a lot more than we have. I understand how you feel. Believe me; I do. Please relax and calm down for a moment. Let me get us a cup of tea to settle us down."

"I don't want tea. Get me a glass of wine," she said angrily. "I can't believe you have even given thought to the idea of volunteering. I'm going to give Donovan a piece of my mind. Who does he think he is? He is asking you to go to war when the United States is not even involved in it. The bastard!"

"Please, honey, don't get mad at Donovan. He is only doing his job. He is aware of more than we are. Hopefully, he will tell us more when we see him. I know it is personal for us. We have much more to lose. The question becomes, what if the United States gets involved? What do we do then? Do we stand back and let someone else fight the war for us? It is an interesting scenario, isn't it? It gives us something to think about," Carlton replied to Maggie's emotional outcry.

"Don't get mad at Donovan, you say. Who else is there? He is the one who caused all of this furor. Then there's your brother and father. How do you want me to respond? Just roll over and say, 'Go ahead, honey. Do what you want.' I'm sorry I can't do that. You are my whole life and soul. I will fight tooth and nail to keep you safe and at home with us. Just remember that. Hopefully, I we won't have to worry about that. I'm sorry I'm so emotional over this. It is my makeup. We are talking life and possible death. I'll just shut up and drink my wine. I apologize," said Maggie.

The remainder of the week the subject didn't come up again. They both had too much to do. Carlton had to be in court for three days. Maggie was preparing costumes for the kids' Halloween trick or treating. They couldn't make up their minds as to what they wanted to be. Finally, Carlton, Jr., settled on the Lone Ranger. Charlotte quickly opted to be Tonto, his ke-mo sah-bee.

Shelly followed up with a phone call on Tuesday to remind them of the meeting in the morning with Mr. Donovan.

The following day, there was a knock on the door at 8:15 a.m. sharp. It was Major Best. Maggie opened the door and hugged the major, saying, "Good morning, Major Best. Nice to see you."

"Good morning, Maggie," he said as he hugged her back. "It is great to see you too."

"Are you both ready to go? The general is anxious to hear your report. Before you ask, I heard from Emily. she and the chargé d'affaires are doing fine."

"Let's get moving," said Carlton as he led Maggie and the major to the car. "How are you doing, Major?"

"I'm fine. Are you both back to normal living after the trip?" the major asked.

"Almost," said Maggie. "We had a lot of catching up with the children and, of course, Oma. She had been very interested in what happened while we were gone." Carlton has been catching up with his practice, and I with costumes for Halloween. Did you have a good visit home?"

"Yes I did. But the general kept me busy regarding details of the trip and what I learned. That kept me busy for a couple of days."

Small talk filled the car as they drove to downtown Cleveland.

They entered the FBI building, and the elevator operator greeted them with a smile. "Hello again. Who is this beautiful woman you are with this time?"

"My wife of course." repled Carlton jokingly.

"Just thought I'd check," replied the operator. "Down the hall and around the corner."

Major Best knocked on the door, Shelly opened the door. "Hello, Mr. and Mrs. Fuller. Good morning. The general is waiting for you."

"Good morning, Shelly," replied Maggie. "Before I forget, I want to thank you for your kindness and the note you provided me while on our trip. It made me feel very comfortable."

"You're welcome, Mrs. Fuller. I have made coffee, and we have some Danish for the meeting. Please help yourselves. Come on into the general's office. He will be with you soon. Have a good day."

Unbeknownst to Carlton and Maggie, Donovan had invited David Bruce to attend the meeting. He would sit outside Donovan's office to listen and evaluate the brief. Donovan also asked him to evaluate Carlton's performance. His first impression would be important, as Carlton would be under his direction once, and if, he committed.

The door opened, and in came the general. He was full of enthusiasm and wished everyone good morning. "Good to see you all. Back safe and sound, I hope. It must have been a difficult trip for you both. Mrs. Fuller, I'm Bill Donovan. It is my pleasure to meet you. Hello, Carlton. How are you? Major. Please sit down. Make yourselves comfortable. Shelly, could you please pour coffee for us all. I think we are going to have a long day. I have already debriefed Major Best. Today is for you, Carlton and Mrs. Fuller."

"It is my pleasure to meet you also, General," replied Maggie. "I have heard a lot about you. You have caused me some discomfort, but we can talk about that later. I have a lot of information for you. I want to thank you, first, for helping us get to Germany and back safely. It was an eye-opener for us both—more so than we could have believed when we started the adventure. Major Best did a wonderful job protecting us and helping us get to the places we wanted to go. I felt very comfortable having him at our side throughout the trip. He handled the Germans with respect, and he demanded and received the same in return. He represented the United States with honor and graciousness. We were very proud to have him with us. Carlton, I would like to go first, as I haven't told you what is included in my report. Is that okay?"

Carlton took a sip of his coffee and nodded okay. He couldn't believe his wife talking to Donovan the way she had. He was feeling proud. "Before you start, Maggie, General, I noticed that this office is a lot larger than the one we met in the first time we were together."

"Yes, I needed the added space for a desk for Michelle and all her equipment. The FBI was very accommodating," replied the general.

"I'm sorry, honey, that I interrupted you. Please continue," said Carlton.

Maggie continued, "General, we stayed at Carlton's brother's house. Horst's wife's name is Hildegard. The house was stolen from a wealthy Jewish family by the Nazis. They have three Jewish servants. Horst hates them. Hildegard is very concerned about the servants. She believes that, if he had his way, he would send them to the concentration camp for elimination. She hates the Nazis. I have documented her words in detail in my report. I took her on my tour with Major Best and Emily Bayer.

"We had a wonderful day seeing the sights the Nazis built and cleaned up for the German population. But Hildegard wanted us to see three other sights that the Germans would not like to show anyone. The first one was Anhalter Banhof train station. This station was used to transport Berlin Jewish families out of town under the guise of relocating them to new locations. The Nazis used regular train cars to carry them as 'passengers.' They took the trains to another location, took the Jews off the train, put them in cattle cars, and took them to the concentration camps for elimination. Thousands of Berlin Jews were moved this way.

"The second location we visited was the Plötzensee Prison. This location is used to house enemies of the state. The prisoners were guillotined and hung at this location. Hundreds of prisoners have been killed there.

"Thirdly, we visited the main Jewish synagogue in Berlin. It was destroyed and desecrated on Kristallnacht. On the same night, many Jewish people were killed and their businesses destroyed by the Nazi Brown Shirts. Over ten thousand synagogues were destroyed. Over seven thousand Jewish businesses were destroyed. The German government did nothing to stop the horror. We were involved with several German officers during our trip. I found them vain, cocky, and self-righteous. They are cruel and evil. They are the devil on earth.

"That's my report, General. The written version has much more detail about the other places we visited that day. Again, I want to thank you for giving us the opportunity to see Carlton's father and attend his funeral. May I have a cup of coffee? First, please have Shelly show me where the restroom is."

"Mrs. Fuller, thank you for your report. The information was well put together and well received. Thank you for being thorough. Shelly, will you please help Mrs. Fuller," directed the general. "Carlton, your wife did an outstanding job. It was a very impressive effort. The Nazis made a negative impression, didn't they?"

"Very negative impression, to say the least. I am proud of her, General.

"Before I begin, I also want to thank you for the opportunity you gave us. I was able to meet with my father privately to understand why mine and my mother's lives are what they are today. He was able to apologize to his son and wife for his past. That helped my mother most of all.

"The Nazis gave him a spectacle for a funeral. Maggie and I had an opportunity to meet most of the Nazi hierarchy at the funeral. They were gracious in their condolences, but I felt insincere. I found them to act superior to most who were not believers in their cult. Maggie and I attended a reception after the funeral at Horst's residence. Many personal friends and their wives were in attendance. They strutted around drinking wine, eating hors d'oeuvres, and bragging to each other of their conquests. Their wives were telling Maggie of the wonderful social lives they have and the wonderful houses they live in, which the Nazis gave them. It wasn't fun for us. Horst drank too much wine that evening and got drunk. He and I had words about killing each other should the United States enter the war, and we become enemies.

"I spent a day with my brother Horst visiting his new job location. Horst's rank in the German Army is colonel. He wears an Iron Cross at his neck. He was very active in the Nazi or Hitler Youth Movement. He and his father built the organization to approximately seven million participants. Both are well respected for their efforts there. Horst's new job is with the Oberkommando de Wehrmacht, OKW for short. Please forgive the German accent, it is the only way I can say the actual names in German. They are the war planners for the Nazi military. It is my impression he is well placed on Jodl's staff. He will have knowledge of all that is happening.

"On the way to the location, we stopped in a small town for breakfast. When he got out of the car, the local population treated him adoringly. Apparently, it was his stature and the uniform. It was my impression the local population did not have many opportunities to see or talk to a ranking Nazi officer.

"I was impressed with the Nazi's headquarters location at Zossan. It is located underground. There must have been hundreds of various service personnel working there. It was very clean, neat, and full of energy. It reminded me of a beehive. Everyone was working at a highly productive level. They are very committed to success.

"Horst and I had lunch with Jodl in his office. He was very much aware of what my and Maggie's visit was all about. He was very neat and perfect in every way. His uniform was absolutely perfect. He explained his organization's role and was clearly very proud of how much it had aided in the success of the Nazis to date.

"I had the feeling that something big they were planning was on the way, but I couldn't put my finger on it. I tried during our travels home but couldn't get any details. Personally, I don't believe the Congress here in the United States has any idea of what is happening in Europe. The Germans are in charge. They are killing and maiming the continent. One thing I did see was military personnel and equipment starting to move West. I, like Maggie, find the Nazis cruel and evil. I too believe they are the devil here on earth.

"General, you and I have to talk privately about your other request. Maggie and I have had words about it. That is the discomfort she was talking about. That's my debrief, General."

Maggie and Shelly returned to the office just when Carlton had finished.

"Where have you two been?" asked Carlton. "I just finished my briefing to the general. I thought you would be part of it."

"We started talking about the trip and then got into some girl talk. You understand," replied Maggie.

"Yes I do. How are you feeling? I'm a little tired. This has been a tough day for all of us."

"I'm fine, Carlton," said Maggie. "I want to give the general my thoughts as to the request he made of you. General, I am most unhappy about you requesting Carlton to volunteer for a civilian post in your future operation. The United States is not even involved in this war in Europe. As you know, we have two children, and I am four months pregnant with our third child. I don't believe you have the right to ask my husband to leave us for a war that is killing thousands of people, both civilian and military. The Nazis are bombing England and killing innocent civilians and their children. Having traveled to Germany, I have seen and heard a great deal. I don't want my husband involved. I told you I had discomfort. This is what it is about." Maggie was loud and direct, standing in front of the general's desk.

"Mrs. Fuller, please calm down. Please sit down. I understand your concerns and discomfort. I feel the same way you do. But I have a job to do, given to me by the president of the United States. What happens if the United States enters the war? Shouldn't we be somewhat prepared? I want the best, most prepared personnel I can find here in our country to be in my organization. Wouldn't you? Your and Carlton's insight today have given me hope that I asked a very qualified man to volunteer. I did say volunteer. I know you and he have a wonderful family and a wonderful marriage. I don't want to disrupt anyone's life. We have to pray that our country does not get involved in the war. If we don't, no one will have to volunteer." The general stopped as Maggie had calmed down. "Please, Mrs. Fuller, may I get you something to drink?"

"No thank you, General," Maggie replied. "You make your point very well. But you must understand mine. I hope you do. Carlton, can we leave now?"

"Thank you both for your debriefings," said the general. "They were very complete. They certainly provided a lot of detail that I had no knowledge of. Combined with Major Best's information, I have quite a package of information I will share with my peers and the president. Yes, Congress has passed legislation this month to begin a draft of personnel for the armed services. I understand the first numbers will be picked on October 29 this year. Things are getting serious. Major Best, please take Carlton and Mrs. Fuller home. This has been a difficult day. Carlton, I will be in touch. Thank you both again."

"General, you said Congress passed legislation for a draft of men to meet military needs? The first will be picked this month? What is going on?" asked Maggie, who seemed a bit shaken by the general's statement.

"Yes, Mrs. Fuller it's true. I heard that this morning in my daily update. Apparently, Congress is very concerned about what is happening around the world. They are concerned should the United States have to get involved to protect ourselves."

"Oh my God. I can't believe it," was all Maggie could say. The draft legislation shook her up.

"Maggie, Carlton, let's get going before the general needs something else," said Major Best lightheartedly, trying to break up a stressful moment.

The trio left the office quietly and headed downstairs.

After they left, the general opened the outside door, walked into Shelly's office, and invited David Bruce back to his office. "What do you think, David? Did you get all of the nuances I did from the briefings? From my perspective, the Fullers fulfilled the mission I assigned them before they left."

"They certainly had a fruitful trip," Bruce said. "I'm glad we were able to finance it. The information they brought back with them confirms a number of issues we have heard about. Mrs. Fuller did a wonderful job of observing and listening. She developed a relationship with the wife of Carlton's brother, revealing what the wife was thinking and feeling. She felt the coldness, rudeness, and ruthlessness of the German military officers she met. She certainly empathized with what the civilians and innocents in Europe are going through. I was very impressed with the detail she provided us.

"I certainly enjoyed her dialogue with you. She doesn't want her husband to volunteer for anything the United States is not involved with. She had no problem telling you how she felt. I think that, if she were talking to the president, she would have told him the same thing she told you. She is a strong woman who wants to protect what is hers. I certainly want her as a friend.

"Now, let's get to Carlton. He pays attention to detail. He noticed the local's reaction to his brother when they stopped for breakfast in the village. He was keenly aware of Jodl's dress, look, and attitude, and he recognized the Iron Cross at the neck of his brother when he was in uniform. I liked, too, the way he described his feeling about the energy at the OKW location in Zossan—like a beehive. Given the mission you have for this man, it is imperative he is able to recognize and evaluate what he will be hearing and seeing. He definitely has the traits necessary to accomplish the job we have for him. Physically, he is perfect. He will have to be trained in the physical requirements of the assignment. The question that needs to be answered is simple: Will he be able to kill as required and step into the role? Our trainers will have to make that evaluation. I believe we have the right person to accomplish the mission. Bill, how do we convince him to volunteer? It will take a serious incident for him to make that decision. One concern I have is, what do we tell his wife? If he volunteers, we will have to keep her in the loop."

"David, great questions. Thank you for your astute evaluation of the two briefings. I appreciate your insight and the concerns that need to be resolved. That last concern you stated is yours to solve. Carlton, will be under control by your people. You will have to manage him and his situation when he is in place. I know our allies and the underground will help you and him accomplish his mission. I told the Fullers about the draft starting the twenty-ninth. That seemed to impress them a bit. It caused Maggie to flinch. We may have to use that to pressure him to volunteer. Is that fair? No, it isn't, but the situation the world faces today certainly is not fair," replied the general, feeling the pressure of the day. "David, when we took the jobs we have today, the president did not say they would be easy, did he."

"No, he didn't, Bill. I have a feeling they will get more difficult before they get easier. Thanks for inviting me to listen to the briefings and evaluate Fuller. He is the right man. I must get moving. I have to catch a plane back to Washington," said Bruce as he shook Donovan's hand and left the office.

"Shelly, it has been a difficult day. Please call the president's secretary and see if he can see me tomorrow. We will need plane tickets and hotel reservations," directed Donovan. The president and I have a lot to talk about. He will be very interested in the information the Fullers brought back with them. I'm also interested in the latest from Churchill."

The Holidays, the Baby, and Donovan

T he family finally started to get back to normal. Maggie began to think about Thanksgiving. She was feeling very sad that they would not be able to have her relatives from Germany for the holiday celebration. She was thinking about Hildegard and her daughter Sara. Maggie knew that, although Sara wasn't really Hildegard's daughter, Hildegard treated her as if she was.

Maggie did not even think of Horst as her brother-in-law. He was a Nazi—cruel and evil. The trip to Germany had definitely been an adventure for Maggie. But the reality she had seen and participated in would impact her for the rest of her life. She didn't want the United States to enter the war in Europe. She knew that, if it did, more death and devastation would follow—only the death would be close to home, for it would be Americans who were killed fighting the Nazis and their allies. She and Carlton discussed the situation at length. They had been listening to the radio more than they had ever done in the past. They read all the war news in the paper daily.

Maggie was getting worried that Carlton would volunteer. She dreaded the day that would happen. She had been spending her time with the children. She helped them in the mornings to get ready for school, making lunches, checking homework, and making sure they were dressed properly. Fall was starting to wane, and winter was approaching. The children never put on enough clothing for the weather. Once they left, it was putting the house in order, figuring out the day's menu, and getting Carlton out of the house. Since they'd returned from Germany, he had been lingering at home longer than normal. When she asked him about it, he mumbled something about wanting to spend more time with her, she being pregnant and all. She thought it was the residue from the trip and dismissed his good intentions.

Carlton was trying to get his practice back together. He had to cancel a number of court cases and put off a number of client cases. The clients understood but were getting nervous about their issues. Carlton found himself working more hours than he wanted to. But the practice had to come first. He had to make a living and get back his clients' confidence. He knew that, in time, he would be back to the normal flow of taking care of his clients' needs.

As time went on, he was getting concerned about the situation in the world. Things were continuing to escalate. The allies' shipping losses were the heaviest since the beginning of the war. In October alone, the losses totaled 198,000 tons of material. The submarines seemed to be winning. The Italians, under Mussolini's direction, had attacked Greece and Albania. The air Battle of Britain was continuing. Although their aircraft and pilot losses were high, the Germans continued heavy bombing in England. The English retaliated by bombing Berlin, Naples, Danzig, Dresden, and Hamburg.

Both Carlton and Maggie voted in the presidential election. They discussed who to vote for at length. They both decided to vote for Roosevelt. He was elected to his third term as president of the United States. Carlton told Maggie his election was unprecedented, as he was the only chief executive to have served more than two terms in office. Carlton was ecstatic over his victory. He told Maggie he would be listening to the president's inaugural address.

Maggie didn't have time, as she was planning for Thanksgiving and beginning to think about all things that had to be done for the Christmas holidays. She was going to invite Oma for Thanksgiving and Christmas. She took it for granted that Carlton would not have an issue with that. He was working too hard to worry about the holidays. The trip had really turned his practice upside down. Maggie was listening to the afternoon news on the radio when a news bulletin flashed on. Neville Chamberlin had died. The newscaster explained that Chamberlin was a past prime minister of the United Kingdom. Chamberlain, who'd had to deal with

Hitler's rise to power, was best known for his appeasement foreign policy. He'd signed the Munich Agreement, which had conceded the German-speaking part of Czechoslovakia, Sudetenland, to Hitler. The newscaster continued, saying the signing of this agreement would always be part of Chamberlain's legacy.

When Maggie told Carlton of the former PM's death, all he could say was, "He gave away a part of a country to Hitler. I'm sure the English won't miss him." Maggie was shocked that Carlton even knew who this man was. Maggie was starting to get concerned that Carlton has been paying so much attention to the war and world affairs. He never had before the trip.

Thanksgiving holiday was lesser news, which was overcome by the war. Still, the people of the United States had much to be thankful for this year, as the United States was not yet participating in the horrendous war going on overseas. Maggie invited Carlton's mother over for Thanksgiving dinner. She was ecstatic to be spending the day with Carlton's family and offered to help with the dinner and dishes. Maggie accepted her help graciously.

The Fuller family had a wonderful Thanksgiving. Maggie and Oma put together a glorious dinner. Carlton had been given a fifteen-pound turkey by one of his clients. Maggie, being an American, made candied sweet potatoes like her mother did, mashed white potatoes, gravy from the turkey giblets, and a green bean casserole. Oma made the rolls and baked an apple strudel that dripped butter and sugar. Carlton and the children volunteered to wash the dishes and put the kitchen back together. The weather in Cleveland on Thanksgiving Day was cold, with rain and snow showers. Oma was a little nervous about Carlton driving her home that evening. She asked Carlton if she could stay the night and spend more time with them and the children. Carlton and Maggie were more than happy to have Oma stay. The kids were excited, as Oma could read to them and play games. It would be a grand evening.

December was coming, and the Christmas holidays were not far away. There would be more planning and decorating to be done at the Fuller residence. Maggie loved Christmas and looked forward to the decorating and shopping that had to be done to prepare for the holidays. But it was a lot of work to do, and it would be a little more difficult this year, as she was pregnant and would probably require more help from Carlton.

"Carlton," called Maggie, "How do you feel about helping me this year getting ready for Christmas?"

"Works for me, honey. I know you are pregnant. I had been planning to do most of the heavy work. I'll be pulling down the boxes, getting the tree, rearranging the furniture, and taking the kids to see Santa Claus. Is that okay?" said Carlton.

"Of course it's okay," quipped Maggie. "I am so lucky to have you. You are thinking of me and the effort that we put into the holidays. Thank you very much, honey. Come over here and give me a kiss," she called.

Carlton walked over and hugged and kissed her approvingly. Oh how he loved this woman.

"Maggie I haven't told my mother about Donovan's request. Do you think I should tell her what he wants me to do?" he asked.

"Why should you? It would only upset her. You haven't done anything about his request have you?" she replied, the negativity in her tone clear.

"No, no I haven't," he assured her. But I feel guilty not saying anything to her. With all the activity going on about the draft, she may hear about it from her friends and begin to worry about me. I certainly am the right age. I do have to register."

"I don't think the government will draft you. You have a mother; a wife; and two, soon to be three, children. Let's wait until you hear from the draft board to say anything. Christmas is coming. You and I have too much to do. I just pray the unfortunate in Europe have something to celebrate," said Maggie.

The children came into the room. "Mommy when are we going to see Santa Claus?" asked Charlotte. "Carlton, Jr., keeps telling me that, if we don't get there soon, all the presents will be asked for by other children, and we won't get any presents this year. Mommy, is that true?"

"Oh, Charlotte, that isn't true at all," replied Maggie. "He is just kidding you. Daddy will be taking you both to see Santa Claus soon. In fact, your dad and I have been talking about the man in red today. Haven't we, Dad?"

"Yes we have." Carlton grinned. "How about going to see Santa this Saturday morning? I'm sure he has office hours Saturday at Higbee's Department Store. We'll make a day of it. We'll take the streetcar downtown, visit with Santa, and have lunch at Higbee's Silver Grille Restaurant. What do you guys think about that?"

"Hooray!" shouted Charlotte. "We're going to see Santa. We're going to see Santa."

"Aw, Dad," said Carlton, Jr. "I knew we were going to see Santa, I just wanted to kid Charlotte. I'm also looking forward to seeing Santa. We are going to have a fun day Saturday. I told you so, Charlotte. You just don't remember."

With that, both of them took off running.

"Watch yourselves," called Maggie after them. "Thank you, honey. Let's get started decorating the house. Let's get up to the attic and bring down the Christmas decorations."

Christmas 1940 had begun at the Fullers. The family became embroiled in the holiday season. The United States was looking forward to a joyous time. Stores were full of shoppers, families were spending time together, Congress took its Christmas recess, and the churches were full on Christmas Day. The people of the United States prayed for peace that day. And unbeknownst to them, it would be the last peaceful Christmas for the next four years.

The war news was full of the British fighting the Italians in Africa. The Greeks were making headway against the Italians, but because the army was still using horses and old equipment, progress was slow. The Germans continued to bomb England. England continued to retaliate. Thirty-six thousand Italians were taken prisoner, captured in the Western desert of Africa. On Christmas, King George IV broadcast a message: "The future will be hard, but our feet are planted on the path of victory. And with the help of God, we shall make our way to justice and to peace."

The Luftwaffe did not bomb England on Christmas Day but resumed on the next day. President Roosevelt, setting the stage, broadcast the following message: "We must be the arsenal of the democracies."

Hitler issued his New Year's proclamation: "1941 will see the German army, navy, and air force enormously strengthened and better equipped. Under their blows, the last boastings of the warmongers will collapse, thus achieving the final conditions for a true understanding among the peoples."

Great Britain suffered massive civilian casualties in December—during that month 3,800 were killed and 5,200 were injured. The war went on.

Maggie visited the doctor for her monthly appointment. It was very routine visit. When she got home from the visit, she told Carlton that the doctor believed she would have a normal-sized child and a normal delivery. She has gained eight pounds. He expected the baby to be born in March. Happiness was an uneventful pregnancy.

"I'm happy it went well at the doctor's honey," Carlton told her, adding. "I registered for the draft. The place was packed with men and what seemed like boys signing up. There seemed to be a lot of grumbling going on. From what I heard, the Selective Service Act requires all American males between the ages of twenty-one and thirty-six to register for the draft. The act requires that only nine hundred thousand men at any given time can be in training. If you are drafted, you will serve only twelve months. The act also provides that, once drafted, you can only be located in the Western Hemisphere or in a US possession located in other parts of the world. That doesn't seem to be a bad deal to me. I don't understand why so many are upset about the issue."

"Well you fulfilled your obligation. You signed up." Maggie sighed. "Hopefully nothing will happen. I was talking with my friend down at the market yesterday. She said that her brother signed up and expected to be one of the first ones to go into the army. She said he was looking forward to it. Apparently, there aren't a lot of jobs available. Getting drafted will keep him busy, and he'll get paid while he is in the army. I think that, for that reason alone, the draft is a good thing. But what will happen if the United States enters the war? Will those who are drafted stay longer than twelve months?"

"I don't like to speculate," Carlton said. "It's not my nature to do so. But I guarantee they would be told they are staying in the service. With what is going on over in Europe, if I were drafted, I would be very uncomfortable with my situation."

"Here we are, almost February of the new year. We have settled into a regular routine. You are very busy with your clients, and I'm busy with housework, cooking meals daily, and taking care of the kids. I have even stopped paying attention to what is going on in the war. I am getting a lot of action inside my tummy. The baby is very active. Seems to get more active every day. It is starting to get a bit uncomfortable sleeping at night. I seem to be getting a little more tired every day. I have another doctor's appointment early next month. I'll be starting my eighth month the first of February. We have to start getting the house ready for the baby. Have you any ideas, Carlton?" Maggie asked.

"I haven't given it any thoughts," replied Carlton. "It is getting close to time for the baby to be born. I noticed your tummy growing. You look more beautiful every day. You have had no complaints. Charlotte told me a few days ago how beautiful she thought you looked. She noticed your belly getting bigger. She wondered how the baby was doing. Maybe you should talk to the children about the baby and all the changes that will take place in the house once the baby is born. They should be part of the experience, don't you think?"

"You're right, Carlton. I will talk to the children tonight. Thanks for the suggestion," Maggie replied happily. "Have you been keeping up with the news?"

"I have," Carlton said, adding, "I listen to the radio every day. I've read the newspaper daily ever since we returned home. I even stop at the Telenews movie theater on Euclid Avenue periodically to get the latest war news. I'm very concerned about the situation. I think about Donovan's request morning, noon, and night. Hitler and his Nazis are evil. The world needs to rid itself of him and his kind. I'm sorry, Maggie; what we learned over there affected me differently than you. The Germans have been on the move. They convinced the king of Bulgaria to allow them to move their troops through his country and enter Romania. The Nazis did that to protect the oil there. The Italians and Greeks continue to struggle. The British are gaining ground on the Italians in Africa. The Luftwaffe continues to attack England. The English have lost thousands of innocent civilians—the country must be a mess—but they continue to bomb German cities. There has been major activity in the Mediterranean areas. The island of Malta has been a target of German bombing. The Germans want the island as a strategic location. It would be an excellent place for their aircraft to stage support for the Italians in Africa. You let me worry about the war. I want you to worry about the baby."

"I didn't realize how you felt, honey. Please don't get caught up in this war and the Nazis. The children and I need you here. I am concerned about the baby. All seems normal with the baby; I can assure you of that."

The phone started to ring.

"Carlton please answer the phone I'm busy in the kitchen," called Maggie.

"Hello, Fuller residence," Carlton answered. "Major Best, hello."

"Maggie, that was Major Best. He is on his way to Chicago via Cleveland.

He wants to visit us with news from Emily. I'm picking him up at the train station tomorrow at three o'clock," Carlton called out, deliberately not mentioning the bad news portion of the phone call.

"Oh that's exciting. It will be good to see him. What did he have to say?" she replied.

"Not much other than that. He is looking forward to seeing us," Carlton said.

As he drove to the train station, Carlton pondered what bad news the major might be bringing. Could it be about Emily or Mr. Morris? *Don't speculate, Carlton,* he told himself. *Wait for the major.*

Sure enough, at 3:15, the major came out of the terminal. It was chilly outside, and he was wearing his military topcoat.

"Hello," Carlton said as he opened the car door. "How are you? You look well."

"I'm fine, Carlton. Good to see you, I didn't realize how chilly it is here. Glad I wore my topcoat."

"What did Emily have to say?" asked Carlton as they drove away from the terminal.

"I'd rather wait to tell you both at the same time if that is okay with you," replied the major. "I have a lot of other questions to ask since we haven't seen each other for almost six months."

"Okay. I'll wait until we are with Maggie. I have a lot of questions for you also."

Small talk filled the car as they drove to the Fullers.

Carlton let the Major knock on the door. When Maggie opened the door, she almost jumped into the major's arms. She couldn't quite make it, as her protrusion wouldn't let her. "Major, it is so good to see you. You are looking as handsome as ever," she said excitedly.

"Look at you, a beautiful mother to be. Hi, Maggie. It is good to see you. How are you doing? How is the family?" asked the major.

"I'm fine, getting a little big. The children are doing well—into a routine of going to school, doing homework, and playing. How is Emily doing?" she replied.

"She is doing fine. I have a lot to fill you both in on. Can we sit down in the living room to talk?" said the major.

"Sure. Before we start, can I get us anything?" asked Maggie.

No was the response from both me. "Let's sit down," said Carlton.

The major started, "I had a letter in the embassy diplomatic pouch from Germany two days ago from Emily. Hildegard came to the embassy in disguise as a washerwoman. She was very frightened for her life. There had been a major disaster at the house. Horst and a number of his officer friends came home two weeks ago from a meeting at the OKW very drunk and disruptive. Horst grabbed Hildegard by the hair, dragged her to the library, tore off her clothes, and raped her in front of his friends. He left her and took his friends to Sara's room. Hildegard knew only that she heard screaming and gunshots. When she found Sara, she was lying in a pool of blood naked on the floor. She was dead—apparently raped and killed by Horst and his friends. Hildegard called the police. Nothing came of it. The local chief told her no problem; Sara was a Jew. When Hildegard told the police what happened to her, they laughed and told her she had to take care of her husband's needs. Emily took Hildegard in at the embassy, cleaned her up, listened to her story, and calmed her down. She was very frightened. Once she was lucid and able to communicate, she sent her home in a taxi. When Horst returned the next day, he acted like nothing had happened. When Hildegard confronted him, he slapped her and shut her up. She has been living in a hell since then. She is afraid for herself and the remaining servants. I'm sorry I had to tell you about this tragedy. I know how you both felt bout Hildegard and Sara."

By this time, Maggie was crying loudly. Carlton reached out, hugged her, and talked to her quietly, trying to settle her down. Carlton was seething inside. *What a terrible situation to have lived through,* he thought, thinking of Hildegard, *let alone to be forced to continue to share a life with my brother.* Was this what the Germans had brought into the world?

"Major when did this happen?" asked Carlton.

"I estimate about one or two weeks ago. It takes the diplomatic pouch about two or three days to get to Washington. Emily didn't say in the letter exactly when it all happened. She did say that Hildegard, in addition to being scared, was mad and has become a determined enemy of the Nazis," replied Major Best.

"Honey, can I get you anything to help you settle down?" asked Carlton.

"Yes, you can. I would like a glass of wine. One glass shouldn't hurt the baby, should it?" Maggie answered.

"I hope not," said Carlton. "How about you, Major? What can I get for you? I'm having scotch. That arrogant bastard brother of mine. He and his ugly Nazi friends. Hildegard told us she was afraid of what he might do. I'm sorry, Major, for cussing, it seemed fitting. I wish we could help her."

"Scotch would be fine. I agree with you. Your brother is as you said, an arrogant bastard, as are all Nazis," he replied, thinking about what the general had in mind.

The three of them talked about Emily's letter the rest of the afternoon. Maggie had settled down. Carlton was calm, but he was outraged. This was too close to home.

Maggie fixed sandwiches for dinner. The children were happy to see Major Best. He had become very friendly with them. He brought Carlton, Jr., an army hat and Charlotte a box of chocolates. She offered them to everyone. She acted very grown-up.

The major had to catch a train early in the morning. Good-byes were said, and he left. Maggie was tired out from the bad news. She took the children upstairs to bed and retired herself.

Carlton had another scotch. He sat down and began to think. *What should I do? Should I call the general? Should I volunteer now? Maggie will have the baby soon. She will need help. Can Oma fill the bill?* He had another scotch. The house was quiet. The war news continued poorly. The Germans and Italians continued to expand their takeovers. The German submarines continued to sink thousands of pounds of ships and supplies. *Will I get drafted?* he wondered. *Is the United States going to enter the war?*

He fell asleep in the chair. His mind was reeling. The questions kept going around in circles.

Maggie came down at 2:00 a.m. to get a glass of water. She found him sleeping and woke him up. "Carlton, are you okay?" she asked.

He mumbled, "Okay." She took him upstairs and put him in bed, a bit inebriated.

On January 21, 1941, President Franklin Delano Roosevelt was inaugurated for his third term as the president of the United States. The Fuller family listened to his inauguration speech—the children in school; Maggie at home with Oma (who had been helping around the house lately, as Maggie was getting very large and cumbersome); and Carlton in his office with the radio blaring.

The president began, "On each national day of inauguration since 1789, the people have renewed their sense of dedication to the United States. In Washington's day the task of the people was to create and weld together a nation. In Lincoln's day the task of the people was to preserve a nation from disruption within. In this day, the task of the people is to save that nation and its institutions from disruption from without ..."

The president ended with what Carlton felt were the most important words of the speech

The destiny of America was proclaimed in words of prophecy spoken by our first president in his first inaugural in 1789—words almost directed, it would seem, to this year of 1941: "The preservation of the sacred fire of liberty and the destiny of the republican model of government are justly considered ...deeply, finally, staked on the experiment entrusted to the hands of the American people."

If we lose that sacred fire—if we let it be smothered with doubt and fear—then we shall reject the destiny, which Washington strove so valiantly and so triumphantly to establish. The preservation of the spirit and faith of the nation does, and will, furnish the highest justification for every sacrifice that we may make in the cause of national defense. In the face of great perils never before encountered, our strong purpose is to protect and perpetuate the integrity of democracy. For this, we muster the spirit of America and faith of America. We do not retreat. We are not content to stand still. As Americans, we go forward, in the service of our country, by the will of God.

Carlton was so impressed he stood in his office and cheered. The other people he shared the office with looked at him incredulously. He looked at them somewhat sheepishly and smiled. He thought to himself, *If you had seen what I did in Germany, you would cheer too.*

The president was telling us to get ready, he realized. *Our time to be ready to defend our nation and democracy is coming.*

Carlton picked up the phone and called Donovan's office. The general's secretary answered.

"Hello, Shelly. This is Carlton Fuller. Is the general in?"

"Hi, Mr. Fuller. How are you? It has been a long time. No, he isn't; he's attending the inaugural ceremonies."

"Please have him call me. Have him call me here at the office tomorrow if possible. The number is DI 3689. I should be here most of the day."

"I will, Mr. Fuller. How is your wife doing? She is due soon, isn't she?"

"She is fine. Thank you for asking. Her due date is early in March."

"Please give her my best. I will have the general call you in the morning. Good-bye." Shelly hung up.

Carlton was pleased. He had made up his mind. He would volunteer. He would tell the general he would be ready to report after Maggie had the baby. Hopefully, that would meet his needs.

The phone at Carlton's office rang early. Carlton had just arrived. He took off his coat and answered the phone. "Good morning. Carlton Fuller's office. Carlton Fuller speaking."

"Good morning, Carlton. Bill Donovan here. How are you? Maggie have the baby yet? Have both of you recovered from the trip to Germany? Shelly said you called yesterday. What can I do for you?"

"General, you sound enthusiastic this morning. I'm fine. No, Maggie did not have the baby yet. We think it will be early March. Yes, I think we have recovered from the trip. But Major Best brought us some bad news a couple of days ago. I have made a decision as to your request. I have not told Maggie yet. Please keep it a secret. I am ready to volunteer. But I cannot report until she has the baby and gets settled. I have a lot to do between now and then. I have tried to make sense of all this, but it evades me. Not knowing what you have in store for me scares me. I have no idea how to prepare for what is ahead for me. I'm concerned about Maggie and my family. I hope you understand my trepidation."

"Carlton, thank you," responded the general. "1 I fully understand your position. I know your decision was very difficult to make. Major Best briefed me on Emily's letter. I'm very sorry about what happened. Certainly, neither you nor I can control what the Nazis have done or what they continue to do. The president is optimistic, as his inaugural speech implied. I will keep your decision secret. Major Best will not know until you are ready to report. As I told you when we first talked, the United States will prepare you for your assignment. It will take a personal effort on your part. Given your commitment to the training you will receive, I assure you, you will be fully prepared to accomplish your mission. I want to personally thank you from the president of the United States for volunteering. One more thing. I'm sure you would like to know how much the United States will be paying you for volunteering. I am able to pay you thirty-five thousand dollars per year, plus expenses. Please call me when you are ready."

"Thank you. Good-bye," said Carlton, who felt like a load had been lifted off of his shoulders. *Now all I have to do is tell Maggie of my decision.*

Now he had to find someone to take over his practice. He had to be careful not to let on why he was leaving. He would use the war efforts going on in the United States as the reason. If necessary, the draft would be a good backup reason. Plus, he had a great deal to do at home to prepare for the new baby. He and Maggie had to buy a crib. They had to fix up their room to accommodate the new addition. Maggie would be putting together a list of items they would have to purchase. He would talk with her about those issues. He needed to put together a financial package for Maggie. The money would go directly into the bank. She could draw from the bank as needed. He had to talk with his mother. She needed to understand his volunteering. Hopefully, she would move into his house to help Maggie with the new baby and the children.

The month of February flew by. Maggie said the action inside had slowed down. She could feel the baby dropping. She felt the delivery would be any day. The doctor had said she was ready and directed her to call him when her contractions were getting close together. Everyone in the house was getting anxious.

When Carlton asked Maggie what names they should consider for the new child, she had already picked them out—Sam if it was a boy or Sara if it was a girl. She wanted to name the child in memory of the servant girl Hildegard considered her daughter. Carlton was not going to argue with her logic.

Sure enough, on March 7, 1941, Sara Christine Fuller was born. It was a normal natural birth. She weighed seven pounds, twelve ounces. Mother and baby were both in good health. The family was excited— particularly Charlotte; she had a new sister and was happy about that.

Carlton, Jr.'s, comment was, "Oh no. I'm the only boy in the family. Shucks."

After five days in the hospital, Maggie came home with the baby. Oma had come over to help Carlton with the children and the cooking. She couldn't wait to hold the baby. Oma told Maggie she would stay as long as Maggie wanted her to stay. She was ecstatic about the new little Sara.

The war news on Sara's day was positive. The British Expeditionary Force landed 57,000 troops on Greece to help them defeat the Italians. The German Submarine *U-47* was sunk by a British destroyer. The captain and entire crew were lost. The day following Sara's birth, the US Senate passed the Lend-Lease act, providing war supplies to England and Greece immediately.

Carlton decided he had to talk to Maggie. In his mind, the United States had been edging closer to entering the war; the Lend-Lease act confirmed the issue for me. Oma had gone home, and the family had settled into a new routine that included the baby. Things at home were as normal as they could be given the situation.

It was the first Sunday in April. Maggie had fixed a marvelous dinner for the family. The baby was asleep, the children were in their bedrooms listening to the radio, and Carlton and Maggie were in the kitchen washing dishes and cleaning up after dinner.

"Honey," said Carlton. "I need to tell you something."

"What is it, dear?" replied Maggie.

"I called Donovan. With all of the war news and the Lend-Lease act being passed by the senate, I felt it was time for me to make a decision. I volunteered," Carlton stated as he waited for a response.

"You what?" Maggie said loudly, "Let me calm down for a minute. Please get me a glass of wine. No. Get me a glass of scotch. I knew you were getting very concerned over the past months. Then when we heard about Sara's death and what your brother and his friends did in Germany, you were more upset than I was about the news. I should be unhappy, but I have been expecting you to volunteer.

"Where does that leave me and the children? Where is my scotch? What do we do? How do we manage financially? Who will help me with the baby? Who will be here when I go shopping? Have you thought about these things?"

Carlton brought the scotch and a glass for each of them.

"Prost," Maggie said and then continued. "What about Oma? What are you going to tell her? How about the children? What do you tell them? I do feel a bit relieved that you made a decision. I know it has been causing you to lose sleep. I'm sure with the draft going on and men going to military training, you must feel some guilt going about your normal day working and being a father. I think I will start drinking scotch. This is not bad. What did you want me to say? Did you want me to roll over and be ecstatic? I'm not, but all of us will get through this one way or another. I love you, Carlton Fuller," she said as she reached out and hugged him. "I am proud of you."

"Maggie, what can I say? I did not know how you would react. After you chewed out Donovan like you did, I didn't know what to expect. I have been thinking about all you said before I talked with you. In addition, I have to find someone to take over my practice.

"I don't know what Donovan has in store for me. He talked about training, before I get my assignment. I will have to wait and see what he has."

The Decision:
You're in the Army Now

*C*arlton spent his time the week following the discussion with Maggie talking with his family. The children didn't quite understand, as he did not know the details of his assignment. Oma was very upset that he had volunteered and the United States was not involved directly in the war. They all had a lot of questions that Carlton could not answer yet. He promised that he would answer all questions when he knew more information.

Spring started early in Cleveland, Ohio, that April. Carlton went to his office to contact Donovan's office. The streets still had some ice and snow on them that had not melted. It was sloppy, but the temperature was fifty-five degrees, and it was sunny outdoors. Carlton was feeling good and was confident about his decision. He couldn't wait to talk to Donovan.

"Good morning. General Donovan's office. Shelly speaking. How may I help you?" her voice was full of enthusiasm as usual.

"Good morning, Shelly. This is Carlton Fuller. May I speak to Mr. Donovan?"

"Hi, Carlton. How are you? How are Maggie and the baby?" Shelly replied warmly. "He's in a meeting. He should be back very soon."

"I am fine. Maggie and the baby are doing well. The baby gained two pounds this first month. Have him call me at my office, will you? You have the number," Carlton said.

"I will have him call you as soon as he gets back. Glad to hear Maggie and the baby are doing fine. Wow! Gained two pounds. Have a great day. Bye."

It was a busy morning for Carlton. He was going to interview two men who were interested in taking over his practice. Both were trained lawyers who were working for larger law offices in downtown Cleveland. It was eleven a.m. when the phone rang.

"Good morning. This is Carlton Fuller. How may I help you?" he asked.

"Good morning, Carlton. This is Bill Donovan. How are you? It has been awhile since we talked."

"Yes it has," replied Carlton. "I'm ready to begin, General. Maggie, I, and the family have talked about my volunteering for your organization. They all don't quite understand it, as I haven't any idea what or where I will be going. I certainly would like some answers."

"I know you do, Carlton, but I don't have them yet. The first thing you will do is attend the army's Officer Candidate School at Fort Monmouth in New Jersey. It is an Army Signal Corps training session, and its duration is seventeen weeks. When you graduate, you will be commissioned a 2nd Lieutenant in the Army Signal Corps. When you graduate, you will be given your next assignment.

"Please remember, our organization is a secret one. For the benefit of the public, including your family and friends, you have joined the Army Signal Corps as an officer. I know your wife knows better. While you are in training, you will be investigated for a top-secret classification clearance.

"You will not be able to travel home until you finish the first six weeks of school. Then you will only have a weekend off. You may want to bring Maggie to Fort Monmouth for the weekend. Following graduation, you will get one week of leave before you begin the next phase of training. I want you to report in Washington, DC, to David Bruce's office on May 1, 1941. They will keep you busy until you report to Fort Monmouth on May 15, 1941 for the training.

"I have a suggestion for you. Officer training is both physical and mental. If your physical conditioning is not fine-tuned, I suggest you tune yourself up physically before you get there.

"Congratulations on your start. I will have your orders and the necessary tickets in the mail to you within the week. I'm looking forward to seeing you in Washington. Please say hello to Mrs. Fuller. She is a wonderful gal. How is the new baby doing?"

"Can I say wow, sir? I'm a little overwhelmed. Both Maggie and the baby are doing fine. The baby gained two pounds her first month. I am looking forward to meeting Mr. Bruce. And I'm looking forward to see you again, General. Will I have a chance to see Major Best again?" asked Carlton.

"Yes, you will, Carlton. He is here with me. See you soon. Good-bye," he said.

"Good-bye, General," said Carlton.

Carlton was excited. He couldn't wait to get home and tell Maggie.

The month of April went by quickly. Carlton's orders and tickets arrived. He would be catching a train from Cleveland to Washington, DC. Following two weeks of business in Washington, he would catch a train to Fort Monmouth, New Jersey, via New York City. His orders were to be turned in at Fort Monmouth. He would receive his uniforms following his arrival. He was to bring personal items and two days of clothing. The Army would take care of the rest of his needs for the next seventeen weeks.

Carlton knew there would be more training beyond Fort Monmouth. Until he finished training, he wouldn't get his assignment. He joined the YMCA to get himself physically fit as the general had suggested. Maggie couldn't believe he was going to the YMCA four days a week.

Carlton continued to interview candidates to take over his practice. He advised all of his clients that he was selling his practice. Many of his clients were unhappy that he was leaving them at the end of April.

Carlton's mother told Maggie she would move in with her and the children once Carlton left. Maggie indicated she wasn't ready for that yet but was thankful she would be available to do that in the future.

Oma said, "Whenever you are ready, let me know. I will rent my house and move."

The month had flown by.

The family left to pick up Oma and head to the train station. Carlton hugged and kissed his mother. She was crying. The children were in awe of the train station. They kissed and hugged their dad. Maggie handed the baby to Oma and jumped into Carlton's arms. It was an emotional kiss and hug.

"Take care of yourself, Carlton," said Maggie as the tears flooded down her cheeks. "I love you. Please write. I will miss you every day. I am already looking forward to coming down to Fort Monmouth. I will write every day."

"I love you, Maggie. We haven't been apart since we were married. I will write as often as I have time to. Be careful. Be safe. I made arrangements for my pay to be sent to you every month. There is money in the bank to take care of you all until the checks start coming. If you need anything, contact Oma. I love you."

With that, Carlton headed down the stairs to his train. They were all waving good-bye as he disappeared at the bottom of the stairs.

During the month of April, the war news was grave. Greece and Yugoslavia fall into German hands. Surrender agreements were signed by both countries. The British and Poland expeditionary forces were successfully evacuated from Greece. Thousands of men on both sides were either dead or taken prisoner. England was being bombed continuously by the Germans. The British continued to retaliate, bombing German cities. Many thousands of civilians were killed and injured in England. The conflict in Africa was mostly at a standstill. Rommel's Africa Corps made headway, and the British were pushed back.

Carlton's meeting with David Bruce went well. Bruce was very happy Carlton had volunteered. He gave Carlton the impression that he was wanted by Donovon for a long time. He wondered what his assignment would be more than ever. He spent his time in DC filling out paperwork, reading war reports, and processing information regarding German troop movements. He had a chance to do some sightseeing, and he continued to work out at the gym located at Ft. Meyers.

Maggie kept him up to date with letters every day. Oma's personal things had arrived from Germany. Horst had been able to get them sent to the United States. *Good news for Oma*, thought Carlton. *I bet she was ecstatic.*

Bruce told him before he left that he would see him following his last training cycle and give him his assignment. Carlton tried to get Bruce to tell him what it was, but all he would say was that, after his final evaluation and graduation from the last cycle of training, he would get all the details. He found Bruce to be very cagey.

When Carlton arrived at Fort Monmouth, he received the fifty-page standard operating procedure document for the Officer Candidate School. He was told to become thoroughly familiar with this SOP, which would be his bible for the next seventeen weeks. Thus, he began the toughest seventeen weeks of his life. After reading the SOP, Carlton thought to himself, *What have I gotten myself into? Most of my peers are five to six years younger than I am. My goal is to complete this training. I'm not going to be in the army. But I will compete and be successful during this training.*

He wrote Maggie a letter outlining the SOP. He told her he'd never done anything like this before in his life. He asked her to please pray for him. He also told her that, if she needed him at home, she should contact the Red Cross and explain her issue, and the organization would get him home. But, he added, make sure it was an emergency. He closed by telling her he missed and loved her and the children and, "Please wish me luck." He added a PS, providing his mailing address for the next seventeen weeks.

When Carlton's OCS training began, over 450 candidates were in the class. By graduation time, only 372 had made it through. Carlton was among them.

During the seventeen weeks of training, many war news announcements had been made. By far the most important one had come on June 23, 1941. It was made during the first class in the morning. Normally nothing interrupted the OCS training. This was big war news. Conducting what would be come to be known as Operation Barbarossa, the Germans had invaded Russia with a force of 133 divisions of men and machines. The faculty said it was the largest force of men and equipment ever assembled for an invasion. This announcement had impacted everyone at the school. It was an eye-opener, to say the least. Everyone had talked about it for weeks on end.

What would happen next? That was the question on everyone's mind.

The weeks ground on, and graduation had finally arrived. Carlton had asked Maggie to come for graduation. She was excited to be able to attend. She traveled by train to Washington, DC, and by local train to the Fort Monmouth station. She came directly from the train to the field via taxi, where the graduation was to take place. She hadn't seen Carlton for ten weeks. The last time they had seen each other was the weekend she had come down to see him after the sixth week of training.

The stands were full of people, most of them relatives of the graduates. The ceremony began at 1:00 p.m. sharp. The master of ceremonies on the reviewing stand introduced the ranking officers of the command. The army band then marched onto the parade ground, playing the army song. They positioned themselves on the parade ground facing the spectators.

After the band had played, the graduates marched in groups of fifty, each group with flags flying. As the graduates came onto the field, the crowd stood up and cheered. The band was playing Sousa marches. Maggie started to cry. She strained to find Carlton as the groups passed in review. She found him as his group came by. She was so proud. He looked wonderful. She couldn't wait to hug and kiss him. It seemed to her that they had been separated for such a long time. It seemed that time was dragging as the speakers droned on and on.

Finally, the graduates were announced individually and commissioned second lieutenants. Following receipt of the gold bar signifying their rank, they all tossed their hats in the air. What a scene.

The crowd left the stands and went to meet their graduates. Maggie walked down the steps and onto the parade ground. There was hugging and kissing going on all over the grounds. Carlton and Maggie spotted each other at the same time. They ran toward each other. As soon as Carlton was within hugging distance, she launched herself into his arms. It was a tight hug and a passionate kiss. Maggie couldn't hold herself back. "Carlton, Carlton, it is so good to see you. It has been so long. I have missed you so much." She was crying like a child, with big sobs and a profusion of tears.

"Me too, Maggie," said Carlton joyously. "I have so much to tell you, so many friends to introduce you to. We have a lot of catching up to do. How are the children and my mother doing? How is little Sara doing? Oh, Maggie, I love you."

The couple had a wonderful weekend together before they went home for the week of leave Carlton had been promised.

Before they left Carlton picked up his set of orders. There was a notation on the package: "Not to be opened until you get to your residence! Your eyes only!" It was signed, "Donovan."

When they arrived at home, Oma and the children were waiting for them. It was a wonderful reunion. Oma was very emotional, and the children were excited. Daddy was home for a while. They had a lot planned for the short time he was going to be home.

Maggie was amazed at how he had changed. His hair was clipped short, he had lost weight, and he was stronger. His figure was lean and sexy, she thought. They made love a number of times that weekend, as he was full of energy. She hoped she didn't get pregnant again. What a difference, she thought, from the Carlton that had begun "his adventure," as Maggie called it. She liked the changes. She kidded him about the changes. All he could do was blush. He too was happy with the changes.

On Wednesday of the week, when Maggie and Oma went shopping, he opened his orders. There was a personal note from Donovan congratulating him on getting through OCS. He was now to report to a school run by the British located outside of London, England. "Your point of contact will be Sir Frank Nelson," Donovan wrote. "He is a personal friend of mine. He is waiting for you to report. You will be trained initially by the British. Following completion of their course, you will report in December to Oshawa, Ontario, Canada." Donovan assured him in the note that this training would complete his training for his assignment.

Carlton was getting anxious about what the assignment was going to be.

The package contained train tickets from Cleveland to New York. He would be met at the station and be taken from there to catch a military plane to London, England. Upon arrival, he would be taken to Sir Nelson's office and the British would arrange for his travel to Oshawa upon completion of his training.

"Give my best to Mrs. Fuller," Donovan had concluded. "This information is not to be shared with anyone. Enjoy your leave."

There was also a short note from David Bruce, saying he would see Carlton in Washington, DC, at Bolling Air Force Base following his graduation from training in Great Britain to discuss his assignment. It was signed, "Good luck, DKEB."

What do I tell Maggie and the family? Carlton wondered.

He had a few more days to think about that. *Enjoy my leave, he says. I will, damn it!*

The family visited all the highlights of Cleveland and the surrounding area. The weather was perfect. It was a wonderful Indian summer week.

They spent three days at the Cedar Point Breakers Hotel. What fun the children had on the beach and at the Penney arcade. Oma stayed in a room with the children. Carlton and Maggie stayed in a room by themselves. It was wonderful.

Maggie couldn't believe how many more times they made love. Carlton was her best friend, her lover, and her husband. Carlton told her he would be leaving the following Tuesday. He couldn't tell her where he was going. He blamed Donovan for being the bad guy. She cried and cussed Donovan out.

₵ⱧɆ Ⱥⱳⱥ₭Ɇ₦₣₦₲

Carlton arrived at Sir Frank Nelson's office at 0900 hours London time after traveling for over twenty-six hours straight. He was tired, a bit dirty, and unshaven. He didn't know what to expect from Sir Frank but waited anxiously. He sat in a chair in front of a secretary who was busy typing, filing, and answering a set of large, old-fashioned phones on her desk. She told Carlton when he arrived that Sir Frank would be in shortly. Her accent was very English and very thick. He had to ask her twice what she'd said. He was embarrassed at not being able to understand her. He feigned being a little deaf from the flight over.

"You Yanks just don't understand our accent," she commented playfully. And they both laughed.

In walked Sir Frank. He came into the office quickly, mumbled something to the secretary, opened the door to his office, walked in, and turned around. "You must be Carlton Fuller, sir? Come in, sir. I don't have a lot of time. Come in. Have a seat," he said as he held the door open.

Carlton walked into the office behind Sir Frank.

"I am, sir," Carlton replied. "It is a pleasure to meet you." He expended his hand to Sir Frank.

"You Yanks and your handshaking," he said brusquely as he extended his hand and they shook hands.

"I don't have a lot of time. Donovan was right. Our research was right on the button. You are the perfect specimen—hair color and all," noted Sir Frank.

"What do you mean, Sir Frank?" Carlton was befuddled.

"Didn't Donovan tell you about our research?" replied Sir Frank.

"Oh yes, I remember now. That seems a long time ago. Why were you researching me and my family?" Carlton asked, a little miffed at Sir Frank.

"Now, now, Yank. Don't get upset. We were just doing our job. You will find out why in due time. Bear with us," answered Sir Frank. "You are here for some training. I will introduce you to our training coordinator. He is a Scotsman. His name is Colin McVeagh Cubbins. He is our director of Special Operations Training. He developed our training syllabus. We have trained over fifteen hundred agents since 1940. I invited him to meet you and get you started. Here he is now."

In the door walked Cubbins. He was a smallish man with a mustache. "Good day, Sir Frank," he said with a bit of a brogue "Is this our man Fuller?" he asked.

"Yes it is. Meet Carlton Fuller, Colin," said Sir Frank.

"Damn pleased to meet you, Carlton," said Colin as he extended his hand.

"Same here, Colin," said Carlton shaking Cubbins's hand.

"I understand Donovan sent you here for some training, Carlton. Is that right?" asked Colin.

"That's right, Colin. I just completed our army's Officer Candidate School. Donovan wants me to continue training here with you folks. And then I'm off to another place before I get my mission from him. I don't know what to expect yet," Carlton replied.

"We'll take care of you,' Colin replied. 'The training is in two parts. The first includes physical fitness training, elementary map reading, and basic pistol and machine gun instructions. The second is paramilitary training in Scotland. This includes small arms, silent killing, demolitions, sabotage basic infantry training, and elementary Morse code. You will be involved in field assignments and individual challenges. Following this, you will receive some indoctrination reviews from some of our people who have served in Germany and have experiences with the Nazi Party and their operations. I think you'll find your OCS training mild compared to our training. Do you have any questions?" he asked.

"I have a lot of questions. The most important one is why? I know you both can't answer that question. I appreciate your providing me some insight as to what training I will be attending over the next ten weeks or so. What can I say to my wife about my training?" Carlton asked.

"Tell her you are enjoying England, the weather is lousy, you'll be home in twelve weeks, you miss her and the family, you are fine, the food is good, and the mattress is soft," said Sir Frank.

"I understand," said Carlton. "When do we begin?"

"You start in three days," replied Colin, "We want you to get some rest and have a chance to visit here in London. But remember, the Jerries are still bombing us on a regular basis. Be careful and pay attention to the sirens and air wardens. If you like, I can have someone be your guide for the next couple of days. That okay with you? Let's get started then. I'll take you to where you are staying."

Colin and Carlton said good-bye to Sir Frank and left. Sir Frank thought to himself, *Donovan has told this poor guy nothing. Will he be surprised.*

As they were walking to Colin's car, Carlton told him having a guide would be a great idea.

"Then done it is. She will call on you tomorrow afternoon," replied Colin.

Colin took Carlton to the training center barracks. Carlton checked in with the master-at-arms, found his bunk, unpacked his bag, took a shower, and hit the bunk. He fell asleep instantly.

He didn't wake up until the next morning. The master-at-arms came and told him he had a phone call. *Who could that be?* he thought. *Who knows that I'm here?*

"Hello, this is Carlton Fuller. Who is this?" he asked.

"Good day, Carlton Fuller. This is Ann Basinger, Women's Army Corps. Colin Cubbins asked me to contact you. He asked me to be a tour guide for you the next couple of days before you start your training."

"Good day to you, Ann Basinger, I think that would be okay with me," replied Carlton. "I just woke up. I had a long, bumpy day yesterday. I didn't get much sleep. You sound perky this morning." He thought to himself, *she has a cute English accent.* "How will we get together? I can be ready in about a half hour."

"First of all, it is afternoon, not morning. It is almost time for tea. I think you will probably be hungry. I'll pick you up in thirty minutes in front of the barracks. Tootle loo." She hung up.

It was thirty minutes sharp and the gray-green army car pulled up in front of the barracks. Carlton opened the door in front and climbed in. "Hello. My name is Carlton Fuller."

"Hello. My name is Ann Basinger. Pleasure to meet ya. I thought we could start our travels at a restaurant named the Modern Café Restaurant. It is a bit ways downtown from here. It's a little different, as its windows are gone due to the blitz. But you can have some food, and I can have tea. Hate to miss my tea."

"Sounds great to me. I know nothing about your country or London. Thank you for taking the time to do this for me," said Carlton.

She was dressed in a women's military uniform. Her hat was cocked, and she was neat as a pin. She was a very pretty woman. *The next couple of days will be fun*, Carlton thought to himself. He hadn't spent any time with a woman since he'd last left Maggie. He noticed a slight wonderful perfume smell as he sat in the front seat of Ann's car.

As they approached downtown London, Carlton noticed a large number of barrage balloons floating in the sky across the city. After lunch and tea, Ann took Carlton to see the Tower of London, St. Paul's Cathedral, Whitehall, Bestminster, and the palace. It was a very busy day.

Carlton and Ann learned a lot about each other. Ann was married to a Royal Air Force Pilot. They'd met before the war and were married early in 1938. He had been flying a Hurricane fighter plane during the Battle of Britain. He was shot down over the channel, parachuted into the channel, and was rescued. He had sustained serious injuries to his legs, which had scraped the edge of the cockpit as he'd exited the airplane. He was in the hospital. It looked as if he would recover, but the jury was still out as to whether he'd be able to walk again. Ann had joined the army when her husband was injured. She'd believed being in the service would help her get access to the hospital. Carlton marveled at her attitude. She was very optimistic regarding the war. She believed England would prevail.

He shared some of the details of his life back home with her. She wondered why he had volunteered, and he told her what little he could, given that everything he was doing as top secret. She seemed to understand.

The second day, they traveled out to the country. Ann packed a picnic basket for them. It was a very enjoyable. relaxing day. They were able to forget the war. When they parted, Ann thanked Carlton for spending the time with her. She left him at the barracks with a kiss on the cheek. Carlton smiled and thought, with attitudes like these people have, England may just prevail. Training started tomorrow. He went to sleep with a smile on his face.

The next twelve weeks went by very quickly. Carlton learned things about fighting a war from a different perspective. The students had the opportunity to practice what they'd learned. They were always cautioned that their peers weren't the enemy. They learned to become the persona they were taking on. They needed to understand the daily atmosphere they would be living in. They needed to always think about what they were doing and who they were dealing with, and they had to stay on the offensive.

Never get yourself into a corner you cannot get out of safely. Kill your enemy before he kills you. Stay above the enemy's suspicion. Use the underground to help you in your job. Constantly watch your back. Don't trust anyone. Be suspicious of everyone. Too much trust will get you killed. The British had learned their lessons well.

The trainees all had the chance to test their skills in live training exercises. The physical training strained their bodies to the limit. Carlton had thought the army physical training was tough. It didn't hold a candle to this training. He became an excellent pistol and rifle shot. His use of the machine gun was less proficient but was considered adequate. He initially had difficulty with the silent killing training, but when he practiced or was practiced on, the difficulty disappeared. He learned it was either kill or be killed. He learned that, if you perceive it, it probably is true.

When the training was complete, he was given his orders to Oshawa. He saw Sir Frank and Colin at graduation. He thanked them for their help and support and asked them what his mission was. They indicated they had no idea. They told him David Bruce would see him in Washington, DC.

Before he left, he called Ann Basinger, He wanted to say good-bye to her. They decided to go to dinner in London.

It was a warm reunion. The club they went to had a band. The food was adequate, but the dancing was wonderful. Ann wanted to talk. Carlton felt something had happened since they'd first met. After dinner, while on the dance floor, Ann opened up.

"Carlton, my husband was killed. He recovered from his injuries. They weren't as bad as we'd originally thought. Although his injuries hadn't totally healed, he was anxious to get back to his squadron. He wanted to fly a Spitfire. He felt the Spitfire was an improved plane over the Hurricane he had been flying when he was injured. He was transferred to a fighter squadron with Spitfire aircraft. His wingman told me a group of Jerry bombers were identified on radar coming to bomb London. His squadron scrambled and attacked the bombers. What they didn't see were a group of German Me 109 fighter planes flying what he called CAP for the bombers. The Me 109s attacked the Spitfires. They were involved in a large dogfight. My husband shot down one of them and was beginning to chase a second one when another Me 109 came out of the clouds and, at point-blank range, shot at my husband's aircraft. His plane exploded. He never knew what happened," she told him, the pain in her voice clear. "His body was never found."

By this time, she was crying quietly. All Carlton could do was hug her and try to calm her as much as he could. She drew closer to him and returned his hug. They finished the dance without further words. As they were leaving the dance floor, he asked her if she wanted to go home.

"Yes, Carlton, please take me home," she said.

Carlton hailed a cab to take her home. He put his arm around her, and she put her head on his shoulder as they sat in the cab. It was a quiet ride to her apartment. When they arrived, Carlton told the cabbie to wait. He took her keys and opened the door. He took her coat, laid it on a chair, and turned to Ann.

"Thank you, Ann, for a special friendship. I'm so sorry your husband was killed. He is a hero of Great Britain. I must go. I have a plane to catch and my family to see. I have to say good night"

"Oh, Carlton, thank you. Won't you stay with me tonight? I need you terribly," she said as she hugged Carlton tightly.

"I can't, Ann. My plane leaves in two hours. They will be waiting for me at the airport. I cannot miss this plane. I wish you well. I will see you sometime," he said as he left her grasp, left the apartment, and climbed back into the cab.

As he rode to the air base, Carlton thought about how sorry he felt for Ann. He didn't know what he would do if he lost Maggie. *Maybe I should have stayed to comfort her*, he thought. *No, I did the right thing by leaving*, he told himself.

Then reality set in. *I have been to two very rigorous training sessions— one to be a trained Army officer and one to be a trained killer and a spy. What does Donovan have in store for me? I am in the best physical condition I have ever been in. I am a sharpshooter. I have learned to kill someone in twenty different ways. In the last year, I have traveled across the world. Why was I trained in these terrifying skills? Why—that's the question. No one I ask has an answer for me. Bruce better have it, or I'll quit. I am a volunteer. I'm frustrated. I'm looking forward to seeing Maggie and the kids. We are here at the airport. Twenty-three hours of flying ahead.*

Mission Final Training

The plane landed at Bolling Air Force Base in Washington, DC. Groggily, Carlton deplaned. He had train tickets to Cleveland in his pocket. He headed to the terminal to catch a cab. As he entered the terminal, a familiar face approached him.

"Hello, Carlton," said Major Best warmly. "How are you? You look a little different to me since the last time I saw you. You look meaner and leaner. All the training you've been through has made a difference. There's a gentleman here to meet you. He wants to discuss an issue with you. Please follow me."

"It is good to see you, Major. Your assessment of me is true," said Carlton, as he fell in alongside the major. "I definitely am leaner. But meaner? Well, maybe. Who would this gentleman be?"

The major opened a door that led into a room with a table and some chairs.

"Please sit down, Carlton," Major Best said. "He will be right in. Can I get you some coffee?"

"Major Best," Carlton asked, "why are we being so formal? You act as if we don't know each other. Of course, you can get me some coffee. Cream please."

As the major left, into the room walked a gray-haired, older gentleman, who extended his hand and said, "You must be Carlton Fuller. I'm David Bruce. I work for Bill Donovan. It is my pleasure to meet you. I know you are frustrated about your mission. We kept it from you until we received evaluations from you training instructors. We heard from the Officer Candidate School. You had very high marks all throughout training. In fact, your ranking in a class of over three hundred was fifth. The army wanted to keep you. Your performance during training in England was rated outstanding by Colin Cubbins. His evaluation was outstanding. He wanted to keep you in the British Secret Intelligence Service. Your final evaluation was from Mrs. Basinger. She gave you every opportunity to stray. You didn't. She did say she became very fond of you. But her story about her husband was true. I'm sorry we had to put you through that portion. We had to make sure."

"Here is your coffee, Carlton," said the major as he came into the room.

"Make sure of what?" Carlton snapped, a bit perturbed. "I was put through an emotional ringer. I understand the army and the training exercises in England, but Ann? That was an evaluation? How cruel for her and me. I would like to apologize to her."

"We had to make sure of your abilities. We had to make sure of your loyalty and ethics. It was her idea," retorted Bruce. "She is part of the English Special Operations Training staff." He continued. "We knew how you would respond when we told you. As I said, we had to be sure. Now please let me go on.

"You will get more training at a special base located in Oshawa, Canada. It has been developed for the British, Canadians, and the United States by the British Special Operations Training organization. You will start your training on December 9. You will get additional training on Morse code, your German, parachuting, and propaganda. In the meantime, I want you to go home for leave. Once you complete your training, you will leave on your mission immediately. You won't get back home until your mission is complete. The only communication your family will have will be through my office monthly. Your family or anyone else is not to know what your mission is. Do you understand? Is that clear? You are now carrying a top-secret clearance."

"It is certainly clear. I do understand. I believe I'm ready to learn what my mission is. It has been almost a year since General Donovan contacted me," replied Carlton.

"Your orders are as follows: You will parachute into occupied France. You will be in contact with the French underground. They will work with you to plan your brother's demise. You will then take your bother's place in all aspects of his life. You will go under deep cover and provide the allies with information regarding the German Army's operations until the end of the war. The French underground will put you in touch with the German underground as you see fit. You will be on your own. We will expect communications via Morse code or written word as you see fit. Your methods and movement are to be determined by you. Your code name will be Arc Angel. Your mission is to help defeat the Germans. Your point of contact is Major Best. He will be with you while you prepare for your mission in London. He will parachute with you into occupied France to make sure you meet with the French underground. Once you are connected with the underground, he will return to England," Bruce said as he handed a large package to Carlton.

Carlton was a bit shaken as he took the orders. "I understand my mission, Mr. Bruce. I have to eliminate my brother, take his place, and provide German information until the war is over. Incredulous. I'm overwhelmed at this moment. I need a drink. Scotch and water—a double I think, maybe a triple. Major Best, do you have any scotch with you?"

Major Best reached into his large briefcase and pulled out a bottle of Chivas Regal eighteen-year-old scotch. "I knew you would need some scotch. I'll have one with you. How about you, Mr. Bruce?"

"Don't mind if I do," replied Bruce.

"Thank you, Best," said Carlton. "I didn't know you drank scotch."

"I didn't either," said the major. "But after I heard your mission, I decided I'd better."

After they finished their scotch, Bruce spoke to Carlton. "The president of the United States, General Donovan, and I assure you we understand the difficulty of your assignment. Words cannot describe your bravery and sacrifice. You will know firsthand what the German Wehrmacht is planning and implementing. This information will be invaluable to the Allies in defeating the Germans. The details of your mission will be supplied to you when you get to London. Major Best will travel with you to London. Thank you." He shook Carlton's hand and left the room.

Carlton left the room with Major Best. They headed to the taxi stand outside the base air terminal. As they parted, Major Best said, "Carlton, it was good seeing you. Give Maggie my best. Enjoy your leave. I'll see you in London in about five to six weeks. Locations and orders are in your large envelope."

"Thanks, Major Best. See you in London," said Carlton, climbing into the cab that had just pulled up.

"Please take me to Union Station."

He would overnight on the train and meet Maggie and the kids at the Terminal Tower station in Cleveland the next morning. He didn't think he would sleep much on the train. His mission kept spinning around in his head. *I have to kill my brother, take his identity, and live with his wife.* The idea was mind-boggling. Not only that; he would have to work on Jodl's staff as Horst, pass critical information about the German Army to the allies, continue this circle until the end of the war, and do this all without getting caught.

It went on and on. Finally, it all made sense. Now he knew why Donovan had contacted him. *It may take more scotch,* he thought. *You have leave for twelve days,* he told himself. *Enjoy your family. They won't see you for who knows how long?* Until the war is over, Bruce had said. Based on the latest war news, that could be a number of years. *Hell,* he realized, *the United States is not even officially involved.*

Once he boarded the train and settled into his sleeper, he changed his mind regarding sleep. He headed to the club car to get a drink. He needed one. He had a lot to think about, and the scotch would help clear his mind. At least he thought it would. Now that he knew his mission, he would focus on its implementation. It would be like getting ready to try a case in court.

The days of leave were wonderful. It worked out that he had Thanksgiving as part of his leave. Being naturalized citizens, this holiday was one that he and Oma really appreciated. Maggie and Oma cooked a wonderful Thanksgiving dinner—turkey and all of the trimmings. Oma made strudel; Maggie made pumpkin pie; and Charlotte, with Oma's help, made Christmas cookies.

The children had the next week off. The family enjoyed being together. Carlton had been gone for so many weeks; it was a great homecoming.

Maggie pestered him about his mission and where he was headed. She finally understood that he couldn't tell her. She was tired of hearing that Donovan had created the silence.

Carlton was surprised the children were reading so well. Together, they all read books as a group. First Mom would read and then Dad, followed by Charlotte and, finally, Carlton, Jr. Mom read for Sara. It was fun for the whole family.

One day, they packed up Sara and went to the Terminal Tower. The whole family visited the train station, had lunch in the Howard Johnson restaurant in the terminal, and took the elevator to the top of the tower. What a thrill for the children. They were able to see Lake Erie and all of Northern Ohio. They even had fun looking for their own house. Carlton carried Sara all day. He knew he wouldn't have a chance to hold her for the next years.

The leave flew by. They spent time at Oma's house before he had to leave. He and Maggie agreed they would say their good-byes at home. He didn't want her and the children to come to the train station. He was due in Oshawa, Ontario, at the Royal York Hotel on December 9. He would catch his train to New York early on the eighth and take the overnight from New York to Oshawa that night.

The last day before he left was an emotional one for the family. Sunday December 7, 1941, dawned cold. The temperature was twenty-eight, and the weather forecast said partly cloudy with a high of thirty-seven. The house was chilly. Maggie was up first. She shook Carlton and asked, "Honey, please put some coal in the furnace, stoke the fire a bit, and turn up the thermostat." She thought to herself how wonderful the leave had been. Carlton had spent a lot of time with the children. She and Carlton had made love a number of times. He was a wonderful lover, friend, and husband. She would miss him. *I'm sure he will be home soon,* she told herself.

"Okay. I'll do it," he said as he walked out the bedroom door. "Please wake up the kids and start getting them ready to go to church. It looks as if it won't be a bad day."

Maggie got out of bed and dressed the kids. She was in the kitchen making breakfast. Carlton was getting dressed. The family was going to 10:00 a.m. service this morning. It was the start of a typical Sunday at the Fuller house.

"What a good sermon the pastor preached today." commented Maggie during the drive home from church.

"I think he is naive, Maggie. Hitler and the Nazis have just begun. They are almost in Moscow, and they have taken over France, Poland, and the Netherlands. And on top of that, they're Allies with the Italians, who are in Africa and trying to take over Greece. It will be a long time before peace comes to Europe," said Carlton, his tone very serious. "As long as people of America think like the pastor, this war will continue on. Something has to be done."

"What are you saying, Carlton? Should the United States get into the war?" Maggie asked. "For our sake, I hope not," she added.

"It almost seems inevitable that the United States will be brought into the war," said Carlton as he pulled into the driveway.

After they went into the house, Maggie put a roast into the oven and was continuing to work on her Sunday afternoon dinner. Carlton was reading *The Cleveland Plain Dealer newspaper.* It was full of news of the war in Europe. But another big story was the National Football League. The New York Giants were playing the Brooklyn Dodgers. The game was going to be broadcast on the WOR national radio network. Carlton had decided to listen to it that afternoon. He knew that Maggie liked the Sammy Kaye Sunday Serenade. How was he going to accomplish that? He didn't know yet.

"Carlton, we agreed that you were going to say good-bye to your mom," Maggie reminded him. "Please put down the paper and go to your mother's house. The roast will take about an hour and a half. Can you say good-bye that quickly? Or should I wait an hour?"

"Please wait the hour. Give me about two hours please," he replied.

He called his Mother to ask her if he could come over to her place to say good-bye. She said of course he could. He and Maggie had agreed that he should say good-bye to Oma alone. Carlton did not know if he would ever see her again. Still, Carlton asked Maggie again if she and the children wanted to go to Oma's, thinking she might have changed her mind. She told him she would stay home with the kids, finish dinner, listen to the radio, and make sure homework was done and the children were ready for school. She knew Carlton and his mother were very close.

As he left for his mother's, he wondered how he was going to tell her goodbye.

Carlton knocked on the door. His mother unlocked the door.

"Hi, Mom," he said. "Good to see you. How are you doing? Today, we speak English okay? His mother spoke English with a heavy accent, but she needed to practice whenever possible.

"Okay, okay," she agreed. "You know I like to speak German any time I can. I just love the language."

Carlton's mom lived on the lower West side of Cleveland in an area called Tremont off of Lorain Avenue, where many folks of German descent settled. She was comfortable there. She did her own shopping at German stores and could speak to everyone in German. Carlton was happy she was in a neighborhood that was something like home in Germany.

"Come on, Mom. Let's sit down and talk," said Carlton.

"No, no. Let's talk," he said, walking with her into the living room and sitting down.

"Well, Mom," he started, "I will be leaving in the morning. I'm leaving for a period of time. I came to say good-bye."

He fabricated a story about being drafted and becoming an officer in the Army Reserve. He was leaving for camp. She was not to worry. She had a lot of questions. She stopped him a number of times. He was able to satisfy her curiosity, but it took most of the next hour to get through it with his mother.

"I have been reading the German newspaper," she told him. "The Nazis are taking over many countries. They are writing a lot about what this Hitler is doing. He sounds like a dictator, not a representative of the Germany I remember. Do you think America will get into this mess? I hope not," she added, her tone heavy with concern, "particularly since you joined the army."

"I'll be fine, Mom. We aren't in the war yet," replied Carlton, hoping to calm her concerns.

"Let's have some schnapps and coffee," she suggested. I always have schnapps on Sunday. Your father and I had it every Sunday before you and I left."

She got up and walked to the kitchen before Carlton could stop her. He relaxed and waited for her to return. Once she made up her mind, there was no changing it. He thought about her response to his story. She was right, as was Maggie—the United States was not in this war yet. For a minute, he forgot his mission.

Carlton's mom came into the living room carrying a tray with a coffee pot, a bottle of schnapps, and cookies. She put the tray on the table.

"I went to the Polish bakery and bought some kolaches. They are apricot, strawberry, and prune. They are really tasty. Make sure you have one," she said.

With that, she opened the schnapps; poured some into two glasses, one for Carlton and one for herself, handed one to Carlton, and raised her glass.

"Prost!" she saluted.

"Prost!" he returned the salute.

As they ate the Polish cookies, they talked about Sara and the other children.

Then Carlton asked, "Have you heard anything from Germany?"

"I haven't heard much," she replied. "I had a letter from your Aunt Gretchen last month. She lives in Strasburg. She says that things have improved in Germany. Many people are working. Good food is available. The Jewish stores are closing, but Germans are taking over the bakeries, meat markets, clothing stores, and other types of stores. Most of the debts are gone, as the stores have been taken over by Germans. They don't know where the Jews are going, but there are fewer of them." She sighed. "Seems strange to me why the Jews are leaving. We had a lot of Jewish friends. They were wonderful people. They are generous, busy, and happy people."

"I don't know, Mom, where they could be going," Carlton replied. "I'll have to be heading home. Maggie will have dinner ready and want to get the kids in their baths and ready for school in the morning. I will have to be giving her a hand. Bye, Mom. I love you," Carlton added as he gave her a hug and a kiss.

"Bye, son. I love you too. Take care of yourself." She hugged and kissed Carlton on the cheek.

When Carlton arrived home, he ran up the steps and opened the door. "Hi everyone. I'm home from Oma's," he called out.

When he got no immediate response, he tried again. "Hi, everyone."

"Hi, Carlton," yelled Maggie. "I'm in the living room listening to the radio. They are talking about the war. The Germans are close to Moscow. The Russians have counterattacked. England has declared war on Finland, Hungary, and Romania. I wasn't aware they were enemies. I can't believe everything that is going on. The devastation must be horrendous. All the people that are dying and suffering, their lives completely overturned—it's terrible. Oh, Carlton, is the United States going to help? Are we going to get into this war? Why is this happening?"

Maggie sounded frustrated. "Maggie, what happened to you?" he asked. "Are you all right? What changed?"

"The radio broadcast was so vivid. With you leaving in the morning," she added, and he could hear fear in her voice, "I had never listened to it before like I did this afternoon. I've become so afraid that the United States will be joining this war."

"Maggie, I don't know what is happening," he told her. "None of us in the United States know what is going on. We are helping through Lend-Lease, but we are not in the shooting war. Hopefully, Congress will hold tight on this issue."

The news in early December was full of the war, but other items were also noted by the radio newsmen and the *Cleveland Press*. The New York Giants named Mel Ott as their player manager, replacing Bill Terry, the famous catcher. A gangster in Chicago named Louis Buchalter was sentence to death, along with his lieutenants, Emanuel Weiss and Louis Capone. This was big news to the American public. A new play—Patrick Hamilton's *Angel Street*—opened in New York. Sister Elizabeth Kenny's important medical treatment of infantile paralysis was approved. The announcer was very excited about this issue, noting that many thousands of people would benefit from this treatment. But the eyes and ears of most citizens of the United States were focused on the war. People were concerned about the future.

It was 2:00 p.m. when Maggie called dinner. Sammy Kay was on the radio. The kids, who were upstairs playing, came bounding down the stairs, shouting about how hungry they were. The food smelled wonderful. Maggie had done it again. Carlton sat down, and the family settled in for dinner. He said grace and passed the roast.

As the Sammy Kay Serenade was ending, a newscaster interrupted the network with the following announcement: "The Japs have bombed Pearl Harbor."

Carlton got up quickly and went to the radio. He changed the station to the CBS network, where John Daly had just interrupted CBS with the same announcement. The announcement came from the president's press secretary, Steve Early. He called the three-press hookup with the Associated Press, United Press, and the International News Service and read a short statement. "The Japs have attacked Pearl Harbor, and all military activities on Oahu Island are on alert."

"It has begun," said Carlton to his family.

The family was shocked. Although the networks resumed their normal programming throughout the day and evening, many programs were interrupted with more news, as it became clear that the Japanese had not only attacked Pearl Harbor but were also attacking the Philippians and Burma. Chaos was reigning on the networks, as stories of Manila being attacked were rescinded and Guam was attacked. Ships were being torpedoed; a black enemy ship was spotted off Oahu engaging our ships. British bases were being attacked. A lot of confusing and speculative information was passed over the airways. Radio shows were continually interrupted throughout the evening. The NBC Red Network interrupted *The Great Gildersleeve* five different times. Jack Benny was interrupted two times with a report that the Japanese had taken over the American company, Shanghai Power and Light. NBC Blue interrupted *Captain Flagg and Sergeant Quirt* twice, reporting that 104 personnel had been killed. NBC Blue interrupted *Bible Week* to announce that the Dutch East Indies and Costa Rica had declared war against Japan. The network also interrupted *The Dinah Shore Show* to announce that Canada had declared war against Japan. This rhetoric continued all night long.

What Carlton and Maggie had both hoped for did not happen. The United States was now at war—not with Germany but with Japan.

Maggie and Carlton took the children up for their baths and put them in their beds. Carlton read them a story. The children didn't understand what had been announced on the radio that day. Carlton tried to explain it in plain language. The Japanese dropped bombs on our ships at Pearl Harbor. They declared war on the United States. Daddy would be leaving for that war in the morning. They were surprised when he told them. When would he be coming home? When the war was over? They hoped that wouldn't be too long. They both hugged and kissed him. He tucked them in, kissed them both, and turned out the light. Thank God it was dark, because Carlton had tears in his eyes.

As he left the children's room, Maggie came out of their room, after putting Sara to sleep.

"Carlton, you're crying," she said.

"Yes I am, honey. It was difficult saying good-bye to the children."

He and Maggie had a quiet evening listening to the radio. The announcers from all the different radio stations speculated that the president would declare war on Japan tomorrow.

Carlton told Maggie he had an early train in the morning. He was going to New York to meet Major Best. He couldn't say more. Maggie already knew he couldn't tell her more.

They turned off the radio at eleven o'clock and went upstairs. They fell asleep in each other's arms. He fell asleep quickly. Maggie cried herself to sleep a bit later.

War Begins

$\mathcal{C}$ arlton was up early. He dressed quietly, as Maggie and the children were still sleeping. Sara was stirring in her crib. He looked out the window and saw his cab waiting. He and Maggie had said their good-byes the previous evening. He kissed her on the cheek, picked up his bag and envelope with his orders, and went down to catch the cab. Whether or not he liked it, he was in the war before the United States had declared one against Germany. He picked up breakfast at the restaurant in the Terminal Tower. The train left on time, and he was headed to New York City to pick up another one to Toronto, Ontario, Canada.

Maggie woke up at 7:00 a.m. She knew Carlton had already left. She woke the children to get them ready and off to school. The baby was crying. Maggie ran downstairs to get her a bottle. The house was always busy on school days. She put on the coffee, turned up the thermostat, added coal to the furnace, and headed back to the kitchen to make breakfast for the children.

She turned on the radio and found the news. The broadcaster was saying that President Roosevelt was going to make a speech to Congress and the nation today at 12:15 p.m. It would be carried on this station. She made a note to herself to call Oma and invite her over to listen to the speech with her. She fed the children; checked to make sure they had put on warm clothes; dressed them in their winter coats, gloves, and boots; and sent them outdoors to walk to school. She changed the baby, who'd made a mess in her diaper. She made sure the bottle was finished, put the baby in her swing in the kitchen, and had a second cup of coffee. She finally had time to think. Now that Carlton was gone, she had to make a list of things that had to be done daily, weekly, and monthly. It was going to be very busy for her with three children to take care of.

Oma did want to come over to listen to the president's speech, so Maggie went to pick her up. When they got home, Maggie fixed a simple lunch and then turned on the radio—it was time. The entire nation was glued to their radios to hear the president of the United States speak.

At 12:15 p.m., December 8, 1941, CBS News broadcast President Franklin Delano Roosevelt's speech before a joint session of Congress:

> Yesterday, December 7, 1941—a date which will live in infamy—the United States of America was suddenly and deliberately attacked by naval and air forces of the Empire of Japan.
>
> The United States was at peace with that nation and, at the solicitation of Japan, was still in conversation with its government and its emperor looking toward the maintenance of peace in the Pacific. Indeed, one hour after Japanese air squadrons had commenced bombing in Oahu, the Japanese ambassador to the United States and his colleague delivered to the secretary of state a formal reply to a recent American message. While this reply stated that it seemed useless to continue the existing diplomatic negotiations, it contained no threat or hint of war or armed attack.
>
> It will be recorded that the distance of Hawaii from Japan makes it obvious that the attack was deliberately planned many days or even weeks ago. During the intervening time the Japanese government had deliberately sought to deceive the Unite States by false statements and expressions of hope for continued peace.
>
> The attack yesterday on the Hawaiian Islands has caused severe damage to American naval and military forces. Very many American lives have been lost. In addition, American ships have been reported torpedoed on the high seas between San Francisco and Honolulu.
>
> Yesterday the Japanese government also launched an attack against Malaya.

Last night Japanese forces attacked Hong Kong.

Last night Japanese forces attacked the Philippine Islands.

Last night the Japanese attacked Midway Island.

Japan has, therefore, undertaken a surprise offensive extending throughout the Pacific area. The facts speak for themselves. The people of the United States have already formed their opinions and well understand the implications to the very life and safety of our nation.

As commander in chief of the Army and Navy I have directed that all measures be taken for our defense.

Always will we remember the character of the onslaught against us.

No matter how long it may take us to overcome this premeditated invasion, the American people in their righteous might will win through to absolute victory.

I believe that I interpret the will of the Congress and of the people when I assert that we will not only defend ourselves to the uttermost, but will make it very certain that this form of treachery shall never again endanger us.

Hostilities exist. There is no blinking at the fact that our people, our territory, and our interests are in grave danger.

With confidence in our armed forces, with the unbounding determination of our people, we will gain the inevitable triumph—so help us God.

I ask that the Congress declare that since the unprovoked and dastardly attack by Japan on Sunday, December 7th, 1941, a state of war has existed between the United States and the Japanese empire.

Following the resounding cheers and applause of Congress, the president left the joint session.

Maggie turned off the radio. "Well, Oma, what do you think?" she asked. "I wonder if Carlton heard the speech. Probably not, as his train for New York left at six thirty this morning."

"I think the president was mad," replied Oma. "A surprise attack by the Japanese. What happens now?"

The Mission Begins

The train was right on time as it pulled into Buffalo, New York. The passengers who were staying on the train were given thirty minutes to get out and stretch their legs. Carlton left the train to find the station in chaos. When he went to the newsstand to buy a paper, large headlines announced, "Japan Attacks Pearl Harbor."

Carlton bought two papers, the local Buffalo paper and the New York Paper. The stories he read said almost two thousand five hundred were dead. Most of the dead were Navy and Army personnel. Eight battleships had been sunk. Three cruisers had been sunk or damaged, and so had three destroyers. Almost two hundred US aircraft were destroyed. The papers couldn't accurately provide the numbers, as it was too early yet. Two Army Air Force bases, Hickman and Wheeler, had been destroyed along with the aircraft on the ground.

Carlton couldn't believe his eyes as he continued reading. The Japanese had also attacked the Philippians, Malaya, Singapore, and Hong Kong. An article in the New York paper announced that the President would speak to a joint session of Congress and the country via radio at 12:00 p.m. He thought to himself, *Damn. I'll miss his speech.*

As he reboarded the train, Carlton asked himself, what happens next? He headed to the club car. The conversation among the crowd focused on the attack on Pearl Harbor. Everyone was disappointed they wouldn't be able to hear the president's speech. And everyone was up in arms about "the yellow bastards," as one person in the car put it. People were pontificating about how the United States would "get them."

"I'm going to join the Navy." Were cries of some of the passengers.

"I'm going to join the Army Air Force and bomb them." Shouted an older gentleman full of emotion.

It sounded crazy to Carlton. He had already volunteered but couldn't say anything. He was traveling in secret. The train arrived at Grand Central Station at 5:00 p.m. Carlton left the train and looked for a redcap. He had to board a train to Toronto, Ontario. The redcap was familiar with the station and knew where the train to Toronto was located. It had just started boarding.

Carlton found the sleeping car porter, showed him his ticket, and was boarded. The sleeping quarters were comfortable. He was looking forward to dinner and a good night's sleep. He was to be met at the Royal York Hotel, given a secret code by his contact that Bruce gave him, and taken to a place Bruce called the "farm." Another surprise. He'd had many the last six months.

Carlton was awakened by the sleeping car porter calling breakfast in thirty minutes. He went to the bathroom, washed his face, and got dressed.

"What time will the train arrive in Toronto?" he asked the porter. "And what car is breakfast being served in?"

"At ten a.m., sir. Breakfast is being served three cars ahead of this one—in the dining car, sir," replied the porter.

"Thanks," he replied.

He packed his bag and headed to breakfast. *I had better enjoy a good breakfast*, he told himself. *I don't know what to expect at the "farm" later today.*

When the train arrived in Toronto, Carlton found a redcap on the station platform. The redcap took him to the taxi stop outside the station, where he waited, along with thirty others, for a taxi.

He found himself evaluating the other folks waiting for cabs. Who were they? What were they doing here? Were any of them going to the Farm? What were their agendas? The training he'd received in England was working. He noticed he was evaluating people wherever he was. It had become second nature. *That is good*, he thought, thinking of his mission.

The line went down, and Carlton finally caught his taxi to the Royal York Hotel. He checked his watch. He was about forty-five minutes early. He had been told his contact would pick him up at about 3:00 p.m. He had been told not to look for the contact: "They will find you and give you the password. Only at that time are you to go with the person. Your response to the contact is thank you, and the password is Apollo." Carlton was a little nervous about all this secrecy. He knew he had to get used to it. *Now is the time to practice*, he thought. He bought a newspaper and sat down in the lobby. He couldn't take his eyes off of the people in the lobby. It was a very busy place. A woman walked by him and tripped over his feet.

"Oh I'm sorry. I tripped over your feet. Clumsy of me," she said.

He jumped up and responded, "Oh no. It was me. I had my feet too far out in front of me. I know better than that. I apologize."

"Quite all right. Thank you for apologizing. I wasn't sure, Apollo," she added very quietly.

"Thank you," he said.

She went on down the lobby steps toward the outdoors.

He picked up his paper, fumbled around a bit, and followed after her, trying to be as inconspicuous as possible. Once he was out the door, he found her walking down the street. He followed her around the corner and returned the word. "Apollo."

The woman turned around and said, "Well, it took you long enough. I thought I was going to walk across town before you caught up to me."

Carlton looked at her. Before he could say a word, he recognized her. "Ann Basinger. Is this another test? What are you doing here? You are my contact? Oh my God, you people are devious, always testing."

"Hello, Carlton. It is good seeing you again. Yes, I'm your contact. The SIS asked me to participate here at the 'farm.' You were my first action. Let's get going. They are expecting you. You have a busy schedule ahead before you leave for England and your mission. My car is in a parking lot down the street." She reached out to hug him.

He hugged her back. "I can't believe it. Ann, it is you. It is so good seeing you again. Were you able to hear Roosevelt's speech? Do you know anything about my mission? Here we are on the street hugging and making a scene."

Ann responded, "Yes, I did have a chance to hear the speech. Your President Roosevelt gave one hell of a speech asking his Congress to declare war on Japan. He was somewhat emotional and very convincing. I figured that you probably didn't hear him, given you were on the train at the time. As for the other, I know very little about your mission. I'm sure the head of the staff at the Farm knows all about it. Your training here is based on your mission. Remember you had all the basics and then some in England."

"You're right," he said as they got into her car. "How far do we have to go? What do you know about this place? Who set it up? Who runs it? How is the food? What about the quarters? I know nothing."

"Slow down," she replied with a chuckle. "We have some time. We have somewhere between thirty and fifty miles to get there. I never checked the distance. The training base is located on an old farm on Lake Ontario between Whitby and Oshawa, Ontario, on the Old King's Highway 2. The British set the place up at the request of your Donovan and the Canadians, based on their training operation for the secret war. It is currently British operated—and on a top-secret basis.

"I have been here for a short period of time. I find the food very good. The quarters seem adequate but initially were built for men only. Now that I'm here, and for future women who will be working in the secret war, they have modified a part of the quarters to meet women's needs." Ann answered as best she could, as she understood his need for answers to his questions.

Access to the Farm was via a dirt road off of Canadian Route 2, Ann turned left onto the dirt road. The trees they passed had lost most of their leaves. As they drove down the road, Carlton noted the harvested fields. He wondered what was grown in them.

"It does look like a farm," he commented. "Look at the fields. The trees must have been beautiful this past fall. Fall here must be absolutely gorgeous."

As they left the fields, Ann and Carlton drove into an opening. They saw a group of buildings.

"There is the Farm. It is rather nondescript, isn't it?" said Ann. "Your home for the next weeks. I'll drop you off at the headquarters building. That's where you'll check in. Good luck. I'll see you around the Farm."

It certainly doesn't look fancy, Carlton thought. In fact, the place looked rather dreary.

He knocked on the door. Someone inside said, "Enter." He opened the door, walked into a room that apparently was an office, and was greeted by a man dressed in scrubs.

"Hello," the man said in an English accent, "Sargent Bliss here. Who might you be?"

"I'm Carlton Fuller, checking in," he answered.

"Glad to meet ya," Bliss replied. "The chief instructor wants to meet with you this evening at twenty hundred hours. That gives you time to get settled, get cleaned up, and get dinner. Your meeting will be here in this office. You are in barracks one. Go out the back door, first building on the right. Pick whatever bunk is available. By the way, your camp name is Carl. Introduce yourself as Carl. We don't use real names here."

"Thanks, Sargent Bliss. I'll be back at twenty hundred hours," said Carlton.

At twenty hundred hours, Carlton knocked at the office door. "Enter," came the voice from inside. Carlton opened the door and walked into the office.

"Welcome, Mr. Fuller. I'm Major Brooker, head instructor here at Camp X."

"Thank you, Major. Happy to meet you," said Carlton, adding, "Camp X? I never heard that name for this place. I have heard it called the Farm, but never called the Camp X. Did we meet in London? I'm not sure. I met so many people."

"Please sit, Carlton," Booker directed. "Camp X is the name I was told is the official name. But I have also heard 'the Farm' used as its name. I prefer Camp X. I don't think we met in London. But I, like you, met many people there. I am aware of your mission. I have set up a special syllabus for you. Here is a copy of it. It gives you the locations of the training and the instructor you will be working with. It will place a heavy emphasis on Germany, its language, the country itself, its customs, the Nazi Party, and the Nazis. It will also include parachuting, as you will be parachuting into France. We have added the underground, who and why. Finally, we will review killing techniques and sabotage. You should be here for about two weeks. It will be a very busy schedule. You will get Sundays off. But if you require additional practice at any skills, we will accommodate you. You will begin tomorrow with the German portion of your training. You will only speak German starting in the morning. You will be treated as a German colonel while in the German training. There is a German colonel's uniform at your bunk for you to wear during the first week. Practice who you will be. "Heil Hitler!" The major clicked his heel and gave the German salute.

The gesture took Carlton by surprise, but then he responded, "Heil

Hitler," saluted the German salute, clicked his heels, turned on his heel, and left the office.

A German colonel's uniform to wear during the first week? Someone must have just placed it in his bunk. *Everything is secret,* Carl thought. *These people are really prepared for me. For the first week, I will be Carl. After that, I don't know. What a setup. Ann did he say the training will be based on your mission?*

Two days after he started his actual training, on December 12, 1941, Hitler and his partner Mussolini declared war on the United States. The United States was at war with three countries—Japan, Germany, and Italy. The announcement was made during the lunch hour at the camp. Carlton, who was in his colonel's uniform, received many strange looks from camp personnel and the other participants being trained. All he could do was look at them rather sheepishly and continue on.

His trainers that first week spoke perfect German—both high and low. He was expected to speak high. It was difficult because he had to associate with others in his barracks. They didn't understand why he had to speak German all the time. As the week went on, they understood a little bit. He learned more about the Germans than he'd ever known. His army boot camp training helped him with the German discipline. The Nazis were not just evil; they were also determined. He read *Mien Kampf* to understand Hitler's philosophy. By the end of the week, much to his disdain, he was thinking like a German and acting like a German colonel.

On Sunday after breakfast, he was headed to the laundry when he ran into Ann. She was headed to the same place. They agreed to wash clothes together. It was a cold December day outdoors, so they planned to attend a movie at the theater. The movie playing was *Waterloo Bridge*, starring Vivian Leigh and Robert Taylor. It was a romance with a sad ending. Watching it gave Carlton a chance to immerse himself in something other than being a German. Ann enjoyed the film, as it took place in London. It was like going home for a while. It was a respite for both of them.

Following the movie, Carlton thanked Ann for spending most of the day with him. They parted and went back to their separate barracks. Carlton wasn't looking forward to the rest of his training. He would be starting parachute training and small arms practice and ending the week with killing. He would be catching a military flight to London after training on Friday. The weather that week was cold and wet. Carlton got through it without catching cold. He felt it was a miracle he didn't get pneumonia.

He became a sharpshooter with the German luger pistol and an expert in killing with his hands. His skills at Morse code and setting up and taking down radios and transmitters were second to none, according to his instructor. The head instructor pronounced him ready for his mission. This was the last training he would receive to prepare him for his mission. Ann Basinger was assigned to take him to Malton Airport outside of Toronto. The Americans had an aircraft waiting to pick him up and fly him to England for his final instructions before insertion. He and Ann had a lot to talk about on the way to the airport.

It was Christmas Day. He hoped he could call Maggie from the airport before he left. He knew she would be waiting to hear from him.

He and Ann learned a great deal about each other. Carlton liked Ann a lot. She had lost a husband in the war. Coming to Canada and the Farm helped her mentally, as it took her away from familiar places where she and her husband had shared moments. Carlton was missing Maggie, the children, and his mother. The ride gave them a chance to share their sorrows, and they grew to enjoy other's company. When they arrived at the airport, the good-byes were emotional. They both knew they probably would never see each other again. When Carlton took his bag out of the car and turned around, Ann was right there to hug him. She then kissed him with passion.

"So long, Yank. You have given me more than I could have ever expected. Although I don't know what you are going to do or where you are going, I wish you well, with love and longing. I'm crying now because I probably will never see you again. I don't want your good-byes, as the last time I said good-bye to my husband, I never saw him again. With you, I'm holding out hope. Good luck, Yank." With that, Ann turned, got into the car, and left.

Carlton thought, *I didn't say good-bye or anything. It's the way she wanted it.*

He walked into the terminal, and who was there? Major Best of all people.

"Hello, Carlton. How the hell are you? You are a sight for sore eyes. I find you in all the strange places, don't I? We need to get going. The plane is waiting, and we have a lot to talk about. By the way, you have lipstick on your mouth. Who was that beauty kissing you?" asked the major as they were walking out toward the plane.

"Hello, Major, how are you? I'm okay, a somewhat different person. She is a friend I met in England. One of my evaluators," replied Carlton. "Do you know where is the telephone here in the airport? It is Christmas Day. I want to call Maggie."

"I'm sure there is one here. Don't tell Maggie where you are. There it is, over there on the far wall. It looks as if there are three or four telephone booths," replied the Major.

Carlton ran over to the booths, stepped into one, and dialed zero for an operator. He hoped the lines between Malton and Cleveland were not busy, as he and Major Best had to leave soon. The operator told Carlton she would try to make a connection. Before she left the connection, he asked to reverse the charges. He did not have any change. She put him on hold. Five minutes later, she came back with his connection.

Maggie accepted the call, and they had a wonderful reunion on the phone. He talked to the children about Christmas, Santa Claus, and what he had brought them. Oma was there, and they talked for almost ten minutes. She was going to move in with Maggie while he was gone. He had tears in his eyes as he talked with Maggie, knowing he wouldn't be able to talk with her or his family again for who knows when.

Before he knew it, Major Best was giving him the high sign to say good-bye. It had almost been forty minutes, and they had to leave for England. Carlton and the family said their good-byes, and he reluctantly hung up the phone.

As they walked to the plane, Major Best explained that the aircraft was a Boeing 307. It had been leased from TWA for use by the military. Carlton and Major Best were the only two passengers. Carlton's was a secret mission, and Donovan wanted it to stay that way. Once airborne, the army attendant wished them Merry Christmas and brought box lunches to them. The pilot came back to explain his itinerary. They would fly to Newfoundland and, from there, to Iceland and then down to Biggin Hill Royal Air Force station outside of London. He explained that the final leg might be a little hairy, as the Germans were still bombing England. They may have to land at Prestwick, Scotland, if the Germans were bombing. After the pilot left, Major Best began to explain the details of Carlton's insertion into France. Carlton focused on what the major was saying. Major Best took a large map of France and Germany from his briefcase and spread it out on a table located in the first-class section of the aircraft. In addition, he pulled out a set of detailed orders to read.

"Carlton you need memorize as best you can what I'm going to say and show to you. The names and locations are important. You and I will be boarding an English Lancaster bomber on December 29—hopefully, it will be a cloudy night—from Biggin Hill Royal Air Force station at twenty-four hundred hours. The plane will join a group of Lancasters on a mission to bomb Berlin that night. As the group crosses the French coast, our aircraft will vector southwest toward Vichy. Vichy was picked because there are no Germans stationed in its area. The Free French underground is strong there. The English SIS has many trusted contacts located in Vichy. They have been using them to insert their agents in France. We will fly for three hours until we reach this point. You and I will get the green light to parachute at this point. The French underground will be waiting to meet us in a farmer's field at oh-three hundred to oh-three thirty on December 29. If we aren't there on the twenty-ninth, they will be waiting on the thirtieth.

"They will take us to the rendezvous point eighty miles away at the crossroads here on this map—the border of Vichy France and German-occupied France. The location is rural.

"Your brother will be making a trip to attend a meeting on the thirtieth with the German commander of a panzer division camped in this area. He was sent by Jodl to determine the mobility of the division should they be called to support Barbarossa. This information was provided by one of an English agent's underground espionage rings. It was verified by another agent located in the motor pool in Zossan, Germany, the headquarters of the Wehrmacht. Marcel is our point of contact from the underground.

"When we land, we are to bury our parachutes and travel north. Our contact's identity code is 'Horst.' Our response is, 'Lufft5.' Should we get intercepted by anyone other than Marcel and we or they do not receive the correct codes, it is shoot first. We would then be on our own, captured, or dead. No questions asked. We will work the details of Horst's demise and your transfer to his identity with the underground group. Do you understand the plan?" asked Major Best. "Please repeat it to me."

"Yes I understand the plan," said Carlton. He then went on to repeat the plan in every detail.

"Good. Your training taught you to focus, concentrate, and listen to details. I'm proud of you, Carlton. Maybe I should start calling you Horst," commented Major Best. "Let's get some sleep now, as once we arrive in London, we will be getting our equipment ready and meeting with SIS personnel for final instructions."

"Major Best, please don't start calling me Horst until we meet the partisans and make the transition. Then I will be Horst. Let's change the subject. What have you heard from Emily?" asked Carlton.

"I had a note from her before I left for Toronto. She is now in Sweden. The embassy in Berlin is closed. She and Mr. Harris were moved out of Germany to a hotel in Sweden when the Germans declared war on the United States. She doesn't know when they will leave. They are both doing fine and trying to do embassy business in Sweden. It is difficult for them, as the Gestapo is sneaking around continuously.

"She did say she'd had a letter from Hildegard before she left. The letter was smuggled in by the German underground. Hildegard has been miserable living with Horst since he and his friends murdered Sara. He comes home drunk and rapes her at least once every week. She wants to kill him. Their social life has picked up. She and Horst are visiting people and attending cocktail parties constantly. She attends clubs and the opera on a regular basis. She enjoys that but hates the rest. The cocktail parties at the Nazis houses make her ill. She is living on the edge. She indicated that she is getting to know Horst's peers and colleagues very well. She said to say hello to you and Maggie." The major added, "I'm going to get some sleep. Our first stop is Newfoundland to refuel."

"Please give me the orders to read. I want to commit them to memory. Then I will turn in," said Carlton in a serious tone of voice.

Having read and reread the detail for nearly two hours, Carlton fell asleep. After about four hours of flying, the attendant came into the cabin to advise Carlton and the major the plane was landing in Gander, Newfoundland. They would be refueling for about forty minutes and would immediately take off for Iceland. They would be able to deplane, take a walk, stretch, and reboard the aircraft.

After landing, they were airborne again in fifty minutes. *Very efficient*, thought Carlton. Both he and the major were still tired and were soon off to sleep again. The trip to Iceland would take about seven hours.

The plane landed in Iceland right on time. The flight attendant came into the cabin to advise Carlton and the major that they would have time to eat in the terminal, as the service team here would be fueling and checking the plane over. They would be leaving for London at 0830 hours.

As the two men left the plane, they found out why this place was called Iceland. The tarmac was covered with ice and snow. It was cold. Major Best estimated the temperature to be twenty degrees. Both almost slipped on the ice running into the terminal. They had a sumptuous breakfast, walked around the terminal, and headed back to the plane, again almost slipping on the ice. The plane left, taking the runway to the north. The wind was blowing about thirty knots, and the plane was bouncing around.

After climbing to nineteen thousand feet, the plane settled down to what the pilot called a mild chop. Major Best said to Carlton, "If this is mild, what is heavy?"

Carlton responded to the major with a laugh in his voice, "You look a little green around the ears, Major. Only another eight hours to go. I have been meaning to ask you, Major, why did Donovan send you with me for the start of my mission?"

"Good question, Carlton," replied Major Best, "He wanted you to have a partner on your jump into occupied France. From his perspective, you are irreplaceable. You are not expendable. You are too valuable. After all, you will be on Jodl's staff planning the Wehrmacht's moves for the next years to come. The United States doesn't have anyone on Jodl's staff. The information you send to the allies will be very valuable to the Allied war effort, don't you think?"

"Putting it that way, makes sense, doesn't it?" said Carlton

They continued to talk about the mission, covering a wide range of issues, including where to hide the radio, how and how often to move the radio, and how to use various codes when preparing messages to send. They all discussed the use of perception when dealing with people and situations, using common sense every day in dealing with the Nazis, and how to use *Mien Kampf* to Carlton's advantage. Although all they covered had been taught in the secret schools Carlton had attended over the past months, talking about these things with Major Best further embedded his training into his being. The time for his transition was getting close.

The only thing bothering Carlton was how he would be able to replace Horst in the Wehrmacht. He hadn't figured out that important piece of the puzzle yet.

The time flew by, and after what felt like only a few hours of flying, the pilot came into the cabin to announce they would be landing at Biggin Hill shortly.

When they landed, Carlton and Major Best went directly to SIS headquarters. They met the equipment manager and outfitted themselves with the necessary equipment for Carlton's insertion into occupied France—weapons, including a Tommy Gun and .45 pistol for the major and a German luger pistol for Carlton; ammunition for the weapons; maps of the insertion area and a compass; French and German money, killing knives for both; radio gear for Carlton; black jumpsuits, black face makeup, black gloves, black warm jackets, black boots, black wool stocking caps, and black backpacks; C rations and canteens; flashlights and goggles; long johns and wool socks; and a complete German full colonel's winter uniform and German ID card for Carlton and a French Vichy ID card for Major Best. Once they received and packed their equipment, they met with the director of the SIS to receive their final instructions.

The director explained the details of the insertion and pickup. "Once over spot A, the jumpmaster in the plane would light the red light. Upon the receipt of the red light, the jumpers would hook up their lines; upon approach of spot B, the jumpmaster would light the green light. Upon receipt of the green light, the jumpers would jump out the door of the aircraft one after the other. The jumpers should try to spot each other on the way down. If there was no moon, upon landing, the jumpers should rendezvous at point C on the map. To identify each other on the ground, they were to use the code word 'Lufft5.' If they heard the code word, they were to use 'Horst' as their response. "If you hear anything other than that, it is shoot first and ask questions later. The French underground people meeting you will have the details of your transition," the director concluded. "Good luck. Do you both understand?"

They responded in unison, "Yes, sir. Thank you, sir."

They all shook hands.

Carlton and Major Best were picked up in front of the building and taken to the plane waiting for them on the tarmac at Biggin Hill. Its engines were running. They were greeted by a crew member who introduced himself as the jumpmaster. Once the plane achieved the cruising altitude necessary to meet the air group the plane was joining, he explained the jump procedure. It mimicked the SIS explanation. It was a good review, Carlton thought. He was getting nervous, as he'd never jumped from a plane. All the Farm had had to learn to jump was a ninety-foot tower. Major Best told Carlton he should jump first, as he had jumped a number of times and felt he would be able to track Carlton easier than Carlton could track him. Carlton agreed wholeheartedly. The jumpmaster advised them it would take about three hours to reach insertion point. He suggested they get some sleep. It could be a long night. He expected the moon would be in and out of the clouds, which would make it easier to track one another on the way down.

They felt the plane veer to the south toward Vichy France and their jump point.

When the time came, they gathered their equipment. Carlton didn't think he could carry it all himself. Major Best took what Carlton couldn't. The jumpmaster signaled for them to put on their parachutes, get as comfortable as they could, hook up their jump straps, and check each other over to make sure they were ready. Carlton didn't want to, but he was curious. He had to ask. "Jumpmaster, how high are we going to jump from?"

"With the load you are each carrying, fifteen hundred feet," he answered and turned on the red light.

Carlton and the Major moved toward the open door. They felt the cold air. The green light came on, and Carlton jumped. As he did, he shouted, "Maggie," at the top of his voice. *Bang!* The chute opened, and all of a sudden, he was floating through the air. It was quiet. All he heard was the air in the canopy. He looked around for the major but couldn't see him. He looked down as the moon came out. He could only make out the trees and steered away from them toward an open area.

Before he knew it, he hit the ground and rolled to help absorb the impact on his body. He lay in the snow that covered the ground he'd landed on. It was very still. Then he heard another body hit the ground about fifty yards away from him to his right. It had to be Major Best. He gathered himself up, broke down his chute, and started to where he thought Major Best had landed. Sure enough, he found the major in a patch of what looked like blackberry bushes. Carlton had to hold his laughter.

"Major, are you all right?" he asked. "I did all right—just like they taught me at the Farm."

"I'm okay," the major replied, "just landed in a bunch of bushes with thorns. I now have holes in my jumpsuit. Help me out of here. We need to get out of here quickly. We have to get to high ground so we can cover our tracks. This snow will give us away if the Vichy French might be looking for us."

"We have to head north to meet our pickup group," the major said once he was free of the bushes. "Are you okay? Are you ready to go? Let's try to bury our chutes. It may be difficult, as the ground may be frozen."

"I'm ready to go," replied Carlton. "I think there's a pile of brush to our left where we can hide our chutes. I'll see it better once the moon comes out. There it is. Let's go."

The two men ran over to the pile of bushes, stuffed their chutes under them, and covered them with the bushes and snow. Major Best had his compass out and was finding the way north. The moon would provide them with some light as they made their way to the north.

The snow was frozen on top. No matter how they tried, they were not able to hide their trail. All they could hope for was fresh snow to cover their tracks. If they weren't picked up soon, any search party could find them easily.

They had trekked about three miles when they thought they saw someone moving about a quarter of a mile ahead in the moonlight. They immediately stopped and hunkered down in the snow, waiting to see what was going to happen. They heard someone walking toward them, whistling the French national anthem under his breath.

As the individual came closer, he said loudly, "Horst."

They couldn't believe it. Major Best said, "Lufft5."

The man ran forward and, in perfect English with a strong French accent, said, "Hello. Happy to see you. You two sure make noise. We saw and heard you about a half mile ahead of us. It is a good thing the Vichy are lazy and don't wake up until eight a.m. We are out here with the deer and wolves. The Vichy stay close to their cities. We have a lot to do before we intercept this German. My name is Marcel. I don't want to know your names. We have to travel fast. Let me help you with your equipment. The roads are very icy. We will have to be very careful driving in the wagon."

After an hour of difficult walking through the forest, the trio came to a road where a station wagon was parked. Carlton and the Major loaded their equipment into the back of the wagon and got in. It smelled of cigarette smoke and sweat. It was warm, which was all they cared about.

They were cold and damp. The heater was turned up to high. The driver put the car in gear and started moving up the road.

Marcel began, "I understand that one of you will be taking the place of the Nazi we will be killing tonight. That is very brave of you. We will hijack his limousine, kill him and his driver, and wreck the car. We will take his body and burn it. We will leave the driver on the ground, as if he was thrown out of the car during the accident. The limo will look like it skidded off the road and crashed into a tree. You will be in the backseat knocked out. When you awake, you won't be able to remember anything. It will take you about two to three weeks to start remembering who you are and what your role is. We will have to mess you up a little to make sure the Nazis understand you were in an accident. We will contact the Vichy and notify them of the accident. They will contact your boss, Jodl. Hopefully, he will take you back to Berlin for you to recover and get back to work. You will be able to go back to the Wehrmacht to meet every one the man you're replacing worked with. You not being able to remember will provide you with the time to catch up and fit right in. Obviously, there is risk in the plan. You remembering is the biggest risk. We have used this drug before. The person who took it worked out perfectly. Your part is to remember carefully. You will have to focus once you start to wake up. Do you think you can do it?"

"The plan is unbelievable," said Carlton. "I don't want to take a drug. I will have to act the role. You can mess me up and knock me out but no drug. When I wake up in the Vichy hospital, I will make a case to call Jodl, tell him the story, have him call my wife, and get me home. I then can determine when I return to work. I will tell him my memory is gone. Just make sure all this colonel's papers are with him. The Vichy will have to find out I work directly for Jodl."

"It is important that you take the drug. The Nazis are very leery of anything that is different from the normal for them," replied Marcel.

"Give me the drug," Carlton bargained. "I want to meet with Hildegard first. She is this colonel's wife. I know her personally. Whether I take the drug or not will depend on the response of Hildegard. All I ask of you, Marcel, is that you don't hit me too hard when you knock me out," said Carlton.

"This adds a great deal of risk to the mission, Carlton," said Major Best.

"I understand, Major. But I know me. All of the training I received over the last six months changed me into another person. I am very confident I can bring this mission to fruition. Both of you will have to trust me. If anything changes between now and the switch, I will let you both know. Please remember, this is my brother we are killing tonight. It is a difficult time for me. I fully understand the why and the reason for my mission. But he is my brother."

The conversation in the vehicle became very quiet. They had about thirty more miles to travel to the rendezvous point. The plan was set. When they reached the site, the vehicle they were traveling in was hidden among the trees off the road. Carlton and Major Best stayed in the vehicle. Marcel left and met with his group down the road and hid in the woods, waiting for Horst's car to arrive.

It wasn't twenty minutes later when they saw the headlights of a car coming down the highway toward the intersection. The intersection was a four-way stop. The car stopped at the intersection. What looked like a Vichy soldier walked up to the car and knocked on the window. The driver rolled down the window and exchanged some words with the soldier. All of a sudden, the driver and the passenger, a German colonel, came out of the car, both complaining loudly. There was a burst of weapons fire, and both the driver and German colonel were lying on the ground. Two more gunshots rang out. The French shot each one of the two on the ground one more time, to make sure they were both dead.

Carlton and the major ran down to the vehicle. The French checked the uniform of the dead colonel with the one Carlton was wearing. They were identical. Marcel commented, "You two are a perfect match. I now know why you are here."

They took the German car down the road a piece and came back at speed, swerving it into the woods. They laid the German driver on the street and pinned a note on his coat. The note said, "A gift to the Vichy. We will continue to kill until you are all gone. Viva la France."

Major Best hugged Carlton. "I wish you well in you mission. Your equipment will be delivered to Hildegard's house by the German underground. We will be in touch. Godspeed."

"Thank you, Major. Thank you, Marcel. I am now Colonel Horst Brausch. Heil Hitler." He gave the one-arm salute.

As Carlton was walking into the woods to get in the German car, Marcel hit him on the back of the head with his pistol. Carlton went down, bounced off of the car, and landed in the snow. The men from the underground picked him up and put him in the backseat. They slapped him around until they made his face bleed. After all, this was supposed to be real.

Marcel slipped his memory drug into Carlton's mouth, pushed Carlton down on the floor between the front and back seats, put two more bullets into the backseat, and left the scene. Carlton was on his own.

CRANSICION

Sirens were howling as police cars and an ambulance came down the country road. Marcel had reported the accident to the Vichy authorities. The police found the driver's body along the road. He had three bullets in his chest. They read the note pinned on the driver's coat.

"Those bastard underground," said the Vichy police officer. He folded the note and put it in his pocket. They found the car in the woods. It looked as if the driver had been thrown out of the car and the car had turned right and ran into the woods. The police searched the car.

"Here. Look in the backseat. There is a body on the floor," said the police officer. "Help me get the body out." He motioned to his colleague.

He opened the door, and before he could reach in to get the body, a bunch of papers flew out of the backseat into the snow. "Gather the papers," he shouted to the others standing outside in the woods. He got into the backseat and reached down to the body. His colleague reached through the door, and they lifted the body up and placed it on the seat.

"It's a German colonel. He is still breathing. Get the medics here quickly," the officer shouted at those outside the car.

The medics came running into the woods with a stretcher and their medical bags and equipment. They immediately started to work on the body. As they were checking Horst's blood pressure, he moaned.

"He's alive," said one of the medics. "Let's get him on the stretcher and into the ambulance so we can continue to check for injuries."

The officer in charge of the group agreed with the medics and told them to get the German colonel to the hospital. In the meantime, he was checking the papers that had flown out of the car. The papers identified the body as Colonel Horst Brausch. He was stationed at Wehrmacht Headquarters in Zossan, Germany. His orders indicated he was traveling to meet with the nearby German panzer group's commander in the morning. *I have to get word of this situation to both organizations quickly,* the officer told himself. *I have to alert my boss too. We are going to be overrun by Nazis wanting to investigate what happened.*

Jodl was awakened by his wife and told he had an emergency phone call. He thanked her and asked her to please make some coffee. He picked up the phone and said crisply, "This is Jodl. What is the emergency?"

He was shocked when he heard that Colonel Brausch's car had been attacked. He was relieved that Horst was still alive and being attended to by the Vichy. He learned that Horst was awake. He had an injury to his head and many scratches on his face. He should recover, but at this time remembered nothing that had happened. "He doesn't even know his name," the caller concluded.

"Thank you," said Jodl. "I want him transferred to the Charité hospital in Berlin as soon as he can be moved. Get this information to the Gestapo as soon as possible. I want a thorough investigation of this incident as quickly as possible."

He thought to himself, *Who knew Horst was going to meet the panzer commander in Vichy?* He didn't trust the Vichy at all. Anyone who would give up their country like they had and collaborate with the enemy couldn't be trusted. *I must get this information to Horst's wife, Hildegard, now.*

He opened his briefcase as his wife brought in coffee. "Thank you, dear. I'm sorry we were awoken this early in the morning."

"It's okay, dear. I know it is part of our job. The coffee is hot. Be careful drinking it," she said as sweetly as she could under the circumstances.

He found the number and dialed it.

The phone rang a few minutes before it was answered. "Hello. This is the Brausch residence," Hildegard answered.

"Good morning, Hildegard. This is General Jodl. Sorry to wake you up. Horst has been injured. He is alive. I have had him sent to the Charité hospital there in Berlin. He was on a mission for me, traveling to Vichy for a meeting. His car was attacked. His driver was killed, and the car ended up in the woods. He was injured but is still alive. They will be moving him today. I will be in touch with the hospital and let them know he is coming. Please meet him at the hospital," directed Jodl.

"Horst was in an accident," she responded. "Where? He is alive. He is coming to Charité hospital." Hildegard was almost in shock. "Thank you, General. I will be at the hospital when he gets there."

She finally woke up. *You bastard, Horst. It's too bad you are not dead,* she thought. *Be careful, Hildegard,* she reminds herself. *You have to be a grieving wife. Not good to show the truth in your relationship.*

The ambulance picked up Horst and immediately headed north to Berlin. It would be a long ride. The Vichy made sure that a doctor would be with the colonel until he was delivered to the Charité hospital. They didn't understand why the Germans wanted him in Berlin rather than in a Vichy hospital closer to the accident site. The doctor examined Horst and noted he had a nasty bump and bruise on the back of his head, in addition to a number of scratches on his face. Horst was still unconscious when they started the trip to Berlin. Soon after, he started to come to.

"Where am I?" were the first words spoken by the colonel. "Who are you? Where are we going? What is this vehicle? Who am I?" More questions.

The doctor tried to calm the colonel down. He explained the situation to the colonel. When he told the colonel his name, he couldn't understand the response. "Who is Horst Brausch?" replied the colonel. "I don't know him. I don't know my name. What happened to me?" he asked again.

The doctor was very concerned about the colonel's status. He gave the colonel a sedative to calm him down, as they had a number of hours to get to the hospital. The colonel fell off to sleep. The ambulance was again quiet, with the exception of the flashing red light and the periodic siren to clear traffic ahead of them.

When they arrived at the hospital and announced who they were, they had more help than they needed. Apparently, hospital personnel knew who they were and who the passenger was. They thanked the ambulance crew and invited the doctor into the hospital to enable the doctors at the hospital to get the latest information regarding the colonel's status.

The hospital doctors couldn't believe what the Vichy doctor told them. They immediately examined Horst. Horst was put in the high-level personnel section of the hospital. They then sedated Horst again, to enable him to rest and give the hospital time to evaluate the patient's situation. They also put Horst in constraints, should he awake and want to leave his room.

When Horst woke up, it was dark. He found that he couldn't move. His mind was spinning. *Where am I? How did I get here? What happened to me? What is my name?*

Maybe I am dreaming, he decided. *I'll go back to sleep, and maybe this will all go away.*

The questions continued to go around in his head. He heard a voice calling a name. "Horst, wake up. Horst, wake up." *Who is Horst?* he thought.

He opened his eyes. The first thing he saw was a woman with red hair standing over his bed, saying, "Horst, wake up."

His first response was, "Who is Horst? Who am I? What is going on here? What happened to me?"

The woman took his hand and replied, "You are Horst Brausch, colonel in the Wehrmacht. I am your wife, Hildegard. Don't you recognize me?"

"No. I don't recognize you," he snapped. "Who am I? What happened to me? I need answers."

Hildegard told Horst the story of what had happened to him.

"I don't remember a thing," he told her. "I don't even remember who I am. I appreciate you telling me my name and what happened to me. I don't know if I believe you. I am very frustrated. Who put me here? Why am I tied down in constraints?"

"General Jodl did. He is your boss at the Wehrmacht headquarters in Zossan. The hospital doctors did not want you to leave your bed. They want to fully examine you to determine what is wrong with you. They need to understand what is causing you not to remember anything," replied Hildegard. "I expect the doctors will be in to see you very soon."

"I hope so," replied Horst. "I need to understand what is going on with me."

A nurse entered the room. "How are you, Colonel Brausch?" she asked. "I have to take your vitals and blood for the labs to evaluate. Dr. VonGeert will be in soon to see you. He is a specialist in brain injuries. He should be able to diagnose your situation quickly. He has had a great deal of experience with war injuries. He understands you are a high priority patient."

"I'm frustrated and unhappy," said Horst. "I want to find out what happened to me and why I can't remember anything."

"I'm sorry to hear that," replied the nurse. "I'm sure the doctor will help you. Which arm would you like me to take your blood from?"

Horst gave her access to his right arm, and she went about her business very efficiently. "Thank you, Colonel. I'm sorry I interrupted you, Mrs. Brausch," the nurse said as she left the room.

As she left the room, in came the doctor. "Good morning, Mrs. Brausch. Good morning, Colonel Brausch. I'm Dr. VonGeert. I am a brain trauma specialist. Hopefully, I will be able to diagnose your situation and help get you to recovery. Mrs. Brausch, I will be asking a lot of questions and doing a physical exam of the colonel. You may want to leave for a while."

"Thank you, Doctor. I will. How long will it be until we know something?" asked Hildegard.

"Once I finish my work here and I receive the results of the blood tests, I will try to make a diagnosis based on our findings. Hopefully, no longer than a day or two. I understand the colonel is a high priority patient. I know that he is General Jodl's staff aid. I should be done here in about an hour."

Thank you, Doctor. Horst, I will return in about an hour," said Hildegard.

The doctor started with the physical examination first and then went on to ask the patient a complex set of questions. He completed his tests and told Horst, "Even though you don't know who you are, you are Horst Brausch. Your wife has identified you. That should give you something to think about while we analyze your blood. I expect I will have news for you and Mrs. Brausch tomorrow. I'm sorry I cannot tell you more. Talk with your wife about who you are and your life with her. I expect that General Jodl will come to visit you. He is your boss. He is well respected by Hitler and the Nazis. Have a good evening. I will see you tomorrow."

As the doctor was walking out of his room, Horst asked, "Who is Hitler? Who are the Nazis?" The drug that Marcel of the French underground had put in Carlton's mouth was doing its job.

Hildegard came back into the room. She and Horst continued the discussion about who he was and the life he led. She was very frustrated, as Horst couldn't remember anything. After spending two hours discussing the same thing over and over, she told Horst she was going home and would see him in the morning. All he could say was, "I'm sorry, I am as frustrated as you."

Horst couldn't understand what had happened to him. Hildegard had explained that she was his wife. She had explained who he was, but he just couldn't remember anything.

Late that evening, Dr. VonGeert came into Horst's room. "Well, I believe I have diagnosed your problem," he told Horst. "I'm sorry it took so long. The lab wanted to make sure of the analysis. You have a case of amnesia. It was probably brought on by the head trauma you incurred in the automobile accident when you were attacked by the French underground. The amnesia, I believe, was enhanced by the drug scopolamine, which I believe was given to you by the French underground. Traces of this drug were found in your blood during the labs analysis. I have seen this in the past in spies we have captured. The French underground thinks that the amnesia will last for a long period of time. We have found that, once the drug is out of your system, your memory will begin to come back over a period of time. The time period varies by individual. It takes personal care by family to help get a person back to normal. Therefore, I am releasing you to go home with your wife and begin therapy with her. I have discussed this with General Jodl. He understands the situation but wants you to return to work as soon as possible. He knows it will take time for you to reestablish yourself in the office. He is happy that you will recover. Do you have any questions?"

Horst was taken aback by the doctor's diagnosis. "I'm shocked that the underground would use drugs. They could have killed me. I will get them for what they have done to me. When will I be able to leave?"

"I have advised your wife of my diagnosis. She will pick you up in the morning. Have a good night and sleep well. Part of your recovery will be helped by sound sleep. I have told the nurse to remove your restraints. I provided a sleep drug for you. Good night," said the doctor as he left the room.

Horst felt somewhat relieved. He would recover with help from his wife and being in what would be familiar surroundings. He would be going back to work in the location where he had worked before. The nurse came in and gave Horst his sleep drug. It wasn't very long until he was asleep. There were no dreams, just sound sleep.

He was awakened by Hildegard the following morning at about 10:00 a.m.

"Wake up, Horst," said Hildegard. "I'm here to pick you up and take you home. They will bring you breakfast, the doctor will check you over, and we will go home."

He was dressed in the clothes he had been wearing when the Vichy had brought him to the hospital. They had his blood all over them. Horst looked at the clothes. He was wearing the uniform of a full colonel in the German Wehrmacht. He felt comfortable in the clothes, but he didn't know their meaning.

He commented to Hildegard that there was much damage to the buildings they were passing on the way home. She commented that the British had continued to bomb different areas of Berlin. She was unhappy with the Luftwaffe for not being able to protect the homeland from the British. This sounded familiar to Horst, but he couldn't remember why.

They finally arrived at their home. It looked familiar to Horst, but again, he couldn't remember why. His therapy had begun.

Hildegard spent all her hours with Horst. She went over pictures of their lives together. Every day, she took him on rides through Berlin, reacquainting him with the city. After three weeks of this and much frustration on her part, she took him to his father's grave.

"Hildegard, I remember the day we buried my father." cried Horst. "There was a parade all of the Nazi dignitaries attended. I can't believe it; I remembered. Things are starting to come to mind—people, places, you. My God, I'm starting to remember. I would like to go home. I would like to go to work tomorrow."

Hildegard was shocked. He was remembering, a blessing in disguise. *Will he become his old self—a drunken, cruel Nazi? The same man who raped me at his will? The same man who killed Sara?* "I'm so happy, Horst," she said. "Let's go home and continue to remember your past."

As they drove home, Horst began to ramble about memories from his youth. Hildegard heard stories she had never heard before—stories of how he and his brother had played together and of the outings they had gone on with their mother. He began to cry. She was flabbergasted. She couldn't stop him from talking.

He needs a nap, she thought. *He will be very tired form all this talking.*

When they got home, she took Horst into the house, warmed some milk for him, and sat down with him in the library.

"Horst, please drink the milk I warmed for you. I think it would be a good time to take a nap. You have had a day of awakening from the amnesia," she said.

"I'm feeling very good now that I have started to remember. Thank you, Hildegard, for putting up with me. I'm sure your patience is about worn out. I will take a nap. This has been a busy day, hasn't it?" Horst said as he drank the milk and lay down on the couch.

He fell into a deep sleep. He began to dream. *Who am I?* he thought. He was dreaming about Maggie, his children, his mission, and all of the events that brought him here. He knew his name; it was Carlton Fuller. He had replaced his brother, Horst, as an American spy undercover in Jodl's headquarters. He was living with Hildegard. She did not recognize him yet. *I must continue not remembering all, as I need to learn the role and function Horst had in Jodl's operation. Hopefully, we can start that soon.* He awoke with a start.

"Hildegard, where am I? What is happening to me? Where have I been?" he asked a bit groggily.

"Horst you have been sleeping. You have started to remember. It is wonderful isn't it, Horst? You are coming back to reality. The doctor said you would. I'm so happy for you. I know General Jodl will be too. We can start you back to work early next week.

"I will try to provide you with more information about your current life before you return to the Nazis," Hildegard added sadly.

"How will I get to my job?" Horst asked Hildegard.

"I contacted General Jodl's office and asked them to pick you up and bring you back daily until you can manage the trip yourself," she replied. "The general agreed to do that. He is anxious for you to return to work. He told me you are a valuable asset."

"Did he say when I could start? I'm looking forward to meeting him. I don't remember anything about him or what he does. I know you told me he is the Wehrmacht. What is the Wehrmacht?" Horst asked.

Hildegard went on to explain as much as she knew about General Jodl and the Wehrmacht. Carlton felt he was ready to meet Jodl again—this time in his role as Horst. He knew he had to be careful as to how he acted and what he said. If he was to be successful in his deep cover role, he could take nothing for granted. He wondered when his radio equipment would be delivered. He couldn't communicate without it.

His mind was spinning. *What role will Hildegard play? What will be our relationship?* he wondered. *One step at a time,* he cautioned himself. He had to have a discussion with Hildegard. It was getting on toward dinner. They always drank wine before dinner. He decided to test Hildegard tonight.

"Hildegard, what wine will we be drinking before dinner tonight?" he asked.

"What would you like Horst?" she asked. "We have all kinds of whites or reds."

"Let's have a cabernet. We can celebrate my coming home and our victory in France. We can toast the Vichy for finding me and saving my life. We can celebrate our marriage and our loving relationship," he said, thinking that should get her emotions started. It did.

"Good, a great red wine," she replied. She was so upset, she said, "You want me to celebrate our marriage, our loving relationship? What are you, crazy? We haven't had a marriage for years. Instead of making love, you rape me. You killed my servant Sara. You have taken me for granted for so long I can't remember when I stopped loving you. I have been hanging on as your wife to survive the war you Nazis began.

"Yes, let's celebrate," she yelled at the top of her voice and slapped Horst in the face. "oh my God what did I do. I apologize Horst, please don't hurt me." She was shaking visibly.

It worked, Carlton thought to himself. *She believes I'm Horst. It is time to be a different Horst and see how she reacts.*

"Hildegard, please settle down," he replied. "You needn't apologize. I'm not the same Horst I was before this all happened. I don't know what happened, but I don't remember any of what you just said. Please understand. If I treated, you wrong, all I can do is apologize. I am a different person. I don't know what to believe anymore. What can I do to convince you that I'm not the same Horst? Here. Take this glass of wine and let's drink to the new Horst."

She took the glass and threw the wine in his face. "A new and different Horst. You apologize for all these years—for your drinking, killing Jews, whoring around, raping me instead of making love to me, acting like Hitler. You no-good bastard. I should forgive you. Let's drink to the new Horst. Give me the bottle. I'll drink." She drained the almost full bottle of wine and then said, "Give me another bottle, and I will drink it too."

Carlton went to the wine cellar and found another bottle of cabernet. He went back upstairs and handed it to her.

Hildegard looked at him strangely as he handed her the open bottle. She took another long drink. "Here is the bottle, Horst. You drink it."

Carlton drank the full bottle. When he finished, he couldn't stand up. Hildegard had already passed out in the chair. They never went to the dinner table that night.

The servants found them both passed out in the library and wondered what had happened

About four in the morning, Carlton woke up. He tried to stand up and almost fell. He steadied himself and found Hildegard sleeping in the chair. He walked over, picked her up, and took her up to her bedroom. He found her nightgown on the bed. She stirred as he began to undress her. His intentions were to put on her nightgown and let her sleep. As he took off her clothes, he couldn't not see how beautiful she was for a woman her age—a true redhead.

As he laid her down, she reached up and put her arms around him. "Horst, I love you. Make love to me," she said, now wide awake.

"I love you too," he replied. Carlton was feeling guilty. He had to give himself a chance to think. *What do I do?* he asked himself. He reviewed his morality in those few seconds. I must fulfill my mission. I believe Maggie would understand. He reached down to Hildegard and kissed her deeply. They made love as they had never made love in their lives. They slept in each other's arms in Hildegard's bedroom.

Hildegard awoke first.

She found herself and Horst naked. *Oh my God. What happened last night?* she asked herself. *This isn't the Horst I know. What do I do now?*

Carlton woke up and saw Hildegard standing over him naked as a jaybird, with a strange look on her face. He looked down at himself and saw that he was naked too. "Hildegard, what happened last night? Do you remember? I know we had a loud argument and drank some wine. How did we get up here?" he asked as he covered himself with a blanket.

"I have no idea," she said as she put on her robe. "Did we make love or did you rape me again? No I don't think so. I dreamt we made love for the first time. We have a lot to talk about. Let's go down and have breakfast. You are not the same Horst I know."

"Yes, we have a great deal to talk about. Last night was a test for both of us. Breakfast sounds wonderful, as we didn't have dinner last night.

I'll take a shower and meet you in the dining room. I'm sure the servants will have questions," replied Carlton.

They ate breakfast in almost silence. The servants served breakfast, and the wife asked Hildegard what had happened last night. No one had eaten dinner. Hildegard told the servants that they'd both drank too much wine and had gone to bed early. She apologized that she hadn't let them know to not serve dinner. They accepted her apology.

Carlton wanted to speak to Hildegard in private. After breakfast, they retired to the library and shut the door. They checked the room for listening devices. Every lamp, every nook and cranny was checked by Carlton. He felt assured that the room was secure.

"Hildegard, I am not the Horst you were married to," he began. "I am his brother, Carlton. I am on a mission for the United States to infiltrate the Wehrmacht, replacing Horst and passing information to the Allies in the endeavor to defeat the Nazis and eliminate Hitler."

Hildegard's face turned from pleasant to incredulous. "You what? Where is Horst? How did you accomplish getting here? Taking Horst's place and treating me as your wife. I'm shocked to say the least. What do you expect me to do?" She slapped his face so hard it stung. "Will you kill me while accomplishing your mission? I need a glass of wine."

Rubbing his face, Carlton found what was left of the wine from last night, poured a glass for Hildegard, and told his story to Hildegard. His goal was to get her complete understanding of his mission. He needed her for cover, as well as help to accomplish his mission. He assured her he was not here to kill her.

Hildegard was in total shock as he provided the details of his journey to date. She broke down when he explained the death of Horst and his transition. She apologized for slapping him. She needed to understand what her role would be. She reiterated her hatred for the Nazis. How would they live together? Last night was an anomaly. She did not know if that relationship could continue. She did agree to work with Carlton and help him fulfill his mission. They would work together to defeat the Nazis and Hitler. She wanted to get back to her life before the war. Their focus now would be to get Carlton back to the Wehrmacht and integrate him as Horst. She would be his dutiful wife. He would protect her and treat her respectfully as his wife. There were a great deal of tears and disbelief that Carlton had agreed that his brother would be murdered and that he would replace him, particularly given his and Maggie's visit to Germany.

It was a long morning for both of them. It was a difficult acceptance by Hildegard. In the end, she assured Carlton of her loyalty to him and her commitment to defeat the Nazis and Hitler. It was the beginning of a new relationship for both of them.

Deep Cover

⸻⸻⸻⸻⸻

*C*arlton (Horst) and Hildegard spent a great deal of time that weekend discussing their new relationship. The first people they had to convince of the change between them were the servants. That would be difficult, as they had seen the strain between Horst and Hildegard over the past years. They would use Horst's lack of memory as the catalyst for getting the servants to accept the change. Hildegard would work out the details of how that would happen.

Carlton reviewed Horst's wardrobe. He made sure all of the uniforms and clothing fit him. He would be wearing a uniform daily on the job. He had to dress perfectly, as Jodl was always dressed impeccably. That was the first step. He had a lot to learn and many people to develop relationships with of over the next month's inside the Wehrmacht headquarters.

On Monday morning, his first day at the Wehrmacht headquarters, he and Hildegard awoke early. She checked out his dress uniform and concluded that it was perfect. They had breakfast together while they waited for the car that would arrive to pick up Horst. Hildegard and Carlton hugged, and she kissed him on the cheek. She reminded him that he was Colonel Horst Brausch and didn't remember very much about the people and the job within the Wehrmacht. She also reminded him of the Nazi salute. He nodded in agreement, kissed her on the cheek, and left the house.

The driver was waiting for him. He saluted the Nazi salute and said very firmly, "Good morning, Colonel Brausch. Welcome back."

Horst responded in kind. He settled into the car. He was on his way. The deep cover had begun.

When they arrived at Zossan, General Jodl was waiting for them at the entrance to the building. He welcomed Horst with a salute. Horst was overwhelmed that the general would take the time to welcome him back. He played his role to the hilt. He didn't remember much. The general had a staff meeting as soon as they reached his office.

As Horst and General Jodl entered his office, three of his staff stood up and saluted General Jodl.

"I know you knew these gentlemen before your accident," said General Jodl. "Do you recognize any of them or what their roles are now?"

"I'm sorry, sir, but I don't," replied Horst.

Jodl introduced them to Horst. "This is Major General Walter Warlimont. His group ensures all details of operational planning are worked out and all operational orders are communicated to the OKW. This is Major General Hasso von Wedel. His group is responsible for troops propaganda. This is General Walther Buhle. He heads the army staff. The fourth member of my staff is you. You are my chief of staff."

They all shook hands. "I look forward to working with you all. I look forward to meeting with each one of you to renew my knowledge of your operation and meet your staff members," said Horst. He set up meeting days and times with each one of the generals, beginning with Walter Warlimont that afternoon. It was late afternoon before they finished.

Horst was getting tired and was ready to go home. It had been a good day. He had learned a lot about what was happening on the Russian front. He noted a feeling of concern from the group he talked to. They indicated that the objectives set out for the Wehrmacht were not achieved. Although Leningrad was still under siege, Moscow was not under German control. Fall had brought rains, which had muddied the roads and bogged down the German tanks and supply vehicles. Winter had followed and stopped any advance the army was making. On the other hand, Rommel in Africa was holding his own and advancing.

His talks with the other groups, in particular the troop propaganda organization, indicated organization frustration. The troops on the Russian front hadn't received enough winter clothing. They were suffering from frostbite and hypothermia. Over a hundred thousand horses had died, and the dead horses fed the hungry troops. The Russians have started a counteroffensive and were pushing the Germans backward.

The German generals had asked Hitler to fall back and regroup. He'd flatly denied them. Morale was very poor on this front. Rommel had met with Hitler and asked for more troops. Hitler, being caught up with the Russian endeavor, wasn't interested but had provided a panzer group out of Italy for Rommel. Rommel had left very frustrated. Thinking like Horst, Carlton agreed with the propaganda the Germans were putting out at home. Things were not as bad as he knew they were. Thinking like Carlton, he knew the suffering the German soldiers were enduring at the Russian front. If only the allies knew the truth. He had to get this information to them. It would be the first information he would provide.

As he arrived home that Friday of his first week, the air raid sirens sounded. He dismissed the driver and rushed into the house to find Hildegard and the servants heading to the basement air raid shelter. He had not even known it existed. Thank heavens he caught them on the way down the stairs. He hugged Hildegard, acknowledged the servants, and headed down the steps. The servants responded and gave him a strange look. They were thinking, *Is this the same Horst we knew? Something is different. We will have to discuss this with Hildegard.*

The bombs were exploding very close. They could hear them coming closer to the house. All of a sudden, it sounded as if one hit in the front yard. "Oh my God," said Hildegard. "They will hit us. Hopefully the shelter will protect us."

"We will be okay," replied Horst. "The next one will hit farther away."

Sure enough, the next bomb exploded farther down the street. Horst went on to explain the patterns of bombs to Hildegard and the servants. The all clear finally sounded, and they all went upstairs for dinner. When they reached the front hallway, they found a large backpack left in the foyer.

Horst checked it out. "Don't touch it," he said to Hildegard and the servants. "I will open it up later. It might be booby trapped." Horst knew exactly what it was. The underground, under the cover of the bombing, had delivered his radio equipment. He would share the knowledge of the equipment and how it operated with Hildegard later that night. Now he could communicate with the allies.

He and Hildegard went to the front door and opened it to see what damage, if any, the bombing had caused.

"Horst, look at the yard. It's destroyed. We were very lucky the bomb didn't hit the house. The British are trying to intimidate the population, aren't they?" she asked.

"Yes, I'm sure. Thank heavens we weren't hit directly. Look at that crater the bomb made," he replied. He thought to himself, *What will happen when the Americans get into this war? They will bomb us flat.*

That night, Horst opened the backpack. Sure enough, it was his radio gear, codebooks, and instructions. He had used this type of equipment at the Farm as part of his training. He called in Hildegard to show her the gear and started to train her on its use. She was fascinated by the equipment but even more so by the codes. He stretched out the long wire antenna in their bedroom and coded his first message, which covered the Russian front issues. He turned on the transmitter and receiver. He sent his message signed off, "Arc Angel."

In a staff meeting on March 16, Jodl announced that Hitler, in a speech in Berlin, had said the Russians would be defeated that spring. He'd blamed the early winter for the halt of the German offensive in Russia. The Troop Morale group published the losses suffered by the German Army at the Russian front from January to March— 52,000 killed and 15,000 missing. Horst had heard other numbers of loss ranging to 1.5 million killed, missing, or suffering frostbite and other weather-related travesties. He continued to pass information to the Allies.

He sent this message: Hitler orders Luftwaffe to recall two bomber groups from Sicily to raid historic cities in England in retaliation for a British bomber raid on the city of Lubeck.

Horst settled into a routine at Zossan. He had started to drive Hildegard's car to his office. He spent a number of nights each week sleeping in his office. This restricted Hildegard, and she discusses the issue with Horst. He made arrangements to use an official car for his transportation. The relationship between Horst and Hildegard had improved, to the point that Horst shared everything with her. She in turn treated him like her lover. She was like a new person. Her friends had noticed the difference in her. She told Horst how she felt. He was a little taken aback. He warned her to be less obvious about their relationship. He didn't want his boss and peers to become suspicious. He suggested that he could go back and become the old Horst. When she heard this, she slapped him again, became distraught, and began to cry. Horst was satisfied he'd made his point.

In April, Horst and Jodl traveled to Berlin to listen to Hitler speak to the Reichstag. He blamed their failure to overcome Russia on the worst winter in 140 years in Russia. But he saw new victories with the coming of spring. He threatened to shoot anyone who was not committed to victory in Russia. Jodl and Horst know the reality of the Russian front from reports received by the troop propaganda group. It caused Horst to wonder about Jodls attitude toward Hitler to hear him talk about reality and Hitler's ranting. On the trip back to Zossan, they discussed the issues in depth. Jodl assured Horst of his loyalty to Hitler. But he wondered about Hitler's delusions.

Horst was tired when he came home from the trip to Berlin. He and Hildegard had a quiet dinner. They went to the library to have a glass of wine before retiring.

"Horst, we had some visitors this afternoon. It was the Gestapo. They explained to me that someone in the area was transmitting messages. They know who you are and wanted us to be aware of "the problem," as they described it. Any help or knowledge we may have would help them. They treated me with respect. I listened to them and acknowledged their request. They were here about ten minutes and left."

"You are kidding. The Gestapo. Once they start, they are like dogs on a scent. We have to be very careful. Is there someplace else we can transmit from? How about the car? Do you have any friends in the German underground that you trust? The Gestapo must have a truck that listens across a band of frequencies for transmissions. They can pinpoint a location that a transmission is emanating from. If we get caught, we are dead." Horst took a drink from his glass of wine. "We have to move the equipment quickly. If they even suppose the signal is coming from here, they will search the house. They will just crash the door and barge in."

"I still have the deed to your father's old house. Horst was going to sell it. But he didn't. We can try there. We could use it as an alternate location—send from there periodically and then from here periodically," Hildegard suggested.

"What a great idea," Horst said. "Let's go and visit this weekend. I always wanted to see my father's house. Maybe we can ship more of Mother's old things. I'm getting tired," he added. "I'm going up."

"I'm coming with you," replied Hildegard. "Those Gestapo people scared me."

That night, they slept in each other's arms.

⠀ⅯⅇⅾⅈⅽⅇⓇⓇⒶⓃⓔⒶⓃ

MEDITERRANEAN

orst was aware that a great deal of activity was going on in the island nation of Malta. Heavy bombing had been continuing. Axis aircraft controlled the skies. Many British aircraft had been destroyed. A plan, "Operation C3," had been developed, and Mussolini was anxious to invade the islands of Malta. Hitler refused to order the go-ahead and allow him to implement the plan, as he was obsessed with the Russian front. Axis aircraft continued to attack naval bases on Malta and virtually destroyed most military bases on the islands. British and Axis aircraft continued to fight in the air over Malta. Many aircraft were lost by both sides.

Horst and Hildegard were transmitting to the allies almost every night. In order to stymy the Nazi tracking trucks, they had been using Horst's fathers house as an alternate site for their transmissions. Following Hildegard's suggestion, they alternated between the two houses, using a different coding scheme at each location in order to keep the Gestapo guessing.

Jodl received a message from Berlin: The German commander in chief of the Southern front had completely neutralized Malta. Horst was asked to distribute the message to the propaganda group for distribution to the field. He also sent the message to the Allies.

Hildegard was getting concerned about the frequency of their expressions. She'd had another visit from the Gestapo. She was uncomfortable talking with them and as afraid they would want to search the house. "They always seem to visit when you are not here," she told Horst. "I'm scared. Can't we slow down on sending messages to the Allies?"

"There is too much going on," he replied. "The orders are flying out every day. They are going to the Russian front, to Rommel in the desert, to Mussolini, and to panzer commanders. It seems like something is constantly happening that the Allies need to know about."

"I don't want us to be caught," said Hildegard. "They will shoot first and ask questions later. Please, Horst, let's stop for a while," she pleaded.

"Hildegard, do you have any contacts with the underground?" asked Horst.

"My friend Angel talks about the underground when I'm with her. I don't know if she is testing me or really has knowledge about them and has contacts within the organization. She talks as if she does. How about you, Horst? Do you have contacts in the underground?"

"Only in the French organization," he said. "Why don't you test your friend Angel and see what she says. If she has contacts, we might be able to get information to the Allies via the underground."

"I will test her next week. We are having tea with a number of women we know. I will ask her when we are alone in the car," Hildegard agreed, adding. "I know you will be at Zossan for a few days next week. I know the ride back and forth is trying. Where do you live when you stay there for a few nights?"

"Be careful when you talk with Angel," Horst cautioned. "I normally sleep in my office, take showers in the men's locker room, and eat in the cafeteria in the building. It's not too bad. Many of the officers do the same thing. Jodl is a tough taskmaster."

Orders were issued for the Wehrmacht to counterattack the Russians at Kharkov. Reports of a great victory at Kharkov for the Wehrmacht came to Jodl via Berlin. When the victory was announced at Zossan, a great cheer went up. The victory was the first good news from the Eastern Front since the counterattack by the Russians. Jodl received the bad news that the city of Cologne had been virtually destroyed by British bombers.

Near the end of May 1942, Horst found himself thinking that the news was good and bad for both the Allies and the Germans. Rommel was having success in the desert working his way toward Tobruk. The Eastern Front was not as bad as reported, although the losses of men, horses, and equipment were very high. Hitler was still focused on victory in Russia. He had made Russia his highest priority. He didn't want to hear of need by anyone else. Horst believed it was a personal issue for Hitler. He believed that was good for the Allies.

Reichsprotecktor Reinhard Heydrich was assassinated in Prague, Czechoslovakia, where he was on a special assignment for Hitler. The Germans made sure the Czechs paid a high price for the loss. Horst felt very sorry for the Czechs but was overjoyed that Heydrich had been assassinated. It was a victory for the allies. He and Hildegard celebrated with a great dinner and a bottle of wine.

The English radio center was getting concerned, as nothing had come in from Arc Angel for over three weeks. Speculation was running high that something may have happened to Arc Angel. The allies knew that the Gestapo had tracking vans to find spies who were transmitting information to them. They were aware that the Gestapo killed spies almost immediately when they were found.

Horst intercepted a message from Berlin: Rommel reported that he had defeated the British Eighth Army in the desert and was very close to the border of Tobruk. Another victory for the Axis powers. He passed the message to Jodl, who smiled when he read it.

"General Rommel, what a soldier, what a leader, what a German," Jodl said. "Let's salute him with a glass of wine, Horst." He reached into his cabinet for the wine and glasses. They saluted and said, "Heil Hitler."

Horst determined that it was important for the Allies to hear about Rommel's victory in the desert. He went home that evening, and after he had dinner with Hildegard they headed to Horst's father's house to transmit the message. As they approached the house, they noticed a Gestapo tracking van parked in front of a local café. They stopped and listened. There was a lot of noise and singing coming from the café. Horst stopped the car, told Hildegard to go on to the house and get set up to transmit, and walked into the café. It was full of soldiers, women, and local citizens, all who were having a great time drinking and singing. Horst looked around, and sure enough, he picked out the Gestapo trackers. They were drinking with a group of women. They looked rather drunk. When they saw Horst, they dumped the women on their laps on the floor, stood at attention, and gave the one-armed salute. The noise and singing stopped.

Horst saluted back, went over to the piano player of the band, and told him to play "Lili Marleen." The player began the opening. Horst sang out loud the only words he knew to the song, the first verse, in the hope that everyone in the café would sing:

Vor der Kaserne
Bie dem großen Tor
Stand eine Lanterne
Und steht sie noch davor
So wollen wir uns
Wieder sehn
Bei der Lanterne Wollen
Wir steh'n
Wie einst Lili Marleen

By the time Horst was in the middle of the first verse, the entire café was up and singing with arms around shoulders. Horst finished the first verse and left the café through the side door. The second verse of the song wafted out the windows and the doors. Horst walked down the street singing to his father's house. He went in and asked Hildegard if all was ready to send.

"Yes it is," she said.

"Thank you, Hildegard, for setting the equipment up. That was a close one. I'm glad we spotted the Gestapo van. The Gestapo soldiers were in the café drinking and messing with some women."

Horst took the time to code his message, signaled the Allies, sent his message, and signed in code Arc Angel. They packed up quickly and left for home. As the drove past the café, the Gestapo personnel were staggering out the door. Horst stopped the car, opened his window, saluted the soldiers, and gave them a "Heil Hitler." They almost fell over when they saw he was a colonel.

The Allies were pleased to receive communications again from Arc Angel. It was a great relief to know Arc Angel was alive and well.

The Gestapo was not happy, as one of its vans had picked up Arc Angel's message related to Rommel's success in Africa and the Heydrich assassination. That information was very current and had not been distributed to anyone in the German hierarchy. They were ready to expand their investigation to determine who Arc Angel was.

Horst and Hildegard were attending a cocktail party hosted by Richard von Grosstien, one of Horst's colleagues, at his home in Berlin. Richard was one of the colonels who had been at Horst's house when Sara was killed and Hildegard was raped. Hildegard was not looking forward to the evening. Horst told her that he understood her reluctance to attend. But going was a necessity—it would enhance Horst's identity and role.

It was a large party, with many Wehrmacht personnel attending. Horst noticed a number of unencumbered personnel who he did not recognize. He found a moment alone with von Grosstien and asked him who these guys were. Von Grosstien indicated that they were Gestapo plants and that he was very nervous at their presence. He'd had no choice but to let them come. His boss, General Warlimont, had simply told him they were coming. Warlimont had indicated they were investigating a potential mole in Jodl's organization. The operation had been cleared by Jodl. The word had come down from Berlin.

Horst knew at this point that he would have to be very aware of any ears he was around. He also knew that, if he told Hildegard, she might panic. He had to say something to her that would ensure she would be very careful. The only privacy they had was in their bedroom. He would talk with her tonight. They left the party early, with Hildegard feigning a severe headache. Horst was fearful of discussing the issue even in the car

He would have to be very selective about the information he sent in the near future—as long as the Gestapo and their dogs were investigating Arc Angel, he would have to pick and choose when and where to transmit.

CLEVELAND

"**M**om, the baby is crying," called Carlton, Jr. It was seven in the morning in the Fuller household.

"I hear you, Carlton. I am warming the bottle now," replied Maggie. "Please ask Oma to change Sara's diaper. I'm sure she is wet."

Maggie was busy in the kitchen getting breakfast for herself, the children, and Oma.

She was thinking about Carlton this morning. She hadn't received her monthly report from the government as to his status. The information she normally received basically said, "He is well"—no more, no less. The monthly paycheck was deposited in the bank. She had to visit the bank to make withdraws so she could have money to spend. She still had not found the right amount to get her through each month. *Thank God I have Oma to help me out*, she thought. *It would be difficult if she wasn't willing to stay with me and help with the baby.*

Oma had forgotten what it was to take care of a little one. All she asked was to listen to her soap operas in the afternoon.

School has just finished for the year. Carlton, Jr., and Charlotte were now home for the summer. Maggie had been trying to find things for the children to do over the summer months. Both children had friends in the neighborhood. That would help, as they would be outside playing a good part of the day.

"Good morning, Mom," shouted Charlotte as she came running into the kitchen.

"Morning, Mom," said Jr. as he popped in.

Last but not least came Oma with Sara. Sara was smiling and making all sorts of noise. It seemed as if she was very happy this morning.

They all sat down at the table. She and the family blessed themselves. Maggie began, "Thank you, Lord, for another day. Thank you for the food we are about to receive from your bounty. Please watch over Carlton, protect him from his enemies, and keep him safe. Please return him to us safely when his work is done. Help us through this summer, Lord. Please help those who are fighting the evil in this world. We know many people are suffering and dying from the efforts of the Nazis and their partners. Help those who are fighting against them defeat the evil and bring the world back to a peaceful place. In your name, Lord. Amen," she prayed. "Let's have breakfast."

"Mommy, I have a prayer too," cried Charlotte. "Jesus, please protect my daddy. Please bring him home to us some day. Thank you, Jesus. Amen."

"Thank you, Charlotte. Please eat your breakfast, everyone," said Maggie.

"Maggie, I read in the paper that the circus is coming to town next month. Do you think we might all go to the circus?" asked Oma.

"Sounds like a great idea," replied Maggie.

Charlotte and Carlton, Jr., shouted with glee. Maggie was trying to set a routine pattern for the family. She was considering taking a war job. The paper was full of jobs to support the war effort. Rationing had begun. Maggie was concerned that the family would suffer during these times. Oma was doing a good job with the children. It would be some sacrifice for all during these critical times. She prayed every day for Carlton's safety. She didn't know what she would do if he was lost during the war.

Security Tightens

eneral Jodl called a mandatory staff meeting for the entire
Wehrmacht headquarters staff. Prior to the meeting, Jodl asked
Horst to come into his office. *What is up?* Horst asked himself.
A mandatory meeting for the entire staff?

"Horst, I expect you, as my staff manager, to keep me advised of all
that is going on here at Zossan. I understand that the Gestapo is working
undercover here looking for what they think is a spy, or a mole, as they
call, it here at headquarters. Do you know anything about this?" asked
the general.

"I heard rumors, General, but nothing other than rumors," Horst
lied. "I have tried to confirm them, but I could not. Therefore, I did not
want to alarm you with rumors, General."

"I appreciate that, Horst," replied the general. "In the future, try me.
If I don't want to hear anything, I will tell you. This came to me from
Himmler. He wants to turn the SS loose here in the building, "to root
out the rat," he says is here. You know how the SS works. They will be
in every office looking over our shoulders. According to them, everyone
is guilty before proven innocent. He has turned the Gestapo loose on
us. I certainly don't want the SS here. That is what the staff meeting is
about. I want you to be responsible for either finding the spy or ridding
ourselves of the Gestapo because all there is are rumors. You will be the
main point of contact for the Gestapo or anyone else snooping into our
business. There is so much going on at the Russian front, in Africa and
Malta, and soon in Vichy France. We are having a hard time keeping up
with the orders to coordinate all the services in these areas. I was able

to convince Himmler that we can solve our own problems. He has his own problems with the Jew exterminations. Let's get to the meeting. I want to inform everyone about what is happening."

"Yes, sir. Thank you for the opportunity. I fully agree with you," said Horst. "After you, General." He followed Jodl out of the office to the auditorium.

The meeting was a great success. Jodl knew how to motivate his team. A loud murmur went up when Jodl mentioned the Gestapo and the SS. The staff would keep Horst informed of anything they heard or saw until the problem was solved.

While Jodl talked, Horst contemplated his situation. What luck to have been appointed the point of contact for everyone at headquarters. *I will soon know who the Gestapo personnel are*, he realized. *I can feed them as I need to.*

He also knew that he would have to stay alert, as security would be tighter. He and Hildegard would have to be more careful than ever before. *We must continue to transmit*, he told himself, *but be safer when we do it.*

He also determined that it might be time to contact the underground—not in Germany but in France. The general had mentioned Vichy France. What was going on there? He needed to find out the details. He had to get a message to the Allies and set up a meeting. *First the information, next approval from Jodl to visit the army in France, third the meeting with the underground*, he told himself. *I am walking a fine line.*

After the meeting, Horst needed to discuss Vichy with Jodl. As they were leaving the auditorium, he asked Jodl if he could have a few words with him.

"Of course," replied the general. "What did you think of the meeting? Did we make our point?"

"Yes, General, you were clear and concise. The stir that happened when you mentioned the Gestapo and SS showed me that all were listening very closely. Before the meeting, you mentioned Vichy, among others. I haven't heard anything about goings on in Vichy. I try to stay ahead of things here so I can keep you informed and up to date. You caught me flat-footed on Vichy."

"Oh yes. We are considering invading Vichy France, as they are negotiating with the Allies regarding their ships. Our agents are very suspicious of the Vichy leaders."

"If we are planning to invade, may I participate with the Wehrmacht organization in France during their invasion planning? I have very little experience in that area. I thought it would enhance my knowledge and experience. It would provide me more depth. I would be better able to serve you," said Horst.

"Good idea, Horst," replied Jodl. "Your participating in the detailed planning would give me eyes and ears in the field process. Contact the field general's staff and make plans accordingly. Thank you for thinking of me and our organization. We push a lot of paper through the organization but get very little, if any, field experience. Let me know when you will be leaving for your visit."

"Yes, sir," agreed Horst. "I will be in contact with the field general staff and make plans accordingly."

He couldn't wait to tell Hildegard what had happened today. This would provide him the inside track on a major invasion by the Nazis and an opportunity to meet with the French underground to establish another communications path. He had to get a message to the Allies.

When he finally got home that evening, the air raid sirens were sounding again. He rushed into the house and found Hildegard, and they both went down into the basement. They heard the bombs exploding in the neighborhood.

All of a sudden, a bomb hit their house. Part of the basement collapsed. Hildegard screamed and knocked Horst down, hugging him tightly.

"What happened?" she shouted.

"A bomb hit the house," replied Horst. "We have to wait for the all clear before we can go back upstairs to check the damage. Don't panic, Hildegard. Are you okay? I'm covered with dust from the collapse."

"I'm okay, Horst. I'm scared," Hildegard replied. "What will happen now?"

"There is the all clear siren. Let's go upstairs and find out how much damage there is to the house." Said Horst. As they opened the door to the interior of the house, they first saw that the library side of the house had been destroyed. The rest of the house was untouched. They would have to check the remainder of the rooms and the stairway up to their bedrooms and bathrooms for stability and security. When they checked their bedroom, Horst made sure the radio equipment was safe. One thing they did not lose was power.

"Thank God we were in the basement," said Hildegard. "My favorite rooms in the house were destroyed. The library and the sitting room. We lost the books and paintings. That Göring and his Luftwaffe are worthless. They were supposed to protect us. I wanted to tell you, Horst. The Gestapo van was parked on the street in front of the house today. Did you see it when you arrived home?"

"Yes, I did," he replied. "Let's look out front to see if they are still there."

The front door was intact. Horst opened the door. "The truck is smashed and lying in the street. I don't think the inhabitants are still alive," he said to Hildegard. "I am going to check on them."

He ran toward the smashed truck. He counted three bodies—all dead—outside the truck. They must have been blown out of the truck. Horst went back into the house, as he heard the sirens of ambulances coming into the neighborhood to look for survivors.

"They are all dead," he told Hildegard. "I have to get a message to the Allies quickly, as we are not being tracked tonight."

He accomplished the message, asking for a meeting with the French underground.

"How do we continue to live in the house?" asked Hildegard. "The whole side is open. Will we be able to close the opening? Horst, what do you think?" she asked, with tears in her eyes.

"We are safe. I will take care of the issue in the morning. I'm sure Jodl will be able to help us. I'm glad it's summer. The temperature is in the seventies. We will be warm. And the bedrooms are secure. There may be a breeze in the bathroom temporarily." He laughed. "Just make sure you look before you pee."

They both broke out in laughter. Their relationship seemed stronger than ever.

It took three weeks for the workman to secure the house. It wasn't the same as before, but Hildegard made it livable again. The servants could not believe what had happened to the grand house.

It was nearly the end of August. Summer was waning.

The war continued, with the Germans holding back the Russian counterattacks along the Eastern Front. Rommel continued to attack Tobruk. He had convinced Hitler he would succeed in his endeavor to take over Egypt and take control of the Annz. Hitler told Mussolini to hold off on the invasion of Malta until Egypt was taken.

Horst had received the message confirming a meeting with the French underground during the second week of September. He contacted the Wehrmacht general in France who would invade the Vichy and arranged his visit for the first week in September. He asked Jodl if he could take a vacation in France with Hildegard the week after his meeting with the Wehrmacht. Jodl, who was ecstatic that he would have the inside track to the invasion, agreed. Horst couldn't wait to tell Hildegard. They would stay in Paris.

The increase of security at Zossan had revealed who the Gestapo personnel where. Horst contacted Gestapo headquarters to ask them to remove their personnel at Wehrmacht headquarters, "as we have taken steps to resolve our own security issues." The Gestapo refused Horst's request. Horst took the issue to Jodl. Jodl didn't want to cause an issue with the Gestapo. He didn't want to create an issue with Himmler.

He told Horst, "Himmler is very close to Hitler. Politically, it wouldn't make sense to get into a battle with Himmler. He would love to have the SS all over us. If they want to keep their people here, let them stay. Monitor their movement. You are head of security here at headquarters. Make sure they know that. Develop a relationship with them instead of fighting with them."

"Yes, General, I understand your concern. I will step up to the issue. I will manage the Gestapo here at headquarters," he responded.

Horst started to think about the politics of the Nazis. Apparently, Jodl was not held in the same esteem as was Himmler. He was learning the hierarchy status. *Keep your ears open,* he told himself.

Jodl received a copy of Rommel's report on the state of the Axis in Africa. Heavy losses had been incurred. Rommel felt the Italians where not reliable and suggested they be integrated into the German lines. He further stated that his supply lines where stretched thin and that his efforts to break through to Annz would be postponed until he could realign his forces. The British were continually receiving supplies and manpower. This report caused a great deal of concern. Horst believed that the British were making headway against the Germans in Africa.

He communicated with the Allies that evening. He knew he was taking a risk, but he wanted to make sure the Allies got the truth from his perspective.

Hildegard was excited about their vacation plans. She had always wanted to visit Paris. She hugged Horst when he told her of his plans.

Horst was concerned about transmitting. He decides not to transmit until he could discuss his concern with the underground. He would like a mobile transceiver he could use in his car. This would give him the opportunity to move around while sending and receiving messages, which would confuse the German monitor trucks. They would never be able to pinpoint his location. The more he thought about this idea, the more excited he became.

Reports of success on the Russian front were coming into headquarters. Hitler was driving troops toward the Caucuses. He wanted the oil fields. He was getting an argument from his field commander, who wanted to take over Stalingrad. Horst was fascinated with the infighting of the Germans. Hitler always seemed to win. Horst wondered how long the field generals would stay loyal to Hitler. *How long will the generals put up with Hitler running the war?* he asked himself.

The Underground

He meeting with the field staff planning for the Vichy invasion was long and tedious. Horst had never been through any regimen like this. The detail required by the actual troops that would implement the plan amazed him. Every move, every minute was accounted for. The logistics of moving men and equipment was very complex. It was a learning experience he didn't relish, but he accepted it graciously. He met and made new friends. What further amazed him was the work ethic and the enthusiasm the staff had. He didn't stay for their presentation of the operation to the general. Horst had a meeting of his own to attend.

Hildegard was in her glory in Paris. As a wife of a German officer of stature, she was treated by the Parisians with both respect and distain. They seemed to know she didn't put on any airs of disrespect for them. She visited many shops and bought a number of dresses and lingerie. She used francs for her purchases. She heard a number of stories of German abuse and killings. The locals apparently did not feel that she was one of "them"—the Nazis, that is. She was friendly and did not want to speak of the war or the politics associated with it. Hildegard was careful what she said and who she said it to. She was on a vacation. As she went store to store, she noticed the Gestapo henchman lounging around and trying to look inconspicuous. They were watching her very closely.

She told Horst when he came back to the hotel about the Gestapo. His comment was, "Bastards. They have nothing else to do."

Horst's meeting was orchestrated very carefully. He caught a taxi in front of the hotel. The driver asked him what his destination was. Horst replied, "Notre Dame, please."

"Yes, sir," said the cab driver. It was a short ride.

Horst noted that, as soon as his taxi left the hotel, a car started following them. *Gestapo*, he thought. *Let them come and follow me. We will lose them quickly.*

The taxi stopped in front of the church. Horst left the cab quickly and went into the church.

The car following the cab continued past the church and stopped the cab. They questioned the taxi driver, checked his papers, and asked questions about his passenger. After about fifteen minutes, they let him go on his way. They apparently were satisfied he was just a cab driver. What they didn't know was he was a member of the underground and the cab was a setup for Horst.

Horst went into the church and was immediately impressed with the majesty of the building and all of its trappings. After about ten minutes, he was met by a priest who asked who he was. Horst identified himself as Colonel Horst Brausch of the Wehrmacht.

The priest asked Horst to follow him. Horst was led down a flight of steps and outside to a truck waiting. He was blindfolded. He was told not to say a word.

After what felt like an hour, the truck stopped. Worst was led to another set of stairs that went down. Upon reaching their destination, his blindfold was taken off. The first person he saw was familiar. It was Major Best. He had a beard and was wearing peasant farmer's clothing.

"Major Best, what are you doing here? I didn't expect to see you, I am supposed to meet with the French underground." Said Carlton as he hugged Major Best.

In walked Marcel and a number of others. Horst hugged Major Best and acknowledged Marcel.

"I have been working with the underground since we left you in the woods," Major Best replied. "I am Donovan's eyes and ears here in France. According to what I have heard from our allies, your work has been outstanding. I know you are at high risk. The word we get is that the Gestapo believes there is a mole in the Wehrmacht. They are looking very hard to find you. It is good to see you," replied Best.

"Hello, Colonel," said Marcel. "Good to see you again."

"I'm not sure I feel the same way about you. I figured that you were the one that gave me the pill," said Horst.

Marcel replied, "I felt it necessary for you to really forget. I am sure it helped you adjust to your new role."

"It did. It gave me time to adjust to Colonel Brausch and his wife Hildegard. Let's get down to details. I wanted to meet with you to see if we, Hildegard and myself, can use the underground to pass information to the Allies. The Germans have tracking vans all over Berlin trying to find people sending transmissions. I need an alternative method to get information out. In addition, I want mobile communications equipment. This would enable me to transmit on the run and confuse the German tracking vans. Are these alternatives available to Hildegard and me?" Horst asked.

"Yes and no," responded Marcel. "The German underground is in tatters. There are a few operating at very high risk. The Nazis have been very diligent in eliminating them. I wouldn't trust that avenue.

"As to the other, there is mobile equipment available. We will get you a unit. It is battery powered. We will work out delivery during another bombing of Berlin by the British. We are aware that your house was bombed. That is good. It will make it easier for us to get the equipment to you. Do you have anything for us at this time?"

"Yes I do," replied Horst. "The Germans will be invading the Vichy portion of France. They suspect that the Vichy are negotiating the turnover of their fleet with the Allies. Obviously, the German's don't want that to happen. In addition, the Germans believe the Vichy are too weak in their dealings with the population. They are in the planning stage of the invasion now. I suspect it will be October or November before it happens.

"It is good seeing you all," he added. "We will need to meet again in the future. I am looking forward to that mobile equipment. There will be times when I take myself off the air due to the risk status. I am in a good situation at Zossan. Jodl has made me head of security. I know everything that is going on there from that perspective. Major Best, have you heard from Emily? I know she is in Switzerland."

"As a matter of fact, I have," Best replied. "I spent a week with her in Geneva a month ago. My friends here have great access to Switzerland. She is fine and worries about you and Hildegard. They are busy with the Jewish population leaving Europe to escape the Germans. How are you and Hildegard getting along?"

"I'm happy that you and Emily are able to see each other," said Horst. "Hildegard and I are getting along fine. Be safe, gentlemen. Please get me out of here and back to the hotel safely."

Remembering he was Colonel Brausch, he said, "Heil Hitler," and gave them the German salute.

They put the blindfold back on him, put him in the truck, and took him back to Notre Dame Cathedral. He was led down steps and was met by a priest, who took off his blindfold. The priest took Horst back into the church. He gave him a guided tour of the cathedral. Horst was in awe.

He left the church, and the same cab and driver picked him up and delivered him back to the hotel. On this trip, no one followed.

When he entered the room at the hotel, Hildegard met him wearing her new lingerie. He was overwhelmed.

When Horst returned to Zossan, he was met at the entrance by two SS officers. They asked for his identification papers.

"What is going on?" he demanded. "Don't you people salute senior officers? Why are you here?" He was irritated by the SS personnel's attitude.

"Come with us," the SS shouted at Horst as they took him forcibly by the arm and marched him directly to Jodl's office. They walked right into the office boldly. "General, this officer questioned our presence and became verbally abusive. We believe he may be the mole."

Jodl's face turned red. He shouted, "You idiots, Colonel Brausch is my staff senior colonel. He is beyond reproach. He is not the mole. He is the head of security here at Zossan. I will call Himmler to discuss your attitude. Get out of here. Leave my operation here in Zossan. You have abused your authority."

The two SS left without apology. Horst felt very relieved. "Thank you, sir," he said to the general. "What is going on?" he asked.

"I'm sorry for their attitude. Himmler insisted that he have SS investigating the potential mole here. I told him we were handling the investigation. He insisted. I didn't want to push any harder. I'm sure they will be back with a vengeance. No one takes on Himmler and the SS. Welcome back. How did the planning session go?"

"It went well, General. I learned a great deal. It is a very complex process. They will be ready when the orders are issued to invade," he replied.

"Good. Keep me posted. Glad you are back. I hope you enjoyed your vacation. We have a lot going on. Things are not so good in Africa. We are holding on in Russia. The siege at Stalingrad continues. The fighting is intense. The Russians continue to resist. The loss of men and equipment is horrendous there. But the Führer is insistent that we continue. The first snows have begun to fall. Winter is again coming to Russia."

Ṯбе Ӓṁеrіeӑṅs

ife for Horst and Hildegard had been rather hectic following their vacation in Paris. Horst had been spending more time at Zossan. The German war effort was beginning to stall. Jodl shared that Hitler, in a communiqué to Rommel, directed him not to retreat in the face of a stronger opponent. He directed Rommel to advise his troops that retreat was not the solution. They were to fight and die. There was always the opportunity for a weaker opponent to overcome the stronger one. They should fight for victory or death. Jodl also shared Rommel's decision. Despite Hitler's message, Rommel had issued orders to retreat.

What is beginning to happen? Horst wondered. The generals were starting to question Hitler's orders. *Are they taking matters into their own hands?* He sent along a message to the Allies with his thoughts.

On November 6, 1942, the Americans landed in Africa at Oran, Algiers, and Casablanca. Immediately, Jodl's organization issued orders to the Wehrmacht, Luftwaffe, and the Navy to attack the Allies Mediterranean fleet and ground forces.

Horst called Hildegard and told her the Americans had landed in Africa. He told her that orders had been issued to attack the Americans. Using Horst's father's house, Hildegard sent messages to the Allies regarding the German response to the invasion. She left the house via the back door as soon as the message was sent. The SS stormed the house just as she was leaving. She heard shots ring out from the house. She ran into the neighbor's yard and into the garage. She opened the car door and lay down on the floor. She heard shouts outside. She was running on adrenalin. She did not have any weapons to protect herself.

All she could do was to be quiet and shake. Someone opened the garage door and shined a light inside but then left quickly when someone else shouted for him to leave.

Hildegard waited for what felt to her like all night. It turned out to be two hours. How would she get home? She wondered. The garage door opened, and the neighbor entered. She didn't know the man. All she could do was trust her instincts.

"Hello, I know you are in here somewhere," said the neighbor. "Come out please. I will not hurt or report you. The SS will come back. I'm sure. I will help you."

Hildegard opened the car door and came out. "I believe you," she said. "I need to get away from here and get to my residence. Who are you?" she asked.

"I am Josef. I am a member of the German underground. I live here next to your father-in-law's house. I have seen you and Horst come and go from his house a number of times. I have seen the German tracking vans driving through the neighborhood. You must have been sending messages from here."

"Can you help me?" Hildegard asked.

"Yes, I can. Get back into the car. I will take you home. It may be the long way. We must make sure the SS doesn't follow us. Is there a back or secret entrance to your home?" Josef asks.

"There is a back entrance," replied Hildegard.

They finally reached the area where Hildegard lived. It was bombed out, with large craters where bombs had hit. She left Josef about a block from the house. She thanked him and asked whether or not he could help her and Horst get messages to the Allies. He said he would. They said good-bye, and Hildegard dove into a large bomb crater to make sure she couldn't be seen. She finally reached the back of the house and made sure no one was following her. She was filthy from rolling around in the dirt. She went upstairs, undressed, took a shower, and collapsed into bed. She was so tired and stressed she didn't even put on bedclothes.

The city of Algiers surrendered to the allies about two hours following the landing. Kesselring intervened on Rommel's behalf with Hitler, who relented on his directive not to retreat. Horst saw it happening again. The generals were taking matters into their own hands. Maybe Hitler was learning.

After a long day at Zossan, Horst finally got home. He found Hildegard naked in bed. What happened to her? he wondered. She always wore bedclothes. He didn't want to wake her. He laid down and fell asleep instantly

When they finally woke up, it was late morning. Hildegard told Horst her story. He was beside himself. She had almost been caught. Horst believed the radio equipment was gone. They would not be able to transmit for a while.

The Americans were now into the war and had committed to it fully. Horst felt good about that. They had been bombing in the Mediterranean area and supplying England with arms, food, and war materials. He heard from the Dönitz Navy organization that the submarines were still sinking ships. They had been withdrawn from the American shores, as the Americans had updated their submarine warfare. Hopefully, the war would be shortened. Horst was sure Churchill and Stalin would be happy the Americans had finally cast their lot. He was looking forward to receiving the mobile transmission equipment the French underground had promised.

Not transmitting for a while would be good. Hopefully, this would take off the pressure, and the Nazis would back off their search for the mole.

He kissed Hildegard good-bye and left for Zossan. He anticipated a great deal of orders now with the Americans in the foray. *Hallelujah*, he thought as he headed to the office.

There was excitement in the office when Horst arrived. Direct orders from Hitler had been issued—the Germans were to invade Vichy France. Apparently the Vichy had signed agreements with the Allies. *Such news should be transmitted tonight*, Horst thought. *But I do not have any equipment available to transmit.* The Germans would be tracking tonight. *If I dared to send a message, they would be on to me*, he realized.

Good news and bad for the Germans arrived at Zossan. Rommel had taken Tobruk. The Americans were dropping parachutists across different areas of northern Africa to support the British, French, and New Zealand Armies.

Hildegard was in the kitchen having coffee with the servants when she heard a knock on the back door. Their ears perked up. "Who could that be?" said Hildegard.

She rushed upstairs to get her pistol. She cocked the pistol and went to the back door. She held the pistol at ready and opened the door. It was Josef standing there with a backpack loading him down. "Josef, what are you doing here so early in the morning?" she asked, surprised.

"I have something for you," he replied. "May I come in before someone sees me?"

"Yes, yes. Come into the house," Hildegard said.

Josef stepped inside quickly. He took off the backpack. Seeing the servants, he stopped. "It's okay, Josef," Hildegard assured him. "They are my friends—very safe."

Josef continued to empty the backpack. It contained the portable transmission gear the underground had promised. In addition, he brought a number of extra batteries. "Let me show you how to operate the unit."

His explanation was meticulous; he noted what every switch was for. He covered how to load the batteries and how to set up the antenna and showed her how to load the antenna by drawing a spark with a pencil. He said the unit could be used for voice if necessary. He showed Hildegard how to plug in the key for Morse code. When he was done, he asked Hildegard to repeat his instructions.

She did well but needed a review.

"You will learn and become very proficient at using this gear," he said.

Hildegard thanked Josef for taking the chance to bring the equipment to her.

She offered him some coffee. He turned her down, said thank you, and left with a word of caution. "The Germans are out in force looking for transmitters. Use the equipment successfully. Be very careful when you use it."

Hildegard knew Horst was waiting for this equipment. She thought about how Josef had said they could use it while traveling in the car and how the capability should cause the vans a great deal of confusion.

Word came to Jodl that Hitler was taking over running the war on the Eastern Front. All orders would come directly from Hitler. Hitler ordered his generals not to surrender. They were to fight to the death. Horst thought to himself, *What will the generals do now? Hitler is going mad.*

He needed to advise the Allies of this turn of events. The Russians must be making headway. This information had to get to the Allies. *I still have no equipment,* he thought, frustrated. Perhaps Hildegard's German underground friend could help. But he couldn't call her now. He would have to wait until he got home tonight.

It was raining when Horst finally arrived at the house. Some of the caverns from the bombs had been filled to allow cars to travel through the neighborhood. Hildegard must have seen Horst drive into the yard. She was waiting for him at the door. As he walked in the door, she hugged him. He kissed her hello. *What a welcome,* he thought as he walked into the kitchen.

"Horst, guess what was delivered to the house today," said Hildegard, beaming. "What a surprise. Let me show you."

They went into the dining room. There it was—the mobile radio. Hildegard showed Horst how it worked, right up to the point of loading the antenna.

Horst was amazed. "Who brought the equipment?" he asked.

"Josef, the German who rescued me from the SS," she replied. "He brought it this morning. Why do you ask?"

"You know me. I don't trust anyone. Where does he live? How do we know he is from the underground? Before we use the equipment, we need to make sure he is who he is. Let's visit him this evening. We will go after dinner," responded Horst.

They put the backpack the equipment was packed in into the trunk of the car. The only thing showing was the key in the backseat. They covered it with pillows.

As they approached his father's house, they saw that the house next door was on fire. "Oh my God!" Hildegard exclaimed. "That is Josef's house. Stop the car. We need to find out what is going on."

They got out of the car and ran into a fireman. "What happened here?" asked Horst.

The fireman was just about to answer when a SS junior officer came up to Horst, who was still in his uniform.

"Colonel Horst Brausch," Horst snapped.

"Oh, yes, sir," replied the major. "I'm sorry, sir. I couldn't see your uniform in the dark."

"We had an encounter with the German underground. We killed two of them. When we entered the house, one of them threw a grenade. My colleague was killed by the grenade. I shot the two in the house and left it quickly, as it caught on fire," said the SS officer.

In his role, all Horst could do was congratulate the SS officer.

The officer saluted. "Heil Hitler."

"Do you know who these traitors are?" Horst asked.

"No, sir, but we are sure they are underground. We have been watching them for months," the officer replied and left.

Hillary was shocked. She was shaking and crying as she hugged Horst. It was all she could do to hold herself together.

Horst put her in the car to calm her down. He then went over to the house, which was, by this point, almost burnt to the ground. The fire crew was getting ready to leave.

He found the SS major in his car writing a report. Horst asked him to get out of the car. As the major turned around to close the door, Horst hit him in the head. He fell to the ground. Horst picked him up, took him to what was left of the house, pulled out his pistol and shot the SS major behind the ear. He found a still burning pile of wood rafters and threw the major into the flames. He went back to the car where Hildegard was waiting. They started the car and left immediately.

"Are you all right?" he asked Hildegard.

"Yes, I am, that poor man Josef. That bastard SS killed him. I heard a shot," she replied.

"I took care of the SS officer. He will be found burned in the ashes. I need to transmit to the Allies. Will you please turn the set on?" he asked.

She went to the trunk, opened it, turned the set on, and loaded the antenna. After Horst had sent his messages, they went home and retired.

Ͳꜧe Beginning of ͳꜧe End

Early in January, Zossan was bombed by the British. Although the majority of the headquarters was underground, there was some damage inside from the concussion of the bombs. Jodl was very upset. He contacted Göring directly and screamed at him about the lack of protection his Luftwaffe was providing. Göring responded that his aircraft were at the Eastern Front working for Hitler. He had limited fighters to attack the bombers. Do as you can. Goring said and hung up the phone.

The English bombed Berlin for the first time since the middle of November. Hildegard and Horst had just returned from a party when they heard the air raid sirens.

They immediately went down to the basement. The neighborhood sounded as if the bombs were dropping right on top of it. Hildegard was frightened. She was shaking. All Horst could do was hug her and try to keep her calm, which was very difficult, as he was also scared. The bombs were hitting so close. All he could say to Hildegard was, "There goes the neighborhood." He tried to maintain a sense of humor. It was difficult.

In the morning they went outside to look. All they saw was fire and destruction everywhere around them. The next day, it was more of the same, except the bombs were hitting much farther away.

Horst realized he had to get Hildegard away from the city and out of Germany if possible. He would have to meet with the French underground. He would ask them for their help. He had one question— what would he be able to do for the servants?

Zossan was functioning again after the British bombing. Orders were going out. Responses were coming back. The German general at Stalingrad asked Hitler if he could surrender. Hitler's response was no surrender ever, fight until the last man, to the last bullet. Horst's thoughts were to pray for the men at Stalingrad. What was Hitler doing?

His message that night was one of prayer and sorrow: "Orders go out to mobilize men in Germany ages sixteen to sixty-five. The Russians are gaining ground on the Eastern Front. The German generals are pulling back. The weather is getting worse, and supplies are dwindling."

That evening, Hildegard and Horst left the house and took a tour of the devastation in Berlin. They saw no tracking vans. Horst sent his messages while they were in the most devastated section of Berlin. They were stopped by a police van, but Horst's rank and position carried the day. He told the officer in charge he was reviewing the devastation for a report to General Jodl.

On their way back to the house, Horst told Hildegard he wanted to get her out of Germany. Initially, she hesitated. "What about the servants?"

Horst told her he had no idea but ensured her he was thinking about the issue. He would have to work with the French underground. Hildegard agreed to leave, but something had to be done about the servants. Horst didn't sleep well that night thinking about Hildegard and the servants.

Word came from Hitler's headquarters that the general in Stalingrad had surrendered—a major blow on the Eastern Front for Germany. All activities were closed in Germany for two hours to mourn the loss in Stalingrad. That afternoon in Zossan, Horst privately celebrated the great victory for the Russians.

Negative news from the Eastern Front and Europe continued to pour into Zossan. The British and Americans were bombing around the clock. Although he had been very conservative in his transmissions to the Allies, Horst transmitted the failures of the German Army. He and Hildegard were constantly alert for the Gestapo and SS investigations.

Zossan was bombed again. The heavy bombing was taking its toll. Every day when he left work, Horst saw hordes of homeless civilians in Dossan. Supplies were not able to keep up with the demand. Rommel met with Mussolini and communicated his concern for the Axis position in

Africa. Mussolini stressed that Tunisia must be kept in Axis hands. Over a hundred thousand workers went on strike in Italy, angering Hitler, who exploded to his staff.

Although Horst is receiving information secondhand in most cases, he was in communication with the Allies, keeping them informed of all of the negative news.

The British continued the heavy bombing of Berlin.

Hildegard struggled daily to find food for the family to eat and drink. She and Horst have discussed her leaving Germany. She is adamant, "I don't want to leave Germany" she replied to his suggestion for her to leave.

Horst insisted. "The British and Americans are bombing all major cities and factory locations every day. There are very few locations in the country where you could find safety. The army is still supplied with food. I will continue my work here. I will try to contact the French underground and ask them to help me get you to Switzerland. I have to get to France and meet with them. Please pack what you think will be necessary for you to survive. We will leave as soon as I can set up the meeting."

"What do I do with the servants?" she asked." If I leave them, the Nazis will send them to the gas chambers. I don't want that on my conscience. They have been very loyal. They are my friends. Can we take them with us?" Hildegard asked.

"I don't know," Horst replied. "The logistics will be difficult."

Hildegard had tears in her eyes. Horst knew how close the relationship between her and the servants was. "All we can do is try," he told her gently.

Hildegard hugged him. Through tears, she thanked him.

Driving to Zossan the next day, Horst realized how effective the bombing had been. The roads were a mess, bomb craters were everywhere, villages had been destroyed, and dead animals littering the landscape. He saw throngs of refugees on the roads leaving the area. The smells were ungodly, the sweet smell of the German countryside gone. Although he was happy with the success of the bombing, the ruination of the countryside was terrible.

He finally arrived at headquarters an hour later than normal. It was getting worse every day. He walked into his office. Much to his surprise, Jodl was waiting for him.

"Horst, we lost Tunisia to the British," said Jodl. "This is a terrible blow to the morale of our troops and the Italians. The Yugoslav guerillas are attacking German troops in Croatia. The bombing across Germany has increased now that the Americans have entered the war. The Luftwaffe, it seems, cannot protect Germany. The Americans are bombing Sicily and the surrounding islands continuously. Hitler is pushing for Operation Citadel to be started. He is obsessed with the Eastern Front. He wants to attack the two hundred-mile Kursk salient with two thousand tanks and two million men. I think he is putting all his eggs in one basket. My optimism is waning. Mussolini has been deposed and arrested by the Italian Fascist government. The allies have landed on and taken Sicily. Rommel believes the Italians are negotiating with the Allies for peace. Please do not let on to the staff. This conversation is between you and me."

"I won't, sir," replied Horst. "I understand your concerns. What is happening in France? Have we heard anything from that country? Should I take a trip to find out how taking over Vichy has transpired? Hopefully, that transition has taken place without problems."

"Thank you, Horst," replied Jodl. "No more negative discussion. I needed someone to talk to about it. I appreciate your loyalty. Yes, go to France. Find some good news for me."

After Horst arrived home that night, he and Hildegard put the communications gear into the car and took a ride into a destroyed section of Berlin. It wasn't far from where they lived.

Hildegard couldn't believe the devastation. "This was a beautiful section of the city," she exclaimed. "Beautiful homes, gardens, parks, fountains, and walking paths through the woods. That bastard Hitler and his cronies. They have brought devastation to Germany. When will it end?" she asked.

Just then, a tracking van passed them by. Horst noticed it immediately. "We can't transmit now," he said.

He pulled the car into a path between bombed-out buildings, turned out the lights, and waited. Sure enough, he saw the lights of the van return. The van stopped. Horst took out his pistol. He told Hildegard to open her blouse, mess up her hair a bit, and grab hold of him and kiss him passionately.

There was a knock at the car window. It was an SS officer. He had two men with him. The SS man ordered him out of the car. "What are you doing here? This is a restricted area. No one is supposed to enter this area. Let me see your papers," he demanded.

At that moment, Hildegard rolled down the widow; stuck her red head through the window, her blouse opened, revealing her cleavage; and said, "Horst, what is going on? You get me excited, and now you are talking with someone outside the car."

The SS officer saw the red hair and cleavage and looked shocked and embarrassed. He looked at Horst's identification and replied, "I'm sorry, sir. I'm sorry, madam. Please leave this area as soon as possible." With that, he apologized, bowed and left with his two men. The van left quickly and didn't return.

Horst and Hildegard laughed out loud. Horst made contact with the Allies and set up his meeting with the French underground. He made sure they understood Maggie and two other people would be in attendance.

Horst also set up a meeting with the panzer division staff that had invaded Vichy the previous year. He used Jodl's name for the authority to meet with the general in charge. They would be meeting during September unless something changed.

The only means of travel would be by auto. Allied bombing in Germany and France had destroyed rail continuity.

The year 1943 was moving quickly. The Allies landed on Sicily and were moving toward Italy. Hitler called off Operation Citadel at the insistence of the generals in charge in Russia. Their losses were very bad. The Germans lost control of the sky, and the Russians were counterattacking along the salient.

Horst was able to get a van from the headquarters motor pool for his mission in France. He was also able to get papers for Hildegard and her two servants. The personnel at Wehrmacht headquarters wanted to make sure the wife of Jodl's chief of staff had all her help with her. Horst was surprised but very thankful that they all would travel with papers.

Under the circumstances, the trip would be an adventure. Travel throughout Germany and France was becoming very difficult due to Allied bombing of cities, transportation depots, and factories. Horst mapped out their route carefully. He wanted to be able to obtain fuel at German Army locations along the way to their destination. He decided they would drive through to the panzer division headquarters in Vichy territory in southern France.

It was a long first day, but Hildegard and the servants made the best of it. They brought food and wine with them for lunch and snacks. They were stopped a number of times on the way, and their papers were checked at each stop. Jodl's signature carried a great deal of weight. They were never challenged. The servants being Jewish never caused a problem, as they wore enough makeup and clothing to disguise themselves as members of a German family traveling with a high-level German officer and his wife. The purpose of the travel was a meeting and vacation.

They arrived after fourteen hours on the road. The German guards at the gate were waiting for them. They were escorted to a hotel in the local town. The owner of the hotel welcomed them with open arms. After all, he exclaimed, he very seldom had such a high-ranking German officer and his family staying at his hotel.

The plan was simple. Horst would attend a series of meetings with the panzer division leaders and staff. They would meet and travel in Vichy for three days. During Horst's time away, Hildegard and the servants would visit the local tourist sites. While visiting out of the town at a French war memorial, the underground would kidnap them, take them to Switzerland, and arrange for the American ambassador to make arrangements to house them until the end of the war.

The plan was implemented like clockwork. Following his meetings, Horst returned to the hotel a day later, expecting Hildegard and the servants to meet him for dinner. He feigned loudly his upset on finding them not there to meet him. The hotel owner had no idea where they were and apologized profusely. Horst delated contacting the local police and the panzer headquarters; it was necessary to give the underground as much time as possible to carry out their plan. He needed help; his wife and family had not come back to the hotel to meet him. There were no messages. The more he was questioned, the louder and madder he acted. He threatened to contact the local SS and Gestapo for help.

The next day, the general of the panzer division came to the hotel to discuss the situation with Horst. They agreed that the best organization to find his family was the SS. The general's staff made the contact. The SS responded immediately to the general's request.

Once they found out what had happened, they alerted the Gestapo and local police constabularies across France. The pressure was on the SS to find Hildegard and her family. The next day, Horst was notified the SS found the van he had been driving burnt out in a valley in the mountains close to the Italian border. Horst knew this was a ruse to throw off the SS and the Gestapo.

Horst contacted General Jodl after the car was found. The general was very empathetic. He would send a plane for Horst to return back to headquarters but was concerned an American fighter aircraft might shoot a German plane down and kill Horst. The general would have the panzer commander send Horst back in one of his cars. Horst thanked the general.

The panzer commander was more than happy to get Horst back to his office as soon as he could. He wanted to accommodate General Jodl. Horst's car, as promised by the panzer general, picked him up at the hotel within the next hour. Horst was happy he had been able to get Hildegard and her servants out of Germany. He knew in his heart that the underground had been successful.

When he arrived home, he found the house ransacked. Someone had come into the house looking for his equipment. The SS was sure he was their mole. They were going to find the equipment and kill him.

The equipment was buried in one of the bomb craters alongside of the house—where Horst had placed it before leaving for France. Now he would put the finger on the SS through Jodl. He would get those bastards once and for all.

Jodl sent a car for him in the morning.

When he arrived at Zossan, the city looked as if it had been flattened by bombs. Very few people were outdoors. It was a ghost town, he thought.

He had a staff meeting to attend. The general would want a briefing on his trip and the loss of his family. Horst received a great deal of empathy from his peers. When he told them of the ransacking of his house, the general became very disturbed. He would call Himmler at once, demanding that he call off the SS pigs immediately and answer why his so-called elite organization hadn't found Hildegard. Horst had never seen the general lose his temper as he did that day. It made him feel good.

There was more bad news at the staff meeting. The German Army was retreating or withdrawing up and down the Eastern Front. The Americans had landed at Calabria on the Italian coast. The Italians had surrendered to the Allies. This information cast a pall at Wehrmacht headquarters. What should they tell the staff? How could they keep up the morale?

Jodl had no answers. Tell the staff the truth was the best he had that morning. Hitler was reluctant to give anyone withdrawal orders.

As the war new worsened, Jodl leaned more and more on Horst for support. Horst used this to his advantage. He made sure he would be able to transmit tonight. The Allies would be excited to hear this news. Now that Hildegard was gone, he spent more time at the office and took his meals at the officer's club in the headquarters. He only went home to sleep, wash, and transmit.

The SS had been quiet since Jodl talked to Himmler. Horst remained vigilant. He knew the SS still think he was the mole.

The remainder of 1943 brought more negative war news for the Nazis. Continuous bombing by the Allies throughout Europe and the Mediterranean were relentless. Most German cities had been bombed. The bombing continued day and night. It seemed that Berlin was hit every day. Allied armies were making progress in Italy and in the desert. The Italian fleet retired its navy in Malta. The partisans begin to revolt against the Germans in Italy.

As 1944 commenced, Horst began to think about an invasion of Europe. Rumors had started at the planning center in Zossan. What were the Germans planning? Where do they believe when and where it will happen? What were the Allies planning? German agents in England were busy trying to glean any information possible from their contacts. Horst was keeping his eyes and ears open for any information he could find.

Travel from Zossan to and from Berlin was getting very difficult. It took longer and longer for Horst to make the trip. Living in Berlin was getting more difficult daily. Power went on and off many times every day. Water was no longer safe to drink. Sanitary sewers were broken throughout the city. The city was beginning to smell. He was considering leaving the house and moving to the military quarters located in the underground headquarters of the Wehrmacht at his office. But if he moved, where would he transmit from? That was a major concern.

He had seen people scavenging bombed-out houses for anything they could carry or find to eat. Horst was afraid to leave anything of value in the house, let alone sleep there any longer. He asked Jodl if he could move.

"Yes, move as quickly as possible," the general replied.

"Thank you, sir. I will move tomorrow. I will close up my house tonight," replied Horst.

Horst worked late that evening. It was dark when he arrived at his residence in Berlin. As he turned into the driveway, he saw movement at the back of the house. He removed his pistol from its holster, took a flashlight from the glove compartment, left the car, and entered the house quietly through the front door. He stopped and listened. He moved toward the back of the house passed the stairs to the bedrooms. He heard whispering coming from the bedrooms. Two people started down the stairs, each carrying a load of clothing. Horst flashed the light on the people. They were dressed as SS officers and were scavenging his house. He shouted, "Halt! Who goes there?"

The intruders threw the clothes down the steps at Horst and jumped at him. He stepped aside and fired his pistol at each of the two people in quick succession. One after the other, the two bodies hit the floor with a loud thump. Horst shot them both again to make sure they were dead. He checked their identification papers. They were the Gestapo men who had been investigating for the mole at headquarters.

"They must have been looking for my transmission equipment, found nothing, and decided to scavenge my house," he said to himself out loud. "The bastards. I'm glad I killed them. I don't have to worry about them anymore."

He dragged the two men outside and buried each of them in a different bomb crater. He transmitted from the house, packed up his personal items and his uniforms, checked the rest of the house for intruders, and left. He drove directly to Zossan. As he drove, he thought to himself, *how fortunate I am to have a boss like Jodl. I will tell him in the morning what happened.*

Just as he arrived at Zossan, the air raid sirens started their wail. *I had better get inside*, he thought. *I must settle in quickly.*

The bombs began to fall as he was taking the last load of uniforms into the underground building.

At the morning staff meeting, Horst told Jodl and the staff that he'd killed the two Gestapo men the night before. He emphasized that the man had been in his house scavenging. Jodl turned red when he heard what happened. "That goddamn Himmler. He assured me he would take the pressure off. I'm not saying a word about this. I don't want any of you to say a word to him or his people. You had no idea who they were when you shot them. We will leave it at that. If they come sniffing around here, Horst, you are authorized to throw them out."

Jodl passed on more bad news. The Americans had landed at Anzio in Italy. The Russian counterattack had reached territory very close to the Polish and Estonian borders. Although the Germans were putting up fierce resistance against the Russians, the Russians were continuously gaining ground on their ultimate goal of reaching Germany. Berlin had been bombed again. The city's industrial area had been almost totally destroyed. Bombing across Europe had been relentless. Industrial areas had been the hardest hit.

Hitler was now putting his faith in new weapons and new technology to win the war. Norwegian saboteurs had damaged and sunk a ferry carrying heavy water. Jodl explained that heavy water was necessary to build atomic bonds. This was the first that his staff had heard of this type of bomb. It had to be some of the new technology Hitler was banking on.

I must get this information to the Allies, Horst thought. He began to devise a way to accomplish that goal. Horst was pleased with Germany's deteriorating situation.

Before Jodl dismissed the staff, he noted that Rommel had been transferred to France to reinforce the French coast against Allied attack. Rumors had it that an attack would be coming soon, but no one knew where it would be. Hitler was taking no chances; he was sending one of his best generals, Rommel, to supervise the effort. Now more than ever, Horst knew he had to communicate tonight. The question, he asked himself, was how?

German agents in England were sending in all the information they could gather about an invasion. Wehrmacht headquarters was buzzing with information. Planners where working on troop movement. Hitler had been firm—panzer divisions stationed in France were to be held in reserve until he released them. Orders where issued accordingly. He would not budge for anyone.

When Horst left the office that evening, he found his car damaged but useable. He headed for the city. It was almost totally destroyed. Even the scavengers were not out tonight. The darkness was completely black. No lights were on in the city. It was a good night to transmit.

The air raid sirens began to howl. *Where are they going to bomb?* Horst wondered. *Will I have a chance to transmit?*

There was only one way to find out. He began immediately. His message was long tonight. About 75 percent of his message had gone through when the bombs began to fall about a mile in front of where he was parked.

Just as he finished his message, a bomb exploded only a block away. The explosion was deafening. His ears were ringing. *That was too close for comfort,* he told himself. He started the car, spun the wheels, and floored the gas pedal.

Another explosion impacted the car, blowing it off the road into the side of a building and throwing Horst around. When the car finally stopped rocking, Horst stepped on the gas. The car lurched forward, and Horst takes a deep breath. *Thank God,* he thought. *I was lucky this time.*

When he finally got back to headquarters, the guard looked at him with raised brows and asked what had happened to him. Horst explained that he had almost been killed during a bombing raid in Zossan while taking a ride to relax after a stressful day. The guard understood and passed him into the building.

Another close call, Horst thought. *My car is a mess, I was almost killed, and I'm stressed almost to the breaking point.* He needed a drink; hopefully, someone in the officer's quarters had a bottle.

There was chaos in the office. It was June 7, and the invasion had begun. "The allies attacked? Where?" Horst asked the field planning staff.

"Normandy, a surprise," five of them said in unison, as if they were in shock.

"Illogical," the commander said, "too far away from England. They should have attacked further north. Rommel wasn't at the coast. He was visiting his family closer to Berlin. The panzers are being held. No one wants to wake up Hitler."

Horst went back to his office, chuckling to himself, thinking, *Illogical hell. Smart move. A surprise? I can't believe the German strategists couldn't figure out the attack was going to be at Normandy. There will be hell to pay when Hitler finds out. The services will be fighting on three fronts.* How long would this war last? *A good question,* he thought.

Jodl called Horst into his office. "Horst, what do you think about this latest move by the Allies," he asks.

"It seems to have surprised us—particularly the timing and the location, General. What are your thoughts, sir?"

"I agree with your evaluation. We were asleep at the switch. Our work will get more difficult, as we now have three fronts to fight on. There will be many troop movements. I hate to say this. Is this the beginning of the end?" Jodl sat back in his chair and sighed.

Horst didn't know what to say. He thought to himself, *I'm sure Hitler wouldn't say that. I wonder what the generals are thinking.*

Jodl told Horst that he and Horst would be going to one of Hitler's staff meetings at the Wolfsschanze—Hitler's headquarters. "Hitler invited me personally to attend. It will take place at the end of July. Make all the plans for us to attend. We will drive," Jodl directed.

Orders had been issued by Hitler to fire the new V1 rockets toward London. Over the next three months, two thousand rockets would be fired on England. Rommel advised Jodl directly via message; since the beginning of the invasion, he had lost over one hundred thousand men who were either dead, lost, or wounded. His officer core was being depleted, and replacements had been thin. His message said that the defensive line was weakening. If it failed, the Allies would penetrate deep into France. Horst cheered to himself.

He left the headquarters that evening to find a place to transmit. The Gestapo was back in force, since the organization had lost the two officers Horst had killed early in June. Himmler also flooded the area with SS. He told Jodl in no uncertain terms that he didn't care what Jodl thought. His mission was to find the mole. Horst knew Jodl couldn't protect him or anyone from Himmler. Every time he went to transmit now more than ever before was a life-and-death situation. He used different coding schemes each time he communicated to throw the trackers off base. He moved his base located in his car to a different location. He transmitted at different times, both in the morning and evening.

Horst was beginning to feel the stress. He needed a new car, as his had been wrecked a number of times. Jodl had not questioned his need for a car. Horst felt that might happen soon. He completed his mission that evening.

When he returned, the building guard was accompanied by an SS junior officer. He was very inquisitive and impertinent. "Where did you go? Why did you go? Who did you see? What do you mean relieving stress? Who gives you permission to do this?" he questioned.

Horst, keeping his cool, used his rank. "Who are you to question a Wehrmacht colonel?" he snapped. "I don't require permission to leave the building. My job is very stressful, especially at these times when we are losing the war. My organization is being held together with spit and string. We are trying to hold together the entire Wehrmacht. I don't believe you have the right to question me, Lieutenant. Do you?"

His reply was short. "Uh, no, sir."

He gave Horst the Nazi salute. Horst returned it. He noticed a big smile on the guard's face as he went inside the building.

ḤiꞆꞭeꞧ's Sꞇꜰꜰ ḾeeꞇinꞬ

odl was excited to have an opportunity to attend one of Hitler's staff meetings. Over the past three years, he had only attended one or two of these meetings. Horst was very interested in attending the meeting also. He had not seen Hitler since his father's funeral. They would be traveling to Wolfsschanze, or the Wolf's Lair—Hitler's headquarters in Bavaria. The meeting date was July 20. Horst contacted Hitler's staff and made all the arrangements. He and the general would stay at the building itself. The meeting would be in a smaller building in front of the main building. It would start promptly at 12:30 p.m. Horst made arrangements for a limousine and a motorcycle escort. It would be a good trip. Horst and the general would have the opportunity to further bond. It would be another chance to pick the general's brain—an opportunity to gain more insight on the future planning of the war. With the war being fought on three different fronts and partisans in a number of occupied countries, it would be interesting to learn the next steps that would be taken to win or lose the war.

Word arrived that Rommel had been critically injured by enemy aircraft while traveling by car. This changed Horst's plan for his and the general's trip to the staff meeting. Horst canceled the motorcycles and the limousine. They would take a smaller car and drive at night. The Allied aircraft were out patrolling during the day and were shooting anything that moved on the roads.

Horst shared the change in plans with the general. He was not happy but finally understood the danger. He still wanted to attend the meeting.

They decide to leave Zossan very early in the morning of the twentieth. They made good progress, as the roads were virtually empty. As the sun rose, it became apparent that the countryside had been heavily bombed. Many of the roads detoured around craters, equipment, and burnt-out buildings.

The general turned to Horst and said, "I had no idea how bad the damage was. The Allies have wrecked our country. It will be very difficult to recover from all this damage. I wonder what the Führer is planning for the future. I cannot imagine what is going on at the Eastern and Italian fronts. We know that the Russians and the Allies are making headway in their thrusts toward Germany. The Allies are starting to move in France. Horst, we need to make plans to move our headquarters soon toward the middle of Germany. It seems to me we will be overrun in the next six to nine months.

"I must talk with Hitler and find out what our plans to survive are. What do you think, Horst?"

Horst was shocked to hear Jodl talk like this. But he was also pleased. It meant to him that the war might be over soon. If Hitler or Himmler heard the general's words, though, they would eliminate him.

"General, I don't know what to say. You are much closer to what is going on than I am. I agree with you; planning to move our staff is becoming imperative," he finally said. "The Russians are advancing so quickly; it won't be long before they are in Germany. The Allies in Italy, I understand, are approaching Florence. Do you want me to begin to look for a place in central Germany to move our group?"

"Yes I do, Horst. Start immediately when we return," replied the general.

A loud noise sounded, and the car lurched off the road.

"What was that? Damn it. I'll bet we have a flat tire," said Horst. "Let me get out of the car and find out."

He looked at the front left side of the car. Sure enough, they had a flat tire. The general got out of the car and helped Horst look for a spare tire and the equipment to fix the tire. Everything necessary was in the trunk of the car.

Horst looked to the western sky and yelled, "Hit the ground, General. Here come four small aircraft headed our way. They could be Allied fighter aircraft. If they see movement, they will shoot us up!"

It wasn't ten seconds before the aircraft flew over them. They were Allied planes. Horst picked up the stars on the fuselage and black and white stripes on the wings. He didn't understand the black and white stripes, but he knew the stars. Almost immediately, two of the planes turned around and flew back over them. Horst and the general both burrowed down in the grass and weeds. Apparently, the pilots of the planes didn't see anything of interest and flew off.

Horst and the general worked quickly to change the tire and started on the road again.

"That was a close call. We lost over an hour travel time. We don't need that to happen again," said the general.

They encountered more detours. The longest one seemed to be about ten miles out of their way. They were going to be at least two hours late for the meeting. The general was getting upset.

As they approached Wolfsschanze, they saw smoke rising in the distance. "What happened, Horst? Hurry up. Try to get there quickly," shouted the general.

When they arrived, they found the building where the meeting was being held shattered. An army colonel ran to their car.

Horst rolled down the window and quickly asked, "What happened?"

"A bomb exploded inside the building," the colonel explained. "The Führer is shaken very badly. He has some scratches and bruises, but he's okay. A number of others are badly wounded, and some are dead. We think it was an assassination attempt. Who are you?" he asked.

"I'm Colonel Horst Brausch. This is my boss, General Alfred Jodl, head of the Wehrmacht operations. We are late for the meeting due to road damage and attack by Allied fighters. Who is in charge? Who are you?"

"I am Colonel Claus Von Kliest, staff officer to the Führer. Will you be staying with all this mess going on?"

Yes, I will, until I can find out how the Führer is and what the next step is," replied General Jodl. "Take me to the Führer. I need to talk with him if possible."

"Yes, sir. Come with me. Colonel, stay with your car. It is chaotic here," said Von Kleist.

Horst was getting antsy by the time General Jodl came back to the car. "It is a mess up there," the general told him. "Himmler has taken charge, and SS are all over the place. His organization will be doing the investigating. I told him that, if he needs help, we are available. He will keep us posted. Let's get out of here and get home. We have work to do. I'm afraid many top-level people are going to pay a price for this failure."

Horst knew he had to transmit that night. The SS would soon be all over their organization.

The trip home was dangerous. They were stopped a number of times by German patrols. Jodl was recognized and respected by the Germans. The status of the army fighting the Allies was tenuous. Every patrol told the same story. "We are stretched thin. Our morale is sinking. But we are continuing our struggle to survive." Jodl commended them all. He was trying to hold up their morale. Horst's message tonight would reflect this information.

They finally returned at Zossan at 3:00 a.m. They were both fatigued. Jodl retired immediately. Horst made an excuse to take the car back. It gave him the time to get to his car, drive to a safe area, and transmit.

The next weeks, Horst looked for a safe location in central Germany to relocate Wehrmacht headquarters. He found very little that had not been bombed and destroyed. All industrial cities had been destroyed by Allied bombing. The bombing continued daily. He met with Jodl to discuss the bad news.

Jodl had been getting bad news from Hitler's headquarters. A number of generals and high-level politicians, along with hundreds of others, had been killed by the SS because of their complicity in or knowledge of the attempted assassination of Hitler. The one general's death that Horst could not believe was that of Rommel. He now knew that the Nazis were all megalomaniacs. He would get this information to the allies. He also knew his boss wasn't one of them.

Although the SS had been trying to implicate Jodl and his staff in the assassination attempt, they were unsuccessful.

Hitler continued to issue orders to his commanders at all fronts not to surrender or withdraw positions. Horst understood the field commanders were trying to save their troops from annihilation. Hitler issued new directives to begin firing V2 flying bombs at London. Horst found out that V2s were more powerful than the V1s, more accurate, and had longer range. The general told him that Hitler wanted to impact English morale by sending V2 flying bombs. More information for the allies to digest.

Although Horst felt the war was getting close to its end, he continues to risk sending messages to the allies. By the end of October 1944, the Allies and the Russians were closing in on Germany. Panic was setting in at Zossan. It seemed that fewer and fewer personnel were coming to work daily. They apparently were reading the handwriting on the wall.

During November, Jodl held a secret meeting of field commanders. Horst was invited to attend. The meeting was so secret that all attendees were required to sign a paper promising they would tell no one of the contents of the meeting under penalty of death. They were to implement the plan without question. They were told that Hitler himself had put the plan together. The goal was to surprise the Americans, take over Antwerp, and stop the Allies from implementing their plans to take over Europe. It would be called Operation Watch on the Rhine. It was to start December 16.

Horst had to get this information to the allies. The security in the building was tightened. No one was allowed to leave the building. Horst tried a number of times, but he couldn't find a way to leave without being caught. Jodl had asked Himmler to support the security effort. He had done so by providing over a hundred SS officers and troops to lock down the building.

The attack started on December 16 at 5:30 a.m. Jodl and his staff listened to the effort by radio. It was a complete surprise to the Americans. The attack was finally quelled by the Americans three weeks after the Germans achieved a sixty-mile bulge in their lines.

Horst believed it was a last-gasp effort by the Germans to stop the Americans from taking over Germany. He was disappointed he had not been able to get the details to the Allies prior to the start of the German attack. He felt it was the major failure in his assignment.

Ḣoṁe ꓩꓔ Ḻꓯꓢꓔ

It was January 1945. Horst learned from Jodl that, across the three fronts, Wehrmacht soldiers were surrendering in large numbers. The Russians had crossed the German and Prussian borders. They were driving toward Berlin. Jodl believed it wouldn't be long before they would reach Zossan. He was waiting for orders from Hitler. The Americans had reached the Rhine River.

Horst believed the end was in sight. His concern was for his safety and his ability to return to the American forces. He continued his communication with the Allies. The tracking vehicles had seemed to go away. He paid particular attention to the SS personnel in the office. They were challenging everyone. He was happy that his relationship with Jodl was still strong. Jodl continued to depend on Horst to coordinate his staff throughout February, March, and April. As those months went on, more surrenders were taking place throughout the continent. Horst estimated that millions of German soldiers had surrendered.

Horst signed off as Arc Angel once and for all early in April. He was now on his own.

On May 5, Jodl came out of his office and advised Horst to come with him. When asked why, he replied, "I heard from Admiral Dönitz. He has taken over the country. Hitler and Himmler are dead." Jodl explained that both men had committed suicide. Mussolini, his wife, and a number of Fascists had been hanged in Italy by partisans. And Hitler had told Dönitz he would not be hanged. Hitler had earlier told Jodl that he was to take over the government should something happen to him.

"I am to negotiate the surrender of the fighting forces of the country to Eisenhower at Reims, France," Jodl explained.

"Yes, sir," responded Horst. He acted surprised at the announcement of Hitler and Himmler's suicide. Why Jodl? he wondered. He hadn't packed a bag. He only had the uniform he was wearing. As he followed Jodl out of the building to the waiting limousine, he thought about the long ride they had ahead of them—most of it at night. Hopefully, the Allied fighter planes wouldn't find them during what was left of the light and try to kill them.

As they started, Jodl said to Horst, "Thank you for your loyalty. You have done a great job as my chief of staff. I am very sad that Himmler and his cronies were unable to find your wife. You, like I, lost everything we have. We have been loyal to the Führer. We have done our job as well as can be expected."

"Thank you, sir. I appreciate your kind words. I tried very hard to do my job for my country," replied Horst.

As the journey began, they discussed many aspects of what would happen once the war was over. Horst found Jodl's outlook somewhat positive. Jodl believed he had obeyed the Führer's orders. Everything he had done was at the direction of the Führer. Horst couldn't believe it—the millions of innocents killed, the plunder, and the physical devastation. He had to swallow hard to keep quiet. It would be a long ride. Thank God, it was mostly at night. That way, he wouldn't be able to see the devastation.

Once they reached the Allies' front lines, they were led by an American escort the remainder of their trip. They arrived at Reims late that evening. Jodl was led directly into the headquarters building and began his negotiations shortly thereafter. Horst was escorted by armed guard to the Allies' officer's dining room for dinner. It was the last time he saw Jodl.

He approached the guard at the door of the dining room and asked to see his commanding officer. The guard left and brought back a US Army colonel to meet with Horst. Over his dinner, Horst told his story to the colonel. He explained that his name was Carlton Fuller. The colonel didn't believe his story. It was the colonel's opinion that the German was lying and trying to slip into the United States illegally. Horst stressed that he was a second lieutenant in the US Army. He had functioned over the past four years under deep cover in the German Reich. He explained that his code name was Arc Angel. All the colonel could do was shake his head. He told Horst he had a big imagination. He had heard of a spy with the code name Arc Angel, but he was sure Carlton was not Arc Angel. Carlton, in his frustration, finally asked the colonel to have someone contact General William Donovan, head of the OSS, or David Bruce to determine who he was. Carlton was tired and very upset. He finished his dinner and waited.

About thirty minutes later, a three-star general came into the room. "Mr. Fuller, I am General Lane, US Army. I apologize for my colonel. Knowing what you have done for our country, I understand your frustration with his reaction. His not being able to believe your story. I woke up General Donovan at his home and asked about you. I have never been chewed out like that in my career. We will be getting you home as soon as we can arrange transportation. General Donovan will be meeting you when you arrive in Washington to muster you out of the service. Again, sir, I congratulate you on your achievements and apologize for our attitude. I wish you well in the future."

"Thank you, sir. No need for an apology. I understand the situation. Where do I check into?" asked Carlton.

"A sergeant will take you too our officers' quarters. He will bring in a set of fatigues for you to wear. Please take off that Nazi officer's uniform. In the morning, someone will pick you up and get you started on your way to the States," replied the general. "Good night, Mr. Fuller."

It seemed Carlton was asleep before he laid on the bed. A knock resounded on his door at 8:00 a.m. Carlton rolled over and shook his head. "Yes. Who is it?" he asked.

"It is I, Colonel Best," was the answer.

Carlton jumped out of bed, opened the door, saw his friend William Best, and hugged him.

"Colonel Best? The last time I saw you it was Major Best. How good to see you! We have so much to talk about. How are you?" Carlton had tears in his eyes.

"Carlton, I'm fine. It looks like you lost some weight since I saw you three years ago. Yes, I'm a colonel in the US Army."

All Carlton could say was, "Unbelievable."

He and Colonel Best couldn't stop talking.

"Emily is fine. She is still in Switzerland. She and I will get married when she gets home. Hildegard has been with her since being "kidnapped" as planned by the underground. She is fine and says hello. She understands she will not see you again. She will always care for you. She thanks you for all you did for her. She will go back to Germany and resume her life. She wants to help rebuild Germany now that the war is over. The US government will help her do that."

Carlton and Colonel Best left on the first plane back to Washington, DC. It was a long flight. They had to stop at Gander Air Base to refuel. Once they left, it would be another six hours. The anticipation was building in both of them. Finally, the pilot announced that they would be landing in ten minutes at Bolling Army Air Force Base. Carlton and William each hugged a widow as the plane approached the runway.

Washington was glorious today. The sun was shining, and spring had just sprung. The plane taxied to and stopped in front of a small terminal.

Carlton left the plane first, followed by William. There was Donovan, along with his family, but Carlton first saw Maggie and the children. He tripped getting off the steps from the plane and almost fell down. The tears in his eyes nearly blinded him.

Maggie flew into his arms, followed by the children and his mother. He and Maggie kissed deeply and hugged each other. Then the children hugged and kissed their daddy. Finally, he hugged his mom. There were tears flowing from everyone.

Carlton stepped back and looked at his three-year-old daughter Sara for the first time since she was a baby. He thought she was beautiful. He was happy to be home with the family he so dearly loved. It had been a long war.

After the family greetings, General Donovan gave both Carlton and William bear hugs. He unfurled a sign pennant from his inside pocket. He gave it to Carlton Jr. and Charlotte to hold.

Welcome Home,

Soldier!